HOMETOWNS

EDITED AND WITH AN INTRODUCTION BY
▪JOHN PRESTON▪

HOMETOWNS

GAY MEN WRITE ABOUT
WHERE THEY BELONG

A DUTTON BOOK

DUTTON

Published by the Penguin Group
Penguin Books USA Inc., 375 Hudson Street, New York, New York 10014, U.S.A.
Penguin Books Ltd, 27 Wrights Lane, London W8 5TZ, England
Penguin Books Australia Ltd, Ringwood, Victoria, Australia
Penguin Books Canada Ltd, 10 Alcorn Avenue, Toronto, Ontario, Canada M4V 3B2
Penguin Books (N.Z.) Ltd, 182–190 Wairau Road, Auckland 10, New Zealand

Penguin Books Ltd, Registered Offices:
Harmondsworth, Middlesex, England

First published by Dutton, an imprint of New American Library,
a division of Penguin Books USA Inc.
Distributed in Canada by McClelland & Stewart Inc.

First Printing, October, 1991
10   9   8   7   6   5   4   3   2   1

REGISTERED TRADEMARK—MARCA REGISTRADA

LIBRARY OF CONGRESS CATALOGING-IN-PUBLICATION DATA:
Hometowns : gay men write about where they belong / edited with a preface by John Preston.
p.   cm.
ISBN 0-525-93353-0
1. Gay men—United States—Identity.   2. Home—United States.   3. Community.
I. Preston, John.
HQ76.2.U5H66   1991
305.38'9664—dc20   91-11992
                                                              CIP

Printed in the United States of America
Set in Garamond No. 3

Designed by Steven N. Stathakis

*With thanks to Hugh Nazur, Linda Murnik,
and all the others who have made
Portland, Maine, my hometown*

—JP

ACKNOWLEDGMENTS

To HAVE A HOMETOWN IS one of the major definitions of being supported and of belonging. There are, of course, other ways we find emotional sustenance for our lives and our vocations. As a writer, I've been charmed to have a whole series of people who have made my work possible through their many and varied contributions.

The authors of the essays in this volume have all been especially helpful and cooperative, making this a wonderfully collective literary experience.

My agent, Peter Ginsberg, showed his usual strong belief in my ability and my career. My editor at NAL/Dutton, Matthew Sartwell, and his more than able assistant, Peter Borland, made working on this book as easy and actually enjoyable as every writer hopes his work with a publisher could be.

Celeste DeRoche once again proved her great worth with her help in typing and giving advice on editorial decisions. Tom Hagerty, my own assistant, was as loyal as ever and capable as ever. Robert Riger and other people in my personal life extended great understanding as I withdrew into this labor.

I appreciate and thank all these people who have helped me create the equivalent to a literary hometown.

—JP

CONTENTS

INTRODUCTION

WHERE WE COME FROM IS important to who we are. The context within which we grow up helps determine how we see the world. Individual psychology reduces the important conditions to simply family-related, but our basic community—our hometown—is important as well.

Do we sense that we fit? Do we feel welcome? Do we experience ourselves as valued members of the community? How are we perceived by our neighbors and peers? These are among the most fundamental questions of identity we have to answer.

Most men begin with the promise that we are, in fact, welcome. The boy child is, in almost all our known contexts, the heir. He has a right to assume that he will acquire whatever is possible in his world. If his background includes being the member of a disenfranchised group because of race, religion, ethnic background, or class status, he still has the expectation of achieving the most that background will give him.

A gay man, since he is primarily a man, begins with those

assumptions. It isn't until he comes of age and understands his sexual identity and the ways it separates him from his birth community that a gay man achieves a perception of being a member of this particular minority. A woman's self-identity doesn't include a late discovery of her gender; a heterosexual Jew's character is usually something that's self-evident at an early age; but a gay man's understanding of himself and his world doesn't come into focus until much later.

One of the first questions that a gay man has to answer revolves around the basic issue: Where do I belong? Having grown up as a privileged member of his community, he will now have to ask himself if he can stay there. For years, gay men thought they had only two choices: They could either sublimate their erotic identities and remain in their hometown, or they could move to a large center of population and lose themselves in anonymity. There was no way for a gay man to have a hometown and still be honest with himself. He had to hide his social and sexual proclivities, or else he had to give up communal life in pursuit of them.

In the last three decades the choices for gay men have increased. Those exiled souls who moved to New York, San Francisco, Paris, or wherever it was that there were others like them, coalesced into a community of their own. They became something more than the accumulation of individuals, they formed a social structure for themselves that meant they had a new hometown. Having been thrown out of one tribe, they created their own new tribe. Once their communal existence became known, they presented the man who was coming out with a new option: he could join them. He could assume a new identity by becoming a member of a new clan.

While the new tribe offered an option richer than ever dreamed of before, it seldom allowed the gay man any compromise. To become a member of the new clan meant a move to one of the evolving gay centers, it meant adopting the new hometown to the exclusion of the old. To be gay on Castro Street or in the Montrose District of Houston meant severing connections with wherever one had come from. A gay man was no longer condemned to walking into a social desert, relieved only with an

HOMETOWNS

MEDFIELD, MASSACHUSETTS

MEDFIELD IS ONE OF THE ancient villages of New England. It was established as a European community in 1649, when pioneers from Dedham moved inland to the location near the headwaters of the Charles River, about twenty-five miles southeast of Boston.

The land on which Medfield was settled had been purchased from Chicatabot, the Sachem of the Neponset nation. He was one of those natives who saw the arrival of the English as, at worst, a neutral event. But it didn't take long for the indigenous people to see that the spread of the Puritan and Pilgrim colonies was threatening their very survival. In 1674, Metacomet, the great leader known to the English as King Philip, organized an alliance of the native nations and led them to battle against the intruders.

The beginning of King Philip's War, as it was called, was fought in the Connecticut Valley. The few communities there were attacked and many of the settlers killed. Within a year Metacomet's warriors were pushing closer to Boston. Medfield was raided on February 19, 1675. Seventeen people were killed and half the buildings were destroyed.

Metacomet was defeated later that winter in a climactic battle in nearby Rhode Island. His campaign was the last serious chance the natives had of sending the English away. Smallpox and other epidemics finished the destruction of the aboriginal nations over the next decades. Medfield's new proprietors, my ancestors, quietly prospered.

When the American Revolution broke out a century later, Medfield was firmly on the side of the rebels. The town meeting communicated regularly with the colonial legislature and the radical Committees of Correspondence, encouraging a strong stance against unfair taxation. When it was apparent that hostilities would break out, the citizens organized a contingent of Minutemen who responded to the call to arms in Concord and Lexington (though they arrived too late to join in the battles).

The Revolution was the last striking event in Medfield's history. Once independence was achieved, Medfield simply became a quintessential Yankee town, the place where I grew up, complete with a phalanx of the white clapboard churches everyone identifies with New England, larded through with extravagant forest parks and with a wealth of substantial wood-frame houses.

When I was born, in 1945, Medfield had fewer than three thousand inhabitants. It was assumed that all of us knew one another. It wasn't just that the population was so small, it was also remarkably stable. Our families had all lived in the same place for so long that it all felt like an extended family. (And there were, in fact, many cousins in town. Not just first cousins, but second and third cousins. We all knew our interlocking heritage at an early age.) The names of all the participants in the colonial and revolutionary events were the same as many of my cousins and classmates and the people in the church my family attended—Harding, Morse, Adams, Lovell, Bullard, Wheelock, and Allen.

We lived our history. When the other kids and I played cowboys and Indians, we did it on the same battlegrounds where our ancestors defeated King Philip. When we studied American

history, our teachers taught us the names of the men from Medfield who had fought in the Revolution.

We weren't those for whom this country's history was irrelevant. We weren't left out of the narrative of the white man's
ascension. We were, in fact, those for whom American history
was written. We were of British ancestry—if not English, then
Scots or Irish. We read about people with names that sounded
like our own. "Foreign" was, for us, someone of Italian descent.
"Alien" was the Roman Catholic church.

As I grew older and came into contact with people from
around the state, I discovered a different social criteria. People
started to talk about ancestors who'd come from England on the
Mayflower. I remember going to my mother and asking her if ours
had. She looked at me strangely and replied, "Well, whenever any
family's lived in a town like ours as long as we have, somebody
married somebody who married somebody whose family came over
on the *Mayflower*. But, why would you even care?" she asked.

Indeed. Why would anyone look for more than coming from
Medfield? There is a story about Yankee insularity that's told in
many different forms. A reporter goes up to a lady who's sitting
on a bench in a village common and asks her, "If you had the
chance to travel to anywhere in the world, where would you go?"
The lady looks around her hometown, mystified, and responds,
"But why would I go anywhere? I'm already here!" The first times
I heard that story, I didn't understand it was a joke. I thought
the woman was only speaking the obvious. It's the way we felt
about Medfield.

Medfield was a very distinct reality to me. There was even
a leftover colonial custom that gave the town a concrete definition. By 1692 the settlements around Boston were growing
quickly and their perimeters were hazy because of conflicting land
grants and native treaties. The executive power of each town was
vested in the Board of Selectmen, three citizens elected by the
town meeting to run things between the annual assemblies of the
town's voters. The Great and General Court, the romantic name
the Commonwealth of Massachusetts still uses for the state legislature, decreed that every five years the selectmen of each town
would have to "perambulate the bounds" with the selectmen of

its neighbors. The two sets of townspeople had to agree on the markers that separated them.

The requirement for the perambulation stayed on the books until 1973 and even then the rescinding law said, "However, it is enjoyable to keep the old tradition of meeting with the selectmen of adjoining towns for this purpose. It also affords an opportunity to agree to replacement of missing or broken bounds and to discuss subjects of mutual interest." (The Medfield Historical Commission recently reported, "It is also rumored that modern-time selectmen partook of a drink or two at each boundary marker.")

When I was young, I used to walk the bounds of Medfield with the selectmen. The grown-ups' drinking habits weren't important to me, but I was in love with the stones we found with their antiquated signs and the aged oak and maple trees that appeared on the town records as markers between Medfield and Dover, Walpole, Norfolk, and other neighbors.

The living history of the monuments wasn't all I got from these walks. The perambulations gave a firm evidence to just what was my hometown. I was being told that everything on this side of the boundaries was Medfield. Everything on this side of the border was mine.

It's hard to overstate the sense of entitlement that a New England boyhood gave me and my friends. I remember the first time I was taken to Boston. The city seemed large and frightening, at least it did until my mother pointed to the large body of water between Boston and Cambridge and explained that it was the Charles, the same river that separated Medfield from Millis. I realized I couldn't be frightened of someplace that was built on the banks of *my* river.

Even if America wasn't all like Medfield, it certainly acted as though it wanted to be. The new suburban developments that were all the rage in the sixties mimicked the architecture of the buildings that had been standing around our village for centuries. Advertisements for the good life all seemed to take place in our town. Medfield had a wide floodplain to the west, hills to the south, forests to the north. It was the landscape surrounding the "nice people" we saw in magazines and on television. Our lawns were well kept and our trees carefully pruned. A snowstorm was a community event; my mother would make hot chocolate and fresh doughnuts (from scratch) for all the neighborhood children and we'd build snowmen exactly like those pictured on the pages of *The Saturday Evening Post.*

Of course there were blemishes, some of them so well hidden that only those of us inside could see them. There were broken homes and drunken parents. There was economic upheaval as New England's industry migrated to the South after World War II. There were class divisions that were especially apparent to me, since my father's family—he was from Boston's industrial suburbs—was pure working class. We couldn't have been much better off than my aunts and uncles and cousins living in Boston's urban blight, but poverty wasn't as apparent when it was surrounded by beauty like Medfield's. Somerville didn't have Rocky Narrows State Park; Everett didn't have Rocky Woods State Reservation. And, besides, not having a great deal of money had no impact on our status in town. My mother's pedigree made my father's background irrelevant. Her children were of Medfield, and no one ever questioned that.

In fact, we were constantly reminded that our roots were right there on the banks of the Charles. My sisters and brothers and I were continually assaulted by older citizens who would stop us on the street and pinch our cheeks, "Oh, yes, I can see that you must be one of Raymond Blood's family. It's those eyes. Just like his!" My maternal grandfather had died fifteen years before I was born, but townspeople kept on seeing his lineage in my face. He'd been something of a hero in the town, a World War I veteran who'd prospected for gold in Nevada before he'd returned to take over the family's business, selling feed and grain to the small farmers in the region. To be Raymond Blood's grandson was no small matter. The pinches may have been annoying, but the rest of the message was clear: You are from this place.

Medfield was a town where a boy knew what it meant to belong. It was an environment out of which almost any achievement seemed possible. As we grew older, my friends and I picked and chose from the best colleges, dreamed the most extravagant futures, saw ourselves in any situation we could imagine. Our aspirations were the highest possible and they didn't come out of pressure from striving families or a need to escape a stifling atmosphere. We envisioned ourselves however we chose because we felt it was ours, all of it, the entire American Dream. It was so much ours, we took it so much for granted, that we never even questioned it. It was self-evident.

There must have been many ways I was different from the other kids early on. I'm vaguely aware of being too smart, of not being physical enough, of hating sports. I got grief for all those things in the way any group of peers can deliver it, especially in adolescence. I certainly *felt* different. I certainly *knew* I was different. But the difference didn't define itself right away.

As we became teenagers, things happened that actually eased the sense of deviation. There were forces at work that made us more aware of the things that bound us together and made what might have separated us seem less important. Route 128 had been built in a long arc around Boston's suburbs in the fifties. Originally called a highway to nowhere, it was one of the first freeways whose purpose was to create a flow of traffic around centers of population, not between them. One-twenty-eight quickly got another name: "America's Highway of Technology." New companies with names like Raytheon and Northrop and Digital built enormous high-tech plants along 128. They moved the center of the region's economy out of Boston, toward places like Medfield. The town's population doubled, and then doubled again.

By the time we were in high school, we were faced with new classmates with strange accents and different standards. My friends had earned their extra spending money by trapping beavers and muskrats along the tributaries to the Charles and selling their pelts. These new kids didn't know about traps and they didn't think it was important that their new homes in the spreading developments were ruining the animals' habitat. We were used to having fried clams as a special treat at the local drive-up restaurant; they were only angry that there weren't any fast-food chains. They had strange and exotic—and sexual— dances we hadn't even heard of. We stood in the high school auditorium and wondered how they could act that way in public.

When they hiked up on Noon Hill, they didn't know that it had been the place from which King Philip had watched Medfield burn. They thought we were backward and quaint that we even cared about such things.

The local kids closed ranks. I'm sure, as I look back now, that the newcomers must have been puzzled when Mike, the captain of every team sport possible, spent time with me, the class brain. They must have wondered just as much why I would pass afternoons with Philip, who didn't even go to Medfield High School but commuted to Norfolk County Agricultural School, the looked-down-upon "aggie" school in Walpole. And why would my (third) cousin Peter, probably the most handsome youth in town, walk home with me so often?

We defied the new standards; we held to our own. We had all been in the Cub Scouts pack that my mother had founded. We had all sat in the same kindergarten. We had all been a part of Medfield. I was one of the group, and they wouldn't deny me.

When I return to my hometown now, I see that, in most ways, we won. People like Mike and Philip and Peter—and my mother and her friends—simply sat it all out. They waited for the newcomers to leave and then for a new wave of them to come in, the waves of migrating suburbanites who can't tell the difference between Medfield and Northfield, Illinois, or Southfield, Michigan, they've changed addresses so often. My family and friends simply stayed, they had never intended to move. Now, my mother is the town clerk, Mike runs the reunions of our high school class, and last I heard Philip took over his father's job as groundsman for the state hospital.

But I had begun to leave while I was still in high school. I had heard rumors about a different life and a different world. Its gateway, my books and magazines told me, was a bus station in a city. I began to travel to Boston more often, supposedly to visit my urban cousins, but I seldom got as far as Somerville. I would stay, instead, in the Greyhound terminal and wait for one of a series of men to come and initiate me. They were traveling salesmen from Hartford, professors from MIT, students from Northeastern.

Eventually I'd travel further to meet them. I took secret trips to New York when I was supposed to be skiing in New Hampshire. I hitchhiked to Provincetown, the fabulous center of the new world into which I was moving. And, with every move, I left more of Medfield behind.

There was really no way I could see to combine my new life and my old. There was a man in Medfield who was whispered about. He belonged to our church and was the target for endless sympathy because he kept entering and leaving the state hospital. And there were two women down the street, nurses, who were so masculine that it was impossible to ignore their deviance from the other norms of the town. But they offered me nothing. I wasn't like the nurses and I never, ever wanted to be like the man who was so continually institutionalized.

In some ways I moved into my new life with great joy. There was real excitement in it, certainly there was great passion. My explorations took me to places as far away as a New England boy could ever imagine. When it came time to pick my college, I chose one in Illinois, the far horizon of my family's worldview, as far away as they could ever conceive of me going.

I also experienced rage over what was happening to me. I was being taken away from Medfield and everything it stood for. I was the one who should have gotten a law degree and come home to settle into comfortable Charles River Valley politics— perhaps with a seat in the Great and General Court? I should have lived in one of those honestly colonial houses on Pleasant Street. I should have walked through the meadows and the hills as long as I wanted, greeted by people I knew, all of us blanketed in our sense of continuity. History had belonged to us. But I was no longer one of them. I had become too different.

There had become a label for me that was even more powerful than the label of being from Medfield, something I don't think I could have ever envisioned being true.

I remember trying to find some way to come back to Medfield. I remember discovering a hairdresser in a Boston bar who had just opened a shop in town. I wanted desperately to fall in love with him and move back and find some way to be of Medfield again. Another time I did fall in love with a truck driver from Providence, a man of as much overstated masculinity as the nurses down the street. Maybe he and I could create a balance that the town could accept. He drank whiskey with my father, fixed cars with our neighbors, and knew all about the Red Sox. Maybe, between the two of us, we had enough that we could stay in Medfield. It didn't work. And, in those days, no one ever thought it would work in any hometown.

I stopped trying to fit my life into Medfield. I turned my back on it. I belonged to a new world now, one that spun around New York, Chicago, San Francisco, Provincetown. I was danced and bedded away from home, into the arms of someplace no one had ever even told me about.

JESSE G. MONTEAGUDO

MIAMI, FLORIDA

I GREW UP IN MIAMI'S LIT-
tle Havana, a community like no other. Here, in the southern
half of a once-sleepy Miami, a community of Cuban immigrants,
refugees from a revolution, created, within the confines of American society, a mirror image of a Havana that they believed existed before Fidel Castro and his minions did away with the things
they once held dear.

Though waves of Cubans have landed in the United States
since the nineteenth century, they were largely limited to members of the political opposition or the intelligentsia. The revolution of 1959, by changing Cuba from a capitalist country
dependent on the United States to a communist country dependent on the U.S.S.R., let loose a series of migrations that rid the
island of much of its upper and upper-middle classes and that
incidentally spared Castro an organized base of opposition. While
the American government welcomed this massive exodus as a
weapon in the Cold War, it sought to avoid its consequences by

resettling the refugees throughout the fifty states and Puerto Rico. It did not work. Most Cuban exiles chose to settle in Miami, a city with a tropical climate and a proximity to the homeland. By the mid-sixties a sizable Cuban exile community had emerged in south Florida, a bilingual society that centered around South West Eighth Street, the old Tamiami Trail whose name, like that of almost everything else in the new Miami, was soon Hispanicized into the now familiar nickname of Calle Ocho.

Though Calle Ocho has changed in the last twenty years, it will always remind me of my formative years, the turbulent sixties. Many of the old sights and sounds remain: old men playing dominoes, coffee shops dispensing rivers of *cafe Cubano,* statues of the saints beaming from store windows and car windshields, and fiery speeches shot from street corners or the airwaves. Other aspects of Calle Ocho are more "typically" American: huge U.S. flags waving (along with Cuban flags) from used-car lots, smartly dressed yuccas (young, upwardly mobile Cuban-Americans) driving BMWs, politicians of all ethnic origins seeking the Cuban vote in perfect or fractured Spanish. The language of Calle Ocho is like no other: a driven, fast-lane Spanish, now diluted into Spanglish, that leaves other Spanish speakers amused and everyone else amazed.

Critics complain that Miami's Cuban community refuses to assimilate. Actually, Cuban-Americans have adopted the American Dream with a vengeance. People who arrived in Miami with just the clothes on their backs became, within a decade, prosperous business owners with homes in Westchester or Kendall, brand-new cars, and a voice in government. Since the once dominant Democratic Party is too liberal for their tastes, most Cuban-Americans are registered Republicans, a development that made the Grand Old Party a force in local and Florida state politics.

When I first moved to Little Havana (1964), Calle Ocho was a street in transition, where some of the older, "Anglo-owned" businesses stubbornly held out against the Cuban tide. I remember walking home from school among a variety of supermarkets, pharmacies, and dime stores that tried to outdo each other in their devotion to *La Causa* by displaying large Cuban flags, maps of the island, and portraits of Cuban heroes Jose

Martí and Antonio Maceo. My parents' generation then took it for granted that *el exilio* was only a temporary condition and that they would soon be able to return to *la Cuba libre,* there to start anew where they left off.

Little Havana was largely a self-contained community, which meant that I seldom had to deal with the problems of belonging to an ethnic minority. Where I lived, we were the majority. The world was divided between the Cubans and the *Americanos,* a category in which we dumped all native-born whites (blacks were in a class by themselves). Some of the older Cubans made it a point of patriotism not to learn English, even when they sought public office. More typical of their generation are my parents who, though naturalized and English-speaking at work, spend all of their nonworking hours surrounded by Spanish, whether emanating from their relatives or friends or from radio or television sets constantly tuned to Spanish-language stations.

Having created a replica of Old Havana in their new home, Miami's Cuban community sought to prevent the emergence of a progressive movement that it believed was responsible for the revolution. Seeing itself as a community at war, Little Havana refused to tolerate diversity within its ranks. Political dissent was (and to some extent still is) taboo, and any form of liberalism, progressivism, or socialism is frowned upon as being tantamount to aiding the "enemy." The Cuban-American media broadcasts the party line with no pretense at impartiality, and anyone who dares to disagree is (they believe) either a communist or an idiot. I remember being called communist (at the age of twelve!) for speaking out in favor of the Civil Rights Movement. Calle Ocho did not "go conservative" with Reagan's election in 1980; conservative politics there were a given, even (especially) during the activist sixties. Reagan himself is acclaimed as a hero in Little Havana (as in nearby Little Managua), even if his crusade against communism was more talk than action.

Politics were the least of my problems. As a budding gayboy, I could not fit in, either with my parents' generation or with my own. My parents worried that I lacked the masculine qualities needed to carry on the family name and genes and, perhaps, to share in the liberation of *La Patria.* My peers saw in me a nerdy bookworm who was undoubtedly queer and thus deserving of their constant harassment. I am still amazed that these boys were able to guess my sexual orientation long before I knew it myself, though here perhaps I am allowing them more insight than they really had. The fact that I was different was enough to convince these boys, raised as they were on machismo and the herd instinct, that I was a sexual deviate.

Miami's Cuban community, with roots planted deep in the soil of Spanish machismo and Roman Catholicism (and politically conservative to boot), is still unwilling to accept its gay population. Twenty years ago, things were even worse, especially for gay adolescents struggling to understand themselves. When I turned thirteen my father sat me down and gave me a stern lecture warning me to watch out for prowling perverts. I was the person my parents were warning me against! Whenever change could not be blamed on communism, it was attributed to homosexuals. My father swore that all rock singers were queer, while the kids in school were certain that their male teachers, especially those who gave them less than satisfactory grades, were *maricones*. Male homosexuals were perennial objects of abuse in a community that worshipped virility and equated dissent with effeminacy.

With such attitudes to deal with, it's not surprising that most of Little Havana's gay population prefers the safety of the closet to the risks of gay activism. The only noticeable homosexuals are those whose looks and mannerisms seem to confirm their community's most cherished beliefs and worst expectations. One such character lived in the apartment building my family and I dwelled in around 1968. The man in question was an *artista,* a word which is Spanish for an artist or an entertainer but which, as it was used by my parents, left no doubt as to what the man's sexual orientation was. A bit player in community theater and local television shows, our neighbor, who, to make things worse, bore the androgynous name of Angel, was lean and fastidious and spoke Spanglish with a pronounced lisp (as did I!). I remember the impression Angel invariably gave as he sashayed down the hall, greeting my bemused parents before vanishing into the apartment he shared with his elderly mother and maiden aunt. Though a charming and doubtlessly courageous man, Angel appeared to be rarely happy and always alone. He was definitely not a good role model for a confused teenager who was trying to deal with feelings that he knew would outrage everyone around him (save one).

Though Calle Ocho was not without its share of obviously gay men, they seemed to gather around such professions as hairdressing, studio photography and show business. The prevalence of *maricones* in Little Havana's theatrical industry is somewhat ironic since gay men are popular targets of ridicule in Cuban-American vaudeville, even (especially) in comedies produced by gay-owned theater companies, directed by gay directors and acted out by gay actors. During my formative years Little Havana's leading playhouse, which naturally specialized in gay-baiting farces, was run by an obvious (but discreet) gay couple who apparently saw no conflict between their personal lives and the prejudices they perpetuated on the stage.

Cuban parents would go to any length to save their sons from a fate they believed was worse than death. Many a Cuban boy of uncertain sexuality was subjected to hormone shots, a practice that led to a crop of hirsute, deep-voiced gay men who walk the streets of Miami today. My parents chose a less drastic (though equally popular) measure. Every afternoon after school I would dutifully walk to the local YMCA—where, naturally, Spanish was spoken—and take judo classes, as if my erotic interest in my own gender could be extinguished through physical contact with other males. When that didn't seem to work, my parents sent me to a psychiatrist, an equally futile gesture but one popular with many concerned Cuban parents at that time.

By the time I graduated from high school in 1972, Little Havana had changed. It had expanded its horizons westward as affluent, now naturalized Cuban-Americans began to move to the suburbs. Calle Ocho itself underwent a transformation as the last of the old Anglo-owned businesses closed down and were replaced by Cuban enterprises. Cuban-Americans were ready to assume leadership of the city of Miami from the retreating Anglos, who were now migrating north into Broward and Palm Beach counties.

I turned twenty in 1973. That year I became both an American citizen and a practicing homosexual, no small feat for a man who is naturally reluctant to take chances. My parents had moved into a house just outside of Little Havana and I had moved along with them, commuting to and from college and a part-time job selling shoes at a Hialeah shoe store owned by a Cuban Danny De Vito. I also worked as a dishwasher for a greasy spoon whose manager was a notorious chicken hawk who invariably invited all his young employees to his apartment for some tea and sympathy. Finding both job and boss unattractive, I quit after a few weeks.

Determined to work my way through college, I got a job in the school library, which helped my coming out process in two ways. First, the library carried all the latest "gay liberation" books, which I, an incorrigible bookworm, did not fail to read. Second, the library had a very cruisy men's room, which I used to good benefit during my student years. From tearooms I "graduated" to adult bookstores and then, in 1974, to gay bars.

Though my parents had long suspected, they did not have to face my sexual orientation outright until one night when I, my inhibitions dulled by alcohol, finally blurted it out to them (so much for my education). I offered to move out then and there but my parents, for whom the family unit is paramount, wouldn't hear of it. Apparently they thought that my reputation (and theirs) would be safer if I remained under parental supervision.

Most twenty-year-olds would have taken this opportunity to leave an increasingly uncomfortable parental nest and set up a place of their own. But Little Havana, like big Havana, is a family-oriented society that expects its sons and daughters to reside with their parents until they get, heterosexually, a means of escape that is unavailable to most lesbian or gay Cubans. *La familia* comes first, which means that "little" Jesse (or everyone else in his predicament) was expected to drop everything in order to assist his parents, straight siblings, aunts, uncles, and cousins.

In the Cuban community a façade of heterosexuality must be maintained while living at home. If one's sexual orientation is known it is treated as, at best, an unfortunate vice that should only be indulged elsewhere. It's no wonder that, once away from their parents, many young gay Cubans went wild. This system of repression and hypocrisy also applied to heterosexual singles, though they have the privilege of eventually getting married, thus adding respectability (and children) to their sexual relations.

An institution that developed in order to deal with the plight of the Cuban single was the *posada,* a drive-in motel which rented by the hour. During the early seventies Calle Ocho was home to several *posadas,* places where Cuban gays and straight singles alike went for sexual release before going home to *Mama y Papa.* A couple would check in, do their business, and check out, after which the motel attendant would come in to change the bed and clean up a bit before renting the same room to another couple. To their credit *posada* managers and attendants were very accepting of sexual diversity, though I once tried their sense of tolerance by bringing in a dirty-looking, *Americano hippiado* ("hippyish" American) I picked up somewhere. In any case, with Cuban libidos (my own included) running high, *posada* owners made a tidy profit. I remember trying to find a room on New Year's Eve 1974 only to find an especially long waiting list and impatient couples lining up around the block.

Not having a car or a place of my own, my sex life depended upon the kindness of strangers. Still, I was able to enjoy Little Havana's lively but furtive gay male social scene, one that centered around bars, beaches, a few private homes (for not all gay Cubans lived with their parents), and the newly opened Club Miami baths. Camp humor combined with Latin high spirits to create a light and lively atmosphere, which, within its limitations, offered Cuban gay men a break from the problems of living in a society that hated them. Some gay Cubans stood machismo on its head by adopting outrageously effeminate behavior, at least within the confines of gay space, while others sought to let off steam through heavy drug or alcohol use and promiscuous sex.

Being a relatively handsome and newly uninhibited young guy in his early twenties, I was able to enjoy many of the pleasures Little Havana's gay demimonde had to offer. From other gay Cubans I learned how to dress (bell-bottom pants and platform shoes were then the rage), to stay up late, to hold my liquor, to cruise and deal with rejection (nonchalantly). I even "learned" to adopt an effeminate pose and to refer to myself and others as "she," though this was something I never cared for. Though I did not have a car, I joined friends who did for joyrides to the gay beach on Virginia Key and north to Fort Lauderdale's hot spots. My sex partners—and I was seldom without one—ranged from my first lover, a Cuban eighteen years older than me who eventually left me to join a Pentecostal church, to a Mexican doctor on vacation and the above-mentioned *Americano hippiado*.

To many Cubans, gay men want to be women. Many gay Cubans took them at their word and got as close to being women as finances and opportunities allowed. Some went into female impersonation, an art form that flourishes in South Florida. Others went the whole route, becoming genital females through hormones and surgery. Many of these were unhappy and confused gay kids who, growing up in an atmosphere of self-hatred, saw a sex change as the only alternative to suicide. They should not be confused with the true transsexuals, people who knew what they wanted and usually got it.

The most memorable of the gender benders who inhabited Little Havana's demimonde was Silvia, who, when I first met her, was a large and imposing *transformista* who lip-synched in straight and gay bars in the neighborhood. (Her impressions of La Lupe, a salsa singer known for throwing her shoes and her wig at the audience, were legendary.) Silvia's goal was to save enough money to have a sex change operation, a goal that she eventually accomplished. I remember the party Silvia's friends gave her the night before she checked into the hospital, a combination victory party and wake that I, a friend of a friend, was invited to. The operation was a success and Silvia, "the woman who became a legend" (as the title of a never-produced stage rendition of her life proclaimed), settled down as a lesbian, eventually moving in with a tough dyke who managed a Cuban lesbian bar on Miami Beach.

Though gay life in Little Havana was fun while it lasted, this shallow and somewhat neurotic scene became ponderous after a while. I was never happy with the excessive effeminacy, the heavy drug and alcohol use, the backstabbing and catfighting (I was once robbed by a so-called friend), the self-hatred, and the need to pretend. I wanted to break with my surroundings, to finish college and find a place of my own. I also wanted to find a permanent lover and get involved in gay activism, two commodities that were scarce on Calle Ocho. By 1978, a year after Little Havana joined the rest of Dade County in overturning a gay rights ordinance, I accomplished all of these goals and moved out of Little Havana, not because of the vote but to be with my lover. I moved to Broward County and a chapter in my life came to an end.

In some ways, I never "left" Little Havana. Fort Lauderdale, where I now live, is only an hour's drive from Miami, in the same state and in the next county. As it turned out, I now live in a section of Fort Lauderdale that is becoming increasingly Hispanic, with a social and commercial life reminiscent of Calle Ocho during the sixties. Fort Lauderdale seems to be a near-perfect compromise between living at home and living away from home. Even my parents have accepted my living arrangements—though they still expect me to visit them.

Calle Ocho has changed much during the past decade. It is now a tourist attraction along the lines of New Orleans' French Quarter, though without the *Vieux Carré's* historical authenticity and artistic reputation. Miami's Cuban community has changed as well, though they might not admit it. If Miami is now "a Cuban city"—a majority of the city's commissioners, municipal employees, business owners, and residents are Hispanic—it is equally true that an overwhelming majority of Miami's Cubans have been Americanized, though not assimilated enough to please their critics. My generation of Cuban-Americans, who has now come of age, is largely U.S.-educated, speaks fluent English, and enjoys American careers, tastes, and often American-born, non-Hispanic spouses.

As for me, I have changed my first name, my religion, and my address, and I profess political views and a sexual orientation that are at odds with those held dear by most Cuban-Americans. My English is even more fluent than my Spanish, though I still speak both with a telltale accent (and a lisp!). My lover, most of my friends, and my economic, social, and cultural life are largely non-Hispanic, and I cannot visit Calle Ocho these days without realizing that I do not belong there anymore.

Still, I am Cuban by birth, descent, and upbringing, my

surname is still Monteagudo (a name that remains unpronounce-able for most non-Hispanics), and at times I still count and curse in Spanish. I am proud of the way Miami's Cuban community (*mi gente*) has changed the social and economic life of Dade County, even while electing politicians who hold political views that are diametrically opposed to my own. One of the buttons on my car radio remains tuned to a Miami-based Spanish-language station, which I always play whenever I drive down Calle Ocho.

As an openly gay man, I can never be reconciled with Little Havana, as it is personified by my relatives and by other Cubans and Cuban-Americans with whom I come in contact. I recently made a very reluctant appearance at my sister's second wedding, an event to which my lover was not invited. Many of my relatives were there, accompanied, of course, by their heterosexual spouses and their children. Though my sister and cousins have life-styles that are vastly different from those of their parents—most of them are married to non-Cubans and most of them have been divorced—their views on homosexuality remain similar to those of the generation before them.

In spite of it all, I have made my peace with my past and do not regret having liked it. Calle Ocho will always be a street of memories that, with the flight of time, become increasingly better. Growing up in Little Havana has made me what I am today, and that can't be all bad.

GARDENLAND, SACRAMENTO, CALIFORNIA

I GREW UP IN A NEIGH-
borhood of Sacramento called Gardenland, a poor community,
almost entirely Mexican, where my maternal family, the Acunas,
had lived since the 1920s. Sacramento's only distinction used to
be that it was the state capital. Today, because it frequently ap-
pears on lists of the country's most livable cities, weary big-town
urbanites have turned it into a boomtown rapidly becoming un-
livable. But when I was a child, in the late fifties and early sixties,
the only people who lived in Sacramento were the people who'd
been born there.

Downtown the wide residential neighborhoods were lined
with oaks shading turreted, run-down Victorian mansions, some
partitioned into apartments, others still of a piece, but all of them
exuding a shadowy small-town melancholy. The commercial district was block after block of shabby brick buildings housing
small businesses. The city's skyline was dominated by the gold-
domed capitol, a confectioner's spun-sugar dream of a building.

It was set in a shady park whose grass seemed always to glisten magically, as if hidden under each blade of grass were an Easter egg.

Sacramento's only other landmarks of note were its two rivers, the American and the Sacramento. They came together in muddy confluence beneath the slender iron joints of railroad bridges. Broad and shallow, the rivers passed as slowly as thought between the thick and tumble of their banks.

A system of levees fed into the rivers. One of these tributaries was called the Bannon Slough. Gardenland was a series of streets carved out of farmland backed up against the slough. It flowed south, curving east behind a street called Columbus Avenue, creating Gardenland's southern and eastern boundaries. The northern boundary was a street called El Camino. Beyond El Camino was middle-class tract housing. To the west, beyond Bowman Street, were fields and then another neighborhood that may just as well have existed on another planet for all I knew of it.

What I knew were the nine streets of Gardenland: Columbus, Jefferson, Harding, Cleveland, El Camino, Peralta, Wilson, Haggin, and Bowman; an explorer, an odd lot of presidents, an unimaginative Spanish phrase, and three inexplicable proper names, one in Spanish, two in English. It was as if the streets had been named out of a haphazard perusal of a child's history text. There were two other significant facts about the streets in Gardenland; they all dead-ended into the levee and their names were not continued across El Camino Boulevard into the Anglo suburb, called Northgate. Gardenland's streets led, literally, nowhere.

Unlike El Camino, where little square houses sat on little square lots, Gardenland had not been subdivided to maximum utility. Broad uncultivated fields stretched between and behind the ramshackle houses. Someone's "front yard" might consist of a quarter acre of tall grass and the remnants of an almond orchard. The fields were littered with abandoned farming implements and the foundations of long-gone houses. For a dreamy boy like me, these artifacts were magical. Finding my own world often harsh, I could imagine from these rusted pieces of metal and fragments of walls a world in which I would have been a prince.

But princes were hard to come by in Gardenland. Almost everyone was poor, and most residents continued to farm after a fashion, keeping vegetable gardens and flocks of chickens. There were neither sidewalks nor streetlights, and the roads, cheaply paved, were always crumbling and narrow as country lanes. At night, the streets and fields were lit by moonlight and the stars burned with millennial intensity above the low roofs of our houses.

The best way to think of Gardenland is not as an American suburb at all, but rather as a Mexican village, transported perhaps from Guanajuato, where my grandmother's family originated, and set down lock, stock, and chicken coop in the middle of California.

My cousin Josephine Robles had divided her tiny house in half and ran a beauty shop from one side. Above her porch was a wooden sign that said in big blue letters GARDENLAND and, in smaller print below, BEAUTY SALON. Over the years the weather took its toll and the bottom half faded completely, leaving only the word GARDENLAND in that celestial blue, like a road sign to a cut-rate Eden.

By the time I was born, in 1954, my family had lived in Gardenland for at least twenty-five years. Virtually all I know of my grandfather's family, the Acunas, was that they were Yaqui Indians living in northern Mexico near the American border at Yuma, Arizona. My grandmother's family, the Trujillos, had come out of central Mexico in 1920, escaping the displacements caused by the Mexican Revolution of 1910. I have dim memories of my great-grandparents, Ygnacio and Phillipa Trujillo, doll-like, white-haired figures living in a big, dark two-story house in east Sacramento.

My grandparents settled on Haggin Avenue in a house they built themselves. My cousins, the Robles, lived two doors down. My family also eventually lived on Haggin Avenue, next door to my grandparents. Our house was the pastel plaster box that became standard suburban architecture in California in the fifties and sixties but it was the exception in Gardenland.

Most houses seemed to have begun as shacks to which rooms were added to accommodate expanding families. They were not built with privacy in mind but simply as shelter. We lived in a series of such houses until our final move to Haggin Avenue. In one of them, the living room was separated from the kitchen by the narrow rectangular bedroom in which my brothers and sisters and I slept. Adults were always walking through it while we were trying to sleep. This made for jittery children, but no one had patience for our complaints. It was enough that we had a place to live.

By the standards of these places, my grandparent's house was luxurious. It was a four-bedroom, L -shaped building that they had built themselves. My grandmother put up the original three rooms while my grandfather was in the navy during World War II. My aunt Socorro told me that my grandmother measured the rooms by having her children lie head to toe across a plot of ground. She bought the cement for the foundations, mixed and troweled it, and even installed pipes for plumbing. Later, when my grandfather returned, they added a series of long, narrow rooms paneled in slats of dark-stained pine, solid and thick walled.

Massive, dusty couches upholstered in a heavy maroon fabric, oversize beds soft as sponges, and a leather-topped dining room table furnished the house. Like the rusted combines in the field, these things seemed magical in their antiquity. I would slip into the house while my grandparents were both at work and wander through it, opening drawers and inspecting whatever presented itself to my attention. It was in this fashion that I opened a little-used closet and found it full of men's clothes that obviously were not my grandfather's. Later I learned that they had belonged to my uncle Raymond who had been killed in a car accident. In a subsequent exploration I found pictures of his funeral, including a picture taken of him in his casket, a smooth-faced, dark-skinned, pretty boy of fifteen.

Another time, I found a voluminous red petticoat in a cedar chest. Without much hesitation, I put it on and went into my grandmother's bedroom where I took out her face powder and lipstick. I applied these in the careful manner of my grandmother, transforming myself in the dressing mirror beneath the grim gaze of a crucified Christ. Looking back, I don't think I was trying to transform myself into a girl, but only emulating the one adult in my family who loved me without condition. Because she was the soul of kindness, it never occurred to me, as a child, that my grandmother might be unhappy. Only looking back do I see it.

She and my grandfather slept in separate rooms at opposite ends of their house. In the evening, my grandfather would sit on a couch in front of the television quietly drinking himself into a stupor while my grandmother did needlework at the kitchen table. They barely spoke. I would sit with my grandmother, looking at pictures in the *Encyclopedia Americana,* comfortable with the silence, which, to her, must have been a deafening indictment of a failed marriage.

In my parents' house, the marriage of my mother and stepfather was as noisily unhappy as my grandparents' was quietly miserable. In each shabby house where we lived I would be awakened by their fights. I learned to turn myself into a stone, or become part of the bed or the walls so as to abate the terror I felt. No one ever spoke of it. There was only one house in which my family lived together peaceably but it only existed as a blueprint that had come somehow into my stepfather's possession.

In the evening, he would take it down from a shelf and unroll it on the kitchen table. Together we would study it, laying claim to rooms, planning alterations. At the time, we lived in a tiny one-bedroom cinder-block house. My brother and I slept on a bunk bed in an alcove off the kitchen. At night, I could hear mice scampering across the cement floor, terrifying me when I woke up having to pee and pick my way through the darkness to the bathroom.

When we finally moved from the cinder-block house, it was to another, bigger version of that house rather than to the dream house of the blueprint. One night, my mother's screaming woke me. I hurried into the bedroom she and my stepfather occupied and found him beating her. When I tried to stop him, he threw me across the room. The next morning my mother told me he was sorry, but it was too late. Where I lived no longer mattered to me because I learned to live completely within myself in rooms of rage and grief. Now I think these rooms were not so different from the rooms we all occupied, my unhappy family and I.

Although not literally cut off from the outside world, Gardenland was little touched by it. We were tribal in our outlook and our practices. Anglos were generically called "paddies," whether or not they were Irish. All fair-skinned people were mysterious but also alike. Even TV, that great equalizer, only emphasized our isolation since we never saw anyone who looked remotely like us, or lived as we did, on any of the popular shows of the day. At school, the same homogeneity prevailed. Until I was nine I attended a neighborhood grade school where virtually every other child was like me, dark eyed and dark skinned, answering to names like Juarez, Delgadillo, Robles, Martinez. My own name, Michael Angel, was but an Anglicized version of Miguel Angel, a name I shared with at least three other of my classmates.

I had a remarkable amount of freedom as a child. As I said, we eventually lived on the same street as other members of my maternal family and I roamed their houses as unself-consciously as a Bedouin child might move among the tents of his people. I ate in whatever house I found myself at mealtime and the meals were the same in each of my relatives' houses—rice, beans, lettuce and tomato salad, stewed or fried meat, tortillas, salsa. My grandparents did not lock their doors at night—who did? what was there to steal?—so that I could slip into their house quietly and make my bed on their sofa when my parents were fighting.

But most of the time I spent outdoors, alone or with my friends. In spring, the field behind my house was overrun with thistles. We neighborhood kids put in long days cutting trails through them and hacking out clearings that became our forts. Tiring of the fields, we'd lurk in abandoned houses, empty barns, and chicken coops. When all other amusements failed, there was always Bannon Slough, a muddy brown creek that flowed between thickly wooded banks. It was too filthy to swim in. Instead, in the steep shadows of bridges and railroad trestles we taught each other how to smoke and to swear.

Just as often I would be off by myself. Early on, I looked for ways to escape my family. I found it in the stillness of the grass and the slap of the slough's brown water against the shore. There I discovered my own capacity for stillness. Lying on the slope of the levee, I could hear my own breath in the wind and feel my skin in the warm blades of grass that pressed against my neck. In those moments, Gardenland *was* Eden, and I felt the wonder and loneliness of the first being.

For, like Adam, I was lonely. Being everyone's child, I was no one's child. I could disappear in the morning and stay out until dusk and my absence went unnoticed. Children barely counted as humans in our tribe. We were more like livestock and our parents' main concern was that the head count at night matched the head count in the morning.

My loneliness became as much a part of me as my brown hair and the mole above my lip, something unremarkable. When I came out, I missed that sense of joining a community of others like me that so many of my friends describe. My habits of secrecy and loneliness were too deeply ingrained. I had become like my grandfather, who, in a rare moment of self-revelation, told me he was a "lone wolf"; the most unsociable of an unsociable tribe. Though I've changed as I've grown older, I still sometimes wonder if one reason I write is because I am filled with all the words I never spoke as a child.

Two things opened up for me the narrow passage through which I finally escaped Gardenland for good. The first was books. I learned to read early and, once started, could not get enough of books. In this affinity, I was neither encouraged nor discouraged by my family. Education beyond its most basic functions, learning how to read and write, to do sums, had absolutely no interest for them. My love of reading became simply another secret part of me.

There wasn't a library in Gardenland. Instead, a big white van pulled up to the corner of Wilson and El Camino, the city Bookmobile. Inside, patrons squeezed into a narrow passageway between tall shelves of books. The children's books occupied the bottom shelves. At the exit, a woman checked out books from a standing desk. The Bookmobile came once a week and I was a regular customer, always taking my limit of books.

Everything about the process pleased me. I was proud of my library card, a yellow piece of cardboard with my name typed on it, which I carried in a cowhide wallet that was otherwise empty. I liked taking books from the shelves, noting their heft and volume, the kind of type, whether they were illustrated, and I studied the record of their circulation, the checkout dates stamped in blue on stiff white cards in paper pockets on the inside covers. I loved the books as much as I loved reading. To me, they were organic things, as alive in their way as I was.

Like so many other bright children growing up in the inarticulate world of the poor, books fueled my imagination, answered my questions, led me to new ones, and helped me conceive of a world in which I would not feel so set apart. Yet I do not believe that my brains alone, even aided by my bookish fantasies, would have been enough to escape Gardenland. For this, I needed the kind of courage that arises out of desperation.

I found this courage in my homosexuality. Early on, I acquired a taste for reading history, particularly ancient history. I suppose that pictures of ruined Greek cities reminded me of the crumbling, abandoned houses in the fields of Gardenland. But I was also fascinated by pictures of the nude male statues. There was something about the smooth, headless torsos, the irisless eyes of ephebes that made me stop my idle flipping through pages and touch the paper where these things were depicted. By the time I was twelve I understood that my fascination was rooted in my sexual nature. One day, walking to school, clutching my books to my chest, girl-style, I heard myself say, "I'm a queer."

It was absolutely clear to me that Gardenland could not accommodate this revelation. Gardenland provided the barest of existences for its people. What made it palatable was the knowledge that everyone was about the same, united in ethnicity and poverty and passivity. The only rituals were the rituals of family, and family was everything there. But I knew that I was not the same as everyone else. And I was certain that my family, already puzzled by my silent devotion to books, would reject me entirely if it became known exactly what thoughts occupied my silence.

Had I been a different child I would have run away from home. Instead, I ran away without leaving home. I escaped to books, to sexual fantasy, to painful, unrequited crushes on male classmates. No one ever knew. I turned myself into an outsider, someone at the margins of a community that was itself outcast. Paradoxically, by doing this, I learned the peasant virtues of my hometown, endurance and survival. As a member of yet another embattled community, those virtues I absorbed as a child continue to serve me.

CARMEL, CALIFORNIA

LIKE MOST YOUNG MEN who were suspected sissies, I had learned to make the best of a bad situation from a very early age. By the summer of 1969, I was a master of disguise (or so I thought), coolly hiding my true feelings behind a bland, inscrutable mask. In truth, I was a terrified seventeen-year-old; afraid of being drafted into the Vietnam war, anxious that a decade of heady license was about to pass me by, and apprehensive about nearly everything else.

I couldn't possibly imagine how a ragtag riot in a dingy Greenwich Village bar would soon transform these premonitions of dread into an awkward promise. But, of course, I had no clue of how an event three thousand miles away was going to change my life any more than I knew who I really was at the moment. All I wanted that humid June night was the keys to the car.

As I sat at one end of the dinner table, idly pushing mounds of meatloaf and mashed potatoes across my plate, I could sense my father studying me over the top of the catsup bottle that stood guard on the lazy Susan. This condiment-festooned wheel was more than just an ubiquitous centerpiece to my family's life: it was symbolic of the great divide that separated a father and his oldest son. There were always few words exchanged between us, but tonight the silence seemed deafening. Finally, he spoke.

"Here, you'd better take these or you'll be late," my father gruffly said, holding out the keys to the family's big-finned station wagon.

Not wanting to appear too grateful, I casually plucked the keys from the edge of the table and mumbled a hasty "thanks" as I headed for the door. I displayed the obvious, barely controlled jitters of a boy setting off on a first date, although by now it was no secret that I was not interested in girls quite that way. No, I was determined to be on time for another kind of romance.

For as long as I had been able to remember, the movies and their magic-box images seemed more real to me than the outer world I was so guarded against. There, in the secure darkness of the neighborhood theater, dug down deep in one of its bumpy stained seats, I could let go and claim my most private thoughts. Like so many others, I had found the ideal mirror for secret dreaming.

By the time I was nine, I was going to the movies nearly every Saturday. I would hurry down the cypress-shaded alleys of Pacific Grove, a small California coastal town founded by Methodist missionaries in 1889, eager not to be late. Typically, the afternoon climaxed with the spectacular ruin of modern Tokyo or ancient Rome. These fulsome epics satisfied my overactive imagination for at least another week. Being way too flushed to go right home, I'd have to burn off my excitement by walking around the few quaint blocks of downtown, calming myself with the basso tones of a foghorn announcing the imminent arrival of dusk. Then, as if on some automatic track, my steps took me back to the theater and the Greyhound bus station next door, where I'd spend the last hour of daylight peeking through the pages of men's magazines. These racks were known to be off-limits to boys my age. But at five o'clock, while the clerk attended to the final busload of the day, I'd edge past the sign warning NO MINORS and trespass into the adult reading section.

There, my imagination was fed by exotic fantasies of a different kind. Row after row of lurid covers advertised the forbidden in a frenzy of color and action: men holding big guns blazed at charging stags; gritty soldiers-of-fortune leered at women in torn slips; other women (sometimes tied to a chair or bed) recoiled from menacing shadows. Such stolen moments were my initiation into the world of men. It seemed like an impossibly foreign world, and never more so than after these nervous excursions. After a heart-thumping minute or two, I would dash out of the station and into the street. Inhaling a long draught of damp evening air, I began the walk home, trudging up the dark hill while contemplating a perplexed mixture of anxiety and glee.

During the warmer months, my mother dutifully escorted my younger brother and sister and me to the ocean and the last saltwater pool in California, where we were given swimming lessons from a very early age. Over the years, I found myself growing bolder there as well. While manly mysteries came to light at the Greyhound depot, other matters found exposure at the pool's deep end.

One summer, I was told I could leave shallow water and take on the whole plunge. Wasting no time, I soon learned a new and risky game. Hidden among the bigger kids, I would hold my breath and sink all the way to the bottom of the diving area, where I'd deftly tug my trunks down around an ankle. It felt exciting to be naked in the water where no one could see. And when, at last, I began to feel light-headed, I quickly pulled my suit back on and shot to the surface. This daring act was done without incident for quite a while. But, one day, my trunks slipped to the bottom of the pool and, shamefaced, I had to beg a stranger for help. As I made my way through the grinning crowd, my butt not quite covered by a towel, I realized that the deep end had already lost its wonder. For that year I had also been allowed membership into the dank and murky recesses of the grown-up locker room. It was there that curiosity about myself—and other men—came out of hiding. From that afternoon on, I knew that vicarious living would never satisfy this prickly appetite for knowing.

During my first semester of high school, our family moved

from the five acres of country land we had occupied the previous few years. We had left Pacific Grove when my mother announced that my sister needed a horse. My father countered with the fact that boys need a dog—and off we'd gone. But the problems of rural living were not as easily resolved. So, in the fall of 1965, we moved back to the ocean, on the other side of the peninsula from where I had spent my childhood. Now I was living near Carmel, the fabled artist's colony with a storybook veneer. I wasted no time in adapting to this new environment.

While empty brown hills—and the dog—had provided a certain solitary contentment, I much preferred the abundant countryside that now surrounded me. There was something exciting to discover in every direction: canyons and coves and deserted river beaches, where sometimes my brother and I would run naked, playing a coy hide-and-seek among the willow. Other days, we'd take our motor scooter out for a run through the fields of artichoke plants that grew for miles around; I, driving down the rutted dirt lanes, Kirk, holding on tight. There, among the bright blue thistles of artichokes gone to flower, we gave permission and grace to each other. Years later, I would find that he, too, was a gay man.

Aside from natural beauty, the landscape was blessed with fascinating people: retired movie stars, famous painters, and rugged individualists of every persuasion added to the local panorama. The town had the scent of celebrity, its beaches glistened white, and every vista seemed a perfect photo opportunity. In fact, the area had sustained itself for years on a charming image as cultivated as its scenery. Precocious to a fault, this sophisticated village tucked away in the woods, known around the world for its romantic ambiance, contained about as much reality as a Hollywood back lot. But at fifteen, and still enamored with any world but the one I was in, I could scarcely notice the difference. I lost no time in proclaiming Carmel-by-the-Sea as home. Little did I realize how like a hometown boy I really was.

The village was a tourist mecca, of course. Locals took great pride in recounting the days when the likes of Langston Hughes, Edward Weston, and Robinson Jeffers helped secure Carmel's reputation as an artists' colony. (I can still vividly picture Jeffers's granddaughter, a fellow classmate, arriving at school from her grandfather's somber stone tower, where she lived. Swathed in a great hooded cape as protection against the morning chill, she was poetry defined.) Still, the day had long gone when working artists could afford to live in the village, for poet's cabins were now remade into pricey shops.

Creative pretensions were kept alive, however, by the gay men in town, a kind of queen's guard who kept watch over the expensive boutiques. I was able to single them out from the other townspeople almost immediately; a kind of ineffable gay radar was at work. And the more I saw, the more I became aware of this stylish clique, a homintern among the pines. Cashmere sweaters and manicured good looks seemed the uniform of choice. Conversations were invariably punctuated by witty asides, usually a line from a Broadway show or old movie that escaped my reference. I had heard about homosexuals, and somehow knew that I was one too. Yet I was made profoundly uncomfortable with the thought that someday I might be like these gentlemen of Carmel.

Certainly, they were gentlemen. Aside from an occasional knowing smile, they never overstepped their bounds with me. Polite to a fault, gracious, and with an amusing story to tell, Carmel's gay men tended to its image and seemed to ask nothing in return except to be left alone. But I heard the stories. Like the night the director of the town's small dinner-theater was seen sobbing alone on the beach. Or the times a well-known married art teacher would disappear for days, saying on his return that he had only gone "painting." Or the hushed-up rumors of suicides and bitchy alcoholic spats in public. These currents of innuendo and gossip, which circulated around the town like a malicious ether, became known to me. They penetrated my frightened consciousness. I was afraid—and achingly so—that someday such things might be true about me. So I kept the fact that I knew these stories closely guarded. It was one way, I must have thought, to buy protection against exposure of myself—as if knowledge, in this case, was power. Still, the hoarding of such secrets meant that I was living a life as lonely and prepossessed as the older gentlemen around me. These gay men I now saw with different eyes.

▪ ▪ ▪

Suddenly, I realized how isolated I was from my own feelings. I could understand why some of my new friends harshly criticized Carmel. It was like being in a "gilded cage," they said. They saw the town as an enclave of rich, privileged white people, culturally isolated from the social awareness then angrily fomenting in other places. Now, disillusioned with its glamour, I saw Carmel as indeed a cage, a place for men just like me. Beneath its golden mystique, and the charm of its most avid caretakers, was a sadness and rage turned inward. For the gentlemen of Carmel, gilding the outer self must have been a way of keeping souls heavy with grief from bursting.

During the next two years, I stayed close to school and home and scrupulously avoided going downtown except for the briefest errands. The tiny one-mile-square shopping district, which according to the map was most of the town, seemed unchangeable. Only the seasonal tide of tourists marked its timeless demeanor. The rest of the world around me, however, was in a state of upheaval. I heard about Martin Luther King and nonviolent civil disobedience the day Joan Baez came to sing to my sophomore class on Carmel High's sweeping front lawn. Fritz Perls and many others were preaching the values of "human potential" at the newly formed Esalen Institute, just a few miles down the Big Sur coast. I smoked my first joint on campus the following year, while struggling to put an experimental student paper to bed at two in the morning. And bearded young men hitchhiking on Highway One, which bordered the campus, came forward and talked about peace and the horrors of a war in Southeast Asia. The world was in turmoil, everything was changing. Even me.

As I drove the family car up Carmel Valley Road that warm June night, I reflected on all that had happened the past few years. Carefully steering past headlights on the winding country highway, I thought about my father, too. I knew he was there for me, however distant he usually appeared. After all, he *had* given me the keys to the car. Still, it must be difficult for him, I admitted, knowing his son was gay. And, of course, it was no secret to either one of us that he knew.

By every account, my father was a man's man. Handsome and athletic, he had been a star quarterback in high school. After serving in the navy during World War II, he worked for a while as a forest ranger. He still liked to hunt and fish. Even his nickname was "Butch." And although I was born in the same place as my father and, so far as I know, his father too, I was never, for the slightest moment, ever destined to be called "Butch." He suspected this from an early age. While I felt no less a man on account of different interests, my father nevertheless seemed obliged to compare notes on rare occasions.

He had done this just the previous week. I was about to leave the house for a rehearsal of a play I was working on at the local theater company, when he called me out to the garage. "I hear you've been going downtown and hanging out with that theater crowd," he said, toeing an imaginary line on the cement floor. I was speechless, more from dread than lack of words, for I knew where the conversation was headed. "Well, you know some of the things that can happen," my father continued. "They haven't happened to you, have they?"

I pondered his question in embarrassed silence for a minute or two. Nothing of what he was implying had ever happened; except for one summer-stock performance when, as a member of the musical chorus, I was caught putting on too much eyeliner. Finally, I feebly replied, "I don't think so."

My father stood in the dim garage light, surrounded by the bins of gleaming copper pipe fittings that marked his trade, and looked me straight in the eye. "I just want you to take care of yourself, son," he said. I noticed how tired and haggard he looked. Things had not been going well with my mother for quite some time, and it showed.

We stared at each other for a while longer, tension crackling between us. Then he spoke out again, telling me about a job he had just completed. He had been repairing pipes up the valley, he explained, at the old Tantamount Theatre, and heard that it was in need of a weekend assistant. He had volunteered me, my father said, for that very Saturday night. I was stunned. Any pretense between us had just been stripped bare. Queasy with panic, I wanted nothing more than to run out of the garage.

Instead, I remained motionless, determined not to betray any emotion. My father looked relieved at the decision that apparently had just been made. "I know you'll do well there," he quietly said, his eyes downcast. And that was the end of our conversation.

The Tantamount was treasured by everyone in the valley, and its proprietors were equally held in esteem. François Martin and John Ralph Geddis had come to Carmel a decade before, creative bohemians looking for a quiet retreat. They met in 1931, and had remained collaborators in life and art over the years. During the Depression, they operated a puppet theater on Boston's Beacon Hill. They later toured the nation with their troupe of actors and masterfully carved stick-and-rod puppets, performing diminutive versions of the classics, everything from Shakespeare to *Alice In Wonderland.* After years of performing they settled in Carmel Valley and rebuilt an old barn into a theater and home.

The Tantamount was a magical place; every board and batten was soaked with the spirit of its builders. Dramatically set on a grassy slope, sheltered by craggy white oaks, the theater's soaring roof was framed by the steep valley walls behind it. At night the trees were artfully lit by low soft lamps, and fanciful shadows played against the dry grass and weathered sides of the building. People from miles around would drive down the theater's long gravel drive on Friday and Saturday nights and find François motioning them onward with a flashlight. A trim, elegant man, usually cloaked in some garment he had woven himself, François greeted each arrival with a smile. Meanwhile, Ralph was busy in the theater's tiny balcony loading that evening's featured presentation into the projector.

Having grown older, they reserved their puppets for special occasions only. Now, their main bill of fare was classic films from the "golden age of cinema," as François would declaim. *Dinner at Eight, Los Olvidados,* musicals, *La Belle et la Bête,* the films of Keaton and Chaplin, *Rules of the Game,* Arletty in *Les Enfants du Paradis, Camille.* Each was offered up as the exquisite work of art it was, lovingly introduced to the motley audience of valley folk and village sophisticates.

After ushering in the last carload, François shut the Tantamount's redwood doors and walked to the front of the intimate hall. With the economy of a trained actor, he said a few words about that night's double bill. Then, after the slightest bow, he would excuse himself and dash through a side door and behind the illustrated curtain, a scene from Molière's *Bourgeois Gentilhomme,* which he had painted himself. A few seconds passed before the resonant tones of a gong were heard throughout the room. This was Ralph's cue to lower the lights and start up the film.

There, seated in the back row, my romance with the movies was rekindled. More important, it was where my true and lasting romance with self began. Ralph and François were the first great teachers I had in life. Indeed, they offered the best lessons any young gay man could wish to have.

It was my job to assist people, once they had parked, through the dark to the theater. During intermission, outdoors among the oaks, I served coffee in white demitasse cups. If Ralph was busy mending a broken reel, I was asked to take tickets at the door. After the last patron had left, the three of us would sit and review the evening's program. Their knowledge of world cinema was encyclopedic, but it was their opinion of one actress, in particular, that remains indelibly impressed on me. It was Garbo, and Garbo alone, who stood above all others, they said. I was caught in the swirl of their enthusiasm and agreed. Her androgynous mystery was oddly confirming of feelings beyond my words.

Some evenings after the show they would take me on a tour of the theater and its adjoining studio. Fine prints, Oriental antiques, and shelves of books were carefully displayed. A loom, carving blades, paintbrushes, and other well-worn tools littered their private quarters. They were the creators of a special universe—especially of their own lives—and who they were, and what they said, was at odds with what I had previously observed about gay men. As we grew to know one another, they told me more stories.

"In thirty-one, you could very easily live off five dollars a week," Ralph would begin one such conversation. "Food was cheap and tomato soup that could eat the tin off the can was plentiful." François would chuckle in reply. "Oh, yes, you could make a little go a long way. When we reached a starving point there was always a watch we could pawn. The only problem with that was that they gave less for it each time!"

The men would continue with their tales, often past midnight; love clearly expressed for the other. During the late 1930s, went another story, they designed Macy's windows in New York each Christmas. It took a year to create the dozens of mechanical figures that filled the windows, all brought to life by an intricate system of pulleys and gears. When they finished, "we would go up to the top of the Empire State Building and look down on Thirty-fourth Street where the Macy's Thanksgiving Day Parade would end," François proudly recalled.

"The parade would stop in front of the vast window covered by great curtains. Thousands of people were there as the curtains were drawn and they viewed our work," continued Ralph. That was a long time ago, but "our standards will never change. We try to inject a human quality into everything we do." These words were infectious.

Many stories were told, and as the months progressed my relationship with the men deepened. So, too, did the understanding of my own past. Dim memories and half-forgotten moments found new meaning. I remembered long afternoons spent in the window seat of a seaside library reading the Oz books, each in turn. Now, its loony world of half-cast characters and misplaced souls made sense. The brisk autumn morning when, at the age of six, I marched down Lighthouse Avenue dressed as a bright orange monarch butterfly was also recollected. It was a children's parade in celebration of the butterfly's annual return. But, for me, with wire and tissue paper wings held high, I now sensed that day was an inauguration of my path.

By the following summer, my work with Ralph and François had come to an end—my apprenticeship was over. Soon I would be leaving Carmel; a life further north, in San Francisco, was waiting. That I was helped on my journey in a special way, I have no doubt. My father was right about the job: I would do well.

And today, long after words have failed, we both know this to be his lasting gift to me.

OAK RIDGE, TENNESSEE

"OH, UNCLE BOB, THIS looks like 'Happy Days,' " my niece gleefully exclaimed when she discovered the 1955 *Oak Log* on the closet shelf where my mother kept the high school yearbooks of my older brother, Jimmy, my younger sister, Barbara, and myself. Each of us had gone through the school system in Oak Ridge, the small East Tennessee city to which our family moved in 1945, and the three of us were graduates of Oak Ridge High School. So Mama had in her little archive an unbroken record of life at ORHS from the late forties to 1960, years covering a relatively large chunk of the history of the town that was built over several months straddling 1942 and 1943 on the 59,000-acre reservation in the Cumberland foothills that General Leslie R. Groves selected to play a strategic role in the Manhattan Project. Bordered on the southeast and southwest by the meandering Clinch River, Oak Ridge processed the uranium that would be used in the atomic bombs that incinerated Hiroshima and Nagasaki in the world's first clouds of nuclear destruction.

My own years at Oak Ridge High School were 1952 to 1955, the ninth grade still being held at Jefferson Junior High. And in our yearbook pictures I guess we do look something like Richie, Potsie, Ralph, and Joanie, the boys with their flattop haircuts, saddle oxfords, and rolled-up jeans, the girls in their swirling appliquéd skirts, sweaters, furry collars, and bobby sox. And yes, we even had a few Fonzies, with their looked-down-upon ducktails. So my niece, a child of the first full TV generation, was right in her "Happy Days" analogy. Nevertheless I do not recall those years, nor any I spent growing up in Oak Ridge, as happy days. From the time I entered third grade, after we had moved into a small boxlike flattop house unlike any I had ever seen, I always felt I belonged somewhere else.

Later—sometime in high school, I think—when I came across Gertrude Stein's famous "When you get there, there isn't any there there" quote, I felt the same could be said about Oak Ridge. Certainly the town, which never really overcame the military-base look its army builders gave it, was a far cry from Milwaukee, the older city where Marion and Howard Cunningham, Richie and Joan's mom and dad on the popular TV sitcom, kept their cheerfully fiftyish middle-American home.

The new "secret" town, surrounded by a chain and barbedwire fence, where until 1949 you had to show a badge or other documentation to be admitted (often after a car check) was also far different from the mid–South Carolina rural community where my parents came from or even Columbia, that state's capitol, where I was born. When my parents, during all the years they lived in Oak Ridge, referred to "home," what they meant was their native community, called the Dutch Fork ever since Germans had settled there between the V of the Broad and Saluda rivers in the eighteenth century.

It wasn't until well into the fifties, when the U.S. government began selling the houses (economically designed by the architectural firm of Skidmore, Owings, and Merrill) in Oak Ridge to the people who lived in them, that Oak Ridgers began to think of the place as home, however. At Christmas, I recall from the few we spent there, the town was virtually deserted; most families had gone "home" for the holidays. Lucky ones from nearby Appalachian towns and farms went "home" more often. And every summer when my father got his vacation from K-25, the huge (42.6 acres under one roof!) gaseous-diffusion plant where he worked for Union Carbide as an electrician, we could drive over the dizzying, curvy, pre-Interstate route crossing the Tennessee–North Carolina mountains down to the flatter Dutch Fork and home.

The couple of weeks we spent there were what I lived for with longing the rest of the year. The warmth of my grandmother Ma Ellen's hug and laugh, the large family (uncles and aunts and cousins would be there, too) gathered around the big kitchen table at breakfast, the noon dinner, and supper, with Pa Joe, my grandfather, reigning at its head and everyone by turns regaling one another with stories—that, to me, symbolized home. At Grandmother's, my father's home place in another part of the Dutch Fork, meals were more taciturn, but the food would be deliciously plentiful and unlike any served in Oak Ridge, except at Mama's table or, in a lesser way, at that of my more "modern" aunt, Fannie Belle. My mother's younger sister, Aunt Fannie Belle and Uncle Otis and Pat, their daughter, had moved to Oak Ridge just before we did when Uncle Otis, like my father, joined the hordes of workers drawn by the many jobs the Clinton Engineer Works (named after the nearby seat of Anderson County) provided in a part of the nation that only recently had been claimed from the Depression by the Tennessee Valley Authority and the war effort.

Indeed, my father had been a TVA man. And before he went to work at Oak Ridge for Union Carbide, we lived in Fontana, the town built for the workers' families when TVA was constructing Fontana Dam in western North Carolina. I began school there, although my memories of first grade are hazy. Neither do I recall much about my second grade in Knoxville, the city some twenty miles east of Oak Ridge where we lived temporarily while waiting for our name to come to the top of the list for housing assignments in the new town. But I *do* vividly recall helping my brother with his *Knoxville News Sentinel* paper route the afternoon the headline heralded the death of President Roosevelt, whose name

I was raised to revere; he had made TVA possible, "saved the South" (my parents said), and nurtured the Manhattan Project. Then several months later, on August 6, the *News Sentinel* boldly announced the dropping of the atomic bomb on Hiroshima. Suddenly we and the rest of the world knew what Oak Ridge was all about.

Third grade is more firm in my memory, because by then, our name having come up on the housing list, we had moved to that prefabricated flattop in Oak Ridge. It was on a lane just off Louisiana Avenue, then the westernmost of the major north–south throughways running up the ridge from the Turnpike, which ran east to west and was the town's main highway. Miss Pippin, my teacher, told us wonderful "lessons" whether we were learning reading, writing, or arithmetic. And although she had a class filled with widely diverse speech peculiarities and economic backgrounds to work with, she somehow molded us into the oneness of rudimentary English grammar.

Except for one of her charges, whose name, I recall, was Bobby Joe. He was a sometimes playmate of mine—I was called Bobby, too—who lived in a neighboring flattop. I really didn't care to spend much time with him because of his harsh East Tennessee twang, which was so foreign to the South Carolina sounds I loved. And I didn't care at all for his fondness for daredevil roughness. Mama said he was "a real boy" while, I must admit, I wasn't yet very far from the time when my greatest pleasure was dressing up paper dolls with Marlene, my favorite cousin, upstairs in Ma Ellen and Pa Joe's big white frame house where we delightedly whiled away the long afternoons, out of sight and lost in make-believe. My brother Jimmy, whom Mama called her "little man," scorned such "sissy" things, much preferring action involving a football, baseball, rifle, or rod and reel. Those were his ideas of what a boy should be attracted to. Bobby Joe's involved a bike that would run over things, including animals and, sometimes, people.

But after my year with Miss Pippin, we moved eastward to the section of the town centered by Pine Valley, one of the several elementary schools around which various parts of town were clustered. Each section had a small convenience shopping area, also, although to buy groceries at the A&P or Tulip Town or take in movies Oak Ridgers had to go to Townsite or Grove Center. We moved into an "A" house, the smallest of the Skidmore, Owings, and Merrill cemesto designs; others increased in size the farther down the alphabet they went. But there were only a few "F" houses, the largest individual family units ("E"'s being apartment houses), and they were situated atop the ridge and were reserved for local Atomic Energy Commission administrators, managers of the K-25, Y-12, and X-10 plants, and top scientists at the Oak Ridge National Laboratory.

Still, we saw our "A" house on Vermont Avenue as a great leap upward. We had a real roof (pitched, not flat), a brick fireplace, a porch, a yard large enough for Daddy to have a vegetable garden and enclosed tool shed, and a coal furnace, instead of the space heater that so spottily heated our drafty flattop. And soon we got our first telephone. Sure, we were on a party line—but so were most Oak Ridgers. Just to have it hanging on a wall in our narrow kitchen was, to us, proof of our elevated status.

It did not really matter that my brother and I had to share a small bedroom, or that Mama and Daddy had to find room for my sister's bed in their only slightly larger one, or that we all used one bathroom, that we still had boardwalks to the street, or that we didn't have a tree in our yard. Most Oak Ridgers didn't either; ironically, the trees identified in the town's name had largely been uprooted and bulldozed away when the town was being built. But there were other civic amenities nearby for us to enjoy. In supposedly classless Oak Ridge, everyone—except the relatively few blacks who were relegated to Gamble Valley on the other side of the Turnpike and out of sight after their jobs as janitors and maids were done for the day—could use the large, centrally located municipal swimming pool, the town's few tennis courts, and the recreation centers at Grove Center and Ridge Hall, where the public library was located.

We even joined a church, Grace Lutheran, although its Sunday services were not held in a real church—not like the Chapel on the Hill, one of Oak Ridge's two actual church buildings in those early years—but in Ridge Hall, just as First Methodist's larger congregation gathered in the Ridge Theatre before the movies began later Sunday afternoon. The Summers and the Low-mans, my mother's family, were traditionally Lutheran, so I assume my parents thought that since they were putting down roots they should support the mission church their denomination was establishing in a state that was predominantly Baptist and Methodist. Never mind that the few Lutheran faithful gathered into the small Oak Ridge flock were in large part Midwesterners, one of whom my mother, at a woman's circle meeting, overheard talking derisively about Southerners.

Once when Mama's brother Paul, then a Nabisco executive headquartered in New York City, and his wife drove through Oak Ridge with their two children on their way south, Daddy was chagrined too when Aunt Vivian proclaimed that the town was full of "floaters." Daddy was loyal to the place, even if it was not "home," and Mama was peeved too but let it pass. The Lowmans had never liked Uncle Paul's wife, and this was just another example of her flightiness, I suppose my mother rea-soned. I let it pass, too, since I was much more interested in hearing my cousin Peggy tell all about the Broadway musicals she had seen, Radio City Music Hall, and movie stars she had glimpsed. Already a big fan of such radio shows as Tallulah Bank-head's "Big Show" and "The Lux Radio Theatre" ("Lux presents Hollywood," the announcer intoned each week), I was bedazzled by the glamour of show business.

"Let's Pretend," a nationally broadcast show that came over a Knoxville station—WATO, Oak Ridge's own new station, had mostly local programs—on Saturday morning was another favor-ite, and weekly I would be glued to it after we had gone to see the Oak Ridge High Wildcats play a football rival the night be-fore. Daddy was a big booster, as were most plant workers; there were pregame parades through town to whip up spirit. But at Blankenship Field, where the games were played, I was more interested in seeing what the girls and women in the crowd were wearing, the half-time show, and looking at the players pictured in the printed program with their exaggeratedly masculine scowls, padded shoulders, and form-fitting pants. I even drew some of them when I got home, though I kept my sketches hidden and never showed them to anyone.

Ever since I had realized my attraction to the visual, I had kept a scrapbook in which I pasted appealing pictures clipped from magazines. And when we learned how to use the library at Pine Valley and were allowed to check out books, I would first look to see if those I pulled off the shelves were illustrated. I quickly became an N. C. Wyeth snob, and if he was not the illustrator I assumed the book was not worth my time. But Mama, seeing my enthusiasm for books, had an unillustrated edition of *Heidi* for me on Christmas morning one year, along with the usual gifts of clothes and shoes plus my customary stocking filled with oranges, tangerines, and pecans (South Carolina style). Neither she nor my father cared much for books, and the only ones we had in our house were a Webster's dictionary, a United States atlas, and a King James Bible, which I liked to peak into to gaze at an illustration of a heavily muscled Samson wrestling with the lions.

I also adored Mrs. Cunningham, my fourth-grade teacher. A North Carolinian, she was actually from Ava Gardner's hometown. But what proved more enduring in my memory was the mesmerizing way in which she indulged my fascination for historical tales. To her, history was synonymous with murals, and that year we painted several, including one of the Parthenon reconstructed in Nashville (the "Athens of the South") late in the nineteenth century. Of course, few of Mrs. Cunningham's students had actually seen it, but she brought in lots of brochures and other illuminating information. And we must have done a pretty good job of following the pictures we painted from, since the mural was prominently hung in Pine Valley's main hallway, where it remained for several years—perhaps until the school was later closed because of a shift in Oak Ridge's population after it declined from a wartime high of over 80,000 and stabilized at around 29,000.

Becoming a budding muralist under the guidance of Mrs. Cunningham and Pine Valley's art teacher, I preferred to dawdle over our painting of the month while my classmates hurried out for recess to the large playing field behind the school. I guess I figured that once again when teams were divided up for the day's sport I would not be chosen until last; paints and brushes, probably, were subterfuges to hide my physical awkwardness. But whatever the reason, they held greater attraction for me than a football, basketball, or baseball, even though my brother was beginning to win fame as one of Oak Ridge's best all-around athletes. Back in South Carolina I would close my ears to the *oh*s and *ah*s about him, anxiously awaiting the "old-time" stories told at Ma Ellen and Pa Joe's table, or on their sprawling front porch.

The only stories Oak Ridgers told each other concerned the mud, coal soot, and other inconveniences of living there. Although the fenced-in area included several older cemeteries and other vestiges of the rural people who earlier lived among the hills and valleys upon which the reservation was superimposed, that preceding culture was seldom mentioned. Not until I was in high school did I become aware of John Hendrix, the psychic Ridger from an earlier era who predicted that something like Oak Ridge would replace the area's traditional ways of life.

One of the vestiges of an older culture was a brick school that was left standing to become a part of the added-on structure built to house Jefferson Junior High, which I became increasingly apprehensive about entering as time grew closer for me to leave Pine Valley at the end of sixth grade. My brother had cut a swathe there and I was terrified of having to follow his shadowing reputation. The only things I excelled in were checking out library books, mural painting, and going to movies, usually alone. Daddy had bought a piano for me and my sister (and perhaps as another badge of our improving economic situation), but deep down I knew he would much prefer that I play football. And I was reluctant to bring home a new friend I somehow lucked out in making after Mama commented that he "was nothing but a sissy." So I tried hard to memorize sports scores, batting averages, and so forth when I poured over the *News Sentinel* sports pages each afternoon after I had finished my paper route. I wanted— passionately—to impress my male classmates with my sports knowledge.

I doubt I ever really did, but at least I found a couple of boys I could sit comfortably beside on the school bus and go to football games with, no longer having to tag along with my parents. And I was even invited to join a group of paired boys and girls to go to Saturday afternoon serials at the Center Theatre on Jackson Square. I thought of it as my first date, and somehow mustered the courage to put my arm around my "girlfriend" when I noticed, there in the flickering dark, the other boys doing that with theirs.

The member of the group I eventually became closest to, however, was a shy boy who *was* good at sports but didn't make a big deal out of it, preferring instead quieter, more individual pursuits. Oh, we never grew to be best friends, but we did become well-acquainted enough to trade sly jokes in the hallway between classes; his low-key and easy sense of humor appealed to me. And as he began making his passage through puberty, Jack— a fictitious name—began filling out his body so muscularly that when he went to the Oak Ridge Swimming Pool during the summer, pubescent girls would clamor to find ways to get close to him. But although he played team sports at Jefferson and on through high school, there was something about his self-mocking way that kept him from being one of the boys who hung out at the Wildcat Den, ORHS's recreation center where football victories were celebrated on Friday nights, or who cruised (in cars borrowed from their parents) around the Blue Circle diner on the Turnpike, where everyone who was thought to matter went after the movies on Saturday night.

Occasionally I swung by the Blue Circle also to see the football players, cheerleaders, majorettes, and other ORHS stars shining there. Although Jefferson was a social fizzle for me, I nonetheless held tightly to my fantasy that my status would markedly improve at Oak Ridge High, which by the time I entered had moved into a sprawling brick-and-glass building that was the town's pride. After all, I convinced myself, everyone there would respect who I was: Jimmy Summer's brother. President of the student council, football team captain, the "most outstanding" male senior in the yearbook's superlatives, and a prize catch for a string of Oak Ridge's prettiest girls, he was *the* big man on campus.

Alas, little of that brilliance touched me. Oh, I did get elected to student council, but not as an officer. And I was chosen by my homeroom class to meet Eleanor Roosevelt when the peripatetic former First Lady stopped in Oak Ridge—then a Democratic outpost in staunchly Republican East Tennessee—and visited ORHS in February 1955. I was a prom attendant the year the decorating committee (on which I served) transformed the school cafeteria with blue lights and crepe paper finely shredded to resemble—supposedly—Spanish moss, and, completing the "southern nights" theme, built an ersatz pillored veranda at the large room's end, where the prom king and queen, together with also-rans (including me), were presented. And in the 1955 *Oak Log,* the one that later delighted my niece, I'm pictured among the class superlatives as the "most courteous" boy. That was also the year I became a lifeguard at the Oak Ridge Swimming Pool, another of my little glories.

By then we had moved to a larger house, a "C" at the corner of Pennsylvania Avenue and West Pawley Road. Later, when the federal government offered the town's houses to the families that lived in them, Daddy and Mama bought it, the first and only house they ever owned. Oak Ridge had steadily become what was locally thought to be more normal since the opening of the gates in 1949, a big celebration that, for some curious reason, was attended by Adolfe Menjou, Adele Jergens, Marie "the Body" McDonald, and cowboy Rod Cameron, all lesser movie stars of varying brilliance.

And by 1954 television finally was being beamed through the East Tennessee hills vividly enough that Daddy bought us our first set, though he grumbled that TV was a fad that wouldn't last. Now we too could watch "I Love Lucy," "Howdy Doody," and Dick Clark's "American Bandstand," the latter to learn the new R&R dance steps. Too, we all stayed home to watch the "Ed Sullivan Show" that Sunday night Elvis the Pelvis shook up the nation. Mama and Daddy were shocked, and I thought that was the end for our TV set.

In the mid-fifties, also, Oak Ridge got its first large shopping center, ironically named Downtown. That meant Oak Ridgers no longer had to drive to Knoxville to shop for clothes, shoes, home furnishings, and other items unavailable in satisfactory selections in "the Atomic City," the town's sobriquet increasingly appearing on tourist brochures. Now we had our own Sears, J. C. Penney, Miller's (a Knoxville-based department store), and Gateway, which sold books and the largest variety of magazines I had yet seen. It was there I discovered bodybuilding magazines, one of which I secretly bought from my paper route income and showed to Jack the next day. ORHS did not have any weights among its gym facilities when we were there—the pumping iron era was a couple decades in the future—but he knew what bodybuilders were. "They lift barbells out in California," he explained, "to develop big arms and chests larger than a woman's tits."

I heard about other things, too, from my ORHS classmates that would later crop up in my life. One day when Mr. X assigned his class to read one of Oscar Wilde's better-known plays, a girl in the back of the classroom giggled. In the hall after class I asked her what was so funny. "Don't you know?" she said; "He"—and she dropped her voice to a whisper—"was a homosexual." I had never heard that word spoken before, although I knew that was what "queer" referred to when I heard it bantered around the locker room during my dreaded gym classes, or saw it scrawled on a men's room wall. I had even heard it applied to Mr. X, who was labeled a "queer" in that locker-room talk, although we knew he was married and a father, as well as one of the Wildcats' most vocal cheerleaders; he was always in the bleachers or stands at every football or basketball game and track meet.

I was in Mr. X's homeroom class when the *Brown* vs. *Board of Education of Topeka* decision came down from the Supreme Court, destroying the separate-but-equal doctrine that had prevailed in the South for generations. Mr. X asked us how we would feel about going to school with Negroes, and when it came my turn to answer I smugly drew on my sophomoric "Madly for Adlai" liberalism that had blossomed when the Democrats first ran Stevenson for president. It, I said, would give "us" the opportunity to be good examples to "them." The memory of that, I confess, never ceases to shame me.

I graduated from ORHS, however, before integration; that came during my sister's time. And although comparatively few blacks initially enrolled in Oak Ridge's schools—generally acclaimed as among Tennessee's best—several were in my sister Barbara's graduating class. It upset my parents to see their pretty young daughter walking down the auditorium's aisles with them to receive their diplomas.

I had gone to college at the University of Tennessee in Knoxville, not because I chose it but because my father told me he wouldn't help pay for me to go anywhere else and the in-state tuition was too good a deal to pass up. (Besides, he was a Vol football fan, and once named a couple of beagles we owned after sensational halfback Hank Lauricella; the male was called Hank and the bitch Laura.) But each summer I returned to Oak Ridge to resume my lifeguard duties, although the pool we had once been so proud of was less a public draw, now that there was a country club to the west of town and some subdivisions of new houses with swimming pools.

I had lost track of Jack, since he had gone to another college and spent his summers elsewhere. And I had little social life, aside from the movies and an occasional play at the Oak Ridge Community Playhouse, which together with the town's public library, the Oak Ridge Civic Musical Association (founded by music-loving, classically-bent scientists during Oak Ridge's beginning years), and the Art Center, provided a "cultural" outlet for Oak Ridgers inclined that way.

I continued to be a constant patron of the public library those summers, going through Hemingway and Fitzgerald one year, and Thomas Wolfe the next. But I read other authors also, including Gore Vidal. It was during my Wolfe summer that I picked up a paperback copy of Vidal's *The City and the Pillar* at Gateway. Mama, Daddy, and Barbara had gone "home" to South Carolina, and I was alone in Oak Ridge. Before going to the pool for the evening lifeguard shift, I stretched out on the chaise longue on our porch and read the paperback from cover to cover, excitedly turning the pages. Nevertheless, the ending was shattering, and I headed up Pennsylvania Avenue to sort out the book's impact on me. As I neared the top of the hill in the late afternoon sunlight, it hit me: That book is about what I am, I admitted to myself for the first time—a homosexual. In that second of self-realization, I was pierced with an intensity greater than any I have ever known.

I did not have the boldness, however, to act on my awareness until some years later, guiltily resolving each New Year's to grow out of it. And I never saw Jack again, although I randomly followed him through items I saw in *The Oak Ridger* newspaper when I returned to visit my parents from places I subsequently lived. But one night, at a park on Melton Hill Lake, just outside of town, a furtive police raid on an alleged homosexual ring gathered there nabbed some prominent Oak Ridge men, including, to my stunned surprise, Jack, who had made his home in Oak Ridge and was married and, I think, a father. The resulting scandal was big news in *The Oak Ridger,* and the identified men were forced out of their jobs and out of the area to rebuild their lives elsewhere. Finally, Oak Ridge as home had eluded them too.

HARLAN GREENE

CHARLESTON, SOUTH CAROLINA

Now THAT I NO LONGER live there, I often think longingly of my hometown of Charleston. My heart beats faster and color rushes to my cheek whenever I hear someone mentioning her; I lean over and listen, for even hearing the name casts a spell. Mirages rise up, and I am as overcome and drenched in images as a runner just come from running. I see the steeples, the streets, the lush setting. But Charleston is really less of a place than a feeling; she does not encompass time and space as much as she does an emotional geography. A Charleston girl once told me that she felt better than others because she had been born in that city.

I will not go that far, but I will admit that I was lucky. Looking back, I think that other towns may have given their sons a toy like a jack-in-a-box that erupted to emit Howdy Doody; while I had something else—a fantastic jeweled casket, that could, with the right amount of rubbing, produce a genie. But dangers came out of that box, too, that had an effect on me.

So my memories of Charleston are bittersweet. I know I am not unique in thinking about my hometown the way one might feel about a first lover. Invoking a dream of innocence, I thought the city and I would be together forever, but Charleston broke my heart and made me angry. And the time came when I wanted to leave and succeed just so I could come back and say, "See what I have done without you? Aren't you sorry about how you treated me?"

But even then, I knew the city would never be jealous, would never regret anything she did to me. Even then, I knew that Charleston would always be part of me; she is wrapped round my heart the way ivy can wrap a garden wall down there. I could never renounce her, for imbedded in her history are flecks and pieces of my own. Still standing is the house where I grew up, as are all the places that witnessed my different incarnations of student, hippie, and respectable member of society. I can go further uptown and look upon the house that sheltered my parents when they first came to this country. Visiting these spots and others are narcissistic adventures; whenever I go back and walk the streets, I can convince myself that I never left; I can instantly take up where I left off.

To the newcomer, though, the city may be disorienting, approached, as she is, through a territory of dreams—a vast underwater world where moss hangs down from trees and sadness seems to be the shadow underlying everything. It is a drugged primeval world, murky as the subconscious, where a glimpse, sudden and swift as an epiphany, will reveal a gold savannah of marsh, as serene as one of its herons slowly taking wing.

Being on a peninsula, she often must be reached by crossing rivers; that is how I always see Charleston: rising up in water, like a reflection, too shimmering to be real.

Entering, you are dazed by the heat. The air is often so thick and languid you feel you need gills to breathe. You move in a dream through the narrow streets.

She is old and worn now, but not all of one piece; there is fragile colonial, heavy antebellum, victorian eccentricity. Neighborhoods differ in feel. In the oldest part of town, tiny houses crowd together, with pastel colors blanched by the sea. Dormers peer from tilting roofs; balconies hang like wash over alleys. But at the edge of town, suburban in the 1850s, bland houses sit as high and comfortable as cats looking at each other with heavy eyes over greens. And there along the seawall that protects the lower end of town from the water are some of the grandest mansions in the city. Tourists rush about—in buses, bikes, golf carts, and now even in rickshaws—to see everything, trying to find the one spot where they can sigh and sit down and say, "This is Charleston, right here." Charlestonians themselves go by more slowly, while oleanders tussle in the breeze, and the palmettos move lazily; their fronds rub on one another like flesh. I wonder if it is that which sets desires stirring. Or is it just that Charleston, like anything of great beauty, gets next to you and you long to possess her instantly?

That is how it was for me, at least. For so long I wanted to belong to Charleston, and because I couldn't I thought I had failed. But now I can see that I was lucky.

Growing up, there were certain things in my favor: I was white and male and managed to be raised in the most exclusive part of town—the area South of Broad (whose residents are often called S.O.B.s). But I lacked other things; my "people," so important in Charleston, where it is your past that determines your future, were, to be polite about it, "funny."

They were recent arrivals, to say the least. My older brother had even been born in Vienna (*Vigh-eena* is often what they called it). My parents could not speak English when they came after barely surviving the horrors unleashed by Nazi Germany. We were even different from the Jewish family up the street whose ancestors had been in Charleston for centuries. And the kids who went to Hebrew School with us made fun of our parents' European accents. The Goulmans, our overtly religious cousins, for instance, disapproved of us. They had sat out the war with religious deferments; they were angry at us for being alive; they blamed us for making them feel guilty. For one reason or another, we were estranged from the Jewish community. We grew up isolated and rank as weeds in the summer streets.

Yet in many ways we were like many Charleston kids. We were raised by our black maid, Ida Lee (Momma worked). We ate our main meal at 3:00. Unlike the other families on the street, we did not have a separate bathroom for Ida Lee, nor did she have to eat in the pantry. And after all the maids talked with her at the bus stop, a delegation of neighborhood ladies visited Momma and told her how she was upsetting things by paying Ida a decent salary and paying her Social Security. Momma did not care a jot what other people thought, so we were not off to a good beginning.

Yet I was secure, like those things Momma bought and thought too good to use, those dishes and soaps and lamp shades kept tightly packed in their boxes and original wrappings. We kids were insulated by our surroundings. There was the Cuban missile crisis, when everyone in Charleston, with its huge military bases, panicked. I remember those civilian defense stations and talks of radioactivity. And the jets that broke the sound barrier and sent us home crying. But those moments were the exceptions, and they were from the greater world. Only rarely did the city itself obtrude on our upbringing.

Following each Passover seder we kids would go with Poppa on his walk to White Point Gardens, the park along the seawall, or Battery. There the city seemed menacing. Passover always falls on a full moon, so the gardens were always ghostly. Spring would be trembling in the air; pollen would dust the backs of our throats, the air was too perfumed to breathe, and the moonlight reversed everything, like a negative did. The city we walked through had a strange haunting quality, so we walked on in the night, quietly, as if through a house belonging to someone else, furniture shrouded in sheets, us afraid to disturb anything.

On Saturdays, when other kids were at the synagogue, Ida was off and my parents were working, I was loose and free and I started wandering those streets. Their beauty made me restless, like an adolescent is in spring. I was sure the black kids I passed whom I could not understand, spoke a different language, just as my parents did; they lapsed into Yiddish at the dinner table just when the conversations got interesting. For years I felt isolated in my cocoon, estranged from the old city.

▪ ▪ ▪

It was when I was at the College of Charleston that things began to change. It was not my intelligence, however, or my excelling in my studies, that set those locked hinges on those old doors squeaking; not hardly. (If I got in anywhere it was because I was drawn to history; I became one of Charleston's handmaidens and was taken up into the cult of the city.) The professors at the college were—and still are, unfortunately—less interested in studies than in society. They find a guest list, rather than a reading list, more stimulating. After all, they have tenure, they live in old houses, their children will be growing up below Broad and may be marrying into the city. Charleston, even with its colleges (the homophobic, all-male military school, The Citadel, is here), is an anti-intellectual city. One of my friends told me how as a little girl, she heard her mother's friends speaking of a well-known lady in town. "She's a dilettante," they said wonderingly; for years, until she left Charleston, my friend thought that to be a dilettante must be the pinnacle of intellectual and artistic success.

At college I fell under the sway of a brilliant professor who had not been born in Charleston. I think that he too wanted to belong. Like any convert to the cause, he took it too zealously. He bemoaned many things that Charleston found distasteful, but which I found in myself. There was, for instance, that morbidness that ran through some art that was defined as "Jewish"—that infected me—and there was always the tincture, as well, of "Jewish melancholy." And then there was my homosexuality, which could be tolerated, but only the way things under rocks could— so long as they were unseen. Charleston could not tolerate such honesty of feeling. The city thinks souls are less important than ceremonies. It is too upsetting, too uncivil to speak of such things.

So I tried not to be seen in profile (that way we knew our Jewishness would be revealed); I tried not to let my other mannerisms (like how I smoked cigarettes) betray my homosexuality. I felt as if I were trying to pass in enemy territory.

But in a way, my very outréness protected me, or maybe it was my youth. Though I was always in dead earnest, no one took me seriously. I felt invisible, as the doors of drawing rooms, with air surely as rarefied as that within the holy of holies, began opening. I peered in.

I went in, because I thought there was no other game in Charleston; what drew me on, too, was the rumor of its utter exclusivity; what made it more lavish, however, was my own imaginings. I thought the world I would find under those impossibly high ceilings would be as fabulous and surreal as those Parisian drawing rooms Proust tried to get into. I thought Charlestonians had to be as significant as their setting. But, as is so often the case, my imagination proved more vivid than reality.

I was not graceful in there, where grandmothers, like gorgons, glared at me. My "flaws" were noted. People asked who my parents were, where I had gone to school; I was asked a lot about Israel and where in New York to find good kosher delis. But anti-Semitism is a polite thing in this city, as time honored and polished as many another legacy. Other Jews at these parties would look me over, too, and catching my eye, they would plead, "Don't tell on me." Many were too polite to say that they were discriminated against. They talked about being invited to lunch, but never acknowledged the fact that they, as Jews, could never become members of the Yacht Club at the end of High Battery. It is very fitting that the building sits on land once a bastion in the old walls of the city.

Intelligence can be tolerated; Jewishness can, too. (Both can be used to make money.) But no one in society will want to own up to the burden of homosexuality; for it is too upsetting a truth that unsettles the pleasant fictions of the city. This is not to say that it is not there. It is covert, lurking. There were (and are) gay couples who have been together for years; they are happy and devoted and certainly worth emulating, but they are captives of their own times. Those men, now in their seventies, are still called boys (just as black men are). They have gained acceptance of a sort and if you pay your dues and do not declare your sexuality ("flaunt it" as the phrase goes) then maybe you can be tolerated and invited to dinner parties. (This really makes me angry. Because even hand holding is called flaunting. That I bought into it, that I often was nervous holding my lover's hand in my own hometown makes me angry.) If you follow the rules and obey the social rites and worship the same deities, you can be gay and accepted. (And that seems to me to be the best way to judge an era, a culture, or a city: see what the Lares and Penates are; see what ideals it holds holy.) Follow these unsaid rules and Charlestonians may even mention you with pride and point to you as further example of their own civility and sophistication.

Another writer friend of mine put it more succinctly. You can have sex with an elephant on King Street, he said. So long as you wear a white dinner jacket, it won't bother anybody. What it means is that social life is governed by the same rules as the mighty Board of Architectural Review: in Charleston you can do anything to your interior, you can gut and wrench and falsify your house or your psyche, but what can be seen from the street, the façade, must be kept up and obey all proprieties.

So I kept myself corseted in and was acceptable. And then an amazing thing dawned on me. I realized that the air in those exclusive places was not rarefied; it was stultifying. Once in there, it was like being in France (in that way it was Proustian, at least), for you had to speak French exclusively. You had to speak to Charlestonians only of Charleston things; the only topic allowed was one they found interesting. They lived in a small incestuous world where joy came from the mundane of who knew whom, whose house was being renovated, and who had done what boating. They did not read; many did not even know their own history. Like the children of the rich, they just basked in the golden afterglow of someone else's struggling. They had inherited their houses, their ideas, their beliefs and their money.

I see now that I had peeked in expecting to see Madame Recamier; instead I saw Norma Desmond. Charleston was like an old actress wandering around the polished gloom, holding on to her clippings. It is sad that the beautiful old city has come to believe all the bad promotional copy that has been written about her; that she thinks she stands for the glorious "Old South" that never was, and that she personifies a flimsy fiction. She wanders in a fog of memories, clutching old photographs, and holding them up to those who will view them, as proof, as testimony.

■　　■　　■

So I left that realm—the part that identified itself with the values of the old city. There was—and is—thank goodness—more to the city. "You white people are so boring," friends from "off" often tell me. "The blacks are much more interesting." And of course, Charleston, with its beaches, with its beauty, with its relative sophistication (it hosts an art festival each year), with its colleges and military, has attracted a sizable gay population. There are bars, but I always got the feeling that they were for those better looking than me. It was odd how the bars mirrored the world that the gay men supposedly were escaping. Outside the aristocrats of birth; in there, the aristocrats of beauty. And like the city, they did not have too much room for someone like me. (I once lost a boyfriend who found out *who* I was—not the preppie little S.O.B. he thought me to be.) And once one of the bar's regulars—you know those men who sit at the corner of the bar every night, drinking and looking and serving as the Fates of the place—lurched up and said he felt sorry for me. If not for my semitic face he supposed I could have been happy; he thought it was tragedy. Maybe so. But what I see as the saddest of things is not what my mirror tells me, but that the gay world in Charleston mirrors the larger oppressive world beyond it. Even the dispossessed aren't free of the rites. Like Ida Lee using kink free in the 1950s, trying to be white, so many gay men in Charleston worship the same hurtful deities of the city.

There are still cliques of gay men who would not dare or deign to be seen in a common gay bar, for the damage it would do to their social standing. They vote for oppression; are the same and as sad as their daddies. They stay in at night and compare china patterns and then clench their teeth as they go out with women to places they can be seen. They are as frightened of the truth as if it were a hurricane coming. I know someone who even maintains separate address books for straight and gay. East and west have more of a chance of meeting than the two worlds of these men who straddle the gay world and Charleston society. They go other places to be gay, to New York, or Thailand or San Francisco. They are caught in one of the most unfortunate time warps in the city, and I am glad to see that their numbers are dwindling, though they will never be extinct like the unfortunate

Carolina paroquet. No, a few will always keep that light of their lives hidden from sight; they are the type, they say, who would *never* end up at the Battery.

Yet that is exactly where I would tell someone, tourist or local, to go if he wanted to see the one spot that sums up the essence of the city. It is the point of the peninsula where Charleston's two rivers, the Cooper and the Ashley, meet to flow out past Fort Sumter to the sea, where all the streets eventually lead. Down at the seawall is a park with oyster shell walks and monuments to the city's heroes. Graceful old oaks gloom over the green and arch over the mansions now being split up into condos and being sold off to rich Yankees. It was here we would walk after the Passover seders—where the moonlight disturbed me and later would not let me sleep. In the 1950s, only white families would go there; in the seventies the hippies began to sit cross-legged under the trees. Go down there now on a Sunday afternoon, and you will see only blacks, come from their neighborhoods to take the air. The same thing happened after the Civil War, after the slaves were freed. Old Charlestonians creep out to walk in the late afternoon, joggers dart by continuously. Underneath it all, like the shadows of the trees, is something else; it swells out, like the shadows do, in the evening. Come night and the Battery belongs to the gay of the city.

They all come down, sooner or later. Some circle hopelessly as moths around a beacon, never lighting. They never get out of their cars, their hysteria mounting with their fear. Others pass down the oyster shell paths and pause under lampposts to light cigarettes, call "lost dogs," or lean over the seawall, looking into the water, trying to see who is cruising. They are all here: like the heaven or hell in which so many believe—the drag queens, the priests, and the society queens, scared teens taking their first steps, the daddies and good old boys in their pickups drunk and happy. At night lust licks around the edges of the chaste, charmed old city.

I often watched and saw things I found amazing. Though reacting to the limits set by the town, though driven to extremes, something as rare, as revivifying, as the breeze that soothes the park on late summer nights was down there—honesty. (Or rather, it was what honesty had become; it was frightening what it had suffered at the hands of the city, what transformations it had gone through to surface, what with all the shame and guilt and denying.) And so the Battery then was what the slave markets might have been for Charleston in the nineteenth century—the point where the false façade, where the gentle lie of how graceful and beautiful life can be meets flesh's reality. The gardens have an emblematic quality. Just beyond their walls, tides flow. There is the smell of the rich marine mud. Porpoises, mysterious as urges, swim in the deep. While on the other, in, side of the garden rise the walls of the town and excesses of decoration and filigree. These are the extremes of civilization of the city—its alpha and omega, yin and yang, Cooper and Ashley.

In high school, you and your date walk the seawall. Then you drive down there with friends to "see who's queer" till you are driven there yourself, but you whisper about others instead with a "Guess who I saw last night at the Battery?" It is a prismatic lens in which to look through life and the city. A kind of wild joy would well up in me as I sat under the trees and the moon poured light down over everything. I felt I had a secret; that I looked down in her soul, the psyche of the city.

It was a knowledge I only reflected upon, however. I kept up my own façade, working for years at the same job, being "that nice young man at the Historical Society." It is a place to which people in Charleston paid lip service. There we were supposed to rest as safe and entombed as the dead. But the past is a subversive place, really; for within it lies not the pleasant fictions or lies that most people believe. Walled up is the truth, seething. Though most laughed at her, I understood why that rich conservative in pancake makeup and pink tennis shoes refused to give her money to the Historical Society, calling it a hotbed of liberality. She hated having to use us when she came to look up people's family trees. If blood would not tell, then she would look into the past to find reasons for people's disagreeable behavior and then tell everybody.

But there in that wonderful vaulted old building, where we

cared for the papers of the politicians and poets and oppressed of the city, there I could dream in my disguise. And I could take heart from figures from Charleston's history, those figures, who, like Florence O'Sullivan in the 1600s, were exiled from the city. He was sent to what is now Sullivan's Island for what may have been gay crimes, ironically giving his name to what is now the family beach; gay cavorting goes on at the aptly named Folly. There were other Charlestonians, too; those who stood up for truth, against the cult of beauty propagated by the city. Others stood up against slavery and then segregation; for women's rights and voting. These people may be in textbooks but they have been forgotten in Charleston. When remembered, it is their behavior, not their beliefs, that Charlestonians talk about. They say, for example, that it was not Judge Waring's integrationist views that upset them, it was the fact that he divorced his local wife and married a Yankee that put him beyond the pale. Learning from the past, I knew that there was a tradition that I could belong to, too; I could be of those who loved the city just as deeply as everyone, but who stood up to her. But, as I said, this was a reflective knowledge, unacted upon. I had been seduced by her and was too well mannered to force my truth on anybody.

I wrote a book, however. I made my claims gently, and in her gentle way, Charleston chided me. The book was somewhat based on truth; was set in Charleston, with gay characters, in the 1920s. I was only slightly scared, for I knew that despite their protests to the contrary, most Charlestonians do not really read. Only about five or so years later did it become known in certain circles what my book was about. Until then they were sweet to my face; though behind my back those who had read it said my work was disgusting. Very few people cut me dead on the street. I even thought what the vapid excuse for a newspaper, *The News and Courier*, did was funny. A free-lance reviewer had reviewed my book; the paper did its best to lose it. Only after he called up to complain to them, did they print it in a completely gutted version. The reviewer for the afternoon papers was not allowed to mention any of the characters by name or to say what the book was about. It hurt to be slighted in my hometown, but really, the *News and Courier* is so bad that no one takes it seriously.

▪ ▪ ▪

Other reactions disturbed me more. I had thought that now maybe the gay men in town would not think me so odd. But I noticed that they would not return my glance in public or say hello. They began to either ignore or condescend to me. I was a threat to them now. Being seen with me in public was poison. It was tantamount to advertising their own homosexuality. Others complained that they felt my book had tipped their cover—by telling straight Charleston what went on at the Battery. And one comment from a boy at one of the better addresses in town froze my blood. He and his older lover were trying to rise in Charleston society. He deigned to speak to me at a garden party and told me that yes, indeed, he had read my book; he was pleased to see that I had talent. Couldn't I, however, turn it toward a more dignified and deserving subject? There were so many other more interesting things to write about in the city, he assured me. If there is ever a hall of fame of Charleston, I think he should be ensconced in there, still living, labeled as one of her most loyal subjects. For all my work, my book had just alienated me further from the city.

But I grew excited when a high school teacher called up and asked me to address her class; I thought, "Aha! here is an opportunity to be honest about everything." But on the day of the event, she came up to me with panic in her face; she had not bothered to read the book and had just glanced at the dust jacket and discovered what it was about. "Don't make me lose my job, please," she begged of me. I had been in Charleston so long by then that the haziness of the place that softens the sky and even blurs thinking had got to me. Being a good Charleston boy, I became part of the silence. I didn't say anything.

But I do now, now that I no longer live in the city. It has taken me some time to realize what happened—how the city slowly tried to gut me, make me into a drone, a cultist in her service. But, ironically, the city herself helped save me. For one of the best things about Charleston is who she attracts. I was lucky to meet Olin there. He came to medical school from the upper part of the state, where they look upon Charleston warily. Olin is younger than me, and he made me realize that one need not go through one's life begging everyone's pardon. You do not have to keep choosing your words carefully as if every utterance were poetry. He showed me what I knew—but had not acted upon—that there are other things to life than those that the fictional Rhett Butler returned to Charleston to look for: grace and beauty. He made me make the choice between surface and reality, and fiction and fact. I took Truth over Beauty, albeit reluctantly. Manners may be nice, but they are not as important as integrity. Olin showed me there is no use living in a culture that demeans you, no matter how politely.

The time came for a choice: either I follow Olin or stay in my city. We left. Olin has, in his way, become my hometown now; his love defines the limits of my emotional geography. We have the oneness that I once fancied achieving with the city.

Olin lectures me still, for he can see that look in my eye when I gaze back like Lot's Wife, or when my voice gets husky.

But it is the beauty, the inexorable pull of the weight of the air, her dreaminess that still makes me think of her. I have to render her her due; she has helped me. For as I look back, and see her still standing, I can see that Charleston still has a metaphor for me, as if expelling me from Eden, she has leaned down to whisper a blessing. I think not of her slavery, her wars, her falsity. No, I think of her sadness, her beauty and her silence, her resilience and endurance. These are the beginnings of wisdom for me. For whatever time will bring and do to deter me, I know that there are truths to treasure and protect, memories that must go on living. In rhythms older than the city herself, I had to be blinded to see; I had to see through the camouflage of beauty to the truth beneath. For this I am thankful.

But I still think of Charleston; I return to her often and always will. I think of her warmly. I claim her now; even though I know she will never claim me.

JOHN CHAMPAGNE

GREENFIELD, WISCONSIN

THE DUST JACKET OF MY
first novel asserts that I was born and raised in Milwaukee, Wisconsin. This is only partially true. While I was born in the city
of Milwaukee, I grew up in Greenfield, a suburb about twenty
minutes on the Interstate from downtown Milwaukee. When I
wrote the copy for that dust jacket, I deliberately erased Greenfield from that version of my history. I thought it a fitting gesture,
considering the fact that I often locate my beginnings as a writer
in a series of journals in which I complained bitterly about my
life in Greenfield.

These journals, begun when I was about twelve or so, were
not coincidently modeled after the diary of Anne Frank. The
entries consisted of letters addressed to a fictional friend named
Jude (as in Saint Jude, the patron saint of lost causes). Even then,
I fantasized about the day I would lean across the couch toward
Johnny Carson to deliver a scathing and witty diatribe against
the horrible, claustrophobic, small-minded, culturally underde-

veloped community in which I'd grown up. Erasing Greenfield—
in writing—from the dust jacket of my very first book seemed an
appropriate act of revenge—especially considering the fact that I
will in all likelihood never be invited to Johnny's couch to tell the
story of my life.

I'm not certain that I know how to write about Greenfield.
I've spent so much time in acting classes and therapy learning to
"let go" of my anger, I'm no longer sure that I am capable of
conveying much of the pain and humiliation I felt growing up
there. Besides, I am soon to turn thirty, and time has taught me
how to dull the memory of those haunting feelings of powerlessness
I felt so often as a child. Now that I am no longer trapped in
Greenfield, it is sometimes difficult to reconstruct how it felt to
live among people whom you felt hated you, and from whose hatred you couldn't possibly escape. Compounding it all is the fact
that I wasn't *just* hated in Greenfield, for Greenfield was also the
place I called home, the place where my family, friends, and teachers first taught me how to nurture and respect those very qualities
that might lead other people to dislike me. No matter how much
I may disdain Greenfield, it will always necessarily be a part of me.

Greenfield. A true suburb. Certainly not rural; while there
was one family who kept a few cows, the local government had
decreed that once these animals were gone, that was the end of
livestock in Greenfield. Yet Greenfield made no claims to urban-
ity. Until quite recently, there were very few sidewalks. Vacant
lots, shopping malls, a gigantic nursing home. Box-shaped buildings, characterless ranch-style homes covered in aluminum siding,
flat and rectangular churches and schools indistinguishable from
one another. These bland and descriptionless places—a legacy
from the 1950s—are what I see when I imagine Greenfield. There
were no factories in Greenfield, nor any ballet nor opera nor even
community theaters. In short, Greenfield was predictably boring.

But it wasn't the dullness of Greenfield that made me hate
it so. I could have tolerated that, at least until I was old enough
to drive away and escape to nearby Milwaukee. In addition to
being relentlessly bland, Greenfield was also the place where I
heard myself called a fag over and over again, from the time I
was eight until I turned eighteen and moved to an apartment in

Milwaukee. Long before I had any sense of myself as a gay person, Greenfield had taught me that my differences from other boys—the fact that I did well in school, that I loved playing the piano, that I hated sports, that most of my friends were girls—these differences made me a fag.

I'm not sure what the relationship is between my sexuality and the fact that I was considered by my peers to be "effeminate." I'm not sure that there is any relationship at all. What does intrigue me is the possibility that, were it not for the fact of being called a fag with such regularity, I might not recognize myself as gay today.

I'm not suggesting that I wouldn't still have sexual feelings for other men, regardless of what I was called by others. But there is a world of difference between sleeping with men and identifying oneself as a gay person. Culture's insidious equating of gender and sexuality not only leads gay men to be perceived as effeminate; it also allows for an identity to be constructed through that equation. In providing me with this identity—fag—an identity based primarily on my (unintentional) refusal of gender norms, Greenfield in some sense made possible my eventual recognition of myself as gay.

To put it bluntly: having been called a fag for so many years by my peers, because I didn't behave according to their conceptions of how a boy ought to behave, it came as no surprise to me that I should be sexually attracted to men. I always knew I was different from other boys. When I was a fag, it was because I didn't act like them. When I was gay, it was because I didn't sleep with the kind of people—women—that they did. The difference between being a fag and being gay seemed minimal to me, partly because I had been taught by Greenfield to think of that difference as minimal.

It is difficult for me today to unravel the difference between those terms as they may have operated in the minds of my classmates at school. Was I disliked because I was someone's idea of effeminate, or was I disliked because it was suspected that I desired men? Obviously, so long as the two things are equated, the question is impossible to answer. Greenfield provided me with plenty of evidence that I was probably hated for both reasons.

I was told over and over again by my peers that my interests were unmanly. Whenever I achieved any academic recognition, I was called a fag. Whenever I played the piano for a school function, I was called a fag. Whenever I expressed my lack of interest in sports, I was called a fag. Many times I was ridiculed in this way by people I didn't even know.

I still can recall quite clearly standing at the blackboard in my seventh-grade math class, attempting to work out an algebra problem, while two other guys in the class discussed whether or not I was in fact a fag. That same year, my English teacher decided that, since my abilities seemed to exceed the work of the course, she would create projects for me to complete on my own while the rest of the class did other work. This led to my being constantly harassed by one boy in particular, who punched my arm, called me a fag, and threatened to beat me up after school. Once, I attended a piano recital at a small women's college in Greenfield with two of my best friends, daughters of my piano teacher. At some point during the recital, I overheard two young women seated behind us arguing over whether or not someone was a fag. At first, I told myself that I was being paranoid, that they couldn't possibly be talking about me. What was I doing, other than sitting and listening to the music? But when I saw the looks of embarrassment for me on the faces of my two friends, I knew that it was in fact me who was being discussed. These recurring instances of being humiliated in this way made it pretty clear to me that I was different from other boys in Greenfield. I was obviously not behaving according to "appropriate" community standards of masculinity.

In addition, there were a number of instances where the community at large expressed its disdain for homosexuality in particular. When word got out that the teacher of a family-living class at the high school had invited two lesbians to speak, the locals became incensed, writing condemnatory letters to the *Greenfield Observer* and telephoning the school administration. When I was a senior in high school, a choreographer who had been hired on my recommendation was fired when it was learned that he was gay. The community at large was extremely intolerant of any cultural differences. The school board refused to participate in a *voluntary* desegregation plan with Milwaukee. When I attended high school in Greenfield there was only one African-American student in the whole school, and to my recollection, not a single teacher who was a person of color. It thus came as little surprise to me that whenever the topic of homosexuality would be raised, either in class or in the local news, people's reactions would almost uniformly be those of disdain and disgust.

The funny thing about being called a fag, this hybrid identity that ridicules one's lack of masculinity as well as one's sexual preferences, was that it hurt me most when it couldn't possibly be naming my actual sexual behavior. When I was too young to be sleeping with men, I found it intensely disturbing to be called a fag. I lived in perpetual fear of hearing myself called that name, so much so that I avoided school assemblies, recess, lunch—any occasion where I would have to face a group of people who might decide to humiliate me. Yet, once I was actually having sex with men, being called a fag no longer bothered me. Instead, it was somewhat amusing. Whenever someone would yell, "Hey, faggot," I would laugh and think, If you only knew. Before I recognized myself as gay, it was as if I could hear only the part of the word *fag* that insulted my masculinity. But once I was actually sleeping with men, it was only the other part of the word I began to hear, the part that named me as someone whose primary attachments were to other men. The word began to sound like an affirmation rather than an insult.

Of course, by the time I was having sex with men, I was sixteen and generally less concerned with what my classmates might think of me. In addition, I had managed to find a number of friends who had taught me how to say "fuck you" into the faces of the people who made fun of me. These friends were like me in that they were also disliked by the other people with whom we attended school. They were girls who were considered too smart and not pretty enough and boys who went out for band instead of football. One such friend, the one who probably influenced me the most, was a girl named Jen.

Jen moved to Greenfield from Flint, Michigan, when we were in eighth grade. It was apparent from the beginning that Jen was not going to fit in in Greenfield. She looked nothing like the other girls. Her long blond hair fell wildly down her back, and she wore much more makeup than her classmates. But what was most distinctive about Jen was her way of dressing. On her feet, she wore a pair of silver glitter–covered platform shoes, the open toes of which revealed her brightly painted toenails. These toenails were blood red, the same color as her fingernails, the longest fingernails I had ever seen. With her platform shoes, Jen usually wore jeans, a glitter-infused top, and an open blouse. And she never wore a bra. She said it was too confining.

I met Jen in the school cafeteria one day. I had heard on the bus that she played the piano. I knew of no one else in Greenfield who played, and I was anxious to meet someone with whom I could discuss music. So, I walked up to her, and introduced myself—very uncharacteristic behavior for me, considering my fear of being ridiculed.

Jen and I became friends immediately. She was a good pianist, and probably would have played better than me, were it not for those fingernails. Like me, Jen was also considered intelligent by her teachers and tested into the "accelerated" math and English classes. But unlike me, Jen couldn't be convinced to "apply" herself in those subjects for which she didn't care, and so her grades were not always that good.

The most striking thing Jen and I had in common was the fact that our fellow classmates disliked us. They often made fun of her weight and the way she dressed, and disapproved of her outspokenness in class. But unlike me, who thought that the best way to avoid criticism was to attempt to draw as little attention to myself as possible, Jen practically sought out other people's disapproval. Whenever someone tried to make fun of her, she would laugh in his or her face, and call the offending party a jock or a bitch or a dumb redneck. Rather than sneak away to the band room during assemblies as I did, Jen would go to them to yell "fuck you" while everyone else was yelling "go Greenfield." Her clothes and makeup got more outrageous all the time, and she became even more outspoken in class, anxious to inform our classmates of their small-mindedness and stupidity. I adored her bravura.

Whenever we were alone together, Jen and I would talk about our future plans to escape Greenfield, she as a club singer or flutist or ballet dancer, I as a concert pianist. Jen promised me that there was a world outside Greenfield, a world where we would be respected for our abilities rather than ridiculed. She was certain that by the time we were seniors, everyone would want to know us and be our friends. All we needed to do was to find a way to make it through high school. After that nightmare was over, then our real lives would begin.

I told Jen of my interest in men when I was sixteen, shortly after my first sexual experience. She didn't seem all that surprised. She already knew a number of gay people. Because Jen looked so much older than her age, she had been going to bars and discos since she was thirteen. The first discos she ever frequented were gay. Jen lived with her father—her parents were separated—in an apartment complex, and two of her best friends were a lesbian couple who lived in the same building. She often accompanied these women to dance clubs. It was the late 1970s, the height of the disco craze in Milwaukee, and Jen had found, in these bars, a means of escaping the dullness and hostility of Greenfield. She was an excellent dancer and was constantly entering contests. She also found a job teaching ballroom dancing at a small studio. Jen's partners were usually gay men, men who loved her outrageous sense of style and her sometimes lewd sense of humor. She was extremely popular at these gay discos, the kind of person who people either loved or hated but always wanted to know.

When Jen found out that I was gay, she offered to take me to the bars with her. But before I could go, I would have to be instructed as to how to behave as a gay person. Being gay in Milwaukee was definitely an achieved identity. It was not merely a matter of showing up at a gay club once you figured out that you wanted to fuck men. Instead, being gay involved, at least in my case, a certain transformation of the self.

First to be altered was my appearance. My hair was unfashionably long, a holdover from my parents' hippie days. Jen suggested that I change the part to the middle and took me to have my hair cut by one of her gay hairdresser friends.

Next to go were most of my clothes. I had always dressed in blues and browns to avoid drawing attention to myself, and always wore jeans so that I wouldn't have to worry about trying to match my pants with my shirt. Jen made me buy jeans a size tighter than I was accustomed to wearing. The gay men Jen knew all wore pants with double and triple pleats to emphasize the thinness of their waist and the shape of their ass. But I was so thin to begin with that most men's pants would barely fit me. So Jen dragged a reluctant me into places like The Limited, women's stores that sold pants with a somewhat unisex look. Rather than the blue and brown shirts I wore to school, I wore, whenever I went out with Jen, an outrageous assortment of tops she had chosen for me: backless black leotards, rhinestone studded T-shirts, collarless shirts worn belted outside my pants, sweaters tied diagonally across my chest. And on my feet, I usually wore my dancing shoes, a tight pair of orange and brown wing tips with stacked Cuban heels.

Once I had learned to dress correctly, I needed to be taught how to dance. Jen and I practiced for hours at our homes and in the band room at school. Every sixth-hour study hall, we would sneak away to practice our latest moves to the tune of "Supernature." The band room had a great stereo system and plenty of floor space near the percussion section. I had had a brief affair with the band director, a married man with children who later went to jail for his sexual advances toward a young trombone student. He never reprimanded me for cutting study hall and gave us free reign of the room—partly due to his affection for me, and partly due to his fear of Jen, who disapproved of his former relationship with me.

After learning to dress and dance, I had to learn what might be termed "comportment." Jen warned me that if I walked and talked in a gay bar the way I normally did, I would immediately be suspected of being underage. All those years of being called a fag had taken a certain toll on my self-image, and I tended at times to behave as if I wanted to erase my physical presence. I walked with a slight shuffle, my head bowed slightly to the ground so that I appeared even shorter than my five-foot-six-inch stature.

I also spoke with a strangely hoarse, self-effacing voice, a voice that led people to believe I was perpetually suffering from sore throats. Jen tried to force me to act as if I had some sense of self-confidence. She warned me never to drink too much, never to talk too much or too little or too seriously. Never act afraid or as if I believed I didn't fit in. Never draw too much or too little attention to myself. And never, ever let it slip that I was still in high school.

Jen's favorite place to dance, The Red Baron, was a real test for the new "gay" me. The bar was practically run by a group called The Disco Sluts, a handful of gay men, lesbians, and a straight woman or two, who performed lip synch drag shows every few months at the bar. The leader of the group was a three-hundred-pound caustic man called Disco Doris who worked at Baskin Robbins by day and harassed people at the door of the Baron every evening. The Disco Sluts could be vicious; if they decided they didn't like you, they could make things very unpleasant and were not beyond making sure you never set foot in the club. They could easily goad the normally lax doorman into checking someone's (in our case, fake) identification, or demanding several different forms of I.D.

The Red Baron and the other dance clubs in Milwaukee were Jen's lifeline out of Greenfield. If anyone ever found out that she was underage, it would mean the end of her dancing. The disco competition circuit was incredibly cutthroat. People were always saying the nastiest things about each other's dancing, stealing each other's moves as well as partners, and most couples were willing to do anything to ensure they won—including having the competition disqualified.

Jen was risking a great deal by taking me to the bars with her. If it were discovered that I was in fact underage, it wouldn't take much effort to learn that she, too, was still in high school. If I were thrown out of some disco, it would just mean that I'd have to try and meet men elsewhere. My escape from Greenfield was accomplished not as a result of going to these bars, but through my realization that I was gay. Once I decided that being a fag had nothing to do with my masculinity or lack thereof, but was instead about who and how I loved, there was little anyone in Greenfield could do to hurt me anymore. But Jen's escape depended on going to these clubs. At them, she was someone important, someone whom people admired and wanted to meet. Without them, the hell of life in Greenfield would continue unabated, at least until she could manage to escape it through graduation.

I never really enjoyed going to the gay bars in Milwaukee. It just took too much effort to become the right kind of gay person. I find it particularly ironic that some months after beginning my trips to the dance clubs with Jen, I met a man at The Red Baron with whom I fell in love. This man insisted on altering my appearance yet again, this time transforming me into his image of a "respectable" gay person: looser jeans, Izod shirts, hair parted on the side, and no more Cuban heels.

If gay liberation involves some kind of freer expression of one's identity, there was nothing "liberating" about The Red Baron or the other discos. I always felt in these bars as if the whole place were watching me. One false move, and everyone would be laughing at the little kid pretending to be an adult. It actually felt quite similar to life in Greenfield, where one wrong move—a gesture, a word, a sound—would reveal the secret effeminacy I never recognized, yet had to struggle constantly to conceal.

What strikes me today about my experience of being called a fag in Greenfield and my efforts to "fit in" to gay life in Milwaukee is in fact the similarity of the two experiences. In neither case was I encouraged to share with others the things I most valued in myself. My classmates in Greenfield thought I was a freak because I did well in school and played the piano. The Disco Sluts didn't give a fuck about how smart I was or how well I played the piano, so long as I danced reasonably well and stayed out of their way. Traveling from Greenfield to Milwaukee seemed primarily to be a matter of trading one restrictive identity for another one equally as restrictive. While all identities are necessarily restrictive, they need not be restrictive in the same ways. "Greenfield fag" and "Milwaukee gay" seemed ultimately to be two sides of the same coin.

I now live in Pittsburgh, where I am pursuing a Ph.D. in Cultural Studies, a field that encourages me to think about things like how I have come to perceive myself as gay, and what roles the places I have lived have played in constructing that identity. I am still uncomfortable at most gay bars. I still feel as if I am being asked to inhabit a version of style that I find too restrictive—whether that version be muscle queen, sweater boy, or leather clone. But the strict lines demarcating these identities seem to be breaking down as of late, so that we are much more free to create hybrid kinds of gay styles. Now, I can sing show tunes *and* wear leather without feeling like a social outcast.

Recent work in gay and lesbian studies has insisted that our identities are the result of social and historical circumstances and not the product of some gay "essence" hidden inside us. With this recognition has come an awareness that we have the ability to create ourselves as gay, to invent identities less restrictive than those historically bequeathed to us. Gay liberation thus becomes not primarily the "discovery" of one's sexuality, but an opportunity to use that sexuality to create new styles and places, places where being gay means more than merely attempting to conform to certain preexisting notions of gender and sexuality.

I still visit Greenfield at least twice every year. Surprisingly, I feel very little remaining animosity toward the people with whom I went to school. In fact, I recently went so far as to attend my ten-year high school reunion. Most people were quite friendly, though I grew pretty tired of answering the question of whether or not I was married. While many of them had heard of the publication of my first book, few had any idea what it was about. Many of them insisted that the very next day, they would run out and buy themselves a copy. I suppose I will have to wait another ten years to hear how they reacted to that fag Champagne's first novel.

WAKEFIELD, MASSACHUSETTS

I WAS A SLOW BLOOMER. It took me a long time to figure out that my hometown was not my home. In contrast, my friend Stephan ran away from his hometown when he was fifteen, knowing full well that he needed to be somewhere else. That somewhere else, in order of succession, turned out to be Provincetown, San Francisco, Los Angeles, Fort Lauderdale, and New York—all before Stephan was twenty-one. By the time *I* was twenty-one, I'd lived in exactly two places: Wakefield and the city where I'd matriculated to college.

Now, Stephan and I are different in many ways, and the difference in our hometowns—he hails from Quincy, Massachusetts, a small, working-class city just south of Boston—may not really have been the decisive factor that drove him to flee while I stayed happily put. Maybe it was the difference in our families or the difference in our personalities or the fact that I got good grades and he did not. I believe in the unpredictability of life, which is why I'm not a sociologist. Still, I can't help but think that there was something about growing up in Wakefield per se that acted to delay my feelings of gay estrangement.

Wakefield, during the years I lived there, roughly the fifties through the mid-sixties, was the kind of place that kids didn't run away from. In fact, the only person I knew who did "run away" from Wakefield was my classmate and sometime girl-friend, Earlene Weller, who left high school a year early—she had enough credits to do so—in order to start college at age sixteen. (The high school authorities so disapproved that they denied her a diploma until she satisfactorily completed her first year of college.) A history of the town, published by the Tercentenary Committee in 1944, four years before I was born, described Wakefield as "a progressive community of happy homes and a contented people." Aside from the obvious boosterism of the claim, this is, at least from the perspective of my preadolescent years, a fairly accurate description. Even Buffy Sainte-Marie, the folksinger and another escapee from Wakefield, stayed long enough to graduate.

Progressive, happy, contented. Yes. As a youngster, I was so at home in Wakefield that I once set about, with crayons and huge sheets of brown wrapping paper, to map every street and every house in town, an absurd task given the size of the place, about 22,000 people. But there I was, wandering the streets of my immediate neighborhood—Yale Avenue, Avon Street, Chestnut Street, Walker Terrace—meticulously jotting down in a little notebook the address of each house for future transfer onto my *mappa mundi*. I soon realized, of course, that my project was too ambitious ever to bring to completion, but during the week or two I did work on it I spent long hours contentedly coloring in matchbook-sized drawings of every address I'd catalogued, giving each home a bit of Crayola green lawn and a lollipop tree in the side yard. Stephan ran away from Quincy; I embraced Wakefield with a cartographer's zeal.

Like most of the towns north of Boston, Wakefield was founded by Congregationalists—English Puritans—in the seventeenth century. In 1639, a number of citizens of Lynn petitioned the General Court of Massachusetts Bay Colony to be allowed to settle "an inland plantation." By 1644, that settlement, ten miles north

of Boston and eight miles from the sea, had become large enough
to be incorporated as a separate town, called Reading or Redding,
as the vagaries of seventeenth-century spelling would have it. Soon
a sizable village grew up around the south side of the lake the
native Indians called Quannapowitt. There, local lore has it, they
built a log cabin house of worship. On a grassy, maple-shaded
embankment behind the present Congregational church, the original Puritan graveyard still stands. A plaque, erected in 1950,
announces that the town won a commendation from *Better Homes
and Gardens* for the creation of a floral pathway on the edge of
those cemetery grounds.

During the years I grew up there, Wakefield indeed fancied
itself to be a *Better Homes and Gardens* kind of town. It still does.
The focal point was, and is, the town green, or common, which
extends southward from Lake Quannapowitt toward the "Rock-
ery," a pile of granite boulders in front of which stands a bronze
statue of a Spanish-American War soldier, erroneously referred
to by everyone as The Minuteman. Rifle in hand, he looks out
over the business section of Main Street, a sentinel marking the
boundary between the commercial district and the more picturesque area to the north.

I remember the common as picture-postcard perfect. With
its gracious, elm-lined pathways and old-fashioned park benches,
its tall Soldiers and Sailors Monument and black pyramid of can-
nonballs, its granite fence posts and freshly painted pipe railings,
the common focused the town around an image of stateliness—a
homey, New England town stateliness—neither too grand nor too
Yankee-shabby. That modest stateliness was echoed in the Fed-
eralist and antebellum homes that faced the common, and especially in the four Protestant churches that more or less defined
its four corners: the white-steepled churches belonging to the Baptists and Unitarian-Universalists; Emmanuel Episcopal, with its
shorter, English country church steeple; and the dark, heavy,
granite edifice of the Congregationalists.

The common reflected the ideals of the town itself, its moral
as well as esthetic ones. Wakefieldians strove to make their town
a handsome place, though not overly quaint, not like the towns—
Groton, Pepperell, Ashby, for example—of northwestern Middle-

sex County. They wanted it to be a gracious town, but not a snooty one. Not like Newton. Not like Wellesley, Wakefieldians must have told themselves. They promoted it as a democratic town, honestly working class and down-to-earth, but not in any coarse, vulgar way. No, sir. We were not a Chelsea or an Everett, or even, just two towns to the south, a Malden.

The town fathers were proud of the balance they had maintained between residential amenities and "solid manufacturing concerns." Under the masthead of the local paper, the Wakefield *Daily Item,* was printed the motto: "The Most Enterprising Business Community North of Boston." Business, when I was growing up there, meant the new industries that had arisen around Route 128, the circumferential highway built around Boston in the fifties. Light manufacturing, electronics, and service industries such as the American Mutual Insurance Company, which in 1958 located its main office on the north shore of Lake Quannapowitt, were the major employers in town.

These businesses replaced Wakefield's earlier, nineteenth-century industries—shoes, knitwear, cast-iron piping, rattan furniture, pianos—which had provided jobs for large numbers of ethnic workers who, like my maternal grandparents, came to Wakefield sometime between the late nineteenth and early twentieth centuries. Italians, Irish, Poles, French, Jews, Lebanese: most of my friends and classmates throughout my twelve years of public school education in Wakefield were the grandchildren of such immigrant families.

My maternal grandparents' story is probably fairly typical of the family stories of many of my childhood friends. In 1917, my grandfather, Louis DeVita, built three greenhouses at the corner of Yale and North avenues, a few blocks from the Wakefield depot. There he established a successful wholesale carnation business, one that he eventually moved to a larger facility at the other end of town. I remember the tall brick smokestack rising above those new greenhouses and the name, DEVITA'S, in black brick letters running down its length. It was visible from a long distance.

The DeVitas—there were two sons, my uncles Pasquale and Dominic (Pat and Dom), who took over after Grandpa died in

1926—were certainly not the wealthiest nor the most prominent family in town, but I now see that they were fairly typical of the first generation of ethnic newcomers: successfully making it in what had previously been a WASP-dominated culture.

By the early sixties, when I entered Wakefield High School, Wakefield's transformation from a Congregational village into an ethnic suburb was complete. Where previously men with names like Eaton, Sweetzer, Atwell, and Beebe had run the town, now those names were found only on street signs and public buildings. Replacing them were names like Colucci (my high school principal), Sardella (the vice-principal), and McGrail (on the board of selectmen). John Volpe, the governor of Massachusetts during most of the sixties and later Secretary of Transportation under Nixon, was a Wakefield boy. So was Israel Horowitz, the playwright. My classmates all through school were kids with names like Santoro, DeGruttola, Martello, and Galucci; McShane, MacLaughlin, MacDougal, and McIsaac; Leavitt, DeMarteau, Mooradian, Abdinoor, and Hanoosh.

For me, then, a Baby Boomer and member of the third generation ethnic influx, Wakefield was a town full of postwar optimism and melting-pot camaraderie, a town where the economic and social ascendancy of the ethnic middle class had reached its peak. Yes, of course there must have been some kids who ran away, but for most of us the life we were offered was pretty comfortable.

Wakefield was a town where everything worked: the utilities, the schools, the trash and snow removal systems, the all-day, town-sponsored Fourth-of-July celebration that began in the morning with the doll carriage parade (an event I knew I wasn't supposed to be interested in, but was); continued into the afternoon with a colorful, noisy full parade; went on to late-afternoon barbecues and carnival events, including an auction called by Al Delaney, the nasal-voiced janitor from my elementary school; and culminated late in the evening with a fireworks display and band concert given by the Red Men's Band on the polychromed Victorian bandstand that stood in the center of the common. (Most of the members of the band were not Native Americans, although our neighbor, Dick Bayrd, was. Dick's father, Leonard Bayrd, who was half Narragansett Indian, started the band and also ran an Indian crafts and jewelry shop out of a stuccoed, wood-frame teepee at the north end of Lake Quannapowitt. He was the most exotic citizen in town, followed, I suppose, by our one "black" family, the Encarnacaos, a clan of dark-skinned brothers of Portuguese Azorean descent.)

The housing stock consisted primarily of comfortable, modestly maintained homes. On my street, Yale Avenue, laid out just after the Civil War, the architectural style of choice seems to have been a restrained Italianate. But all the Victorian styles—Queen Anne, mansard, neo-Colonial—were, and still are, represented. There were newer neighborhoods, too, dating from the twenties, the thirties, the forties, the fifties. There was no "bad" area of town, no "other side of the tracks." The streets were all lined with maples, beeches, oaks, and, before the blight in the fifties, elms.

When I was growing up, there were about a dozen elementary schools in Wakefield, including an 1840s vintage "little red schoolhouse," the West Ward School, which is reputedly the oldest schoolhouse in continuous operation in Massachusetts. There was a junior high (new the year I entered it in 1960), a high school, a parochial school, and a private girl's academy, Nazareth, run by the Sisters of St. Joseph. There were three Roman Catholic churches (including the "Italian church," St. Florence's, on the Italian West Side), a Jewish temple, and, in addition to those four churches around the common, a Protestant church for each and every other denomination.

There were baseball fields, tennis courts, playgrounds, a YMCA. There were two railroad stations. The kind of station you only see now in quaint model railroad setups—long, low brick buildings, with the station name in large gold letters on a shingle out front—one for Wakefield and one for the village of Greenwood, at the southern end of town. There were branches of the Rotary Club, the Old Fellows, the Lions Club, the Knights of Columbus, and the Elks, my father's club, to which he brought me and my brothers for the annual father-son picnic, an event I secretly dreaded. The Catholic kids had C.Y.O. The Protestant kids had DeMolay. And everyone had Pleasure Island, an amusement park built around 1960 on forested land at the outskirts of town, a park that was supposed to rival Disneyland and "put Wakefield on the map."

In short, Wakefield was the kind of town where, say, an FBI man might comfortably locate himself, blending inconspicuously into its happy, middle-class fabric while he pursued a secret life as a double agent. This, in fact, is exactly what Herbert Philbrick, of "I Led Three Lives" fame, did, a piece of information that any Wakefieldian in the fifties and sixties would have proudly told you.

Double lives. Blending inconspicuously. Hiding out in the most enterprising business community north of Boston. It would be nice to use Herbert Philbrick as a metaphor for the life that I, and all gay kids growing up in Wakefield during that era, had to lead. But that was not my experience. Not that I didn't have my secret crushes and secret adolescent sex play to hide. I did. But the overwhelming sense of differentness, and the need to flee a stifling, unsympathetic environment that many gay teenagers feel—I think of my friend Stephan again—seem to have bypassed me. As I said, Wakefield was a town where you didn't have to run away.

Or was it?

It was around my sophomore year at Wakefield High School that I first heard the rumor about two girls (I think they were in the class ahead of me) who were . . . well, what words *did* we use back then? lesbians? dykes? queers? lovers? I can't remember, though I do recall that the news was spread in suggestive whispers and hushed asides at lunch, where my friends and I often met. Most of the time our lunch table conversation was innocuous: typical adolescent stuff about friends and school and our favorite pop singers, the Beatles. (All the girls in our group thought Paul was the cutest, an opinion I feigned no interest in.) But occasionally someone brought up the names of the two girls and for a few moments the talk turned catty and wicked—a conspiracy of ridicule and ostracism that transformed these hapless and I think frightened young women into freaks. I take little comfort in the fact that I did not participate in passing on this gossip. I'm sure that the only reason I did not was because I couldn't bring myself to speak *any* words related to homosexuality.

And yet, I seem to have made little or no connection between the two lesbian girlfriends and the nature of my own sexuality. Perhaps because they were women, which meant—since I was using impeccable adolescent male logic—that their acts were truly perverse whereas mine were simply examples of "messing around." Or perhaps because they were lovers whereas my connections with other boys had none of that sense of final commitment. Or perhaps because, after a year in eighth grade, when I engaged in mutual masturbation sessions with a friend (we did it after Tuesday afternoon Confirmation classes), I'd actually stopped having sex with other boys. Whatever the reason, it was somehow possible for me to listen to the sneering comments of my classmates and not feel that their hostility could ever come my way. Wakefield was a safe place.

I am trying to capture the particular quality of my experience of myself and my hometown during my teenage years. As I look into that dim past, uncovering memories I'd long ago forgotten, I realize that my awareness of myself, particularly of my sexual identity, was subsumed into a safe little suburban world. I was living in a cocoon, a cozy, warm, friendly cocoon that I had unconsciously spun out of all the pleasureable experiences that my town—and especially my high school—had to offer. It was a world of good grades and extracurricular involvements and C-block lunches with friends. If I was hiding amid all of this, I wasn't even aware of it myself. The truth is, it was easy to repress or ignore the occasional evidence of homophobia ("Don't wear a pink shirt on Thursday"; "Don't carry your books against your chest if you're a guy"; "Donna and Paula sitting in a tree/ *k-i-s-s-i-n-g*") when otherwise life was so attractive. For me, more than anything else, that meant extracurricular life.

During my four years at Wakefield High, I went to every varsity football game, home and away. I hate football, but I was a member (first French horn) of the high school band, and this meant that from early September through Thanksgiving I had to participate in the marching band. Our band director, Mr. Boisen, was one of my high school heroes. He loved good music and exacted high standards of musicianship from us. He was also honest. He told us he hated having to lead the marching band. He would have much preferred to rehearse us in the Vaughn Williams English Folksong Suite or the concert band arrangement of "Good Friday Spell" from *Parsifal,* both of which we did play during my years in the band. But, Mr. Boisen told us, if we had to have a marching band, then Wakefield High School's marching band was going to be top-notch. And it was. We rehearsed several afternoons a week, high-stepping through elaborate routines while we played tricky arrangements of John Philip Sousa and the latest Broadway tunes. It was innocent and exhilarating and made me feel like one of the gang. Marching band, concert band, orchestra, Junior Choraleers, madrigal singers, French horn lessons, Future Teachers of America Club, sophomore hop committee—I was an extracurricular activities junkie. These were the years when you could take music theory classes at W.H.S. (I did), when you could organize your own chamber music groups (I did), when you could find a faculty member to help you compose and orchestrate a large choral piece (I did). In college I met people who had gone to the High School of Music and Art in New York, but at Wakefield High I had put together my own arts high school out of the bits and pieces the school had to offer. Sophomore year I even joined a nearby civic symphony.

I now look at the life I was leading back then and realize how gay it truly was. *Esthetically* gay. My friend, Bob Smith, a wonderful stand-up comedian, who along with two other comics is in a group called Funny Gay Males, has a line about how his high school (he grew up in suburban Buffalo) had a Head Start program for gay kids. "It was called drama club," Bob says, a line that always gets a big laugh from his largely gay audience. In place of drama club, I had music.

Remarkably, no one ever called me a sissy for pursuing such an extracurricular career during high school. I've heard so many stories of guys who were ridiculed in high school for behavior that seems far less obviously gay. Was my escape from such notice a result of the benign character of the town? Or of the naïveté of the times? Or of the strength of my personality? (Yes, I was popular.) Or of the cleverness with which I (consciously or otherwise) managed to "pass"? Was the town protecting me, or was I protecting the town?

I don't know the answer to any of these questions. Clearly, my feelings about Wakefield would have been very different if the life I was leading during high school—blithely doing lots of music, getting straight As, being mediocre at gym, not playing sports, not dating girls, generally being a "nice boy"—if that life had brought me ridicule and threats. It did not. (As it turned out, I was even asked to be one of the graduation speakers, and I gave an appreciative little talk about Leonard Bernstein, a topic that surely must have raised some eyebrows.) When they let you get away with that kind of thing, what was there to complain about?

What there was to complain about dawned on me only very gradually. And I owe that knowledge, at least in part, to the Boston & Maine railroad.

In the annals of the history of my hometown, it has become a commonplace to trace Wakefield's evolution from an agricultural village to a modest industrial community to the year 1845 when the Boston & Maine opened a branch line to Wakefield. With the railroad came easy commuting back and forth to Boston. My grandfather and my uncles took the train into Boston in order to go to the flower market. My mother commuted by train during the one semester she attended Boston University and later art school. And it was on that very same line that I took the train into the city for cultural outings.

I think I started to take these train excursions during the summer after my sophomore year. That was the summer a group of us, encouraged by the high school choral director, signed up to sing in a teaching chorus for students of choral conducting at Boston University. Every morning for two weeks we'd catch the train into North Station where we'd switch to a trolley to Park Street and then out the Commonwealth Avenue line to B.U. (The Boston rapid transit system, at that time known as the MBTA, had not yet adopted the color-coded system by which all the subway and trolley lines are identified today. We took what has become known as a "B" car on the "Green Line.")

More than the choral program itself, I loved these train and subway rides. I loved being with my friends, traveling into the city, a world that had always previously been mediated for me by adults and into which we were now venturing without adult supervision. I loved that sense of freedom and adventure. I loved the possibilities that taking the trains and subways gave me. I'm not talking about erotic possibilities; the idea of using Boston as a place to pick up men never even came to my mind. The possibilities were still only esthetic, but they carried with them the tingle of adult pleasures. I learned how to use public transportation to take myself to the Museum of Fine Arts, to Harvard Square, to Beacon Hill. And to a wonderful discount book and record store, The Book Clearing House, where I bought my first classical album, a Russian recording of the Schumann Concerto for Four Horns.

You could not buy classical albums in Wakefield. You could not see foreign films there—in Japanese, Italian, Swedish—such as I did at a little foreign film theater on Norway Street. You could not buy a cappuccino there, such as I did at the Café Florian on Newbury Street. And Wakefield's public library, the Lucius Beebe Memorial Library, as good as it was, could not hope to match the treasures—all those scores to Bach cantatas!—that I found at the Boston Public Library in Copley Square. (It was *years* later that I learned you could cruise the men's room at the B.P.L.)

Maybe all this adolescent passion for high urban culture was just a way to sublimate other, more somatic passions. What's certain is that these trips into Boston planted the first seeds of what was later to blossom as an important awareness: Wakefield could never be my adult hometown. It just couldn't offer me *enough*.

One more story. During the summer of 1964, the summer between my sophomore and junior years in high school (the same summer as the choral program at B.U.), I auditioned for and got the part of Polonius in a student production of *Hamlet*. We were a pickup troupe of artsy types from Wakefield High, kids who had come under the spell of a young, dynamic, and controversial teacher named Polly Hogan.

Miss Hogan—perhaps we called her Polly, though my recollection is that we kept to the formality of "Miss Hogan"—had come to Wakefield High School the previous fall, where she quickly became immensely popular with the students. In addition to her youthful (mid-twenties) vitality, she brought fresh ideas, a love of working with kids, and a mildly disrespectful attitude toward the administration.

With the exception of my cousin Fred, who had gone to art school and who had taken me to Greenwich Village the previous year, Miss Hogan was the first bohemian I had ever encountered, a suburbanized bohemian to be sure, but by Wakefield's standards a bohemian nonetheless. She wore jeans to rehearsals, cut her hair short, drove a Volkswagen. She was also one of the first teachers to wear contact lenses. These had scratched her cornea, forcing her to don a black eye patch, a fashion accessory that brought Miss Hogan great notoriety. Her teaching methods were considered quite notorious, too, though in retrospect they consisted of little more than role-playing exercises with her students.

Perhaps every high school has a Miss Hogan, a teacher more comfortable in the world of adolescents than in that of the adults. She was one of those teachers whom students know to be wholeheartedly on their side. "Kind of like Robin Williams in *Dead Poets Society*," my brother told me, when I asked him what he remembered about her. Polly's apartment was the place kids went to for coffee and counsel. She threw a grand cast party there after the fall musical, *Brigadoon,* a show the principal fought her on and ultimately censored because of Meg's song about being born out of wedlock.

"The old biddy English teachers hated her," my brother reported. Apparently, the administration did too, because they fired her after that first year. And so, in addition to giving us teenagers something creative to do during summer vacation, Miss Hogan's plan to put on *Hamlet* that summer of 1964 was a chance for her to give the finger to the school board and for us, in turn, to show our undying loyalty to her.

The production never came to pass. A combination of factors—erratic schedules on the part of us kids; lack of rehearsal space; the intervention of parents, who, I believe, were as disapproving of Miss Hogan as were the school authorities—all conspired to make short work of our ambitious plan. Or maybe Miss Hogan just gave up, realizing that bringing her version of *la vie bohème* to Wakefield was futile. In any event, shortly after we scuttled *Hamlet,* she moved out of town, into Boston as I recall, where years later, as a gay man living on Beacon Hill, I saw her in a production of *A Doll's House* at the Lyric Stage on Charles Street.

I haven't thought of Polly Hogan in years. Indeed, because I was really on the fringe of the drama groupies, she never even figured that prominently in my life that year. (I'm not even sure I've remembered all the facts correctly.) But when I came to think about my relationship to my hometown, the incident of the short-lived production of *Hamlet* was one of the first things to come to mind. Why?

Working with Polly Hogan, even for so brief a time, taught me many things. First of all, it gave me a taste of the real world of artists, not the one officially sanctioned by my high school, but a world where imagination took precedence over organization; where spontaneous, messy creativity was more important than final products; where self-expression, even if it risked offending someone, gloriously flourished. Working with Polly also introduced me to *Hamlet,* a play about a sensitive young man with a confused, troubled heart and lots of love to give. (I remember a lot of clasping of shoulders and affectionate embraces whenever Hamlet would encounter a friend. I remember wishing I didn't have to play Polonius—I wanted to be Hamlet's friend, too. I remember the boy playing Hamlet was very cute.)

Most of all, being a part of that summer troupe helped to muster my cynicism for the kind of unimaginative authority that Polly and, by extension, people like her—me, for instance!—were up against in that town. And I soon realized that it wasn't just a few stodgy town officers who were the enemy. The troupe had talked about doing a cabaret production, a kind of coffeehouse *Hamlet.* But we had run into resistance there, too. Now, with adolescent indignation, I began to question why there were no coffeehouses in town. What was the matter with this place that it was so . . . so . . . well, again, what words did we use in those days? Conformist. Unsophisticated. Establishment. I was learning a whole new vocabulary with which to evaluate my hometown.

Unsexy, too. That becomes another word to describe Wakefield. There was something terribly unsexy about the place. There was no charge in it for me. No electricity. No allure. Sure it had its charms—the lakes, the parks, the unusually wide Main Street with its blocks of trim stores—but these were the kinds of things a parent might ask you to appreciate. Esthetically and culturally, the town felt parental. Without being able to articulate it, I was coming to see that I could never have the kind of "erotic" relationship with Wakefield that I could have with an urban area like Boston.

Someone (I've forgotten who) once said that one of the functions of a city is to confuse and disorient, to shake up one's sense of what is real and true and good and acceptable. The city enriches and deepens one's experience of the world and the self. Towns cannot do this, especially childhood hometowns. Which is why, for instance, the classic shape of the bildungsroman, the novel of self-discovery, often takes the form of a journey from the town to the city. Think of *Great Expectations*. Think of *Tom Jones*. Think of *The Beautiful Room Is Empty*.

My generation in Wakefield was the first to leave town in large numbers, mainly to attend college. Many, to my surprise, eventually came back, choosing to settle in the town that had nurtured them. But as the years go by, and I discover who in my high school turned out gay, I see that we, the gay ones, never really did return. Despite all that a town like Wakefield can offer—and a recent visit back (I took the train) showed me all the amenities are still there—as long as it remains a town and not a city, it cannot offer *us,* its gay sons and daughters, what we need. Which is the chance to put together lives and families in new and different ways, ways that are much more diverse, global, unpredictable, erotic, and celebratory.

I now see that all those extracurricular activities I did in high school provided me, for a little while anyway, with a kind of alternate family: a family organized around the mutual love of beauty, around energies and passions that could be both divinely foolish and exquisitely serious, around aims that had nothing to do with the usual teenage (read heterosexual) preoccupations. Polly Hogan's *Hamlet*—wild and disrespectful and full of foolish seriousness—helped me, as did those train trips into Boston, to see something more: that the town was willing to go only so far in its support of the arts and of the kind of outlook the arts embrace. In Wakefield, the arts would always remain extracurricular. Which meant, though I couldn't have explained it then, that as long as I stayed there who I was would always remain extracurricular, too.

I never ran away from Wakefield, but once I left for college I rarely came back except for vacations. And pretty soon, I stopped coming back for vacations as well. I did not run away, but I had learned, though still only from the point of view of esthetics (sex with a guy wouldn't happen again until my junior year in college), that the city was where I would get my life, and get it abundantly.

GEORGE S. SNYDER

NORTH EAST, PENNSYLVANIA

LAKE STREET HAS BEEN shaved; occasional raw, zippered sores and puckered wounds show through the snow along the curbs. Everything is exposed now. Unrestrained, the winter afternoon light shines more harshly, throws asbestos shingle siding into high relief, reveals traces of old advertising painted on brick walls, buckled sidewalks, mounds of pale frozen dirt clods, patchy asphalt.

They have cut down all the trees. The 150, even 200-year-old trees lining, or rather that used to line, Lake Street as it passed through town. And not from another attack of the Dutch blight, which ravaged us over 30 years ago and left Elm Street ironically named. These were perfectly respectable maples, oaks; they were harmless old shade trees. Cut down to clear the way to bury the power lines. A project that has to do with Civic Pride, my sister in the front seat next to me tries to explain; something about downtown rejuvenation, a Main Street revival. Which ought to be something I can understand, something that ought to be right up my alley, she suggests. Something about an esthetic decision and telephone poles.

Leaving this town, I explain to my sister, was an esthetic decision. But my sister, never much of a wit and less of a cynic, turns and stares more intently out her window, so that I will concentrate on driving. We stop at the only traffic light on Lake Street. We have come back to bury our mother. And having returned, sitting there in a rental car in what is euphemistically referred to as our hometown, I want to make a connection; somehow I am feeling bitter enough. But it is not the moment. We drive through the intersection of Main and Lake and continue north.

Lake Street connects the Interstate on the ridge south of town with the lake to the north. Main Street, or Route 20 as it is known, runs east and west. Where they intersect constitutes the commercial, social, spiritual, and literal heart of North East. A town whose very name, derived from the northeasterly winds off the lake (the local newspaper is named, appropriately, *The Breeze),* connotes direction, as if the inhabitants have always been in some deep sense concerned about which way they were coming from or going to, as if living was measured by weather vanes and compasses more than anything else. As if telling direction was the whole point.

In many ways, it was, and is. Main Street runs east into New York State, and west through our little piece of Pennsylvania into Ohio, and even (I am assuming; I do not know for certain) all the way across to the West Coast. Route 20 is Everybody's Main Street, the old highway west through all the small towns of America. From North East across the state line east to Ripley, Fredonia, on up to Lancaster and then across to Alden, Bethany, Geneva, Auburn, Skaneateles, and on to Schenectady. Or across the other state line, west into Ohio to Conneaut, Ashtabula, another Geneva, Painesville, Mentor (home of President Garfield), and past Cleveland to Norwalk, Bellevue, Clyde, Fremont (home of President Hayes), Perrysburg (for Admiral Perry and the Battle of Lake Erie). A landscape of forgettable presidents, pedestrian wars, small towns.

And of all these small towns of America, ours was, and is

still, typical of them, even nicer than some: North East has a park, with trees (mostly spared in this latest purge) and war memorials. Also green iron benches and a fountain on which all sidewalks converge. Dead center, a circle of painted concrete surmounted by a lady endlessly emptying a jug. She is, in style, antique: Greek or Roman. She is (one assumes) perpetually pouring out what we knew from Latin class was *aqua vitae,* the water of life. Walking around her, you have a view of everything, the Methodist church, the corner store, the bank, the Presbyterian church, the library, the Presbyterian manse, several other prosperous homes, and the old high school. Our entire world, our town. Which sent, per capita, more men than any other town its size in America to the war. As we were reminded at least annually every Memorial Day. "The war" meant World War II, always referred to as if it had just recently ended, and blackout shades, unmistakably dark green with tassel pulls, reminded you from most windows, even into the days of dotted-swiss priscillas, even surviving into the times of harvest gold and avocado green and sliding porch doors.

An unstylish little town in some respects, proud but uncommunicative, especially about those years during the war when you would only have found women and children and a few old grandfathers in the park, only women trying to keep the farms going, and then the ones who moved back into town with relatives. Not a man to be seen. You can't imagine what it was like, my mother told us, nothing but the women left in the town, you can't imagine, she explained. And we did not try.

Not like Pittsburgh (far south of us) with the mills going night and day, part of the war effort, not at all. "Like Pittsburgh on a Sunday during the war," was the expression. Meaning (one assumed) a kind of unnaturally frantic, even devil-may-care sort of energy and activity. Not like our town, not like North East, grim, dedicated, not taking anything lightly.

I was born at the beginning of the Eisenhower years, after that nearly (ever present) ended war. I developed my esthetic sophistication under Mamie and Ike, in an era of powder blue walls and eggshell trim. It was a time in which patterns grew smaller, quieter (violets instead of peonies, houndstooth check instead of palm fronds); it was a time of white lead paint and hunter green shutters. It was ultimately a time in which Williamsburg Colonial evolved into as much a sensibility as a style. And a goal, so that we made the trip to Virginia and the pilgrimage to Deerfield outside Detroit in our wood-sided Plymouth station wagon and bought the handmade soap and candles and rock candy that were the emblems of our heritage. Postwar tourism being a quest for the Early American ideal, what Our Fathers had fought for, we sought out the beauty and virtues of the rural good old days and came home disenchanted. What ought to have been in full abundance in our own backyards—simple pleasures; decent, honest post-and-beam construction; center halls and roaring hearths—became accessible by car, what you drove and parked and took time walking to, paid to get in. Kept at a distance. Meanwhile what you came back home to seemed less and less looked after, cared for, less desirable for being within walking distance perhaps. Everyone getting away until only the skies ended up being friendly. Everyone on the road. Because you can't go home.

Home was shabby even. You could only do so much mental redecorating. You could imagine a pine dry sink under the window, a butter churn by the stove, a corner cupboard disguising the Amana, the dinette into ladderback chairs and a maple dropleaf, but how could you ever control the looks of an entire town? After all, progress is usually a matter of opinion, downwardly mobile an opinion strictly in the eyes of the beholder, no matter how relentlessly pursued. Gas stations on every corner, more asphalt rolled out every year, neon and aluminum siding like some kind of unstoppable and unsightly growth, every ill-conceived addition of an attached garage a blatant reminder of the unattractive times we lived in.

It was the beginning of my disenchantment. Remodeling was in the air, we were traveling in the fast lane; who was going to let progress pass on by? Adolescence in the late sixties would come as a kind of relief, in some ways, and a distraction. I decided I would never survive as a purist of the picturesque, outside of recreated villages where no one really lived anyway. Small towns were underdeveloped countries in miniature, picking up on the worst the dominant nation had to offer, strip malls and fast-food drive-ins, and a coin laundry on Main Street next to the public library, a mobile home park between the center of town and the cemetery along with a Dairy Queen, the last of the romantic ruins in Paper Mill Hollow buried under fill and chintzy split-level low-slung, low-brow three-bedroom ranches. Drive-thru banking next to the Methodist church.

I took picture windows punched in the façades of decent Greek Revivals as personal affronts, I cringed at basketball hoops and frowned on Florida rooms made out of butchered Victorian verandahs. They were terrible times. Wasn't a respectable old farmhouse left that was safe from the ravages of modernization, not a sturdy old Queen Anne someone didn't want to renovate the daylights out of. My best friend Skip used to say the only ones spared would be those they turned into funeral homes, since at that time any other possibilities—bed-and-breakfast ventures, day-care centers—hadn't been invented.

And so as Jackie gave us tours of Green and Blue Rooms, and inspired our historical conscience, at least where decorating was concerned, our own landscape came to seem more and more a disappointing pastiche, the subdivisions cropping up in former orchards and vineyards, the cinder-block bunker erected for the Church of God evangelicals just another vulgar display of shoddy construction and cheap enticement. Evidence of a vaguely sinister disrespect for the past.

And now, I point out to my siblings, they have to chop down venerable oaks and maples and think they're improving the look of the place. Like taking the ivy off the Methodist church.

It was the ivy or the church, my older brother observes, always the practical one.

Then they should have let it grow on the Sunday school wing, an unhappy and uninspired addition where we are ushered before the service. The charm of a fallout shelter. But I say nothing. We know better.

We all know better, because we left this town, even if it has always been home. My father took us for a time to another town on Route 20, in Ohio, where he died just across the border, an hour and a half drive, and we came back, only to grow up and leave again. We left for lots of reasons, not simply esthetic. There were other catalysts. And for a while, one small town is going to be the same as the next, calling one of them home is, of course, to define a state of mind. For my brothers, the women they ended up marrying were not necessarily more cosmopolitan than the North East girls, just that they hadn't grown up next door; they were from other small towns that presumably they too wished to get away from; so that along with the locations of lucrative careers, you could say that wives sometimes determined the course your life took. As for my sister who married one of the boys next door, well, eventually they left together and are now almost more outspoken than the rest of us about their mutual disdain, perhaps because they are doubly aware of what they left behind. Or perhaps, on this occasion, they are reminded of what their lives were like when mother lived down the street from them, what it is like to be adults with parents living in the same little town.

We, the family, wait in the Sunday school room while the friends of our mother gather in the sanctuary, and her friends in the choir with whom she sang run through a scale quietly next door. Her friends from her days of teaching arrive, at least those who are left from those days; who are, were also our teachers in first and second grade, and who will remember each of us even when we do not recognize them. Her neighbors and the ladies from the Methodist home and Eastern Star, and all the other widows and little old ladies with white hair who helped her keep the church going, who ran the guilds and the Sunday evening classes and the Methodist women's groups. For this, as my brother will say to them later, standing and turning to face the little congregation, with a nod to the choir loft, this was her church. She loved this church, he will say to them, speaking for us, her children and grandchildren, her family sitting quietly at the front of the sanctuary in front of the casket, in front of the plain wooden altar. And he will speak from his heart. The way a man who has been away and become successful can speak. For a moment weak winter light will play across the wall where the famous picture of Jesus hangs, tiny dancing splotches through the stained-glass window, skipping beams of rose and turquoise and amber, flickering across the faces of Jesus and my brother looking out and down at us. She loved this church, she loved this town. She loved all of you.

And yet we left, each of us. Even she did. Even our mother, stranded in Ohio after Dad died, and instead of coming back, hesitated, wondered what to do with herself, though it didn't matter where she lived, sat for a year in a condo community around a pool in Florida, until she came back. Because, she explained, her furniture all looked out of place, and because, although she would never really miss the snow, she missed the seasons. We found her a new little ranch, in a subdivision that had once been a vineyard, and from the front window on very clear days she might have a glimpse of the lake, of a narrow line of deeper blue near the powder blue of the sky. For she had admitted to me, even before she returned, that she missed the water. Sitting on a tropical terrace in that unnatural, close, scented twilight of Miami, with the glitter of a gaudy Deco coast in the distance, past the stage prop palms, "I miss the lake."

Oh but how could she, I had thought, wanted to think, don't want to think now, or then, flying in for her funeral, gliding in over that gray water. I live in Chicago now, I live on another of the Great Lakes and I understand, but differently. For living in Chicago is a choice based purely on convenience, on life-style as much as landscape, and has to do with opportunity as much as view. "By myself," she began to explain twenty years ago, a preface to an explanation or apology, and then let the rest of her words pass in a sigh and a wave of her hand, speculation not worth pursuing, brushed off in the direction of the horizon line. Where the sky and the water seem to touch.

Lake Street runs north to the lake, past the vineyards where the new high school is now, past the housing developments where there used to be vineyards and orchards, and then dwindles down to dirt at the last stretch to Freeport Landing. Where we were told they smuggled slaves across to Canada from this rocky little strip of beach; where my sister and I searched for beach glass; where my brothers built bonfires out of driftwood and tried seducing girls they would never marry; where I'd sat and contemplated an escape to Canada, that invisible shore on the opposite side, in the face of another war. I was not the only eighteen-year-old looking across that lake in those days, but a lucky draw in the draft lottery and I canceled the trip. My best friend Skip did not have to go, his father had died a hero in Korea, so we were both spared, one assumed we were spared to stand on the shores of other lakes and oceans, from Race Point on the Cape to the Hudson to the Island to Russian River, wasn't that the point? Or to stand, the night of her funeral in the bitter cold sweeping in across the shallowest of the Great Lakes, and try to summon up an emotion other than homesickness. Which I try to fend off, because I am supposed to be home, even if I do not feel it.

Storms rise up faster on Lake Erie than on any of the other Great Lakes, Skip would explain to people in Manhattan, when we were living there together. Faster because it is the shallowest of the lakes. Shallow and prone to violence, he would add facetiously, like our lives.

The lake is north, I would tell them, and we tell direction by it. Water is always north and that's how you know where you are, how you keep your bearings, how you know which way you are facing. But a river called East and the Hudson off West Street, and living on an island—I wave my hands, pretending to be nonplussed, at the various horizons.

And what sort of life would you have had there, Skip would ask, when I would try to think about the consequences if we had never met and try to imagine us back in small towns along Route 20. What sort of lives would either of us have had, he would ask rhetorically. Of course. For we knew perfectly well, both of us had spent enough time in the provincial backwaters, in little towns that were on the way to somewhere else.

America after the war was on the move. I was a boy watching them build that Interstate. These little towns, these rest stops along the way, none of them were ever going to be our final destinations, our final resting places.

We were certain. And I had known this for a long time. At the age of ten, old enough to ride a bike—an old Schwinn without fenders—I rode out of a town on Route 20 and south to the Interstate, where I would lie down in the shoulder's tall weeds and feel the shudder of the ground, the shivering of the milkweed pods and Queen Anne's lace. The throbbing in the earth was the pulse of the rest of the world passing in and out of mine, running an index finger down my back. Outside the town's limits, where Lake Street dwindled on down to size, the Interstate roared along the ridge in lofty disdain. Later, at the age of fourteen, I would ride alongside or stand and lean with hands like claws on the cyclone fence, studying the preoccupied drivers headed toward the exotic east or limitless, expansive west of the amber waves of grain and purple mountains. What was Route 90 anyway but a faster way than old 20 for these semis and Coupe de Villes and mobile homes to get beyond my little town? The two worlds barely converged, there was no genuine overlap, the local never really merged with the express, the transition was posted with cautionary tales: divided highway ends, reduce speed, slow children playing. Pedaling passionately out of town I did the warnings in reverse, over and over again. Down a road memorized by a pounding heart.

For the geography, the lay of the land, was not my only interest. And eventually I made contact with the outside world. Inevitably I made a connection. Not, to be perfectly fair or honest, while we lived in North East, but in another of the towns along Route 20, and does it matter? They were all alike, these little towns; they were different only in degree. All of them close enough to the rush of traffic, all of them with gas stations and opportunities. And checking the pressure on your tires often enough would finally pay off. A boy and his bike. Nice bike, boy. What you got there? How old are you anyway? Which way you headed? Old enough. I bet you are. I'll take care of that. Enough time.

What is a gas station anyway, but a stage set, cinder block faced with white enamel in front, exposed in back, squatting on a leveled-off plateau of gravel and fill. From underneath the edge of the tarmac the culvert pipe poked out and dribbled into the high weeds sprouting from the original lay of the land. Brown in almost every season, broken, determined brush and tenacious burdocks and flourishing sumac, mulberry, wild grape, ragweed, cheered up at night by crickets. I link this landscape in my memory to desire: unfriendly and tough, not very pretty but unequivocable and real. On a night without even stars or much moonlight, in the fuzzy hot blue dark of a washroom, surrounded by the pale glow of tile and porcelain, drunk on disinfectant and Old Spice aftershave.

After Williamsburg, I would ask Skip, loving to speculate, what was the most important influence in our growing up?

"*After Dark,*" he replied without thinking. "And Donna Summer. I saw them make enough candles to last a lifetime. What changed our lives were the photographs of Ken Duncan. One of his ballet dancers was worth all the handmade balls of soap in Sturbridge Village."

"Deerfield Village. But what about Jack Kerouac? *On the Road.*"

"*L'Huomo Vogue.*"

"Sherwood Anderson. Winesburg was Clyde, Ohio, dear. You remember Clyde."

"What I remember is the hitchhiker on spring break from Penn State."

"That too."

"Outside of Painesville."

"But what affected me most in those days, what changed my life? I keep thinking about—"

"Blow jobs from truck drivers."

"Not just that."

And yet you chalked up experience along that stretch of highway. And you wondered about what might be farther down the road. You took your chances. Like the trucker from Nashville, who wouldn't let you out of his cab without relinquishing your BVD boy's medium briefs. You kept your eye on the road, you pedaled on home, but you knew you'd go back. "Some, they get their name put in, their moms do it, with a laundry pen." It is a detail that strikes him as memorable, examining the waistband, sniffing at the all cotton, balled up in his hands like a dirty handkerchief. So whatever else, you knew you weren't entirely alone. If you could only get to where they all were. And then that seventeen-year-old, a lifeguard type, visiting for the summer, and the first unforgettable examination of someone else's tan line. Adolescence

is a series of adventures, with the rise and fall of traffic rushing
by like the rhythmic splash of waves on a beach. Or both. All on
the way to somewhere else, to somewhere beyond the vanishing
point, beyond the horizon line, beyond the place where the sides
of the road seem to meet, where the pale sky touches the dark
water.

And so this little town could never really be home to me,
and was just briefly. And I will not return, after this, I remind
myself. This is not home. Home was with Skip. He and I left this
part of the country, grew up, moved away, had our adventures
played out on a much grander scale than anything we might have
hoped for back here. There is nothing left here for me now. For
this is not my first trip back for a funeral, but it will be my last.
There is no one here, and now that Skip is gone too, home is
anywhere else.

This is not home. Even the house itself is gone, the farmhouse with the powder blue walls and eggshell woodwork, the
house I so carefully redecorated in my mind, the old white clapboard house with green shutters, which the developer promised
my mother they'd restore to the way it would have looked 150
years before. Restore its original beauty, back to its original glory,
was the phrase. They wanted her to know this, one assumed, so
that when they pulled it down and subdivided the land for another development, and plowed new roads back in through the
orchard and the vineyard, they could explain it had not been
their original intention. They could explain how costly restoration
would have been, how putting things back the way they would
have been simply wasn't feasible.

It is that kind of a town. It is that kind of a people who live
in that town, who have just so much sympathy for old clapboard
and green shutters and old mills and old shade trees. You can go
drive to see history and rural charm. Early American is long
distance; strip malls are local. And because I have a certain contempt for this way of thinking, I have a certain contempt for the
town where I learned to think this way. I make Chicago my home,
where I try to forgive them and perhaps also forgive myself. Home
is Chicago. Because as I tell people, you have to go somewhere,
and I have always lived near water, so that I could be anywhere

on the Great Lakes, Chicago as easily as another place. I have always lived near water and tell direction by it. By yourself, one beach is as good as another.

After this funeral, when I have said good-bye to my siblings, I drive south. And I wonder whether I will see them very often now that the center of our family is gone, now that our mother no longer is the point of intersection for our lives. I turn my back, metaphorically as well, on the lake and the town and head for the Interstate. I am alone, I drive a rental car, without even thinking I stop for gas. And for a moment I reflect on how quaint, how old-fashioned it is, not even exclusively self service; it is all still that provincial. So that when the boy with a dirty overall and ski vest and white blond hair and ice blue eyes peers in at me, I am caught off guard; I am wondering which side the tank is on, I never pay attention to details like this in a rental car. "Which way you headed," he says, as if there were no reason to pretend it into a question, as if there were any other reason for a conversation. And I look up.

His eyes have that oddly familiar look, like that of animals caught in the road by headlights at night. Or like a raccoon I frightened once, held for a moment by a flashlight beam, in the woods, by a boy more afraid than the animal. And is it fear now, or something else? Is it curiosity or loneliness out here, on a bleak winter day with a pale, thin, timid kind of light?

He is not a cute kid. He could be (I realize with genuine dismay) the son of anyone I went to school with. My mother could have taught his father in the fifth grade. I have been away too long; I can't imagine sorting out the connections of his very young life to mine. I don't even know who owns this station, if there was a time when I did. I don't want to know. This is not a high school lifeguard with a perfect tan line. The memories are tough and not very pretty to think about anymore.

"Cold enough, isn't it," he observes, and I see the long underwear at the neck, gray and grease-stained, his hands are in his pockets while I find my cash; he is not as cute as either Skip or I was at his age, but his cheeks are ruddy from the cold and his youth is striking if only because of being unexpected. Except not on this day, not after—so soon after would be in such bad taste.

On up the ridge, onto Route 90 itself, where for a moment there is a vista. There is a break in the lay of the land and you can look out, north, across the trees and slopes of vineyards and orchards, past a couple of steeples, and all the way to the lake itself. In the winter it is almost invisible, a thin line between white and gray, the horizon almost indistinguishable, so you would not know, if you were a stranger in this part of the country, you might not realize that what you were looking out across was a coastline and a lake and a sky. They are almost the same colorless expanse. And as I turn to look, I think only that I can tell the direction, that in the distance is North East, that I am looking north. But I am headed in another direction. I am headed home now, which is no longer here.

BALTIMORE, MARYLAND

Henry James once wrote of Baltimore that the houses, especially, possessed an unmistakable manner, a certain vividness he had never seen before in another city. To some, the block upon block of marble steps that mark the entrances to the Baltimore row house mean only uniformity, the banality of repetition. Some straight people believe that gays are always the same garden-variety homosexual too. But just as each row house reveals the individual challenge of personality on the inside, gay people have souls and elbows, dimples and despair.

There is a doorway, number 5 on Mt. Vernon Place, that means as much about being gay to me as the Stonewall Inn does. It's where Alexander Stokowski pushed me, late on the night of November 13, 1978. I was supposed to take my GREs at Hopkins the next morning and I was fatally wavering, lingering on the brink of going home, of abandoning this man whom I had met the week before. My indecisiveness worked as an adrenaline surge might, and Alex pushed me into the doorway, partially hidden by the columns of the small portico, out of the light, and kissed me; then he put his hands into the pockets of my overcoat, pulling me by the coat pockets closer to him and closer, as yellow cabs, almost white in the moonlight, jostled and rumbled across the uneven cobblestones of the circle around the Washington Monument. I have ever-mounting evidence that Alex's kiss that night may have been the one of a lifetime, the one against which all others will be measured.

Alex Stokowski was laid off from the Bethlehem Steel plant. He was younger than me, twenty at the time, but he taught me things about being gay with the patience and precision of a sixty-year-old elementary schoolteacher. He lived on the east side of the city—Highlandtown, the area is called. Originally the land was surveyed with an eye to promoting the property as a place where people could build houses above the fetid air of the inner city basin. It didn't work out that way, and now, along the strip called Eastern Avenue, Greeks, Poles, Lithuanians, and other Eastern Europeans lived, most attracted, since the turn of the century, to the port and the jobs it engendered. Like a majority of the people he grew up with in Highlandtown, Alex finished school and then went to work at the steel plant, making far more money than many white-collar jobs paid; more, for instance, than an associate professor might make at Hopkins. By the time he was twenty, he owned his own house—three blocks from his parents; paid cash for a 1977 Chevrolet van—with "Alexander the Great" painted in calendar art on both sides of it; had gone to the Bahamas every year for his vacation since he'd started work; and had settled into a life that included both his neighborhood and his love. When I asked him if his parents knew he was gay, he laughed at me gently and showed me a photograph taken at one of the Polish ethnic festivals held every summer at the Inner Harbor. In the picture his mother, his boyfriend from high school, and Alex stood, sort of in totem-pole fashion: Alex with his arms around his boyfriend, Mrs. Stokowski with her arms—and ample ones they were—around the two of them. They are all wearing flower wreaths on their heads with ribbons dangling down, just like the Polish national folk dancers wear.

Being gay was, apparently, just like being Polish: he lived it, danced it, wore it.

When I finished work in the afternoons, teaching at old Seton High School on Charles Street, Alex would be waiting for me to take me home to his house, where he cooked us wonderful dishes, the names of which I couldn't pronounce. Sometimes we bought steamed crabs, spreading them out on newspaper on his kitchen table. Afterward, we would make love, then go to sleep in the big carved oak bed his grandfather made and brought with him from Poland, the bed that Alex's father gave to him the day that Alex moved into his own home. "Love is a proud thing," his father told him. I would ask him to tell me that story over and over as we lay there night after night. And he would, running his finger up and down the length of my spine, hypnotizing me, making certain with his finger, like a careful traveler plotting the distance, the route of adventure on a map.

The day he left town—his house sold, the bed passed on to his brother, an aspiring law student who'd moved out of the city, north to the suburbs of Towson—Alex stood on the curb, half hidden behind his open van door, and cried. I cried, too, but it was for myself. I couldn't go with him. The steel plant was closing for good, and Alex was moving west to see what he could find. I'd just come back to Baltimore, having been away too long in school and in New York; I had just come home, and Alex was leaving home, so we stood there together crying on the curb. "You be here when I get back," he said, " 'cause I am coming back." I suspect now that he was really crying for me, too. I think he knew about the kiss he'd given me that night at number 5 Mt. Vernon Place. That beautiful old building, stately and quadrilateral on the square, Alex's kiss, and Alex himself, are artifacts of my love life.

There is another place that functions as a kind of monument to being gay here in Baltimore. The old Alcazar Hotel on Cathedral Street is where the Assembly is held every year. For those of you who don't keep the social register by your bedside or have Debrett's memorized, you will need to know that the Baltimore Assembly is one of the oldest dances held in the country. It remains a mystery as to how one may become invited to the Assembly, but once done, only death removes your name. Wives may bring husbands, husbands may bring wives, but no one unmarried may bring an escort. The stag line there is the stuff of legend.

I was having a tragic love affair the year that my friend Stacy Carlyle Wentworth was first invited to the Assembly. I was devoting most of my energy that winter to desperate relations with a first-year resident at Hopkins. My young doctor was a farm boy, up from the Eastern Shore of Maryland, and I couldn't understand why he kept choosing the hospital, his patients, and his career over me. One night, just a few days before the Assembly, the doctor called to tell me he was not coming home after his eighteen-hour shift was over and that, in addition, he couldn't continue with me *and* the rest of his life: It was over; he was moving into doctor's quarters at the hospital. Hysterical and dramatic, I began playing a form of Russian roulette with the telephone, calling all my friends to tell them my life was ending. As usual, I called Stacy first, and by the time I was on my third call Stacy barged into my apartment, snatched the phone from my hand, and said to Randy Pumphrey who was dangling on the other end, "Never mind. I've got her," and hung up. He collected me and a few things and took me to stay with him until I was all over my "country doctor," as Stacy referred to him. So, on the day of the dance, we stood across the street from the Alcazar, shivering in the raw January weather, Stacy plotting his entrance for later that night.

The Alcazar Hotel had been part of Stacy's and my childhood. Every Christmas, the Wing School (where Stacy and I had met, at the age of nine when I saw him thrown in a perfect arc from the back of a very tall horse) sent the Wing School Chorus downtown to the Alcazar for the DAR Christmas Charity Bazaar. Stacy and I stood side by side as darling cherubs until, at age fourteen, we were expelled from the chorus for sneaking off from the group to smoke cigarettes and flirt with the men we'd heard cruised Mt. Vernon Place a few blocks away. We'd been gay together for most of our early lives and had returned to Baltimore, years later, after college, almost as though we were survivors: the only two passengers left alive from a shipwreck. And just like survivors, the lives to which we returned were forever changed by our survival.

My heart, or what I actually had of one then—for I think hearts grow with age—was breaking. My Hopkins resident was everything to me, and nothing feels quite as separate as heartbreak. But worse, perhaps, was that Stacy, for the first time in my life, seemed different from me; our lives actually pointed in different directions. He was serious about his social career, something that meant nothing to me and was closed to me. I was miserably alone standing with him across from the Alcazar. I hated him, my doctor, and the whole claustrophobic city of Baltimore.

Near us two people, a man and woman, were arguing loudly just at the entrance to the hotel. Finally, after the man said something close to the woman's head and kissed her, she started beating him savagely with her pocketbook, eventually chasing him, his arms up, trying to fend off her blows, down Cathedral Street toward the Pratt Library. An old black man, heretofore unnoticed by us, said from behind us, "Just like Baltimore; everybody act like that when they in love in Baltimore. Good thing I'm from South Carolina," and he moved off shaking his head.

Stacy touched my arm. "There's the man for you, dear, someone exotic and from out-of-town, too."

"Can we go, please?" I said wretchedly. "I really can't devote any more of my time to this silly dance of yours." I stalked off toward Stacy's apartment, my arms wrapped around myself.

By eight o'clock that night Stacy's tails were pressed and laid out on his bed. He stood, trouserless, in front of the mirror in his bedroom tying and untying his tie. I was sulking, hard at work on his patent leather evening pumps with a handkerchief and Vaseline, hoping to create a good sense of guilt he'd carry all around the dance floor with him. "Goddamn it!" Stacy shouted from his bedroom. I finished what I was doing and went in to see what was wrong. He thrust his right arm out at me as though it might as well be chopped off. I sighed and snapped his cuff link into place.

"I don't even know why I'm going to this goddamned thing!" he said, "I'm going to feel like a freak there. I know: Why don't I just forget it. We'll order a pizza and you can tell me all about

Dr. Heartthrob, how your life is over and all that. I really don't want to do this without you." He turned to look at himself in the mirror. "I am fucking terrified. Gorgeous, of course, but just about to piss vinegar!"

"You'll be fine," I heard myself saying instead of saying what I thought I was going to say, which was, "Good, forget all that, I'll forget my life, too; who needs this shit?"

Stacy looked at me in his mirror. I arched one eyebrow, what I thought was provocatively.

"Do you know who you look like?" he asked me.

"Who?"

"Me," he said. "You look just like me. And if you were me, you'd go get one of the pistols Daddy left me, take a cab to that hospital, find that country doctor, and give him a *real* choice."

"You mean I'd have to kill him," I said.

"Seems likely," he said. "But, honey, what's life without you, anyway?" He turned to smile at me. "You *know* how love is in Baltimore!"

As he left, I watched him from the tall windows of his living room. He hailed a cab that was conveniently passing, and, as he stepped into the street to open the taxi door, he turned back, looking up to where he knew, instinctively, I'd be standing, and blew me a kiss. Then he swirled into the cab, his evening coat disappearing with him like the last puff of smoke from some ceremonial gunfire behind him.

I think I tell you about Stacy and Alexander only because they were significant relationships for me, and only because they were actually relationships with my city as much as they were anything else. If cities are human constructs—and who could really argue they are not—then I love my city as I love each man in it. To begin to know a city, love its men.

I would never live anyplace else now. Baltimore is where I've come back to stay, to raise myself all over again, to remind myself what it means to be gay, for there is nothing so important to me as being gay in the place where men first seemed outlined in fire as they walked idly by me, a kid so overwhelmed with his own desires and difference, he could barely hold the Coke bottle that trembled in his hand as he watched those men saunter by in the heat of a Baltimore summer. We are the gay men from the gay cities beyond New York and San Francisco, the heart-red dots that cover the country. Outposts and border towns like Baltimore mean something only to the millions of men like me.

Perhaps what I've told you, then, is not really about being gay in Baltimore, but about being you and me, as we are, where we are, about building our nests above the floodwaters. For me, certainly, number 5 Mt. Vernon Place and the Alcazar Hotel—my gay history of Baltimore—are the twigs that make my nest, the soft strong home into which I entrust my life.

AMETHYST, TEXAS

TWICE A YEAR FOR THE last ten years, in high summer and again at Christmas, I have made the journey back to Amethyst.

Texas is a long way, on the map and otherwise, from San Francisco. "Steven," said my mother once, "you live in another country out there." She was right, and what I feel when I fly from California to Texas must be what an expatriate from any country feels returning to his childhood home. I make the trip to see family and friends, but also to step into my own past, to reclaim my youth, to see how much I've grown, to confirm the choice I made in leaving. Texas is home, but Texas is also a country whose citizenship I voluntarily renounced.

The trip has become a ritual. There are clearly marked stations along the way. It begins at the San Francisco airport. Filing onto the plane, I can spot the more obvious Texans among the passengers—good-ole-boy businessmen in Stetsons coming home from conventions, children in boots, families who talk back and forth in twangy voices. I can close my eyes and almost smell the barbecue.

In Dallas I change planes for the short hop to Austin. Dallas–Fort Worth airport is a living showcase of the worst aspects of Texas attitude. Women wear their makeup in the style of Tammy Bakker and pile up their hair in lacquered bouffants. Instead of Hare Krishnas selling incense, Republican Ladies for Nuclear Power hawk "Nuke Jane Fonda" buttons. The gift shops are full of Texas memorabilia: decorative plates painted with bluebonnets and wicker gift baskets stuffed with hot sauce and jalapeño jelly are popular, but Texans are most proud of the distinctive outline of the state of Texas. Anything at all that can be imagined in the shape of Texas is offered for sale—ashtrays, serving dishes, memo pads, key chains, buttons, baking tins, cookie cutters, belt buckles, charms, barbed-wire wreaths, refrigerator magnets, jigsaw puzzles, even a branding iron for branding steaks. My favorite is a laminated cow pattie glued to a wall plaque in the shape of Texas. Could Zanzibar be stranger?

But Dallas is only a station on the journey, a distraction and an illusion. I have no use for the place; it embodies the very worst excesses of Texas—the racism, the intolerance, the greed, the hanging judges, the blazing heat reflected off endless parking lots, the frigid shopping malls, the oppressive flatness, the J. R. Ewing morality, and the Miss Ellie esthetics. It may be the heartland for some Texans, but not for me.

There is a sweeter, gentler Texas in the rolling, lake-studded Hill Country of Willie Nelson and Lady Bird. In the 1960s there was a virtual civil war in central Texas between the dopers and the shitkickers, until it was discovered that the dopers liked country music and the shitkickers liked grass; a great mellowness ensued in the seventies, with its center at the forty-acre campus of the University of Texas. I was there. I love to come back. Before I go to Amethyst I always spend a while in Austin.

The flight from Dallas is so short the stewardesses have to run down the aisles to serve everyone a drink. Students and assorted academic types fill the plane. Even the businessmen seem more relaxed and humane, closer to Bobby Ewing than J. R.

We fly over Lake Travis, where I spent many a summer in

a marijuana haze, diving naked into green water from limestone cliffs. We descend on the Hill Country and pass the high antennas west of Mount Bonnell. Ahead I see the tiny, toylike skyline of Austin. To the north, the University of Texas (the campanile where Charles Whitman played sniper when I was a boy, the LBJ Library with its bombastic Egyptian façade); at the center, the sublimely graceful capitol dome and the pink granite state office buildings; and down by the river, the glittering glass towers that mushroomed all over the quaint downtown during the phony boom years of the eighties.

The plane touches down. On a summer trip, the heat will hit me in the face like a blast from a blow-drier as soon as I step into the gangway. At Christmastime, the cold is likely to be more bitter than any wind that blows in San Francisco. Either way, there's no mistaking I'm back in Austin. Emotionally, I'm halfway home, only a hundred miles from Amethyst.

The best years of my life were spent in Austin. Fortunately, I knew at the time that they would be my best years, so I didn't waste them.

During the mornings I bicycled to classes wearing a T-shirt and cut-off jeans. I studied what I wanted to study: history, literature, fencing, archery, design, French. During the afternoons I got stoned and went to either Hippie Hollow (the nude beach at Lake Travis) or to Barton Springs, a vast spring-fed pool in the heart of town, superbly landscaped by the WPA and populated, now as then, by the most achingly attractive set of young men and women to be found anywhere on the planet on a warm afternoon. At night I went to the gay bars (there were three in town), saw my friends, drank, danced, and if I were lucky (which I often was) went home with another boy as eager and tender and sweet as I was, or else with an older man who had a taste for the eagerness I could offer.

Sex and pleasure are the currency of the young. I spent mine happily, already suspecting that some day sex and pleasure alone wouldn't be enough. I indulged without guilt or worry; these were the years after Stonewall and before AIDS, when maximizing sexual discovery was not just an indulgence but a cultural and political duty. I found a lover early, when I was nineteen, but we always worked extra hard at having an open marriage.

Hanging over this Eden was a vague, free-floating anxiety. It came not from disease but from bigotry. Sodomy was and is illegal in Texas; I never knew that law to be enforced, but it hung there always, an implicit threat when figures like Anita Bryant and Jerry Falwell began appearing on the scene. Austin was and is an oasis of tolerance, but a small oasis—the harsh desert is always visible beyond its leafy edges, even from its shaded heart at Barton Springs.

Too soon, I graduated from college and started living in the world at large. In those years the fundamentalist, right-wing menace was booming. Austin and the opportunities it offered began to seem small and confining. A larger oasis beckoned. After Reagan was elected and before he took office, Rick and I made up our minds to move to San Francisco; I told friends and family (especially the ones who'd voted Republican) that there was no way I was going to spend the Reagan years in Texas.

I left Austin with mingled regret and exhilaration. I was desperately homesick for the first year or two. I still suffer acute relapses of homesickness, especially when the fog recedes and a rare ninety-degree heatwave passes through San Francisco. I can close my eyes and breathe the warm morning air and almost believe I'm in Austin. The nostalgia I feel for the place is not just the nostalgia any man feels for the place where he came of age; my life there really was rich and sweet, and in my daydreams it could be so again.

For a time in the mid to late eighties, Austin lagged behind San Francisco in terms of the plague and all its attendant side effects. The pall had settled over San Francisco, a fog of despair so thick that it seemed to swallow up even life's simplest pleasures; but the party was still rolling in Austin. San Francisco became one of the hardest cities in the world in which to get laid. Austin remained one of the easiest.

In the bars I always had the New Face in Town advantage. Austin is small enough so that even with an influx of students every semester, by the end of term all the bar patrons have begun to recognize one another. When you're in town only once or twice a year, you're always the New Face.

But the sweetest men and the otherwise most inaccessible students were not to be found in the bars but in the adult bookstore arcades, the peep shows. While I was still living in Austin, the peep show phenomenon reached its audacious peak, with three major arcades located a block or so from campus and the extraordinary Mr. Peeper's downtown on Sixth Street. Mr. Peeper's was a kind of Disneyland of gloryhole sex, with its black-painted walls and ultraviolet lights, its single booths and double booths, its catwalks and balconies where, without putting too much strain on the neck, you could peer down into the booths below. The insatiability, versatility, and acrobatic imagination of the clientele amounted to something like performance art. The nights were steamy, but so were the afternoons when downtown office workers dropped in on their lunch hours or coffee breaks. To enter you only had to buy a dollar's worth of quarters.

Mr. Peeper's eventually fell victim to the upscale gentrification of Sixth Street, but the scene continued hot and heavy at the campus venues. Austin was X (for Ecstasy) capital of the world in the eighties, and quite a few of the users seemed to be hanging out at the arcade across from Dobie Mall. To arrive in Austin one morning from doom-laden San Francisco, where the men were afraid even to look at one another, and to drop by the arcades later that afternoon and find myself jammed half-naked in a dark booth with an X-driven nineteen-year-old business major was to venture, as my mother might well have put it, into another country.

During that bittersweet period before the plague caught up with Austin, I was the one who had to insist on safe sex—Austin men either didn't know about it or were in a state of denial and afraid of admitting mortality by dealing with condoms. Students might legitimately have been a bit wary of a visiting San Franciscan in his late twenties but seemed blissfully unconcerned. In San Francisco I was part of a dubious generation from which younger men shied away, but back in Austin I was no longer a potential carrier of lesions and killer pneumonia. I was a hot number again.

Time caught up with Austin. A firebrand fundamentalist

named Mark Weaver began a campaign to "clean up" the arcades, and the State of Texas likewise started having doubts about the prudence of gloryhole sex. Just as the baths had been shut down in San Francisco, ostensibly for the public good but largely from homophobia, the arcades in Austin were, if not put out of business, emasculated. A metaphorical guillotine closed on the gloryholes. They were boarded up, and the flimsy wooden doors with latches were replaced with black curtains. Ever resourceful, one Austin arcade obeyed the order to seal the gloryholes by installing transparent Plexiglas over them. Patrons could still peep, although the view was often obscured by translucent layers of dried semen.

The attitude of the men began to change as well. On one of my Christmas visits everything seemed the same, in spite of the new obstacles to intimacy in the arcades and the emergence of the crusading Mark Weaver and his vitriolic homophobic ranting at city hall. Then, on my next visit in August, I felt it like a chill in the air. I felt it in the bars, in the arcades, at Barton Springs, at Hippie Hollow. I heard it in the voices of my friends down at Liberty Books, the legit gay book shop. The college boys were more furtive and distanced. The clientele at the arcades suddenly seemed sadder, older, depressed, and rather bewildered. I recognized the symptoms all too well.

For the first time ever, I visited Austin and I did not get laid.

Then I went back for Christmas. And I didn't get laid again.

Surprisingly, I didn't mind too much. I have a lover, after all, and in my thirties the long, hectic reign of my hormones seems to have entered a natural decline; getting spectacularly laid is no longer the highest aspiration of my life. And there is so much more than sex that still draws me to Austin—family, friends, the sun and water, the singular mood of the place. But it saddens me to see the paralyzing clutch of the plague close in on Austin, like watching a much-loved friend fall ill.

If Austin follows the pattern of San Francisco, the long funk has only begun. Eventually it will bottom out; the plague will not be over, but the initial paralysis will pass and gay men will get on with their lives. They will learn the lessons the plague teaches, about mortality and survival, and they will cautiously allow themselves to smile, relax, and enjoy life again. The process may be faster in Austin, given the city's innately mellow constitution; or it may be slower, given the gay community's loose-knit, laid-back structure and the vindictive tenacity of its enemies.

The future is uncertain, the past is inviolate, but one is no less mysterious than the other. To explore the past one needs what any explorer needs—the right gear, some experience, reliable transportation, and the luxury of time. In some ways, my trips to Texas are only a tool I use to let me enter the past. I feel it all around me whenever I go to Austin, more poignant and concentrated for me, no doubt, than for those who spend their lives there.

I remember one trip I took in spring instead of summer, when the campus was in full semester swing. I wore shorts and a T-shirt, strapped on a backpack, borrowed a friend's bicycle, and pedaled to campus. I arrived during a break between classes as thousands of students poured out of the ornately decorated Mediterranean buildings and across the pecan-shaded malls. As I passed among them, dressed as I might have been in 1978, on two wheels, with a satchel on my back, a wave of nostalgia crested inside me, filling me so full I could hardly contain it. It is one thing to remember and meditate on the past; it is another to make visceral contact with the exact state of mind you might have experienced on a given day ten years before. The sensation of déjà vu, like orgasm, usually peaks in an instant and passes. To experience it full force for a long sunny afternoon is so sweet as to be almost maddening.

When my mother was dying in an Austin hospital in the spring of 1985, I flew in for the death watch. I took an afternoon off from the gloom and tension of her sickroom to lie on the grass at Barton Springs. The sun was mild, obscured now and again by the big puffy clouds that dot the central Texas sky. The grass was impossibly green. Swimmers glided through the cold water. Sunbathers dotted the hillside on the opposite bank. Death was on my mind—my mother's cancer, and the threat of AIDS hanging over Rick and me. But the sun, the clouds, the impossibly green grass, and the cold water were oblivious of death. In the timeless power of the place I found peace. In memory I found forgetfulness. My mother would soon live only in the past. In my memory of the past, she would live forever.

Amethyst is two hours by car from Austin, and twenty years from San Francisco.

Amethyst is very small; so small, in fact, that I've chosen to give the town a pseudonym, in deference to the privacy of certain people mentioned here. Since leaving it, I have never met anyone who came from a town as small as Amethyst. People shake their heads in disbelief when I tell them that there were twenty-five students in my high school senior class.

My brother and sister and I grew up poor and without a father in Amethyst, but poverty is a relative thing in a town so small, especially for a child. We had many relatives. We went to the Methodist church, which in the sixties was abuzz with psychological interpretations of the miracles and a secular emphasis on curing racism and social ills; this provided a considerable head start in life, considering that we might have been Baptists instead and had the evils of dancing drummed into our heads. Most important, we did very well in school; my mother (who I later learned had been a wild and loose teenager herself) would settle for nothing less that straight *A*'s. In the small classrooms of Amethyst I never lacked for personal attention.

I first discovered the existence of homosexuality when I read an article in one of my mother's *Cosmopolitan*s titled, "I Married a Homosexual." This must have been around 1966, when I was ten years old. It was a typically lurid (and I imagine completely fictitious) first-person confession, with little redeeming educational or literary value, but I can still recount the finer points all these years later, especially the part where the neglected bride discovers her husband and his "best friend" in the living room. The description was intentionally pathetic rather than pornographic, but it electrified me nonetheless: best friend wrapped in the wife's silk robe, lying on the sofa while the naked husband knelt beside him stroking his face.

Cosmo set me searching for more tawdry glimpses into a world of possibilities that seemed very remote from Amethyst. The information I could get from books was fragmentary, contradictory, and always tainted with condescension and squeamishness—clinical disdain in something called *A Marriage Manual* among my mother's books, vicious jokes in Dr. Reuben's *Everything You Always Wanted to Know about Sex,* the lurid cover painting of two nude men on a paperback edition of Mishima's *Forbidden Colors* in a catalogue of paperbacks.

Then, from a convenience store in a town thirty miles away that sold liquor to underage customers as well as porn paperbacks, I acquired a copy of a novel called *Pretty Boys Must Die.* It satisfied my curiosity about what homosexuals did in a way that the *Britannica* had not. I was excited out of my mind. Next came *The Corporal's Boy,* and then *Military Chicken.* As a sophisticated reader, I knew there must be a difference between pornography and real life, just as there was a difference between Middle Earth and Dallas, but I also knew that somewhere out there, beyond Amethyst, someone had to be doing something remotely like what leather hustler Riley Jacks did to naïve young David (the "Pretty Boy") for it to have ended up in a book. I was ready.

But I had to wait. To have sex with another boy in Amethyst simply seemed impossible. Beginning at about age ten, Amethyst boys learned to use the word "cocksucker" as the worst imaginable epithet, and fear of being called a cocksucker kept everyone in line; to actually *be* a cocksucker was too scary to think about.

Meanwhile I was a perfect student. I played trumpet in band. I worked as a sack boy at the grocery store. I dated girls, and even did a passable amount of making out. I holed up in my room or escaped to the ancient oak tree on my grandparents' land and read for hours and hours—fantasy (Tolkien, Heinlein, Cabell, Dunsany), Russian novelists (Tolstoy, Dostoyevsky, the then-fashionable Solzhenitsyn), best-selling "trash" (my mother's word for Arthur Hailey and Leon Uris), and everything ever written by Larry McMurtry. I gorged on new porn when I could get it, and otherwise reread *Pretty Boys Must Die* until I had all the sex scenes memorized.

Mostly I bided my time, waiting to get out of Amethyst, putting life (which for a teenage boy means the hunt for sex) on hold. When I was a junior I visited my brother in the marijuana haze of his student apartment in Austin, and I saw the future. Until it arrived, I was content to read for hours, and masturbate for hours, and imagine a life beyond the wildest dreams of Amethyst.

On my trips to Texas, I used to be jealous of the time that Amethyst took from Austin. Days spent in Amethyst were days that could have been spent looking for sex at Hippie Hollow, swimming at Barton Springs, strolling across campus, checking out the arcades, or eating Mexican food and drinking beer with Austin friends.

Now I find myself drawn more and more to Amethyst. This did not happen until after my mother died.

I think perhaps that her death freed me to experience the past in Amethyst on my own terms, without constantly having to deal with the present. So long as my mother was alive she dominated any visit to Amethyst. Time there was time spent carefully choosing words and reactions and never quite relaxing. My mother was accommodating but never comfortable with my sexuality. In Amethyst, in her house, I could never be myself. I disliked causing my mother pain, and I was no good at dissembling to protect her from the truth.

I believe that my mother did come to grips with my sexuality, on her own terms and in her own time. Before her illness my mother had made plans to see the Methodist minister in Amethyst for counseling. Among the conflicts that fretted her, I was clearly high on the agenda. But when the lung cancer was diagnosed she canceled the counseling, saying that the problems that had seemed so staggering were now too petty to be bothered with. What did it matter that I was gay when her life could be—would be—over in six months?

Surrounded now by plague and suffering, I have tried to remember and take comfort from the priorities my mother learned in her extremity.

The family house in Amethyst is not exactly ramshackle, but it is not pretty. My paternal grandfather, a carpenter until the day he died, built the thing when he was in his eighties with no helper except my older brother, who was hardly in his teens. My mother did her best to civilize it with carpet and paneling and paint. The floors are mostly level and the windows rattle only on windy nights.

Now that my mother is gone, my grandmother lives alone there. She began living with us shortly after my parents divorced in the early sixties. In her eighties now, she has been on crutches or in a wheelchair since before I was born, one of the original victims of polio. She lives alone and prefers it that way, but there is a constant stream of visitors who check up on her, do her shopping for her, post her mail, and bring her little gifts of garden vegetables in season or homemade pie.

My grandmother is often extravagantly praised to me behind her back by those who have known her since creation (a truly good woman, a fine example, so strong); her equanimity and determination are qualities I've always taken for granted. A few years ago she broke her arm in a scary tumble from her wheelchair and had to live in a rest home for eighteen months. Stumped by weakness and pain, her confidence ebbed at times, but she never lost sight of her goal of regaining her strength and moving back into the house.

The time I'm able to spend with her now in Amethyst is precious. The best times are when no one else is there, before the others arrive for the Christmas holidays or in the summer when I can have her and the house all to myself. I take long walks down the country roads that circle Amethyst, climb the towering oak tree where I read so many books as a boy, hike through the rolling fields of cactus and mesquite I explored as a child.

Best of all are the afternoons when my grandmother is in the mood for a drive. I help her into my rental car, stow her chair in the trunk, and off we go. The change of scenery makes her talkative and relaxed; we drive past the overgrown baseball field on the outskirts of town, by the site of her old family homestead, over the ancient suspension bridge on the Colorado River. We head into the unexplored hinterland of the county and get lost in the skein of little dirt roads, and my grandmother will laugh and say, "Well, Steven, I reckon I don't have any idea where we are. Do you?"

▪ ▪ ▪

It was on one of those drives that she told me the truth about Jerry B. Jerry B. was a grade or two ahead of me in high school, a sweet-faced Baptist boy with a doting mother. He was born a sissy, and while I suppose he was sometimes cruelly talked about behind his back and razzed about his gushing mannerisms, he was outgoing and bright and, in such a small town, pretty much accepted for what he was. After he graduated he moved away, probably to Dallas or Houston.

My grandmother first told me about his death over the phone. "Of course Billie Lee is real torn up about it," she said. "He was her only child. They say it was cancer."

I looked out my window onto Castro Street and I knew the truth.

The next time I was in Amethyst, I took my grandmother for a drive. We took a loop through the little city park and up by the American Legion Hall, where I went to dances in high school. Out of the blue, my grandmother said, "You know, they say that Jerry B. died from AIDS. Isn't that terrible?"

I only nodded and sighed. Even here, I thought.

Except for family, I have only a nodding acquaintance with most of the people I run into at the grocery store in Amethyst or on the small main street. It used to be that old ladies would stop and make a fuss over me while I desperately tried to remember who they were, or some vague school acquaintance, changed beyond recognition, would say a few words. That happens less often now; the old ladies die one by one, and I no longer look quite so much like the boy I was. The people who were closest to me in high school left Amethyst when I did, and they return less often than I do. Someone tried to organize a ten-year class reunion in 1984, but there wasn't much interest.

To pass the time in Amethyst, sometimes I look through my old school yearbooks and wonder.

I remember H., who was a little older than me and had red hair and brown eyes and a beautiful body; all through high school we did a dance around each other, flashing signals and having strange eye contact and pressing our legs together on long bus rides. But the fear of being cocksuckers was on us, and neither one of us would reach out quite halfway. He was the object of my jack-off fantasies for years. A few years ago I heard he was married and living in a larger town not far from Amethyst. I felt like rushing to his rescue, but I should have had the courage to do that in high school.

I remember K. Tall, skinny, big-boned, a practical joker, and congenital troublemaker. He wore cowboy hats and boots and chewed tobacco. We were both Methodist boys and buddies in high school because we worked together at the grocery store. He was always scheming to seduce girls who wouldn't give him the time of day. I gave him a nonreciprocal hand job once in his pickup on a dark country road. It was his idea; I would never have dared to suggest it, and I did my best to act like I didn't particularly enjoy it. For some reason he wore a lubricated condom, I suppose because rubbers were forbidden and dirty. His cock was the first one I ever touched besides my own. I remember being a bit startled at the thickness. He married and had a kid or two and apparently never stopped being wild. He died in a car accident a few years ago.

I remember L., who had a very precocious body, superbly defined and muscular even in junior high, with an extraordinarily clefted chest and smooth, downy skin. I got to take good looks at him when I'd sleep over at his house. There was no fooling around. We later grew apart; I was too bright and he was too thick. I imagine he's married now, and I often wonder if he's kept his looks; his father was a handsome, sexy man, so he may well have.

I remember poor J. Starting in first grade and continuing for year after year, he was the class scapegoat, a role I always thought I might have been stuck with if I hadn't been securely pegged as the class brain. One day in junior high, after gym class, one of the school bullies cornered J. in the locker room, roughed him up and wrestled him down. While everybody watched, the bully forced J., red-faced and struggling, to kiss his dick. It was a despicable act of brutality that shocked even a roomful of cruel schoolboys. J. cried afterward, trying desperately not to. He ended up being a rocker, a bad boy into metal and dope. I never figured he was queer, just unlucky.

▪   ▪   ▪

Winter in the Hill Country is often quite mild, but on my 1989 Christmas trip temperatures reached record lows. For several days, before my sister and her husband arrived from Denver and my brother and his family drove up from Austin, I was alone in the old family house with my grandmother. The cold was like a siege. We set quartz space heaters in front of the kitchen sink to keep the pipes warm through the night, and in the mornings I scrambled in the crawlspace under the house checking for damaged pipes. The frigid air sweeping down straight from Canada was so cold it penetrated gloves and ear-muffs like needles.

On the morning after Christmas, just when I'd had enough of idling inside day after day, the cold spell broke. I took a long walk in the hills north of the house. I tramped along the over-grown trails we used as children, surrounded by gray-green oaks and naked mesquites hung with mistletoe, sprawling cacti, and outcrops of rock the color of weathered bone. The underbrush was filled with thousands of migrating birds, flitting about so loudly I kept thinking I heard human footsteps around me. In the indeterminate distance someone kept firing a gun, probably a boy who'd gotten a .22-calibre rifle for Christmas and wanted to do some target practice.

I left the hills and walked through town. Except for a boy on his way to the convenience store on the highway and some children riding around town on bicycles, no one else was stirring on the streets of Amethyst. I walked by the courthouse grounds, where the bandstand built by my grandfather was torn down long ago and replaced by a sterile, misguided attempt at landscaping. A few blocks away is the hotel he built and oper-ated in the thirties, when the railroad still brought visitors to Amethyst; it was a rest home when I was a boy, and now stands derelict and abandoned. A little away from the heart of town is the modest little library where I became addicted to history by reading the *We Were There* series as a boy and later discovered *The Persian Boy* and Mary Renault. Across the street is the Meth-odist church, which I last entered for my sister's wedding. I was officially a member for many years after I left Amethyst, the chief advantage being a subscription to the church newsletter, which kept me up to date on who was in the hospital and whose kids were home visiting from faraway points. A few years ago, after the latest flap over gays in the Methodist ministry, I wrote a letter of protest to the minister in Amethyst and asked him to remove me from the rolls; I haven't seen the newsletter since.

Down the hill from the church there is an old overgrown creek bed that runs through a series of culverts beneath dirt roads. When I was a boy, ten or twelve years old, my little sister and I would ride our bikes across town and go trekking through the culverts, taking along snacks and books and exploring a tiny secret world. For the first time since then, I hiked along the creek bed and through the little tunnels. Overhead on the road I heard the children I'd seen earlier on their bicycles. One of them stuck her head around the edge of the tunnel, glimpsed me, and disappeared.

For a brief, shivery moment, I was twelve years old again and a virgin boy in Amethyst.

Tears came to my eyes. All that had died lived again. The world was the closed and tiny world of Amethyst, a place of waiting and postponement, opened up by books and imagination and sustained by hope.

What struck me most as the moment subsided was the *hope*. It was not something I remembered, a distant emotion, but something that for a brief moment I felt and lived again, mixed up with all the complexities and emotions of any given moment of living, not filtered through memory but concretely reexperienced. I recaptured a truth I had long forgotten about my boyhood in Amethyst. Growing up I always had confidence that there would be a place for me in the world, that the future was bright with promise—not here, perhaps, but somewhere; not now, but eventually, if only I were patient. In subsequent years I concentrated on my alienation from Amethyst. My values, my sexuality, my interests took me far away, and I dwelled upon the discontent of my boyhood and adolescence. But deeper than these there was a sense of belonging in Amethyst, never again so strong in any other place: the feeling of home. A part of me would always belong there, because a part of me, if I could only find it again, would always be twelve years old.

                                                    •

I never go immediately back to San Francisco from Amethyst. Instead I make the journey in reverse: San Francisco–Austin–Amethyst, and then Amethyst–Austin–San Francisco.

The final days in Austin before flying back are bittersweet. I drop in on my brother and his children one more time, and try to get in touch with friends I missed on the first leg of the trip. In winter I may go biking up the trail alongside Barton Creek, suffused with the last subtle colors of autumn and the evergreen of juniper and cedar trees.

In summer, my last day is always planned along the same unvarying schedule. The plane will leave in late afternoon, and before that I will eat lunch (Mexican, of course) with friends and then spend a few final, stolen hours at Barton Springs. I swim long, long laps until the frigid water begins to seem warm, then pull myself onto the grass and feel all my muscles relax. At the fashionable end of the pool, the beautiful young things recline on air mattresses, so thick on the water's surface that on busy days you could walk across from shore to shore. Away from the armada of floats, the water is deep green, reflecting brilliant points of sunlight; the sound of faraway children, splashing divers, murmuring voices, and the rush of water over the dam melt into an endless green beneath a blue sky and a procession of magnificent white clouds.

The changing room at Barton Springs is built on the model of a Greek gymnasium; shaded porticos surround a square open to the sky. The showers are in the center with clay tile beneath, interspersed with plots of lush grass and banana trees. All-over tanners lie nude on the grass. Men and boys come and go—young fathers with toddlers, muscular athletes, willowy college boys, graying academics. They strip, shower, and change into swimsuits. They stretch on the grass; some of them linger on the benches and check each other out. The same things bring them here that have brought men to the gymnasia for thousands of years—sensual pleasure, the exercise of the body, relaxation, the enjoyment of sunlight and fresh air, the visual delight of healthy, naked flesh.

I shower and wash my hair. In the hot sunlight the chill of the Springs begins to fade and the humidity closes in. A light sweat forms on my naked skin. I dress in short pants and a T-shirt, leave the changing room, step through the turnstile, get into the rental car, and head for the airport—refreshed, relaxed, renewed, a grown man again returning to his life in the present in faraway San Francisco.

CLINTON, NEW YORK

IT WAS A WARM SPRING
day when the phone rang in my graduate student's apartment in
Berkeley and a woman, speaking in a heavily German-accented
voice, invited me to apply for her position at Hamilton College,
in upstate New York. I would teach German and Russian, she
explained; I would be her replacement for the upcoming 1988–
1989 academic year.

The offer seemed like a dream come true—a full-time job,
an exclusive liberal arts college, and only two counties away from
where I had grown up. When the descriptive brochures and promotional video I had written for arrived at the end of June, Hamilton College appeared every inch the genteel rustic ivy-covered
haven for the quiet but passionate pursuit of knowledge. Magically, a drawbridge had been lowered and scholar Wright was
bid to shed the garments of his humble past and, like Cinderella,
cross the moat and enter Castle Hamilton.

My family background is poor, white, working class. Of the

fifty or so first cousins, including spouses, that make up my generation in the family, five of us went to college, three of us have acquired advanced degrees—all three in the field of education. Growing up poor and being raised by people who, like their parents before them, had been poor all their lives, our generation had been taught we could better ourselves through education.

Today, as I approach the top of this particular staircase, where education has led me, I find, preponderantly, alienation, and I am confused, frustrated, and disheartened from the journey. Family expectations for social and economic betterment, it seems in retrospect, were informed by a public school system, by popular images from movies and television, and by the ethos of a former time when fighting the good war had been the answer to chronic depression.

My own graduate education has placed me in a social reality far different from the fantasy that the American media assures me, on a daily basis, is real—of a three-bedroom suburban house with attached two-car garage, the daily commute to an industrial park, and weekly *hejira* to the local shopping mall. And, having cultivated myself out of working-class sensibilities, my reality, as a gay man or as a humanities scholar, lies beyond anything I gleaned from my collective family's imagination.

When I was in high school, my family lived in a rented house way down Preble Road, the single east-west junction in the village of Preble, New York, population three hundred, in the County of Cortland, population fourteen thousand. It was an average house in a poor dairy-farming community, suffocatingly stuffy in summer and unheatable in winter. We had given up a railroad flat on the east side of Syracuse, and left the four-family tenement occupied up until then by the four of us and by several of my father's siblings, their spouses, and their various broods of Catholic or Episcopalian children.

In the country and away from so much family, our economic plight became apparent to me. Giftless Christmases, fried Spam and eggs for dinner several times in the same week, violent arguments between my parents over the lack of money to buy coal filled me with fear and despair in my teen years. I would unload chunks of lumber my dad had obtained from the local mill into the cellar and chop them, along with my shame and despair, into kindling. But no amount of tears or chopping could efface the shame in my heart.

I went through high school in the late 1960s, the very last years before Stonewall and the spread of gay liberation. In high school I was never popular, but I had a gift for music and foreign languages and mathematics; I excelled in all of them. This, however, did not make me popular, not did it teach me the rudiments of the social graces.

Also, I could not imagine myself graduating into any living situation I was familiar with. I fully expected my future to consist of a stultifying routine of nightshifts at the local typewriter factory or of a tortured life divided between a daytime teaching job at my alma mater and a secret double life in nocturnal shadows— a future I could not quite discern but which I anticipated nonetheless.

I hid my homosexual self from what I imagined to be the piercing gaze of all my classmates at Homer High—down in fancy-shmancy Homer, New York, where all the doctors' and lawyers' and old-moneyed families lived, while having sex with other guys who lived up the road from me in Preble or with their fathers or with the friends of their friends. At school I had a steady girlfriend. She spoke to me, at first hesitantly and with shame, later more freely and relaxed, about her crushes on other girls. But, since there were no role models for what was happening to us in our community, she and I assumed, like everyone else at school, we would graduate from high school and get married; a few years later in college Sally came out as a lesbian.

I dedicated myself to my studies and was a model student. Above all I coveted the idea of being elected to our high school's honor society. But one balmy afternoon in late May 1970, when the whole nine hundred of us had been assembled in Homer High's auditorium for honor society induction, my nemesis came.

Uncle Wilbur, as we called Principal Dunn out of earshot, made the usual significant-sounding pronouncements, speechified a bit, then turned the program over to the president of the honor society.

The lights went down, the honor society president paused meaningfully, the silence crackled with anticipation.

The first inductee's accomplishments, activities, and personal attributes were read out into the darkness. At all once we recognized the mystery person—Jon Canale, tall and meticulously groomed, scion of a local lawyer and headed for Princeton. The lucky winner came bounding up to the stage, and his name was read out for the benefit of those who hadn't recognize Jon by his accomplishments.

The ritual was repeated perhaps a dozen times, each time my heart pounded in my ears and I stopped breathing. As I sat in the front row of the balcony in the darkness in a cold sweat, poised between sheer terror and delicious anticipation, I thought I recognized myself in each description. Twice I thought it was me—for sure. But each time it was someone else: Laura Gustafson, determined, indomitable, and from a brainy family (her father was a biology professor at the local college). Then, gangly, conversational Jeannie Owen (whose mother was a librarian at the school), marched briskly to the stage, her black-framed glasses, as always, perched halfway down her nose, and her natural platinum blond hair flying away at odd angles from her face.

As the number of inductees onstage grew into a crowd and I failed to find a match between myself and the descriptions being read out, something very unpleasant sputtered into life inside my chest, burst into flame, and burned with a mouldering heat. In this cold medieval night deep within me, shame welcomed this humiliation to its company, and they hid themselves away. My throat constricted so that I could not breathe: I knew that they knew. And that this was their way of telling me.

I knew this beyond any shadow of a doubt.

The lights came up and we stood to file back to homeroom. At just that moment, Ed Wright (no relation, but a classmate who had just been inducted) caught my eye by accident. Ed had ruddy red hair and green-gray eyes, rugged good looks, and an artless air about him that made me think of Lincoln. I thrust my hand out to bid a hasty congratulations. He bent his face to my ear and he whispered, "I'm sorry," and returned my handshake.

Nonetheless, my gift for languages took me to Germany,

then to college in Albany, New York, then back to Germany and more universities. In college and thereafter I sought clues to understanding my life in my literary studies, and I began to see myself as a gay radical and a budding member of the radical avant-garde intelligentsia; I would unite American gay liberationist and German marxist principles. Thus began Cinderella's long evening at the ball—living in Germany, in open and openly gay relationships, in large provincial towns of castles, cathedrals, and regal residences, in small university towns of less stately castles, minsters, and *Spitäle,* traveling to the major cities of northern Europe and their leather bars, and back and forth along the transatlantic circuit, from the Mineshaft to the Coleherne, from Sporter's Bar to the Black Jail and Gusti's Ochsengarten, and thereby creating a movable feast entirely of my own making.

And when this party was over, I thought, I will assume my rightful place as a sage and worldly-wise scholar, the epicurean now intoxicated only by his quest for knowledge. I suspect I had read too much Herman Hesse. When this thinking carried me to San Francisco in 1979, at the height of the noble experiment in gay community building, my reality had degenerated into daily handfuls of pills and two-fisted drinking. Drugs to wake up, drugs to stay up. Drugs to enhance the effects of alcohol, drugs to counter the alcohol, drugs to put me out cold at the end of a run.

I moved directly into the Castro and had visions of myself as a young, gay Jack Kerouac. However, the gay theater group I had fallen in with when I first came to California dubbed me "the young, gay Zelda Fitzgerald," and kept me at arm's length. When the young, gay Zelda broke someone's arm in a drunken rage, the party ended. And, on the doorstep of "incomprehensible demoralization" and clearly perceiving my destruction to be imminent, I chose sobriety over death. In 1981, I found my way to gay gatherings of Alcoholics Anonymous.

For the next ten years I commuted between Berkeley and the Castro. The heedless decade of chemically-induced bohemia would be followed by a decade of contrition, of salvage and rescue, as I plodded through the deadening rigors of graduate school. I became involved in the Gay History Project in San Francisco, and cofounded the San Francisco Bay Area Gay and Lesbian

Historical Society. I hoped such commitments on either side of the Bay would bridge the post-alcoholic distance I felt within me between the "professional homosexual" and the humanities scholar. Sometimes I felt connected to the gay community, sometimes to the academic community, but never at the same time. I was still not quite at home in my own skin.

I felt safe in gay AA meetings, where everyone is considered an equal, had an equal say in all affairs, and where you are encouraged to speak whatever is on your mind; our common denominator is admission of defeat to alcohol. I "hid out" in meetings for years. Consequently, I made acquaintances easily with fellow recovering gay alcoholic men, with whom I could strike up deeply personal, intimate conversations, anywhere, anytime—on street corners, on the MUNI metro subway, at the supermarket, on line at the movies, anywhere in public. But over my first decade in sobriety, these throngs of intimate acquaintances dwindled. People fell away, one after another, in twos and threes and clusters of half a dozen at a time, all falling ill and dying, slowly, painfully, horribly, of AIDS.

The voices at AA meetings raging against the unrelenting ravages of this disease fell silent too. They were replaced by other voices that, all too often, also fell silent and were replaced, until the roar of the silence of the missing voices left everyone vulnerable and afraid. Many united in common cause in San Francisco's gay community, far too many isolated themselves in their fear. All of us had become exhausted and found ourselves battle weary, incomprehensibly surviving in a state of siege.

I viewed the call from Hamilton as a reprieve from a slow death sentence, as if I were being mustered home from the battlefront. The randomness of intimacy in gay San Francisco, and the rapacity with which people were dispatched from the ranks of the healthy and the living, left me longing for stability among steadfast friends. I wanted to get to know my new lover in this new environment. I hoped to cease passing through other people's lives as smoothly and seamlessly as they were passing through mine. I desperately wanted a reprieve from encroaching death.

When Hamilton called, it seemed the prodigal son, finally, could vindicate himself: I wanted to go back and show "them" that I had succeeded. Through the romantically veiled eyes of an inveterate city dweller, I now saw the rustic life-style of upstate New York, of both the townsfolk of substance and the working people, as somehow simpler, more open-minded, more satisfying in its ease. When Castle Hamilton threw open its gates to me, I thought I had finally been chosen, that the years of exile and searching were about to conclude forever.

There was no question in my mind I wanted to go home. When painful memories from childhood or youth crept in, I banished them with Kodachrome-glossy visions of New York State, its burgeoning greenness in summer, its vast open spaces of rolling hills and broad valleys. I recalled to my lover vivid memories of tramping through the woods in the fall, the pungent scent of autumn leaves. And I recalled summers when the corn grew so fast you could hear it clicking in the fields.

I recalled absentminded daydreams from high-school German classes, when I imagined myself as a university student in the Black Forest, a modest but respected scholar who got along famously with his landlady, who baked him fresh *Apfelstrudel* and *schwarzwälderische Kirschtorte*. In the geography of my memory German landscapes blended into New York countryside, distant German and Dutch ancestry jumbled with high school history and local folklore and family stories. In this rush of sensations, of urban alienation and alpine fantasies, I leaped at the illogical conceit that this mythology was actual personal history, and I wanted to go home to it.

I imagined having relatives again, reintegrating into my family as a gay man, introducing my family to my gay lover. I was filled instantly with the inflated pride of the newly arrived. But I also had thoughts, half-formed, that I scarcely articulated to myself—about the prodigal's return with the first slight signs of a terminal illness. I wasn't sure that I wasn't really returning, in a roundabout manner, to say good-bye.

I cautioned my lover about the remoteness of upstate New York, about the lack of sophistication he'd encounter there, about the small-mindedness, the isolation, the lack of cultural opportunities or gay community, and especially about long, dark, snow-filled winters. In the snow belt, this meant a season of getting dressed and undressed every time you went outdoors, it meant shoveling snow off the car and out of the driveway every time you wanted to go somewhere. It meant pitch-black darkness by four. But didn't it also mean plenty of cozy winter evenings indoors with good friends, all hibernating together?

The more I weighed the factors, the more ambiguous the proposition seemed. And yet, as these two voices within me deliberated, the rational points against moving fell on deaf ears. There was no dislodging the converted from the grip of his conviction.

In June we made the decision to move. My lover and I gave up our respective apartments, sold off all our furniture, and shipped off to New York State my personal library and a few other valuable possessions—valuable because they were familiar and would bring a sense of home from California.

I wrote away to the Oneida County Chamber of Commerce for information. The glossy pamphlets that arrived in the mail a week later assured us that Utica, ranked as the thirty-fourth most desirable place to live in America, was "America's Best-Kept Secret." The cost of living was a fraction of that in California, shopping malls proliferated, the train to New York City stopped at Utica's Union Station every hour, the countryside was photographically beautiful with every change of season. Employment prospects in the region for my lover, we averred, must be reasonable.

I flew to Syracuse alone, leaving Dennis in San Francisco to finish business there. I landed in the sweltering heat of an East Coast July. My mother and father and sister met me at the airport. Our greetings were perfunctory, an old family ritual. I could detect no sense of deep affection. I found myself standing before strangers, as the waves of humidity soaked my clothing, feeling suddenly defenseless before these people who knew so many intimate details of my childhood. I felt like an inveterate criminal, caught at the border, being prepared for the shakedown. I was glad I had flown alone and had time to compose myself before Dennis's arrival in mid-August.

On the face of it, my family seemed glad to see me back, seemingly healthy, happy, and newly employed. On the way to the car, they warmed up to me, filling me in on years of family gossip, excitedly reporting who had worn what to whose wedding, graduation, funeral, and baptism, who had borne a child, in or out of wedlock—many of these events in the lives of relatives I had never heard of. Similarly, my descriptions of California, my new lover, my new job, all fell on uncomprehending ears. That I was employed was important, what I was doing at Hamilton incidental, that I was not yet quite through graduate school a clear disappointment.

I got on the phone right away, tracked down an apartment, arranged to borrow furniture and to buy a car. By the time Dennis arrived in mid-August, everything was prepared for our new life together in Clinton.

It was a two-hour drive across endless picturebook countryside. As we drove through Clinton, the grand houses of the eighteenth and nineteenth centuries stood in ominous silence, as if watching. Every Victorian gingerbread flourish, every Greek Revival cornice attested to the presence of very old and very traditional money in residence here. And, as in Homer, low, squat, and cheaply constructed tract housing of the 1950s and 1960s trailed off behind the imposing double file of mansions lining the main streets, dissipating into cornfields and pastures at the edge of the village.

We drove up the hill and across Hamilton campus enchanted. We really had landed at some fantasy East Coast college. Graceful ivy-covered post-Revolutionary buildings were arranged symmetrically, as in some giant formal garden, in the manner of Thomas Jefferson's architectural designs. The many fraternity houses, situated downhill from the campus, rivaled the village mansions in the valley further below for elegance of style and the quietly stated opulence of their inhabitants.

The college rented us a townhouse apartment, a boxlike affair that consisted of three tiny rooms upstairs and a single room down. The floor and the south wall, built into the side of the hill, were of poured concrete and covered with linoleum. The entire north wall, floor-to-ceiling, was double-paned plate glass. Yellowed drapes could be pulled shut across this wall of glass, to keep out the biting cold winter wind, but this created an ambience suggesting the lobby of a roadside motel.

Our first days in Clinton were strangely tinged with a kind of panic. Dennis was disoriented by the abrupt change of scenery, finding himself in a place he knew only from books and films. I felt a different, vague anxiety, I had the urge to keep moving.

As they say in AA, when you don't know what to do, go to a meeting. And so, our first contact with the community occurred in the rooms of AA. Our first meeting was at the Court Street Alano Club of Utica, where street people and mental outpatients congregated. To my embarrassed chagrin, I was uncomfortable among the local underclass in their efforts to get "straight." The address for the next meeting turned out to be a parking lot. The third meeting, we sighed with relief, was a gay group; but when we got there, no one had anything to say, so the meeting was adjourned in fifteen minutes, after the Californians had spoken their piece. We left each meeting like Martians who had failed in their attempt to communicate their mission of peace to the earthlings.

At the weekly Clinton meeting, most of the meeting time was taken up by two local curmudgeons, who baited each other over the size of rifles each used to shoot deer and rabbit and who continued a political argument in the meeting that they had been carrying out in the letters-to-the-editor column of the *Weekly Clintonian*. The frank lack of focus on recovery was shocking to us, the two outsiders everyone stared at without extending a hand of welcome. AA is the same everywhere around the world, you always hear, but I guess no one had ever been to the environs of Utica.

As the fall semester rapidly approached, the annual preseason faculty social calendar burst into life. Suddenly I was expected everywhere. My department chair offered to chaperon my lover to these affairs to give the appearance of heterosexual orthodoxy. We declined, insisting that we go as an openly gay couple. Dennis had never been exposed to the life of faculty spouses, and, finding himself offered day-care programs and faculty wives' teas as a distraction, soon beat a hasty retreat.

The informal reception the new college president and his wife gave at their mansion was typical of these gatherings. Sydna, my department chair, assured us this was a casual affair, so we came casual, in jeans and polo shirts. Other couples came in matched well-heeled pairs, one attired in slacks and tie, the other in a fetching summer frock or demure cocktail dress. Spiked punch and white wine were the only drinks provided, so we stood nervously to the side of the buffet table while one of the caterers went to the student union to find a nonalcoholic mixer. One guest or another might inquire of Dennis's academic credentials and, discovering that he had none, would become momentarily perplexed, then drift away. When the bursar's wife introduced herself to Dennis, he extemporized, "I'm Mr. Wright's guest." She looked back and forth at the two of us, and without dropping a beat, responded, "Oh, I see. And I'm Dean Harrington's guest. Pleased to meet you."

We tried frequenting the gay bar in downtown Utica, a dismal cavern of a place that was inevitably empty before 11:00 P.M. The social rituals bore similarity to those of every provincial gay bar I have drunk and caroused in, from Germany to England to California. The social pecking order was fairly precise, one was introduced by mutual acquaintances, promiscuous sex was disparaged, but furtively pursued. New faces were unheard of in Utica, and the regulars tended to band together and whisper back and forth; a direct approach seemed inadvisable.

Having long since abandoned bar practices out of dire necessity rather than any personal disdain, we nonetheless quickly lost interest, driving up to Utica only on a rare winter's evening when cabin fever had gotten the better of us. A couple of cranberry juices and a couple of hours later, we'd don scarves and coats and suit up our frustration, and creep back home in the car through the hypnotizing swirl of a blizzard.

I had imagined a small but united cadre of gay and lesbian academics. Instead, I found within my department the dubious refuge of belonging to what the college considered a group of eccentric, artistic misfits, and which was made the butt of many a campus joke.

The campus grapevine thrived on racy hints at who might be gay, but no one outside my department seemed willing to be associated with the openly gay couple from the German/Russian Department. We learned, too late, that the manager of the local bookstore was an openly gay man; he moved to an Adirondack resort town just as we were settling in. We learned there was another openly gay couple a hundred miles off in a Catskill resort town, and heard rumors of an openly gay chef who ran a restaurant in a village somewhere south of us. At the gay AA meeting in Utica we eventually befriended another gay man who had himself recently returned to his hometown in the area after twelve years in Los Angeles; he had AIDS. Over Christmas break a leather dyke, also on visiting faculty status, risked coming out to me. And we heard rumors of others, but it seemed incomprehensible that there could be so few gay people over such a vast geographic area.

Dennis spent a long time searching for work, but rarely got an interview. One potential employer called his previous boss in San Francisco and asked her, quite plainly, if Dennis was "a homosexual." She later called Dennis to tell him this, assuring him she had not answered the question but had counterposed another—what possible significance could that have on one's ability to work with computers? "Well," the former had huffed, "we have no experience in dealing with people like that," to which the latter rejoined, "It's about time you got some."

This turned out not to be an isolated occurrence in Dennis's job search. In the end he gave up on the idea of permanent employment and settled with being placed as a Kelly temp at G.E., the local manufacturer of radar surveillance equipment for the Defense Department. Personnel placed a tail on Dennis the first three months he was on the job at minimum wage entering coded data. In time he became friendly with a coworker (who, it turned out, lived in a trailer park with her woman friend) who did him the mixed kindness of tipping him off to the tail placed on "Tinkerbell from California," and to the concomitant office gossip.

Meanwhile, I was rapidly growing disillusioned with my students. It seems students choose to come to Hamilton as a kind of second choice; either they didn't get into Harvard or Princeton, or they decided they weren't going to work that hard in college. I was teaching three classes a semester, in the course of the day moving from German to Russian to English, and feeling rather elated at the stimulation of my new routine. But the students were not responding, most were unwilling to speak in class, they handed in homework done before last evening's party or completed just moments before on their way to class. They showed no enthusiasm for the subject matter and, since I taught only elective courses, I could not understand why they pursued subjects that did not hold their interest. The students in Russian seemed undisciplined and unmotivated. Their language ability seemed very poor, and I attributed this to weak instruction (no homework, no mandatory memorizing) in their first year. Because the language is difficult for English speakers and the discipline to learn it quite rigorous, the constant chore to push and prod the class enough to make any progress at all grew to herculean proportion.

The students in my German classes were even more puzzling to me. They seemed put out by the idea of having to hand in homework and challenged me whenever I held them accountable for literary or cultural content of any of their readings. Halfway through the semester I polled my language class on why they were taking German. *"Ich weiss es nicht,"* most of them responded, "I don't know."

In the department we brainstormed to dislodge this traditional apathy, known as "Hamilton cool." Sydna organized the German Club, but no students came. I organized a Russian table for Friday lunch and again no students came.

My German literature students were the single beacon of light in this collegiate swamp. They were interested, they were motivated, they made suggestions about readings and essay topics. They eagerly anticipated viewing films and discussing them afterward, and they wrote engaging papers. But, as the fall semester unfolded and everything else seemed to go from bizarre to inscrutable, this small band of students just could not offset my increasing depression.

We survived by traveling. My entire salary, after expenses, was spent on escaping Hamilton. From fall to late spring, every weekend the roads were passable, we drove to visit friends or be tourists in Albany, Rochester, Ithaca, Syracuse. On Thanksgiving we watched the Macy's parade from Columbus Circle and dined in an Indian restaurant in the East Village. After a perfunctory Christmas dinner with my parents, we flew to New Orleans for a week of conventioneering and sightseeing. We rang in the New Year at a leather-sex party in San Francisco. As long as we kept moving, we might create the illusion that we were really just on an extended vacation.

In the spring I attended some Quaker meetings, in lieu of AA, and reflected on what I was looking for in upstate New York and what had gone so wrong. We had had regular contact with my family and, while they seemed little interested in what I did at Hamilton, they considered my return as part of the order of things and accepted Dennis and my relationship with him. Old friends that we visited on our weekend escapes were as loving and affectionate as ever. The people to whom I had wanted to "prove" my success were phantoms of my memory, figments of my imagination.

On the surface, Hamilton faculty were avowedly elitist and clannishly exclusive, shunning temporary faculty, overt homosexuals, Democrats, and Californians. They made constant sport of the indigenous population, alleging them to be dim-witted and poor as a result of generations of inbreeding. At times, I found myself mirthfully indulging in this verbal local-yokel bashing, but feeling much like a closeted homosexual offering rejoinders to antigay jokes.

Somewhere deep within me, all of this—Hamilton College, Utica, all my family in upstate New York—hit a long-forgotten raw nerve. Something pierced unerringly through my fears and neuroses and the forgetfulness woven so densely over the old shame and dread. I was confronted, by my own unwitting choice, with the shattering discrepancy between my long-nurtured fantasies and the realities of life outside the twin cocoons of the Castro and Berkeley.

I have been out of the closet for twenty years, have lived with the freedoms of a graduate student. And I have lived so long as an expatriate that I had completely forgotten my state of expatriation, of being at home everywhere as a stranger. I had not anticipated myself as an expatriate in my own hometown—in my family, in the social class of my origin and aspirations—nor that

I no longer understood the languages spoken around me in New York State.

"People who have disappeared from the face of the earth," Oscar Wilde once alleged, "have reportedly been seen walking in the streets of San Francisco." I returned to San Francisco that summer of 1989 with Dennis. And now, a year later, I find myself in an unexpected transmutation of the same quandary: as an openly gay man who embraces the urban American gay culture, where will I find a home? As a humanities scholar facing a minute and still dwindling job market, how do I respond to the professional dictate that a humanities scholar must accept any offer of a teaching position, wherever it might be? And, as a person living with HIV infection (and no medical insurance), just how far dare I stray from the Bay Area?

Today is another balmy day in San Francisco. A drought has been officially declared for San Francisco and we are back on water rationing. It has been an unusually hot summer so far. From June to mid-August the fog usually rolls in at dawn, burns off shortly before noon, and the afternoon fog comes rolling in, cascading over Twin Peaks by two in the afternoon. This summer each day of fog has alternated with a day of a beating hot sun in a clear blue California sky: the heat of one day creates a vacuum that the following day draws in the fog bank off the ocean, which in turn creates a counter-pressure that draws the heat in from the Central Valley. But there has been no rainfall in the process. Every summer the refrain attributed to Mark Twain gets repeated dozens of times, "The coldest winter I ever spent was one summer in San Francisco." Even that isn't true anymore.

And so this morning I sit at my desk and watch the fog pour in over Twin Peaks, not quite sure whether I'm coming or going. While I do not know how long I can continue to eke out a marginal existence, as I have this past year back in San Francisco, I am as torn as ever between staying and leaving my adopted home again. And I think again of Wilde, as gay San Franciscans are wont to do, who also wrote, "Sometimes we must leave in order to arrive." And I think the journey is more important than reaching the destination.

MICHAEL LASSELL

BROOKLYN/LONG ISLAND/
LOS ANGELES/NEW YORK

Do I HAVE A HOMETOWN?
I never thought so. I know where I was born: Flower Fifth Avenue Hospital in New York City. My parents lived in Brooklyn at the time, in Greenpoint, in one of two identical railroad flats over a "shop" where the pickle-making business founded by my maternal grandfather still turned out Old Reliable dills. My mother grew up at 8 Lombardy Street, and in its unglamorous confines my earliest memories took form: my father tightening barrel hoops with a rubber mallet, the small desk under the girlie calendar where my aunt kept the books, the sour smell of brine seeping through oak staves. My grandfather had died of bleeding ulcers at the Mayo Clinic during the war while my father was off with General Eisenhower invading Normandy (ancestral home, it is supposed, of his own family). My grandmother, a sofa-sized, sad-faced woman in every photograph, followed her husband within months, dead of a broken heart, or bone cancer, depending on who's telling the story, how much alcohol has been con-

sumed, and how much sentiment is wafting through the room. Cancer was considered shameful in those days, so my mother's not really sure how her mother died, a statement that embodies a sorrow all its own.

In any case, I was a postwar Brooklyn boom baby, and my father, Purple Heart in hand, was working for his brother-in-law making pickles and horseradish and selling them to places in Manhattan, some of which still exist, and a few of which—like the Empire Diner—I've patronized just for the sake of continuity. From 1947 to 1950, we lived in one of the Eight Lombardy Street flats; across the landing (where our bathroom was) my mother's brother Jack lived with his wife (my beloved godmother), and their daughter, fourteen years my senior and my first baby-sitter. At 6 Lombardy Street lived Helen and Alex (known then, before balding, as Whitey) and their daughter Linda, my first playmate and the only "sibling" I would ever know (remember her name; it recurs).

Alex and my father worked in the same machine shop after high school and met their future wives at their employer's compound in Rocky Point, then the antipodal outpost of Long Island. My parents and Helen and Alex dated together in the late thirties, while the women were stenographers in Rockefeller Center and the men cranked out tools for Martin Swanson, patriarch of a tribe of Swedes (and Helen's uncle). There are pictures of the two couples at the World's Fair in Flushing, all decked out, the women in fox-collared coats and broad-brimmed hats; the men in suits and fedoras, carrying walking sticks (a momentary rage). Both couples married in 1940; Linda was born during the war, I after.

So there were countless relatives and near-relatives around me in my early years, and scores of Greenpoint photographs to document the emotions my parents rarely spoke of: Michael in his high chair pulling his uncle's tie, bundled in a sled in snow, chasing pigeons in a spring park, with Uncle Doug's blue-ribbon rabbits. They are photographs of contentment and love, and I hold them as proof positive that I was happy once, although it was many years ago.

These many relatives, each of whom was referred to as aunt or uncle in one Northern European language or another, came

together in my maternal grandparents' summer house in the Catskills: my father's parents (American-born father, English immigrant mother); his three sisters—my aunts Lottie, Carrie, and
Rose—and their families; my aunt Helene, her Polish mother,
Granny (the knitting genius who bruised cheeks with two-fisted
kisses), her sister auntie Anne, brother Joey, their spouses and
children; and all the Swedes. My first trip to Palenville was in
August of 1947; I was three weeks old. My first birthday, shared
with my cousin Gloria's fifteenth (duly reported in the local newspaper) took place on the lawn by the huge blue hydrangeas.

To a toddler let loose from the confines of Brooklyn, this
immersion in the countryside, every need attended to, was Eden.
On Lombardy Street, you could smell the gasworks, just down
the block. The view from our front window was the Trunz meat-
packing plant, now only recently demolished. And Linda, who is
just enough older to remember, tells me there was a slaughter-
house where animals were skinned for furs, but I don't remember
it. I don't exactly *remember* the happiness of Palenville, either, but
the photographic record of those days is, for me, an absolute
truth: potbellied and flaxen haired, new at walking but running
through sprinklers in diapers or less, surrounded by strong young
men in T-shirts and shorts, by benign seniors lounging in the
shade, by laughing women in flowered sundresses with enormous
buttons and pockets that held scented handkerchiefs embroidered
with violets or strawberries. How could a child not be happy?
There was even a swimming hole nearby—icy creek water cours-
ing through a natural rock formation.

In the huge trees were birdhouses carved like cuckoo clocks
by my grandfather before he died with half a stomach, the best
doctors in the country helpless to save him, his long-suffering wife
keeping a diary of her accumulating grief, a document my mother
saved and intends to dig out of a trunk to read again. It will find
its way into my hands one day, and I will pass it along to my
cousin's daughter, or to a child of hers (the first, a boy, made his
debut the week of my parents' fiftieth anniversary). My father's
mother was born in London, to a Jewish upholsterer and a concert singer who had given a command performance before Queen
Victoria. She died shortly after I was born. There are pictures of

my grandmother's last Easter, gaunt, wasting, holding an infant me in her spindly arms, trying to smile, undoubtedly delighted to be cradling the first child of her younger son, the last of her five children to reproduce. I look at those pictures and wonder if she ever got over the stigma of being half-Jewish in the Ellis Island days of New York, a biographical detail obliquely alluded to all my life, but never stated until I was nearly forty and my father was telling stories about his own Depression boyhood: skipping out on the rent month after month at night, playing hooky and sneaking into Broadway theaters to see Franny Brice. The things my parents leave unsaid say more about them than most of the things they proclaim.

In many ways, the selling of the house in Palenville after my German grandmother's lonely death—"She just reached behind her to zip up her dress," my mother told me, "and her arm broke; she died a few months later"—marked the end of a certain innocence in my life, and the beginning of a profound feeling of restlessness, a spiritual homelessness that has always dogged me, a mutt you can't discourage by kindness or cruelty.

In 1950, just shy of my third birthday, my family joined the great exodus from the tenements of Brooklyn and the Bronx to the tract homes of Long Island, to the "developments," the "bedroom communities." With visions of middle-class materialism dancing in their heads, the children of the immigrant working class, aided and abetted by the G.I. Bill, poured whatever money they had managed to put aside (or inherit) into five-room Cape Cods on streets of nearly identical addresses (our street was named Campbell, I've been told, as a bribe to a sewer official who subsequently reversed his refusal to approve the builder's proposal for this new neighborhood). Futures secure, and photo albums bursting with snapshots of their houses in each stage of construction, they went about the business of raising lawns and children.

For the next fifteen years—there are photos galore: Michael with a snowman, a puppy, a crew cut, a swimming pool, a tuxedo and a girl—I lived in that unincorporated and altogether undistinguished section of Nassau County's New Hyde Park, on land that had only shortly before been occupied by gracious estate farms (one of the local manor houses still survives, choked by a sprawling "recreational facility"). Our fellow homesteaders came from similar metropolitan backgrounds and shared dreams of peaceful nights, safe streets, and Wonderbread kids protected from epidemics like the one that took my mother's bookish brother George and pudgy sister Anna (the only member of my family I've ever resembled). And I'm told by my parents that I took to suburbia like a duck to water (they are a repository of maxims, platitudes, and aphorisms) and struck out on my own to create whatever three-year-old excitement I could muster. I was shielded from life's disasters by a back-stoop mother network, a kind of over-the-hedges telegraph system of "I've got yours, have you got mine?" If Mrs. LoPresti had made stuffed shells and sausage, she had me.

The cyclone fence in my parents' yard was meant, my father tells me now, not to keep anyone out, but to keep me in. "It didn't work," he adds with a chuckle, sipping his salt-free seltzer and flipping the filets mignons on his gas-fueled grill (sprayed with PAM to cut down on cleanup). Along the fence his roses grow, some of the bushes almost as old as I am. "Your mother gets such a kick out of those roses," he says with pride. There are hundreds of snapshots of this yard, of the roses, and family barbecues on Memorial Day, Labor Day, and my birthday, when I'd always ask for hot dogs and hamburgers, corn-on-the-cob, and watermelon—photos that record the decline of the Brooklyn/Catskills crowd, and the gradual reduction of their number.

But for all the good times, the singing around the patio, I always felt that I did not fit in. I was one of the only "only children" I knew. Except for Linda, whose family soon moved into the house that kitty-cornered our yard, next to the LoPrestis. All my cousins—in places like Seaford, Plainview, Westbury—had brothers and sisters, none of them remotely like me. My mother had had a second pregnancy, in 1949 I think, but submitted to what was then called a "therapeutic" abortion after she came down with German measles at a critical phase of gestation. Since this was *never* spoken of, I do not know the details to this day, or why she held me tighter than any mother in the neighborhood, and I ached for freedom and for a younger brother with a passion that was almost lyrical. (As late as high school, I stealth-ily poked holes in my father's condoms, hoping to induce an "accidental" pregnancy.)

By the time I was five, before I started school, I had become an inward, moody child, suddenly unphysical, given to crippling headaches, obviously bright, even precocious, but fat, self-conscious, awkward, and neurotically dependent, a crybaby, an embarrassment.

At a neighborhood wedding when I was in my twenties, a woman who had lived down the block the whole time we were growing up together said to me, "I've known you all my life, but I still think of you as someone from someplace else." She could not have put it better. I was so convinced I was adopted, I stayed home from school one day to look for the adoption papers. Even now, no matter where I am, I seem to be from someplace else, looking at the world from a minority perspective, and I've had to rethink the concept of "home" over and over again. Is it a place or an attitude, a feeling of well-being, serenity, an ease of self? Hideous as Oz could be, I couldn't for the life of me figure out why Dorothy ever wanted to go back to Kansas, yet I was plagued by nightmares in which my mother died or disappeared, leaving me abandoned.

Like many people, when I hear the word *hometown,* I conjure the kind of place where middle-aged men don comical uniforms and play oompah songs in gingerbread gazebos on the Fourth of July. A place where everyone is known and cared for, and the common good is not only good but common, a tangible thing universally agreed upon; where the smell of fresh sawdust means a barn is going up, and once a year a circus sets up a big top and boys leave off baseball to stare at the tattooed bosoms of the hootchie-cootchie bearded fat lady.

Where this idealized image of small towns comes from, of course, is literature, films, and TV. Before *Twin Peaks,* it is to be remembered, there was *Peyton Place,* the book before the movie, the movie before the series. The claustrophobic stagnation of small towns was exposed, along with the steamier belly of small-town indiscretions, but Main Street, U.S.A., is a powerful myth—like that of your immigrant ancestor's bucolic village in Alsace, where great-grandparents sat in their vineyard for an itinerant photographer, not really knowing what was going on. To me, a "hometown" is a place where family feeling extends to neighbors and friends, a place, of course, where families allow their children breathing room to become themselves instead of carbon copies of imperfect elders, and where no child ever grows up quivering with anxiety for becoming something the common good has decided is uncommonly bad: a communist, for example, a serial killer, or a homosexual.

And a "hometown" should look like Litchfield, Connecticut, a whitewashed, wood-framed, eighteenth-century hamlet complete with potpourri-scented Christmas shop and steepled church on a central green. It's widely known, but my parents and I discovered it by accident one tight-jawed afternoon driving through the flame-leafed autumn, ignoring the presence of my lover beside me in the backseat, a lover who would surely have been fiercely doted on, had he not been both male and Latin.

Neither Brooklyn nor New Hyde Park look like Litchfield, but the truth is that the naïve virtues we associate with towns that look like Hallmark cards were more than amply evident inside my family. We had enormous Christmases of abundant gifts (my parents were generous, my godparents outrageous). Every holiday was spent with the clan, which was moving family by family across the county line. Auntie might dance on the table in her underwear on New Year's Eve, and Uncle Jack's jokes might be crude and corny ("Eat every carrot and pee in the bowl"), but Uncle Roy sent postage stamps from all over the world in his Coast Guard travels—from Papua, New Guinea, to Antarctica—and Aunt Mildred was overcome with emotion trying to read me *Black Beauty*. And if a firecracker went off in a boy's hand or a pack of matches ignited in his pocket, he would be circled by a crowd of caring women who would rub ice on his blistering skin and wipe away tears with kisses. But this was the age of innocence, and the innocence seemed to dwindle to a trickle before I was ready. I took its loss personally.

Even places that look like back lots for the kinds of movies no one has made since the death of Louis B. Mayer are far from guileless. And New Hyde Park, as I came into my school years,

proved neither innocent nor particularly wicked, neither picturesque nor ugly in the way that people who hate cities think cities
are ugly. It is just a narrow place (an isthmus of the imagination)
without a single distinguishing feature. Esthetically void, New
Hyde Park was, and is, a grid of boxy houses lived in by white,
mostly Christian, mostly Republican families living mostly unex-
amined lives and not being bothered about it one bit. There was
a wooded section once where we played Tarzan or Indians, but
they tore it out to build the dullest shopping center ever erected
on Long Island. There was a Currier and Ives–like skating pond,
too, on the old Ritter farm, but it's been paved over, fenced in,
and made into a County Park that's always empty because it's
been claimed by Canada geese—who no longer migrate—and it's
full of their finger-sized droppings.

It's near the house where my friend Ralph lived. The summer of my senior year in high school I'd wait up for him until
he came back from his night job at the airport. He was four years
older, and although we'd known each other since childhood, we'd
only recently become friends. He was a former state track champion, and the first heterosexual I ever told I was gay. He expressed no shock or disgust, but became a closer friend than ever.
I spent my eighteenth birthday getting drunk with Ralph and
Linda. He was shot down in Vietnam, and all that I have of him
now is a photograph of his name on the Vietnam War Memorial
taken by Linda on a recent trip to Washington. Even the happiest
hometown memories hold sadness now, like fossils in amber. I
think of my life sometimes as Bergman's *Fanny and Alexander*: the
beginning a wild and loving Christmas feast; and a sudden
change, without warning, to the strict, unloving fanaticism of
fundamentalist Lutherans, which, by the way, my parents are.

Whatever needs New Hyde Park may have filled for my
parents' generation, it met few of mine. And the more like an
outsider I became, the fewer hungers were satisfied. Whatever
decencies New Hyde Park and my loving extended family might
have possessed, they had no tolerance whatever for eccentricity
or difference, for contradiction or deviation. For these, my formative years, my unsensationally unhappy childhood, unfolded
at the height of the Eisenhower-McCarthy era, and well-behaved

children of upstanding citizens were fed a steady diet of conformity salad and what-will-the-Joneses-think stew. We were the good people and values were absolute (like the black-and-white television of the time: "Lassie," "Howdy Doody," "The Lone Ranger"). People who were like us (white, Protestant, Republican) were good people; people who were different (you name it) were not.

And it was not considered a good thing for a male child to be a lisping sissy who hated baseball; who got good grades and loved eating, drawing, and Jesus; who managed to charm parents and teachers with his mastery of manners, but who was afraid to go outside for recess; who was threatened by bullies and teased by everyone else; who spent his leisure hours designing gowns for Brenda Starr's trousseau and hiding them because he managed to intuit that he was a transgressor every time he exercised his free will. And the lengths to which New Hyde Park, Trinity Lutheran Church, and the Parkville School went to normalize me, which felt humiliating every time, were astounding. Even more astounding, I suppose, is their complete failure to saddle and bridle me with their outworn assumptions of appropriate behavior. Nowadays we might talk about exceptional children of unexceptional parents. Then I was just a tormented kid who could not obey but who was forced to obey, and the only way I could handle the expectations was to split into halves: the goody two-shoes who sang in the choir and did what he was told; and the anarchistic hellion who took suicidal risks on bicycles, who smashed and broke and set fire to things, who stole flagrantly from the time he was eight years old. Well, that's the suburbs for you: decor by Disney, script by Stephen King.

Almost nothing has been able to depress me faster than a visit to my parents, who are retired now, my mother from Sperry Rand, my father from the Pepsi Cola Corporation. They live in the same house they purchased with the money they inherited from my grandparents. Many of their neighbors have died or moved away—to Florida mostly (another K-Mart dream)—but the tempest-in-a-teapot world of suburban life goes on. My father and his next-door neighbor are no longer speaking after sharing a property line for four decades because of a contretemps over a hedge and a garden fence. Alexander Pope could have had a field day with these characters ("The Rape of the Locked Gate"), not to mention Jonathan Swift. It all seems so illusory, so fantastical.

We had our share of reality in New Hyde Park: infidelities, teenage pregnancies, unmarried motherhood, even a little Mafia action: my best friend's uncle was shot through the head, gang style, in the parking lot of the Sterling Lanes, the underground bowling alley on Union Turnpike (the opening of which, complete with the town's first elevator, was the highlight of my long-delayed puberty). We were, of course, dying to see if Johnny's uncle had left any bloodstains behind, but we were dutifully forbidden to go near the scene of the crime, just as we were prohibited from attending any movie displeasing to or unflattering of Pope Pius XII (who had turned his jewel-laden back on the Holocaust), even though my family was not Catholic. This Romanizing of my mother's sensibilities can be traced to her maniacally hygienic circle of coffee-klatching Canasta pals—Lucy, Joan, and Santa—all of them addicted to the League of Decency. Which is what led to the fight when I was barred from seeing *The World of Susie Wong* in 1960, an injustice I rectified by flying to Hong Kong in 1989 to visit the kinds of bars where girls like Suzie led unsuspecting artists like William Holden astray—only there weren't any girls.

Sex, like everything else in the suburbs, was a secret. The overt racism was a secret, the anti-Semitism, the physical maladies of children: the boy with epilepsy, the girl with "blue-baby syndrome," even my own cousin Ginny, who died—a saint—of an increasingly debilitating disease the name of which I don't think I ever knew. (Was it polio, the bone-twisting specter of our early summers?) I was not, in fact, even told when Ginny died, my closest cousin in age and a friend by virtue of her frailty. She simply disappeared, like Mrs. Roche, who hanged herself in the basement one fine day, only to be discovered by her ten-year-old daughter Paula when she scampered across the street from school for lunch. None of this was ever spoken of over dinner on Formica kitchen tables.

I was thirteen years old in 1960 (yes, I remember exactly where I was when Kennedy died, and yes, I saw Jack Ruby kill Lee Harvey Oswald on live television, and yes, the funeral was the first occasion my parents and I had to weep together for the same reason). My father had left my uncle's inept employ, and my mother went back to work to save money for my college education. And I was to leave the relative security of a grade school right down the block to be bused to Great Neck, two miles and a galaxy away. If I hadn't felt enough like an outsider before, I was now an alien. Clearly over my head academically, I was a social outcast by virtue of modest family means and Christian heritage (I wasn't exactly from the wrong side of the tracks, but I was definitely from the wrong side of the Long Island Expressway, which divides the haves from the haves-a-lot). Seemingly all of my well-to-do classmates had lost their grandparents in Nazi concentration camps—undoubtedly at the hands of my own relatives, I was assured. I became *personally* guilty in their eyes after the release of *Judgment at Nuremberg* in 1961.

I entered high school a paranoid, introverted kid afraid of everything, but most terrified of being excluded. I had been raised to think I had no right to express an opinion that differed from my parents. And here I was awash in a sea of kids who had been trained that a rugged individualism, fierce competition, and outspokenness might be the keys to their very survival in a hostile world. I started to crack. I started to cause trouble for the first time in my life. I will be full of remorse until my dying day for the extortion, or attempted extortion, of money from a smaller classmate named Lenny Katz. I was nearly expelled for a quarter, but I was that desperate for attention, for power, for some arena in which I did not feel entirely inferior. A failure at criminal behavior, I settled, at the suggestion of a gruff but caring teacher, on academic prowess, which was within my grasp. Largely to impress Emily Miller, I started to get straight A's. I did not stop hating myself. And it wouldn't be long before the A's became harder to get: I was starting to drink, more and more often, more and more heavily.

By the time I was in high school, I knew I was homosexual. I had a massive crush on the school's star actor, Ray Singer (who was to become a friend years later in Los Angeles), and I had had an immediate and unequivocal physical reaction—a body gasp—when a fellow student stripped down to postpubescent nudity in gym class. The combination of his fully developed genitalia, his clearly defined adult musculature, and his radiant black skin (for he was one of the dozen non-Caucasians in this student body of three thousand) made an impression that duplicated in my mind and groin what Columbus must have felt like when the *Niña*, *Pinta*, and *Santa Maria* dropped anchor off the shore of Hispañola. Like Archimedes in his tub, I had found it. But I had no idea what it was, what it meant to be a homosexual, or how one went about becoming one. It would take years of mistakes to find out, years in which lovers of both genders would be left behind, quizzical looks on their faces, wondering what they had done to drive me away. Years in which I became convinced that I was incapable of love, that I was undeserving of love, that love did not exist. Years in which I downed more than my share of double scotch boilermakers, my jump-start cocktail of choice.

I visited my old high school recently, on a beautiful early autumn day, and walked around its wooded campus. I felt almost nothing for those interminable years of pain and panic, which I take as a good sign. Ultimately I'm grateful to Great Neck, though it is one of the most loathsome places I've ever been. If I'd lived just a few blocks further south or east, I would have gone to New Hyde Park Memorial, Ralph's alma mater, home of football champions and prom queens of legendary pert-nosed beauty. Sister-person Linda thinks she would have been better off there, among those unobsessed by wealth and achievement; I would have been crushed. For among the crowds of popular kids who needled me incessantly for not being rich, for not being Jewish, for being fat and ill-at-ease, were a group of Great Neck students—a loose federation of thinkers—who had inherited from their grandparents that rich and poignant tradition of Jewish humanitarianism, a love of music and literature and justice. A tradition that inspired many of my classmates to spend their summers in Mississippi on the now-famous but then quite dangerous freedom rides that eventually broke the spine of legal segregation.

It was in this subculture of Great Neck South High School in the early 1960s that I began to see myself as one of the underdogs, one of the wronged, a lover of truth and beauty, a creature possessed of the will and talent to move others by word and deed to greater understanding and compassion for the downtrodden of this our imperfect earth. It was in high school, too, that I first began to spend time in Greenwich Village, where I took guitar lessons at a place where Joan Baez and Bob Dylan hung out, though I saw them only once. And that's when I began to find some kind of spiritual home: not New York, per se, not the district known affectionately as The Village, although that's where I live today, but a metaphoric place, a cosmopolitan bohemian enclave of kindred souls. Without ever having really lived in one, I had become a city kid. Before I knew what was happening, I fulfilled all the demographic criteria to call myself an urban gay male.

I owe it to my early idyllic summers in the Catskills, I suppose, and four intensely angry undergraduate years at Colgate University (a lovely vile place, with the exception of a handful of visionary teachers, most of them now dead, a bastion of the worst in bourgeois thought, word, and deed) that I am moved to tears today by nature in all its glory: sunsets in the Canary Islands, the tumultuous gray of a storm off the coast of Normandy, the oncenightly collective howl of the coyotes of Yosemite, a sound so close, so enormous, you feel it rather than hear it. Despite the cynicism of years, I can believe in God when I'm so congruent with nature. But it is in cities, the biggest ones, that you meet people from all over the world, that you abut the myriad traditions of society, of the many societies. In Los Angeles, where I lived for fourteen years, I was drawn to the Latin tradition of Mexico, of Central and South America, although I'm clearly a stranger in that Spanish-surnamed world. But "outside" is a place that's comfortable to me because it is, finally, familiar territory (despite my constant, pathetic attempts to fit in). If I were to identify my "hometown" as a concept rather than a place, it would be "The City, Outside."

In the last twenty-two years, I have lived for the most part in New Haven (as poor an excuse for a city as has ever been beset by the urban redevelopment cartel) and Los Angeles, with briefer stints in San Francisco and New York. I lived in London for the better part of a college year and have visited cities in Europe and Asia. In all of them, it is the city of night, to borrow dear John Rechy's penetrating phrase, that holds my imagination, the city of throwaways, of runaways and the damned, the city of the neglected, abused, and misunderstood, the city of those who sleep through banking hours and emerge from their crippling ostracism to find simpatico fellow travelers in the portion of the day abandoned by the respectable and the condemning majority. After midnight everything feels like love.

They have their ludicrous pretensions, God knows (just thumb through *The New York Times*, the *New York Review of Books*, or drop in on any underground club any night of the week), but to me cities are still places where you can be yourself, whether or not you'd kill for attention. You don't have to explain yourself to anyone. And because I was smothered as a child for being a nonconformist in the making, I enjoy breathing through both my nostrils now wherever I go, filling my lungs with the air of permission cities manufacture with their smog. On Long Island I constantly found myself on the verge of an apology: I am sorry I'm not more normal, sorry my hair's too long, sorry I'm not a Christian, a Republican, sorry I couldn't produce grandchildren for the days dwindling down. The suburbs induce an asthma of the psyche, wit, and soul. In New York, London, Paris, I begin to hear the poetry of my life as some kind of liturgy offered to an elusive but bounteous "higher power." It is in cities that, in Whitman's definitive words, I can sing the song of myself. No rural poet of the nineteenth century came close to Whitman's unrestrained, raw, pulsing authenticity, which I admire and respect. Barbaric yawp? Amen!

In the Bible, of course, cities are associated with sin. And I like that aspect, too, of the universal metropolis, since the Bible seems to define as sin everything that is most natural in human behavior. Maybe it's the suburban obsession with aerosol cleansers that makes sex seem so filthy there—all those odors, those sticky and potentially hazardous fluids! But sex doesn't seem nearly as dirty to me in cities, just more vital. I've had sex with porn stars for cash that was as virginal in its way as one of my earliest encounters: in a field at dawn, along the banks of the

Mohawk River, in the shadow of a ruined mill. It wasn't until a fighter jet took off about ten feet over our heads that we realized we were making love at the weedy end of a military air strip. Wild blue yonder, indeed!

Cities are not spotless; they are not orderly or polite. They have, however, sensual charms: I have been overwhelmed by the scent of a cab driver's leather jacket, his heavily lidded gaze in the rearview mirror, by a whiff of pungent aftershave on a young waiter in a Greek coffee shop on a blustery day, by the pull of Spandex across a bicycle messenger's rock-hard thighs. This is the stuff of cities. On a recent Saturday night I was walking down Eighth Avenue near Forty-second Street (where I had just seen a Pulitzer Prize–winning playwright in a "boylesque" joint where nude Puerto Ricans let you touch their dicks for a dollar). A gay little person (that's "dwarf" in the vernacular) walked up to me, put his hand on my overample belly, and tried to pick me up. Cities are full of such adventures. Maybe they don't spill out of *Huckleberry Finn,* but they're not always out of *Salo* either. There's always a hint of Fellini evident in cities, but there's a dose of Fellini anywhere there's a jolt of life.

Nowadays I do my nocturnal prowling clean and sober. It's been fifteen years since my last drink. I'm proud of the longevity, but the original decision was not a moral one. In the beginning my choice was between drinking and suicide; later life offered the options of sobriety or death.

I have had to surrender a lot of old ideas in order to preserve my sobriety, and one of the first to go was my need to condescend to anyone. Although my male thirst for competition never seems to wane, I prefer to see commonality rather than difference, inclusion rather than exclusion. I have found that "bottom of the barrel" people can be among the sweetest, most loving, and most generous people on earth, far kinder and gentler than any government official I've ever met. The hustlers, strippers, and other denizens of the night who frequent my writing are sometimes dangerous and often untrustworthy, but they have their own dignity, their own dreams, their own limits and frustrations. Certainly they have their own pain, and it is to be respected rather than belittled. In any case, it is not these soulmates of my id who manifest themselves in nightmares as the dark, pursuing "other." These men are what I am: prodigal sons who never went home to dinner.

But I have not always been sober, and the last and worst of my drinking was so associated with New York that I had to flee. Los Angeles, last refuge of people on the run, seemed a perfect place to go. I suffered through one more family barbecue (a disastrous Bicentennial Fourth of July) and the loneliest birthday of them all (my twenty-ninth) and touched down at LAX on July 28, 1976. It was raining.

I arrived in Los Angeles physically, mentally, emotionally, spiritually, morally bankrupt. I know in my heart that I'd be dead by now if an old school friend hadn't opened a door for me into a healing way of life that requires no artificial stimulation, no sedation. In a very real sense, the home I found in Los Angeles was not a *place* to live, but a *way* to live, and a group of peers to do it with—an eclectic group that included pimps and prostitutes, doctors and deejays from Southland Jesus stations. In little more than two years I had a lover and a clique of friends that I admired and, in some cases, adored. I got thin in Los Angeles, and tan. My hair crept back toward childhood platinum. I danced all night in the hottest discos, paced the halls of the preferred bathhouses, pumped iron in the coolest gym, basking in the occasional lustful glance. Men approached me on the street and invited me home for sex. I had become everything I had ever dreamed of or prayed for: accepted, inside, in demand.

And yet of all my memories of L.A. my happiest is of a Christmas spent with a collection of sober gay alcoholic friends. A full turkey dinner with all the gourmet trimmings, the event was hosted by my closest friend Kenny and his lover Roy; and prepared by them along with Michael and Bill (another interracial couple) and other members of our circle. It must have been around 1980, and it was the first time in my life that I was fully relaxed for a holiday, the first time I was entirely comfortable, even serene in a group of equals, judging no one, feeling no pressure to assert myself. I was a man among men, a friend among friends. The pictures from that day are as silly as we were, all of us dressed in red and green and all of us in love with each other and with life. I am tempted to say that this group of good men was, for years, the "hometown" I had always felt I'd missed. It would be very close to the truth. There was nothing I couldn't say to these men, nothing I wouldn't have done for them, or asked them to do if I needed help. I had regained Eden, rediscovered laughter and innocence; I had been reborn.

And then my friends began to get sick. And then they began to die.

And I began to notice that L.A. was very much like suburban Long Island. My tan started to fade; the sun started giving me cancer. My hair started to darken. I stopped going to the gym and began putting on weight. My lover and I started to bicker over nothing. There didn't seem to be much energy for dancing. We hung on, but that was not the same thing as celebrating our existence. When Kenny died in 1987 (a week after my return from Spain) and my dear friend Clark Henley died in 1988 (a week before my trip to France), and my lover called it quits somewhere between the two, taking up with a flashy programmer for PBS (which will never see another dime from me), I saw no more reason to stay in a city I had come to detest, though it's hard to imagine any city could have withstood the enormity of my rage.

I have nothing original to say about Los Angeles. I hated all the same trite things other New Yorkers hate who tried to make it in L.A. and failed (although this summation might be a bit self-deprecating). I tried to stay neutral, but I threw in the towel; I couldn't take the driving anymore, the relentless redundancy of the weather (hot, white, hazy, dry), the earthquakes in ascending numbers on the Richter scale. Perhaps it was the rampant racism and the vigorous suppression of the Asian, Latin, and African-American majority. Maybe it was just the stiffening redneck heart that beats beneath the public persona of Hollywood or the "cultural Renaissance" that failed to materialize. At root was a pervasive discontent with the citywide solemnization of lowest-common-denominator mediocrity; this ritualized anti-intellectualism made the City of Angels seem too much like New Hyde Park with its homogenized traditional American values contradicting every humanistic or humanitarian principle of my own. It didn't help that the gay community was growing increasingly Republican (I called it the Rise of the Limp-Wristed Right).

I miss my friends in L.A., my "family," the headstones that mark the graves of some of the closest, the T-cell charts that record the precipitous decline of others. I was deeply attached to those men. The grief has been deep and the mourning long. But in the end, after fourteen years, L.A. was easier to leave than a decent party you drop in on between more important engagements.

I returned to New York in April. My parents picked me up at the airport—as they'd done many times (it's a nod to family feeling that reminds me of happiness). I stayed with Linda for a while, then moved into a second-story apartment in Greenwich Village. There were pink geraniums in a window box down the street, and a cherry tree was in full bloom. The bright spring green of the new ginkgo, sycamore, and ailanthus leaves—almost chartreuse in the sunlight—was a pleasant contrast to the natural red brick and the painted Chinese red of the townhouses down by P.S. 3 that date from the early 1820s. The history of New York is one of the things I love most about it. Cities are like that, they have histories.

Here's another corner of New York: The orchestra of the Metropolitan Opera House at Lincoln Center. Beside me is a young dancer named Julio (pronounce the J, he's from Brazil). The American Ballet Theatre is dancing up there onstage. It's the fourth time in two weeks I've been here. I love the ballet. I felt starved for it in L.A. without even realizing it. Julio's an excellent dancer. I've seen him, at one of those Times Square dives where young men strip between fuck movies. They don't earn a lot of money dancing, but they meet the men there who pay them for sex—either on the premises or off. Julio (as in Juliet)—whose birthday, not coincidentally, is, like mine, in July—cut his foot today during an audition for a new company he wants to study with. He's tiny, looks sometimes like a child. I'm crazy about him. During the Gay Pride parade in June (I was in the first one, in 1970), he struts from Central Park to Christopher Street, a distance of several miles, in Carnival-inspired Carmen Miranda drag: lots of headdress, lots of beads and crimson flounces, black spike heels. I took a photograph, which came out beautifully. I'll keep it in the mock-wood cardboard box with all the others.

For my birthday this year, Linda gave me Terry Miller's book on the history of Greenwich Village (*Greenwich Village and How It Got That Way*). As an inscription she wrote: "Always your spiritual home, now your physical home as well." And maybe it's as simple, as unmysterious as that: I'm finally living where I belong, where I've wanted to live all the time. "It's what you've wanted for twenty years," my mother said as she inspected my apartment, having had to see it herself to approve the wisdom of my extravagance (I'll pay more in rent for eight months than she and my father paid for their house in 1950).

Greenwich Village isn't a symbolic place for me anymore, a kind of rive gauche Gotham where suburban kids go to take guitar lessons. It's real now, a place where unimaginative people come to sin. It has broken water pipes, noisy heterosexual neighbors, obnoxious tourists, homeless panhandlers. But it's a place where the neighborhood drunks know you by name and wave as you walk home from another insane day at work or a night at the Philharmonic or a hotel roll in the hay with a dazzling new boy from the Gaiety, or a dinner with a dozen sober gay and lesbian poet friends—a birthday dinner, as it happens, for two of you (the other Moon Child a friend from L.A. who lives in SoHo now). It's a place where dogs know each other's trees, where you can see the Empire State Building, the Chrysler Building, the World Trade Center, the Hudson River, and the Macy's Fourth-of-July fireworks from your own tarry roof, or sit on the stoop and watch the New Kids on the Block catapult from a pair of limos into the Pink Tea Cup, the local soul-food diner across the street.

It's a place where "hometown" seems like a reality, a place immune to nothing, a city place with all its organs intact, all its juices flowing, and all its emotions available for use, a place where I don't feel robbed of ethnicity but part of a multiethnic whole. It's a place where strangers seem like family because of a wink or a smile, a shared ironic take on life's little absurdities, a place where weather changes every day and every day is an excursion into the unknown. A place where nothing is resolved, but everything might be resolved. Where anything's possible, nothing unlikely. A place like Oz and Kansas rolled into one—at least for me.

I was forty-four in July. I'm fat again, balding, alone—without even a fern or a goldfish to distract me from my work, from myself. And if that sounds hideously self-obsessed, you'll have to forgive me. I've never felt more complete in my life. Even New Hyde Park has lost its power to undermine my equanimity. And maybe that's why coming back to New York feels so much like coming home.

Quick! Somebody take a picture.

MICHAEL BRONSKI

CAMBRIDGE, MASSACHUSETTS

"The resemblance of knowledge to truth is like that of the wild almond to the sweet paste; it must be ground and destroyed before it is palatable." —JANE BOWLES

"I want no part of a revolution which does not allow me to dance." —EMMA GOLDMAN

"There is great comfort in knowing that our bodies may be used in all manner for a supreme Glory." —ST. TERESA OF AVILA

"Geography is of little importance so long as the heart is exact." —RONALD FIRBANK

I WAS CALMLY PAGING THROUGH A DUSTY, WORN edition of Wilkie Collins's *The Law and the Lady*—the first novel, someone had just told me, to feature a woman detective—

when I heard footsteps resounding through the marbled room. Ears alert, I followed each step as it passed in front of me. I listened for the click of the metal latch, the unbuckling of the belt buckle, the soft clicks of the zipper, and the slow slide of the pants to the floor. Then, that amazingly serious moment of silence.

Suddenly an eye appeared in the small, diligently carved hole in the booth wall to my left. I placed Wilkie Collins gently on the floor—marking my place with a sheet of white tissue—and, jutting my hips, exposed my hard-on to the gaze of the disembodied eye. After a minute of posing and preening I sat down again and placed my eye to the hole. I was not disappointed. Within the tiny, round field of vision allotted to my eye—I've always thought of the size and detail of this privileged view as resembling a miniature by Parmigianino—were a strong set of thighs supporting a well-shaped cock whose owner would, every few seconds, use his thumb and forefinger to slightly pull and stimulate the head. I took a ballpoint pen from my knapsack and on the full roll of paper next to me printed a short note expressing interest and inquiring what he desired. He wrote back in clear Anglo-Saxon terms and within seconds I slipped into his booth.

After we finished—in my agile youth I could do so much more in a confined space—we slipped out of the men's room together and with an air of civility exchanged names. He glanced at my book (I was not one to leave a good Victorian novel behind, even after sex) and asked if I was enjoying it. I was taken aback; I mean, hardly anybody reads Wilkie Collins, and *The Law and the Lady* is *obscure* Collins. But it turns out that Ian (I remember because he was the first Ian I ever met) was a graduate student at Harvard writing his dissertation on *Social Mobility, Gender, and the Victorian View of the Body in Dickens and Collins.* I was entranced. We proceeded to the not-quite *faux* bo-ho Café Pamplona for coffee. This was my idea of heaven: spending time in well-stocked libraries, discovering new novels, meeting handsome men in bathroom stalls, and then five minutes after having their cock down your throat, going out for coffee and discussing the theoretics of the Victorian novel. It was what I had wanted since

I was a child. It was also one of the last times that Cambridge seemed a perfect place to live.

It was 1973. I was twenty-three and had just moved into a rent-controlled apartment several blocks from Harvard Square with two roommates. In a very vivid way I felt as though I had achieved the *n*th degree of happiness. My life had come to revolve around three axes: books (or at least what they represented of my self-image as an "intellectual"), politics (particularly gay liberationist and feminist), and sex (getting a lot of it). Cambridge, with its demeanor of intellectual stimulation, its reputation for political activism, its air of tolerance, and its quirky architectural look—sort of a Puritan version of the West Village—seemed to be the paradise about which I had always dreamed. It was only later that I realized that the stimulation was many times narrow-minded pedagogy; the activism mired in homophobia; the tolerance actually emotional repression; and the city's architecture about to fall prey to insensitive urban development: talk about Paradise Lost.

But before Paradise was Lost it had to be Found, and my journey to Cambridge, or at least the *idea* of Cambridge, had taken more than twelve years and several sheddings and acquisitions of identity. Although I knew that I was a homosexual from an early age—my vivid sexual fantasies were clear indication even in a 1950s childhood—my gay *identity* was more protean and had undergone several metamorphoses over the years.

My desire to be well-read, which has at times become obsessional, not only came out of my working-class childhood vision of what it meant to be an intellectual but also from my first conscious deliberate attempt to define myself as a homosexual. For one thing, like many lesbians and gay men of my generation, I had to turn to books to find out about *any* sexuality, especially *homo*sexuality. There were, of course, dictionaries—I've been partial to the term "invert" since I discovered it at the age of eleven as a synonym for homosexuality; it seemed to mean a quiet, bookish sort of person—and the sex manuals and medical directories, which always yielded small gifts of information.

But as I read further I discovered also that what was commonly called "literature" was fraught with signs, codes, and sometime explicit information about what being "homosexual" might entail. I began having fantasies not only about the Hardy Boys (the older, darker, seriously sexy Frank as well as his younger, blond, but better built brother Joe), but their mature, attractive father, Fenton, as well. This was so exciting that I quickly graduated to the half-naked antics of Natty Bumpo and his Native American cohorts in James Fenimore Cooper novels and the enticing torture scenes in Scott's *Ivanhoe*. Even the heterosexual Edgar Allen Poe managed to excite my oversexed and impressionable mind with his tales of misfits exhibiting the most extreme kinds of sexualized identities. Once I had mastered the art of culling sexual fantasies from fiction (and as Brigid Brophy points out all fiction is nothing *but* sexual fantasy), I began to discover and explore overt gay literature. I learned about real gay lives and truths from James Baldwin and John Rechy, Allen Ginsberg and Tennessee Williams. With a little bit of digging it was amazing what you could find in 1964.

But inflaming my sexual fantasies and finding out about the actual gay world was only a part of why these books, this amassing of knowledge, were so important to me. As I had become aware of my sexual desires around the age of ten or so, it became clear to me that the prevailing culture expected male homosexuals to be "artistic"—that this was the acceptable social identity.

This was not odd for the time. I was determined to fit the mold, to justify my homosexuality, my erotic desires, by becoming an intellectual, an artist, a writer—whatever. It was salvation through truth and beauty. (Culture—both high and low, academic and popular—has always been a way for gay men to both create and control the world around them.) And while I was in touch with my sexual desires I was also very aware that they were unacceptable to the rest of the world. Never expecting to escape criticism—I had been queer baited too often in my younger years for that—I sought instead to have a way to deflect it. My rush to gain knowledge was a desperate attempt to recreate myself into a person whose sexuality would be permissible, if secondary. I was determined to be a *smart* homosexual, an extremely well-read homosexual, a cultured homosexual. Of course this implied, at least to me, that I was also not *just* a homosexual; that my sexual desires were no basis for an identity. And while I spent much time feeling isolated—reading is not a particularly communal activity—I also felt safer and acceptable. When I arrived in Cambridge, with its overtly bookish atmosphere and its patina of cultured class mobility, its bookstores and its cafés, I felt as though I had attained this goal.

But books were not the only filter through which I had learned to experience my sexuality. Even while reading compulsively, seeing art films on triple bills, attending the theater indiscriminately, becoming a pop culture addict (joining the homo-cults of Judy Garland and Barbra Streisand), and even developing a taste for opera—somewhere deep inside I knew that something was missing. In college—a dreary, inner-city state university settled in old office and factory spaces, whose lack of basic economic resources stifled its mostly working-class student body's imagination and possibilities and whose only strong point was that it was a twenty-five-minute train ride to Greenwich Village—I discovered politics. In 1967, this meant progressive politics. We had a small SDS chapter and participated in anti-Vietnam war as well as community-based projects. Then in 1969 the publication of Kate Millett's *Sexual Politics* heralded an onslaught of exciting feminist writing—Shulamith Firestone, Ti-Grace Atkinson, Jill Johnston—all of which spoke to me and my gay male friends. (It was only much later when I realized that what attracted me most about these writings was not only their sense of new community, but that their critique of gender, subtextually, spoke to my disenchantment with being a gay man involved in a mostly heterosexual world.) Being an "intellectual" was not enough. By the time of the Stonewall Riots of that year, and I began attending Gay Liberation Front meetings in Manhattan, it was impossible not to see the world, and my own life, through political eyes.

Gay politics opened the possibilities of uniting my sexual identity with my "intellectual" interests. It was a way to connect with others and gain a new, collective identity. Although I had gay friends, as well as lovers and boyfriends, through college I never really felt part of a broader gay male community and never even went out to bars. While I was fairly open about my gayness—the prevailing hippie ethos of my circle made this possible—I did not really see myself as a member of a defined group with shared political or social interests. There was always the erotic connection to other men, but I had learned as a child to de-emphasize the importance of my sexuality and did not view shared erotic desire as the basis for a community.

Gay liberation spread like prairie fire—college gay groups blossomed across the country within a year of the Stonewall Riots—but the flames seemed to burn particularly bright in Cambridge and Boston. The radical, anarchist *Fag Rag* was one of the first gay liberation newspapers published, there were several gay male living collectives, and Good Gay Poets was sponsoring readings and publishing broadsides. Boston also had a reputation for other political activities—antiwar work, radical feminism, and student activism. The potential for combining gay liberation with these other struggles was exciting and important to someone like me, who was coming out of the New Left, and I moved to Boston in 1971, ostensibly to attend graduate school but determined to pursue my political life.

I was shocked to discover that after gay political meetings in Cambridge everyone would go out cruising in Boston; to the funky, mob-run, Other Side, a drag/dance bar in Bay Village, or to the Victory Gardens in the Fenway for sex under the stars. This didn't happen among my political set in New York. I did not consider myself sexually repressed, but anonymous sex, sex in tea-rooms, at rest stops, in the bushes or in the baths seemed, well, *wrong*—impersonal, objectifying, and certainly not politically correct.

My gay political training had reinforced the idea that our newly emerging political community was distinct from and better than the rest of gay life. Bars, we thought, were oppressive institutions owned by straights, where we were forced to go because of a lack of social options, and queens who frequented bushes and bathhouses were plagued by internalized self-hatred. While these ideas had some truth in them—the social oppression of New York gay life was tremendous during the fifties and sixties— they were inadequate as political theory. And to a large degree my attachment to politics was to political *theory*. Having constructed an intellectual identity that downplayed my sexuality—as well as my gay identity—I began to reinforce it with a politics that did the same thing. Fearful of the intensity of my sexual longings and still wary of being punished if I admitted that being "gay" was about sex and not books or politics, I felt fragmented and even more isolated. Though I had constructed a life that revolved around my identity as a gay man, I refused to admit the importance that sexual desire played in this.

After a few months in Cambridge-Boston political circles, the idea of combining books, politics, and sex began to appeal to me. I came to view myself as part of a diverse gay male community whose life took place in the bars as well as at meetings, at bathhouses as well as protest marches. I began to discard the notion that "gay politics" had little to do with gay life and started enjoying going out to bars, not only to meet sex partners, but just to be in an all-gay environment: Sporters on Beacon Hill with its quirky mixture of postcollegiate and hippie men; 1270, around the corner from the Fenway Victory Gardens, with its upscale disco beat; even the slightly dangerous-feeling Shed complete with a sexually active bathroom. I discovered that I had an affection for all sorts of gay men—men with whom I shared few common interests or politics—based only on the fact that we shared similar erotic desires. It was a period of continually coming out, refining and expanding what it meant for me to be gay: exploring my sexuality and understanding how it affected all of my physical, emotional, and intellectual experiences. After the bars I discovered the joys of cruising the bushes and tearooms and soon it was sex, and a community brought together by a shared sexual desire—not books or politics—on which my identity was based. Sex became a form of political and emotional transcendence—an identity and community that made sense of my life and experience and left the half measures of my earlier life feeling singularly empty and vague.

It was during this time, in this flush of sexual excitement and intellectual enthusiasm, that I felt most happy about living in Cambridge. My past relationship to books and politics seemed impoverished, emotionally bankrupt, and, most of all, lonely. Now fifteen-minute bathroom romances seemed to have the potential to lead to stimulating discussions and friendships, nights in the bar felt like being part of a giving community; it felt all right to be *just* a homosexual. My fragmented identities finally appeared to fit together like a quirky, slightly pornographic puzzle.

Looking back, my love affair with my adopted hometown developed like a bad marriage: incredible expectations, an enticing courtship, a vibrant but short honeymoon, and then considerable trouble in paradise. That first flush of excitement about the ways that the separate parts of my life seemed to be pulling together was more the glimpse of a possibility than an actuality, and I see now that in many ways Cambridge was a hindrance rather than a help in this process. My coming-out quest for psychic freedom that encouraged and fed my fantasy of Cambridge also, ironically, allowed me to leave Cambridge behind.

Books and knowledge, in my mind, have always been associated with intellectual freedom, which in turn has signified sexual freedom. And while this is maybe nonsense, I used to find it a comforting thought. Cambridge, with its myriad bookstores and massive university library collections, gleamed as a beacon after the darkness of my inner-city college days. But although my limited access to the Harvard libraries (as a nonaffiliate I had to sneak in) was an improvement—I certainly could never have found a copy of *The Law and the Lady* back in Newark—sexual freedom was hardly ever the result of intellectual inquiry. If anything the rarefied environment of the university setting seemed to breed and enforce closetedness. Gay writing, publishing, and scholarship were becoming more public and more bold, but you would never know this at Harvard. Even feminist scholarship was viewed with disdain and distrust.

I was shocked to discover how difficult it was for people to be out at Harvard in the seventies. Concerned about social standing, careers, tenure, and future prospects, both students and faculty seemed terrified of life outside the closet. This social, psychological, and emotional repression seemed to spill out of the staid brick-wall boundaries of Harvard Yard and onto the streets. Cambridge back then and even today does not have the same gay street presence, the sheer queer visibility, that Boston does. When

I first moved to Cambridge I was impressed by little things—Reading International or Temple Bar bookstores were likely to carry new gay and lesbian titles from both mainstream and small press publishers—while choosing not to see larger problems. What I, and others, took as an ambiance of freedom in Harvard Square was actually a result of a Brahmin-style emotional repression, which would ignore you rather than cause a scene—not exactly tolerance. It was possible, for instance, to walk through Harvard Square holding hands with your boyfriend without feeling that you were endangering your life. And while this is infinitely better than being queer bashed, we did not seem to realize that the permission to do this came more from our own brazenness than from social acceptances.

The brazenness that came from a newly found, liberating, and exuberant political identity set me and my friends apart not only from the intellectual aspect of Cambridge but also from its established political culture. Cambridge had a long-standing reputation as politically progressive and active from the civil rights organizing of the fifties to the multitude of antiwar groups such as the Indo-China Peace Campaign of the sixties. It was impossible to walk past the Harvard Coop—the center of the Square—without being deluged with political leafleteers, petitioners, or speakers. Even Joan Baez had gotten her start in the (literally) underground folk Club 47 on Mt. Auburn Street. Much of this activity was still happening in the early seventies, but it was clear that no matter how much gay liberation and feminism may have established themselves they were not really accepted as equally important political endeavors. Women were still expected to make the coffee in many progressive groups and any mention of gay liberation was written off by heterosexual males as a sign of pernicious individualism. This was not all that surprising. Gay liberation and feminism were radical breaks from traditional leftist thinking in their insistence that the personal was the political. Their challenging established progressive groups on misogyny and homophobia made few friends. What was surprising, however, at least to me, was how ingrained this hostility became in the alternative cultures that thrived in Cambridge.

I remember being very surprised at the resistance to gay

writing in both the "alternative presses" like *The Real Paper, The Boston Phoenix,* and in local literary magazines. For example, *Ploughshares,* one of the more prestigious of these, would not print any openly gay poems by John Wieners, in spite of his established reputation as a Beat poet. Countercultural yoga and dance classes such as The Joy of Movement actively discouraged men from choosing one another as partners, and alternative theaters had two-for-one couples nights but would refuse to recognize same-sex couples. The list was endless; my sense of isolation became more and more acute.

In the excitement of early gay liberation we had so convinced ourselves of the obvious truth of our politics and feelings that we occasionally became blinded to the harsher realities of the world around us. Of course it was also this fervent belief in ourselves and our lives that led us—forced us—to invent an alternative to that alternative culture: gay poetry readings, literary magazines, and newspapers; gay folk dancing groups; and gay singing groups. And while all of this was, and is, necessary and good, I still feel a lingering resentment, disappointment about having to give up fantasies of unity that Harvard Square seemed to symbolize to me.

My image of Cambridge as an intellectual and political utopia was now demolished, leaving only my sexual paradise to be exposed as a fantasy. Without a large visible gay street presence the eye-contact factor was very low. There were at one time very active bushes along the Charles River next to the Anderson Bridge, but from the early seventies onward these were constantly under siege from both Harvard and the ever-vigilant Metropolitan District Commission, a state agency whose main purpose seems to be to prevent outdoor cruising. After years of pruning, transplanting, and uprooting this sylvan sex spot no longer exists. ZumZum on Brattle Street used to have a very busy bathroom, but the restaurant closed in the late seventies. That left the many Harvard bathrooms—Lamont Library, Paine Hall, Burr Hall, the Science Center, Widener Library. And while these were fun they were also somewhat hazardous, their safety dependent on unpredictable administrative policies.

Beyond problems of finding easy places in which to pick up

men, the problem with much of Cambridge cruising—especially at Harvard—was the uptightness and the closetedness of so many of the men. For every encounter I had with someone like Ian— in which sex might be casual and unencumbered by emotional traumas—there were at least ten that were full of anxiety and fear. Many times the men I would meet in Harvard bathrooms refused to tell me their names or gave obviously false ones or lied about where they lived or attended school. Furtive was clearly the tone, which did not enhance the sex; the situation was frustrating and politically nettling.

And while some Cambridge liberals in the arts and poetry circles gave lip service to pro-gay sentiments, this tolerance was only accorded to those homosexuals who were deemed respectable: no talk of sex, no obvious cruising or queenly mannerisms, and certainly no connection to such activities as tearoom sex, s/m, leather, or drag. Like me in an earlier time, they were only comfortable with a homosexuality that did not exhibit much sexuality.

During the mid to late 1970s I was becoming more and more involved in a gay-centered community. I worked on *Fag Rag* and Good Gay Poets, wrote for *Gay Community News,* helped to found and publish *Boston Gay Review,* in part because I discovered that you could never count on either mainstream or counterculture establishments to help promote gay and lesbian causes, but also because working with other gay men and lesbians was an end—political, emotional, and psychological—in itself. So much of my early attachment to books and "knowledge" had been a way to avoid dealing with the importance of my sexuality in my life, to isolate it in a dim corner where it would not attract much attention. And while my political leanings were at first coalition-oriented I soon discovered that you can only build coalitions with those who want to work with you. I also discovered that a politics that did not address sexuality and gender was not very useful to me and that my early willingness to avoid those questions came from an unwillingness to explore seriously my own sexuality.

Looking over the last twenty years I see that my early fantasy of Cambridge as a paradise and haven of safety was based on many factors. It was better than where I came from—there is more of an intellectual and political atmosphere than the New Jersey suburbs or downtown Newark—and whatever its failings it is an easier place to be gay. But the fantasy was predicated on sidestepping the centrality of my sexuality—my gayness. I don't mean to shoulder some huge metaphysical blame here. I am a product of my time, and my growth as a person is inextricably bound to the growth of the gay liberation movement. What was most comforting about my fantasy was its suspension in time. The Cambridge of my mind was untouched by the reality of everyday life: its knowledge was contained neatly in books lined up on the shelves of bookstores and libraries, its politics were set in the not-long-ago but somehow nostalgic sixties (as opposed to the real-life ones) when the difference between right and wrong seemed less complicated and Joan Baez held all of the answers in her pure soprano, and its sexuality was simple erotic attraction devoid of human complications or disease.

Over the years I have made discoveries about myself that have transformed who I am and how I see the world. The adventure in sexuality I used to find in novels I am now more likely to find in my own life. My sexual desires are also less separated from my political identity than they were twenty years ago, making life clearer and less conflicted. In many ways I have outgrown the need that I had for the fantasy of Cambridge. I still go to Harvard Square, although it has grown in many unlikable ways: there are no cheap restaurants like Cardell's where customers— from distressed Cantabridgian gentlewomen to bearded anarchists reading Berkman's *Prison Memoirs*—could sit next to one another lingering over another cup of coffee; many independent bookstores have been taken over by chains like Wordsworth, which do not stock small press titles; and even its street population seems to be made of kids from the suburbs more interested in shopping for trends than inventing them, like the hippies of two decades ago. Although much of what I wanted from Harvard Square was based on a fantasy, it was a fantasy led on by a reality that prized, if it did not promote, individuality. That is not true anymore.

Now I walk through the Square with clear eyes and little longing for what I used to hope I'd find there. However I do feel some nostalgia for wonderful moments like walking across Mass Ave with Ian, his smell still on my face and hands, looking forward to coffee and talk at a café. Moments when it seemed as though everything might be possible. However, such possibilities exist not in geography but in the heart and mind.

CHRISTOPHER BRAM

PERRY STREET, GREENWICH VILLAGE

I'M OUT ON THE FRONT stoop early one evening, talking with our neighbor Cook while I wait for Draper to get home from work. We're continuing an old argument about gay sensibility, something Cook believes all gay men share and I doubt even exists. "If there's a scene in a movie with a lamp in it," says Cook, "a gay man will notice that lamp where a straight man won't." I disagree, citing as evidence two recent conversations about *Vertigo.* The film has an inquest scene where everyone wears suits of the same peculiar shade of phosphorescent blue; nothing in Hitchcock is accidental and it's a puzzling detail. When Draper and I mentioned the suits afterward to the friend who saw the movie with us, that observant gay man said, "What suits?" When I talked about the movie a few days later at the bookstore where I worked, a straight man who'd seen it excitedly asked, "And how about that scene with the weird blue suits?" Cook patiently hears me out, frowns, and says, "I dunno. It'd mean what you think it means if it'd been lamps. Suits are an entirely different animal. Just how straight is this straight man anyway?"

On another night, Draper and I sit on the stoop after dinner, delaying the moment when we climb the five flights to our hot, airless apartment. A man hurries past, then doubles back to ask us something. He's four feet tall, built like a muscular fire hydrant, and grinning with a jumbled mouthful of crooked teeth. His mind races ahead of him on amphetamines. In the course of asking directions to Greenwich Street, he tells us about his happy childhood, unhappy adolescence, battles with a conventional-sized father, and a brief career in midget wrestling that ended when the manager skipped town and stranded the troupe in Florida. "Love to chat, love to jaw with you guys, but I got a hot date and I'm late already, three days late because I had to go to the bank and the cash machine said my mama's check hadn't cleared and I love my mama but her second husband lives out at the track and . . ." He's already halfway down the block, continuing the conversation without us.

Or, on yet another night, very late, I sit alone on the stoop in shorts and black socks, reading tomorrow's *New York Times*. A few cars are backed up at the traffic light in the narrow street. The smoked window of a long limousine suddenly whirs down. "Hey, buddy! Buddy?" A hand comes out of the shadows to point disapprovingly at my feet. *"White* socks. Okay?" The window whirs shut, the light turns green, the limo drives away.

And so on. Most of my neighborhood life seems to take place on the front stoop of our building.

We live in Manhattan, in West Greenwich Village on a side street fifty yards off one of the main avenues. New York City for many people is not so much a place as an abstraction, a frenzied state of mind, an intersection of fast lanes. Home is just a room where you keep your answering machine and go to sleep, a space as private as sleep, often stacked in high-rises with a hundred other private sleeps. You'd go crazy knowing everybody who lives around you, so many New Yorkers prudently screen most of their neighbors out. But there are still real neighborhoods here and there, side streets off the fast lanes. Draper and I have lived here for eleven years. And our building has a stoop.

Seven brown-painted concrete steps climb from a cramped sidewalk to a vestibule full of mailboxes and buzzers. Flanking the steps are two fat concrete walls the color of old chewing gum. The cement flower boxes at the tops of the walls are filled with candy wrappers in the winter and petunias in the spring, diligently tended by our neighbor Peggy and her nine-year-old daughter, Regina. Above the door, caked in flaking nicotine paint, is a droopy stone face with deep-set eyes and a droopy moustache and, above that, the ubiquitous iron zigzag of a fire escape. A five-floor walk-up with sixteen apartments, our building was constructed in 1899, one year after the Spanish-American War and a year before the death of Oscar Wilde. Across the street are older, smaller brick town houses, very neat and pretty between their cast-iron gates and Federal cornices. There's a similar set of town houses to the left on our side of the street, thick oak doors shaded by ginkgo trees whose trunks are protected by iron cages. We're probably the ugliest building on the block, but we don't have to look at ourselves when we're on our stoop.

"You got a minute?" asks Cook when I come out and find him sitting there in a Hawaiian shirt, menthol cigarette in one hand, his walking cane hooked over the handrail. "I want to get your opinion on this movie I saw on cable last night—"

Conversation begins with movies, but goes on to political affairs or affairs of the heart or Judyism (Cook doesn't try to convert me to Judy Garland, only explain her cultural importance) or the old Pogo comic strips.

It's chiefly because of Cook and Fred that our stoop is a social institution. I like to think Draper and I helped initiate it, two transplanted Southerners using the front steps as a Yankee equivalent of sociable porches and patios back home. But it's Cook who provides the continuity. He lives on the first floor and the stoop is right outside his door. His narrow apartment is packed with knickknacks, posters, videotapes, books, a ceramic parrot on a perch, all kinds of ashtrays and over four thousand long-playing records alphabetized by artist—Cook likes music. When he needs a little room to breathe, Cook goes out on the stoop. He knows everybody in the building and half the people in the neighborhood. Those who might be intimidated by Cook's forwardness or strange green eyes (contact lenses, although no-body's supposed to know) are put at ease by Fred. Fred is Cook's dog, a friendly mixture of collie and harp seal with a white face, short snout, and bushy copper coat.

"Sweet dog," say perfect strangers as they walk by and see Fred grinning behind Cook. "You wouldn't say that if you had to live with him," Cook replies. Many stop to pet Fred. By the time they leave they've gotten to know Cook.

Cook is a real New Yorker, Brooklyn-bred and born, still lean and quirkily handsome after turning forty. When we first met him, he was a social worker, a city employee who worked with the mentally retarded. He visited families in the outer bor-oughs, counseling parents, arranging health care and schooling and, sometimes, institutionalization. Cook threw himself com-pletely into his job, even taking kids without families home to his mother's in Brooklyn on holidays. This was before multiple sclerosis tore up his nervous system and damaged his coordina-tion. The MS seems to have stabilized, but Cook walks with a cane now and tires easily. Although he had to leave his job nine years ago, he remains ferociously social. He founded EDGE, Ed-ucation for a Disabled Gay Environment, a group for lesbians and gay men with physical disabilities, founded the organization because he suddenly wanted to join such a group and discovered no such thing existed. Betrayed by his body, he's more spirited than ever. Cook can get irritable, especially in hot weather when his muscles give out, but I've never heard a word of self-pity from him. He remains stubbornly independent.

One Sunday afternoon, a bedroom-eyed blond chats with Cook for five minutes, then moves on without Cook introducing us. "Who was that?" I ask.

"Crip queen," Cook says contemptuously. "The creep has a fetish for handicaps. He's sleeping his way through EDGE, and I refuse to be another notch on his bedpost. People sleep with me for my sparkling personality," Cook declares, prettily batting his eyes. "Or they don't lay a fucking hand on me."

We're sometimes joined on the stoop by Sam, a large yet graceful man who lives on our floor. Draper calls him Sam the Adult, to distinguish him from Sam the Baby, the two-year-old on the third floor. Sam the Adult smiles a lot with his gopher teeth and walrus moustache, but rarely says much unless the subject is dogs. Sam is enormously sentimental about dogs, far more than Cook. He owns a frisky white mutt named Blanca and is very good friends with Linda, the equally sentimental dog owner who lives downstairs from him. Linda was so devoted to her ancient German shepherd she continued to coax and plead the poor rubber-legged beast up and down the stairs twice a day long after anyone else would've had the animal put to sleep. Linda is quite old herself, a fact we frequently forget because of her energetic chirp and apparent alertness. She has a petite body and a large head of ghost-white hair. When her dog finally passed away one night on her kitchen floor, it was Sam who carried the bulky animal downstairs in his arms and rode in a cab with Linda to the veterinarian, indulging her insistence they get an expert opinion before admitting the dog was dead. "Poor Linda," Sam sighed afterward. "I know just how she feels. You think a dog is forever. Unlike a man."

Straight people are still the majority in the West Village, although just barely. Our landlord is gay, a retired New York City cop who divorced his wife after leaving the force and went at his new life with the fervor of a teenager fresh off the bus. "You *are* one of us?" he proudly asked the first time Draper spoke to him on the phone, about a leak in the roof. Our mailman is gay, I think (he's certainly friendly enough). Most of the people who join us on the stoop are gay, except for Ricki, who lives in the basement with her boyfriend, and Bill.

Bill is Peggy's husband and Regina's father, the family down the hall from me and Draper. Eleven years ago, Bill and Peggy were a bohemian couple, from two different bohemias. A balding, round-faced man with a goatee and motorcycle, Bill was a throwback to the Greenwich Village of the early sixties, coffeehouses and abstract expressionists and folksinging in Washington Square; he supported himself driving a cab. Peggy, with a mimosa stripe of pink in her hair, seemed positively New Wave, all anomie and intellectual paranoia. Everything changed when Regina was born. Bill sold his motorcycle and Peggy became a dedicated Greenwich Village mother, wearing the role like a suit of armor. "We're visiting Regina's friend in Staten Island," she'd tell us on their way out, suggesting her only social life now was her baby daughter's. We've seen Regina grow from a curious infant to a painfully shy toddler to an impossibly arrogant little girl who tromps through us on the stoop in roller skates as if we weren't there. "Regina, don't walk on people," Peggy says indifferently and continues to water the petunias.

Bill, however, remains friendly and interesting. He started law school a few years ago but has kept his cabbie's gift for gab. He has street-smart opinions on everything under the sun, from the politics of dumdum bullets to the old Cinema 16 underground movie circuit. "Did I hear someone say *Jackson Pollock?*" he asks when he comes up and hears us talking about a recent biography. "That takes me back to days of yore." And he smiles, puffs up his chest, and delivers a well-informed verdict on action painting. As the oldest married straight man in the building, Bill often plays the role of being everyone's smarter, more practical big brother. If the subjects turns to anything gay, he politely listens a moment before excusing himself with, "Well, gentlemen. Time to trudge up to the wife and family."

Two muscular boys sashay past in those black Spandex bicycling shorts that suggest old-time prostitutes in garter belts and hose. All heads turn, but the conversation about "Outweek" and outing continues without missing a beat. Attractive men walk by every hour of the day. A particularly striking one might elicit, "Hmmm?" from someone, followed by Cook going, "Nyaah," but further comment would be superfluous.

I hate to admit it, but, when I first moved in with Draper, I was uncomfortable with the prominent numbers of obviously gay men on the street down here. My discomfort was not because of anything like self-hatred or even temptation. It was the unrealness of the situation, the fact that something once secret and rare could become as natural and commonplace as bread. It's not a normal situation, although it should be. I can flip through *Torso* or *Mandate* at the local newsstand (for the book reviews, honest) without fear of a snicker or slur from the Yemenite cousins who own the place. If I run into Draper on his way out and my way in and we exchange a kiss on the stoop, the only reaction we might get is Bill glancing skyward or Sam saying, "Isn't that nice?" suddenly as sentimental about us as he is about dogs. There's safety in numbers, and there's the safety that comes of custom. Surrounded by openly gay men and women, straight neighbors take homosexuality for granted and notice only if you're a good neighbor (quiet) or a bad one (noisy). What you do in the privacy of your bedroom is of no interest to anyone else, so long as the bass on your stereo is not turned up too high.

Well, no. Not even the West Village is quite as Arcadian as that. Our neighbors are fine. Visitors can be a problem, especially teenaged boys from Long Island or New Jersey who think the city is a jungle where anything goes. It's homophobia's trickle-down effect, beginning in smug moral pronouncements by clergymen and politicians and ending in insults and sometimes beer cans thrown from car windows late at night. It trickles down even to street people, who've become more numerous on our block over the past two years. Actually, most of the homeless are as indifferent to sexual persuasion as our neighbors with homes, and many are gay themselves. But now and then one sees an angry man scuffing down the sidewalk, muttering, "You faggots make me sick, you faggots make me sick," over and over. Unemployed and homeless, insane or addicted, he must know he's at the bottom of things. But he furiously insists there's someone he can look down on, too.

Other New Yorkers often dismiss the West Village as quaint and unreal, as if familiarity and tolerance were less real than anonymity and threat. Nevertheless, so-called real life comes here, too. There was a crack house on our street, eventually shut down by the police with the neighborhood's cooperation. Not even crack drove us from the stoop, only made us more careful about the strangers we talked to. Our building's garbage cans stand on the sidewalk beside the stoop and conversation is occasionally accompanied by the clink of bottles being sorted into a homeless man's grocery cart. These deposit collectors are too proud to ask for money, although they do sometimes ask for a cigarette.

Draper and I are sitting out front one afternoon with Ricki, who was the building's super before her career as a stage manager took off. A woman with a great swoop of hair above her dirty face stops in front of us, stares at Ricki, and hisses, "You horny little girl! One man isn't enough for you, huh?" Ricki throws her arms around our shoulders and says, "No and it's great!" But the woman has already stomped off to bless out two ten-year-old boys swapping comic books on another stoop down the street. A few days later, I see the woman again, sitting on the pavement outside the Yemenite newsstand, her shirt off and her arms folded over her breasts. "Go ahead and stare!" she screams at passersby. "You perverts! You animals!" A week after that, I spot her shouting at a perplexed Labrador retriever whose leash is tied to a parking meter outside a coffee shop. "You stupid animal! You think you're so smart!"

In such a world, the gender preferences of one's neighbors seem like very small potatoes.

People from other buildings in the neighborhood often stop to talk with us on the stoop. Muriel Spark, author of *The Prime of Miss Jean Brodie,* owns a co-op in the new brick monstrosity on the corner. She's never sat with us (I wouldn't know her if she bit me), but we are joined by Michael, who works with SAGE at the Lesbian and Gay Community Center a few blocks away. Michael brings us the world of gay bureaucratic squabbles. Then there's Jim from around the corner, a veteran of the old Gay Activist Alliance who remains politically active and savvy, always good for an angle on the news one hasn't heard yet. And there's Tom from next door, an actor and singer who used to perform in children's theater. Now he gives most of his time and energy to the Community Research Initiative, doing staff work for a group of doctors who study alternative AIDS treatments.

"That was a terrific speech you gave at the fund-raiser on Sunday," I tell Tom.

Tom grins sheepishly. "You were there? I'm surprised at all the people I know who showed up. Was a good turnout, wasn't it?"

"Tom gave a speech?" asks Cook.

"Yeah, weelll—" Tom hums and screws up his face in a self-deprecating squinch. "They needed *somebody* from CRI, and old ham that I am . . ."

Much of the talk on the stoop turns around gay politics and

the politics of AIDS. Except for Jim, we're not a particularly political bunch, or wouldn't be under normal circumstances. I know Cook would rather discuss the joys of "Be My Baby" by the Ronettes than fume over the latest fatuous statement by John Cardinal O'Connor, but the cardinal's influence is too dangerous to ignore. Draper would prefer to talk about Bertolucci's forthcoming movie than GLAAD's antiviolence tape, but the tape moved him so much he sent a copy to a friend in Helsinki, who translated and played it on Finnish radio. Tom would rather be a singing cat in a community production of *Pinocchio* than pour over abstracts of AIDS articles in *The New England Journal of Medicine,* but AIDS has become an undeniable part of Tom's life.

Tom's lover died of AIDS two years ago. It was through Stephen, a biochemist, that Tom originally became involved with the Community Research Initiative. And Tom is a PWA himself. He just got out of the hospital again and this week had a catheter lock implanted in his arm for the intravenous treatments he administers to himself. The other day he matter-of-factly explained to me how the lock works, a chemical in a circuit of tube preventing the blood from coagulating over the puncture. We regularly exchange hopes and skepticisms about news in the *Times,* *New York Native,* and *Village Voice.* Within a week after coming home from the hospital, Tom resumed going to the CRI offices for meetings. Cook, who has no pity for himself, thinks Tom has a right to some self-pity and can't understand why he won't indulge, just a little. I feel awed and shamed by both of them.

Journalists with a melodramatic bent describe the West Village in the age of AIDS as "devastated" and "the killing fields." A young writer who should have known better did a piece about walking his dog in a gay ghost town. The West Village isn't any of those things. Gay life goes on, everyday and commonplace life. Attractive men still notice each other on the street, although they're not as quick to go home together as they once were; there's more conversation nowadays, more flirtation. On our stoop, we continue to talk about old movies and Motown's greatest hits, but we also talk about AIDS and politics. We run into each other at memorial services (Stephen's was in a chapel one block away) and protest rallies. I was startled to realize how much "in the

life" I am, and how political that life has become, when I went
to a mammoth ACT UP demonstration at city hall last year and
could not turn around without seeing someone I knew among the
protesters circling the park in an endless conga line of chanters
and placards. Squads of mounted police covered the approaches
to the Brooklyn Bridge in the distance, epic and ominous in the
hazy morning light, but up close all I saw were friends and neighbors.

I don't know how much thought my straight neighbors give
to AIDS. The young couples appear well-informed and somewhat
concerned. The older people seem to block the topic completely
from their minds. The sentiment of "Love thy neighbor" is not
as effective in keeping the peace as that other American adage,
"Mind your own business," which means tolerance sometimes
shades into a careful indifference. In our building, twenty-three
very different people live over a plot of ground that might be
enough for a single nuclear family in the suburbs. A hundred
different wars, some more private than others, take place simultaneously here. We don't share the same wars. We don't even
watch the same TV shows. Although recently, when Wagner's
Ring was televised over four nights, I was amazed to come up the
stairs the first night and hear the muffled sound of *Das Rheingold*
on each and every floor. Behind Cook's door Judy Garland sang
a duet with Mickey Rooney, but everyone else seemed to be trying
a taste of Wagner. It was both comic and spooky. By the last
night, *Götterdämmerung* was heard only on the third and fifth floors,
but for a few hours the entire building finally had something in
common.

Actually, there was one other shared experience, an incident
that involved more of us than anything else that's happened here.
I have to change details and the identity of one of the participants
so nobody will get in trouble, but the spirit of the story is true.

Linda, the cheerful white-haired woman who lost her German shepherd, lived on the third floor. A nephew sometimes
stayed with her, a gaunt, morose fellow who wore eyeglasses as
thick as his aunt's. Linda was alone one evening when a lamp in
her bedroom shorted out, starting a fire in the bed that sat on
the wiring. Filling a pan with water, Linda quickly extinguished

the fire herself. She thought she extinguished it anyway. The short had blown a fuse and her lights were out. It was getting dark, but Linda expected her nephew that evening and did not want to trouble her neighbors. She sat there in the dark with her two cats and patiently waited for the nephew to arrive.

Draper and I smelled smoke in the halls when we went out for dinner. We passed Peggy coming up the stairs from Linda's floor. Ever since she became a mother, Peggy has been keenly alert to every sinister noise or smell in the building. "I just checked," she told us. "Linda said she burned something, but everything's okay."

When Sam came home a half hour later, there was still smoke in the hall. He knocked on Linda's door and asked if she were all right. "Everything's fine, thank you," Linda called through the closed door. Sam went upstairs.

When Draper and I returned from dinner, the smoke still lingered, a smell of burnt protein, like meat. The ventilation in all the kitchens is bad; we know every night exactly what our downstairs neighbors are having for dinner. Mildly nervous, yet familiar with the building's idiosyncrasies and ashamed of our nervousness, we settled down in our apartment to watch television.

It was Bill, the ex-cab driver, the building's know-it-all big brother, who finally did something. He went down to Linda's and banged furiously on her door.

"Sorry if I alarmed anyone," Linda called out. "But everything's fine now."

"Everything is *not* fine!" Bill declared. "The hall's been full of smoke for two hours. Let me in right this minute."

She guiltily opened the door and Bill saw the pitch-black apartment. In the light from the hall, he saw the thin haze of smoke inside, then the blackened mattress.

"Jesus, Mary, and Joseph!"

"I put it out with a pan of water," Linda explained.

"The hell you did! The wadding in these things burns forever. Can't you see? It's still burning!"

We heard Bill shouting in the stairwell. Then the smell of smoke was suddenly very strong. We ran out to the hall, looked over the rail, and saw Bill and Sam dragging a smoking, blackened mattress down the stairs. The mattress left a trail of smeared ashes on the steps and landings, and flakes of charred cloth like black leaves.

Nobody called the fire department. The fire was all in the bed and everyone agreed the water damage would be far worse than a stink of smoke in the halls. More important, if the fire department were called in, then the landlord would learn what had happened. The consensus, gay and straight, is that Danny's a decent fellow, but he's still a landlord.

"I'm not saying he'd actually do it," Bill argued when he and Sam returned from the street. "But I wouldn't put it past Danny to evict Linda for this stunt, saying she's too senile to stay here, that she's a hazard to his tenants. And it would give him one more rent-controlled apartment he could put on the open market."

Almost immediately, Sam was out on the stairs with a broom, sweeping up all evidence of fire, Draper following him with a dustpan and trash bag. Bill and I hunted inside Linda's apartment with flashlights, looking for her fuse box. Linda couldn't remember where it was and suggested we call the electrician who installed the outside line for her air conditioner. Hearing her air conditioner was on a different circuit, I plugged a lamp into that outlet and we suddenly had light.

"Oh Jesus," groaned Bill. "Will you look at this?"

We almost never see the insides of each other's apartments. Linda's was full of stacked newspapers and magazines, collapsed piles that shingled her floor with paper. The windows were shut tight to keep her cats from getting out; one cat shyly watched us from under a sofa heaped with health brochures. Linda stood by the sink, not in the slightest bit upset or frightened, her eyeglasses slightly askew.

Bill kept his temper. "I don't know if you realize it, Linda. But I just saved your life," he sternly told her. "With that mattress still going and your windows shut, you would've died of asphyxiation if I hadn't come when I did. I don't even want to think about what might've happened next."

The box spring the mattress sat on was charred on one side.

I touched it and felt heat, a slow burning in the wooden frame. Bill and I carried the box spring downstairs to the street.

"I got my wife and daughter to think about," Bill said as we maneuvered down the corkscrew of stairs. "But I don't want to see that little old lady evicted either. If she were thrown out on the street, she'd end up homeless, I know she would. We're going to have to work out something with her nephew."

We set the box spring outside on the curb next to the mattress. The mattress continued to smolder, a smoking slab of springs and stuffing. At that moment, Cook came hopping up the sidewalk on his cane, coming home from a meeting at the Center. "Ohhh shit," he said. "Who's gone and done what now?"

Bill returned upstairs and I told Cook what happened. "That Linda," Cook sighed and filled pots of water at his sink which I carried outside to douse the mattress and box spring. Bill was right: beds burn forever.

Sam and Draper came out the door, sweeping the last of the ashes in front of them. We all stood on the stoop, looking down at the scorched bed in the gutter. "Looks like somebody still has hot sex," Cook muttered, then twitched his eyebrows wickedly and added, "I didn't really say that."

We disposed of the extinguished mattress and box spring that night. An electrician came the next day and made Linda's wiring safe again. Her nephew bundled up the newspapers and magazines and cleaned out the apartment. This all happened several years ago and Linda was not evicted, our building has not burned down.

OKEMOS, MICHIGAN

WE WERE JUST LOOKING—
that's all I had agreed to.

Five years ago, I had reluctantly said I would "look," after
Gersh, my life partner, had called while I was at a conference in
San Francisco. He told me that we should buy a house in Okemos
(where we had separate apartments) instead of trying to rent one,
because there weren't many rentals available in Okemos just then.
I felt both sick and stunned at the idea of owning a house, let
alone our actually living together, and the day after he called, I
came down with the flu.

I had grown up in Washington Heights, that hilly and park-
filled upper Manhattan neighborhood as remote to many New
Yorkers as Riverdale or even Albany, though it's now infamous
for the cocaine sales and murders scarring its Depression-era
buildings and shaded boulevards. Back then, I thought of houses
as completely alien, out in the suburbs, something to visit or
drive by. And I pictured them as negatively as Birkin did in

Women in Love: " 'The world all in couples, each in its own little house, watching its own little interests, and stewing in its own little privacy—it's the most repulsive thing on earth.' "

But Indian Hills, the Okemos subdivision in which we saw our third house one sunny May morning, was not at all repulsive. It is an oak-lined neighborhood of about two hundred houses, a few miles from Michigan State University in East Lansing, with curving streets; old blue spruce, maples, scotch pines, towering arbor vitae, weeping willows, and magnolias; overgrown yew hedges and shrubs; lots of nearly an acre; and thirty- or forty-year-old houses set well back from the road. There are some large homes, but this is not the wealthiest part of a prosperous and stoutly Republican suburb studded with Michigan State faculty members, but dominated by Lansing-area professionals whose wives wear mink and drive Cutlass Cierras, Jaguars, and the occasional Porsche. The houses in Indian Hills are not at all pretentious, like the newer, Tudoresque ones in nearby subdivisions that dwarf their tiny lots with only a scrap of yard.

Indian Hills is even more appealing given that a few minutes away you could be in any featureless part of the homogenized Midwest, swamped by malls and minimalls, wholesale outlets, fast-food and video encampments, and grim acres of parking lots. Best of all, the day we saw our house, we drove off East Lansing's and Okemos' main street, Grand River Avenue, to cross a narrow bridge into the subdivision. The road curved around a golf course, which was studded with groups of shirtless hunky young men as picturesque as baby lambs on an English lord's estate. "Beautiful," I murmured. And it all was, though the four-bedroom house we stopped at looked like a simple ranch-style house from outside. It was fronted at the street by a ginkgo tree—which I recognized from its fan-shaped leaves because one had grown in the park near my elementary school in Inwood. Finding the ginkgo and having crossed the bridge made me feel I had entered some childhood fantasy.

Up near the house was an enormous flowering tree in full bloom, whose wide-spreading boughs started from just a few feet above the ground; the blossoms were pink, edged with white. I discovered it was a hawthorn, the first one I had ever had named for me, and so, like a child learning the word for *table,* I felt suddenly possessed of mysterious but useful information.

Years before this morning, in New York, I had gone apartment hunting with my best friend Kris, and we unexpectedly and angrily fled from one with a sumptuous view of the Hudson because the apartment made us feel very anxious. "This is an *awful* place," my friend said, confused by the intensity of her feeling. "Something *terrible* happened there!" It *did* feel awful, almost possessed, but this house on Chippewa Drive felt welcoming and warm. From a brick-walled vestibule, we stepped into a large open living room–dining room (the "great room") with a stone fireplace at one end. The long wall with large windows facing the back was not parallel with the one opposite it, nor was one in the dining area—somehow these anomalies were delightful. My partner and I looked at each other, and kept looking as we moved through the house, which was bigger and deeper than it had seemed from the street, and far more beautiful. The colors throughout were royal blue, maroon, beige, and orange, and kept appearing in varying combinations in shades, curtains, custom-made rugs. Our tiny, tipsy-sounding realtor with big hair explained it was a red-ribbon house—you could move right in without having to change or prepare anything. That expression made me think of a contest capped by prizes and applause.

Each room drew us into the next. Details kept bursting on us like fireworks: the Italian tiles in the kitchen, exquisite fabric on the living-room walls, honey-colored pine in the room I knew would be my study because it faced that glorious hawthorn in the front yard. We were falling in love not just with the house, but with the idea of ourselves there, with the idea of a home. We fit in. We looked at it twice more that day, brought Gersh's two sons over to see what they thought (since they would be spending about half of their time with us), we looked at each other and said yes, and we made our offer that evening.

Gersh had wanted to live with me for years, but I had never believed it was possible—not because I doubted that gay men could live loving and happy lives together, but partly because Michigan, and more particularly the East Lansing area, had already become my home as an outwardly straight man, and I was unprepared to make the shift, to emerge, to give up my anonymity. I had come to Michigan in 1981 to do a doctorate, but really to escape my family, and more important, to escape New York. It was a city I no longer had the courage or patience to live in: dirtier, noisier, more crowded and dangerous than the city I had thought was the center of the universe when I was growing up. Two and a half years in bucolic Amherst, Massachusetts, had shown me I could flourish outside of New York.

I fell in love with Michigan when I got here, exploring MSU's lush and spreading campus, traveling around the state with its more than three thousand miles of shoreline, up to Hemingway country, to Lake Michigan, Lake Huron, the Keewenau Peninsula, crossing the Mackinac Bridge at sunset. Life seemed simpler here, less oppressive, more inviting; like Jodi Mitchell's free man in Paris, here in Michigan, "I felt unfettered and alive." Of course, being a graduate student is a strange mix in which the elements of slavery are often masked by romanticism, but even as I was finishing my degree, I knew that I would want to stay here: people were friendlier, without the walls that any city demanded for survival. And most important, I could write here. In the mid-eighties, I had finally begun to feel that I had a career as a writer, and an audience.

Gersh was also a transplanted New Yorker (we had even gone to the same high school ten years apart) and felt about Michigan as I did. But having already made his great plunge into the future through divorce, he was ready and eager for a complete life together. The most I had previously agreed to was getting an apartment in the same complex that he lived in. No one would see us, I thought. And here was the other side of living where we did: visibility. There were no crowds to lose yourself in. So this sudden about-face, the abruptness of my decision to say yes to the house, to our living together, was all the more astonishing.

When we finally moved into the house, I was paranoid about being observed every time we were out in the enormous backyard with its two sassafras trees, maples, and oaks, or trimming hedges in the front, or even walking to the front door with groceries. In New York, neighbors had seemed tamer, less threatening, even though they were sometimes just on the other side of a wall. You chatted with them in elevators or lobbies, at the mailboxes, but their scrutiny was something I rarely thought of. Here, I felt exposed and vulnerable, and it didn't help that every year when Gay Pride day came along, letters in MSU's student newspaper and the Lansing State Journal condemned homosexuality with unswerving hatred that masked itself as Christian love and salvation. My partner tried to calm my anxieties with jokes, but it turned out that I was right. We *were* being watched, though not in the way I had imagined.

As we began shaping the house to become our own, we started a series of changes that kept escalating like those series of five-year plans in the Soviet Union. After fruitless attempts to trim back the overgrown yews that were at practically every corner of the house, we started having them removed. Then we began replanting. My world expanded as we became habitués of local greenhouses and entered a community of gardeners. Each conversation I had about soil conditions, sunlight, pests, drought stress, winter kill marked how different this world was for me. I began to worry about how certain shrubs were doing, consulting books and experts, and plants became a permanent and enjoyable part of my conversation as I began to feel at home with them, and with the soil under my fingernails after an afternoon of planting.

The new and more interesting evergreens we planted at the front of the house, under the study window in a raised, stone-edged bed, got our neighbors' attention. On either side of us and across the street lived elderly men and women, and all remarked on how well we were taking care of the house, especially that we were raking the leaves in the fall and not letting them scatter onto someone else's lawn. The lawn itself was a frequent subject of conversation. The previous owners had left it alone, which meant in the summer it was seared, thin, brown, and the rest of the year not much better, but we hired a lawn-care firm and then installed an underground sprinkling system. People walking by on a nice day, from several streets over, would remark on the lovely changes in the property. They had been watching. And I realized I did the same. As we drove into or out of Indian Hills, I found myself intensely aware of changes in people's yards, new plantings, problems with a tree or shrub, remodeling. I was becoming deeply connected to this place.

We also began changes in the house itself. And each alteration, however minor, had the effect of making me feel more stable, more rooted, more secure—whether it was new locks, a French door between the vestibule and the living room, and ultimately an entirely remodeled master bathroom and a new roof. All of this was as exciting as working outdoors on the trees and shrubs because I had always lived in rental apartments, which stayed quintessentially the same no matter how creatively I moved my furniture around.

The greatest change was adding a deck onto what had been a scruffy screened porch and having the porch itself enclosed and heated and made into a sun room. The large windows let in the outside but also made the house more open. I was growing less afraid of that, after we had taken out the ugly chain-link fence the previous owners kept because of their dogs. This was a profound new reality for me. In just two years we had stripped the house bare of its ugly, obscuring yews, and opened up the backyard to the unexpected: a dog wandering through, utility repairmen up on their poles, the glances of strangers in other yards.

This was *my* house. I could do what I wanted. I could be what I wanted. If we hugged or held hands on the deck, it was our business and no one else's. Owning a house and creating a home had this entirely unexpected effect: it made me gradually more proud, aggressive, more determined to be out, to overcome the years of silence and lies. I see now that living in an apartment, or even renting a home would have continued the climate of hiding because the front door opens into transience. Here, I felt committed to living in this place, to voting for a board of supervisors that would slow the rate of growth in our township, to signing petitions about road closures or recycling, to writing letters to local officials so that my voice would be heard. I cared about the environment in this beautiful neighborhood—so quiet you could always hear the mourning doves—in ways I never could have in New York because someone else would be responsible there, surely.

If I had previously felt suspicious and even hostile toward

the idea of living in a house, perhaps part of my distance was the inevitable image of children. With only a few isolated moments of longing, I had never wanted to be a father, but that's what I became when we moved in together, because Gersh shared custody with his ex-wife, who lives a few minutes away. He was determined to stay in Okemos after his divorce, so that he could be near his two boys, and so that they could easily travel to and from school from either parent's home with minimum disruption. Both boys knew me and seemed to like me, but the bonds that developed between us were as powerful as my connection to the physical in my environment. In the last four years, my sense of time has shifted radically, and I am much more attuned to the seasons, as well as to the stages of a life. I eagerly note the first crocuses of spring and feel comforted by the smell of burning leaves in the fall, just as I am aware of the boys getting taller, filling out, leaving the whining of childhood behind for the testing of adolescence.

It was David, the eldest, who at fourteen started talking about doing things "as a family"—a term that Gersh and I were determined not to force on them. David wanted to go out to eat, all four of us, and to play board games and card games, especially ones he was good at. Many nights we played hours of hearts, and like any family, each game recalled wild jokes and terrific plays of previous games. It was clear to me that we were all building a history together.

Gradually, I was drawn into the boys' lives, and have become an acknowledged "third parent" for them. It started with my helping with their homework, especially their writing assignments, and then running errands for them or with them—to their mother's house, to the mall, into town, to a friend's, or just going for a ride. Having two adults in the house made scheduling a lot easier for Gersh, because he didn't have to be the only one the kids relied on. The "backup" has been particularly valuable when there have been family arguments, because we can then break down into teams and someone always seems to be reasonable and in control, able to act as a sounding board.

Each year has brought new levels of closeness—like David telling me things he asked me not to share with his father, or coming in after school and chatting about his day. He has told us that those chats have been the high point of each day, a chance for the two of us to get to know each other outside of the constraints of the group. Aaron, the younger son, and I have gone out by ourselves to see movies or shop, and my feelings for the boys have been a surprise. Talking to people who don't know me, I often reply to a comment about their children with, "Yes, my son does that too." The first time I mentioned this to the boys, they seemed very pleased. They can't have been too surprised, because we've all shared a great deal in the last four years. We have season tickets for the football team, and even went out to the Rose Bowl in 1988 when Michigan State was the Big Ten Champion (and we beat USC!). We have also taken short trips together, seen rock concerts and musicals at MSU's concert hall.

Having two children living with us, and feeling ourselves a family, has unexpectedly helped ground me in the reality of my own identity as a gay man. I have found myself explaining news items to the kids about gay rights, sharing my outrage over Jesse Helms and other troglodytes, letting them, in other words, know what moves and alarms me. I am a news addict, and both boys have become used to watching the evening news and talking about it, asking questions. Living with people who love me has had the effect of making my freedom at home more precious, and the public opprobrium gays and lesbians deal with every day more pernicious. Gersh and I are not shy about being affectionate with each other, nor do we keep our involvement in gay causes secret. If anything, we have been convinced that modeling a healthy, committed, and politically aware and active relationship between two men is crucial. How we live has the potential of being a message to the boys that will hopefully override the sick and destructive messages about gays that they are bombarded with by our culture and by their peers. We don't expect them to battle homophobia on their own, but at least they understand it from the inside.

The sense of security and family we have felt propelled us into an unexpected series of activities. Gersh and I are founding members of a study group of faculty and staff at Michigan State University that meets regularly with the aim of establishing a Gay and Lesbian Studies Program at the university. We are also founding members of a Lansing-area coalition of gay and lesbian groups meeting to bridge the various gaps between the two communities and develop joint political action. Both groups have met at our house on various occasions, and the kids are well-informed of their aims. Gersh has been offering a workshop at MSU's counseling center on self-esteem for gay men. We are both committed to making Lansing and Michigan more open, more accepting, and more protective of lesbians and gay men—because this is our home, and we cannot accept anything less.

When Gersh and I first met, marveling at how much we had in common, our home was the world of ideas, because we started writing articles and then a book together. Everything we have coauthored has been published, and our joint teaching and lecturing has likewise been as powerful for our students and audiences as for us—knitting us together, creating a world of shared experiences. All of that laid a foundation for living together and ultimately making Okemos prove to us what Elizabeth Bowen says in her novel, *The Death of the Heart,* that "home is where we emotionally live."

WASHINGTON, D.C.

THE S2 IS THE SO-CALLED "Avenue of the Presidents" bus because its route is the handsome and seductive Sixteenth-Street corridor. The S2 travels from downtown Pennsylvania Avenue to Silver Spring, Maryland, a suburb that borders D.C. at its northern edge.

The ridership on the S2 is black, white, and variously ethnic. Hispanic, West African, and Caribbean passengers, as well as other nationals, diversify the sophisticated commuter ambience. Newspapers, books, and quiet conversations are standard as the S2 speeds its way to Adams Morgan, Mt. Pleasant, the Gold Coast, the end of the line, and back again.

Sixteenth Street—lined with embassies, churches, respectable homes, and majestic trees swaying overhead from Lafayette Park to Silver Spring—this undulating, rolling hill climbs and descends with deceptive grace. At its side, in the middle of a black gay ghetto called Homo Heights, sits the once glorious, mystical park called Malcolm X by black cultural nationalists, though its official name is Meridian Hill. At dusk it becomes a black gay cruising ground, while during the day it serves as one of the city's open-air drug markets.

Vandalism and graffiti now mar its classic beauty like brutal knife wounds that have become keloids. The shrubbery has been hacked down in an effort to prevent crimes that still occur. The once-green grounds are bald and littered with used condoms and assorted trash. Decay and decline exist here. Gloom and danger are ever-present in the piss-stained air, air that is often thick with marijuana smoke and always filled with the hawker's cry of drug dealers. And though children romp and wrestle on these grounds, and soccer players kick the game ball back and forth, the men appear who cannot contain their loneliness until dusk. They are not zombies. Their eyes are luminous with enormous, living hungers, but no one seems to notice except those of their kind. For black gay men, this park, elegantly appointed with gushing fountains, grand stairways, moonlit plazas, and statues of Dante and Joan of Arc—for black gay men seeking the kisses of one another—Malcolm X/Meridian Hill Park is now nothing more than a tomb of sorrow.

I remember riding the S2 home one evening, a Sunday in fact. I had taken the X2 from H Street, N.E., to Fourteenth and H downtown, where I transferred and waited for my S. From the corner of Fourteenth and H you can view the war-scape of AIDS and the remnants of casual sex zones reduced to rubble by the aggressive development of downtown. It is interesting to observe new postmodern office buildings rise on soil where the seed of gay men was once spilled with reckless abandon.

Ten years ago this corner was a sexual crossroads. On either side of Fourteenth Street, from H to I, there once stood thriving porn shops, movie galleries, and nude dance clubs. A block away, the raunchy black gay club, the Brass Rail, was bulging out of its jockstrap. Drag queens ruled, B-boys chased giddy government workers, fast-talking hustlers worked the floor, while sugar daddies panted for attention in the shadows, offering free drinks and money to any friendly trade. Everybody was seeking a sex machine. White folks were sneaking in for their "black-dick-fix." Sometimes the dose was fatal: Robbery. Murder. The pulsing music always throbbed like an insatiate erection.

A block north of the Brass Rail, Franklin Park was a soft cruise spot primarily because it borders K Street, Fourteenth and Thirteenth streets offering too much visibility for most. But east of its lower end, bordering I Street, on the Thirteenth Street corner, stood the notorious Curiosity Bookshop, complete with back room, movie booths, garish red lights, gusts of heavy breathing, and the popping noise of greased dicks pumping in and out of tight holes. The creaking floorboards were aging with semen and sighs. Every now and then you'd hear a man hiss, "Work that pussy, bitch," as clusters of panting men gathered to watch an ass being fucked.

At that most historic spot downtown, where, on the corner of Fourteenth and H, one could watch the parade of flesh all summer long, the quest for the perfect abuse was keen. Now the area is almost desolate of nightlife, the players scattered, the seekers scared to venture out.

I wait for my bus. Shortly before it arrives, two black men cruise by. They appear to be in their thirties/forties. The shorter, stockier, fair-skinned, clean-shaven homeboy has his arm thrown around the shoulders of the slightly taller, slender, darker daddy. The tall man is obviously older, moustached, and somewhat attractive. Homeboy carries a hustler's air about him. They swagger by, slightly drunk and horny. I am surprised when a few stops later they board the bus and sit at the back.

The bus crosses K Street and continues up Sixteenth without incident. The seats fill quickly. By the time we cross P Street standing room is all that's available. A murmur begins to rise from the back of the bus. It explodes in a startling confrontation.

"You my bitch!"

"No! Uh-uh. *We* are bitches!"

"No! You listen here. *I* ain't wearing lipstick, *you* are! I ain't no bitch! I fucked *you!* You *my* bitch!"

This argument continues without resolution until we arrive at Sixteenth and U Streets. The bus is packed with passengers, and as we approach the stop, I see ten more waiting to board.

just as the first person at the stop steps aboard, a strident, hysterical voice cuts loose from the back:

"I'm a forty-five-year-old-black-gay-man who *en-joys* taking dick in his rectum!" Snap! "I'm not your bitch!" Snap! "Your bitch is at home with your kids!" Snap! Snap!

We are entering the fifth dimension of our sexual consciousness. The ride is rough. There is no jelly for this. The driver is trying to call the police on the bus phone. No one has said anything. No one else attempts to board.

The air is charged with tensions unleashed from an ancient box of sexual secrets. The older man abruptly leaves by the back door. Homeboy follows. They have violent words outside. The children sitting at the front are wide-eyed and speechless. All the homosexuals on the bus have frozen. So have I. The driver is frantically calling the police. The older man suddenly pushes aboard wielding a Flash Pass with Homeboy in hot pursuit. The driver drops the phone and jumps between them. Homeboy pulls out a knife and waves it toward his companion.

"You gonna pay for this dick!" he sneers.

"I ain't paying for that tame shit!"

The children's heads snap back and forth during the ensuing shouting match as though they were watching a Ping-Pong tournament and not two grown black men giving high drama. In a stern voice the driver orders Homeboy to leave the bus. He backs down the steps, waving his blade, threatening to catch the black gay man on the street and make him pay *dearly* for the dick he got. Homeboy is last seen stalking east on U Street with his glinting knife clenched in his hand.

The bus pulls off and begins to climb Sixteenth Street again. Every homosexual on the bus is still frozen. So am I. The police never arrived. The children are quiet for the remainder of their journeys. So am I. Occasionally, a very nervous man, a very terrified schoolboy laughs out loud then subsides into silence. The forty-five-year-old-black-gay-man who enjoys taking dick in his rectum rides the rest of the way without further incident. At the back of the bus he sits—his legs crossed at the knee.

■　　■　　■

The experience detailed here in "Washington, D.C." (a.k.a. "Without Comment") actually occurred. By documenting my experiences on the S2 bus, I discovered an opportunity to speak about the sites of pleasure I had intimately known as I was coming of age in Washington. Those sites of pleasure are known to many a black gay man familiar with D.C. Many of the places I name no longer exist or they've been transformed; thus the possibility of them being absolutely erased from the record is prevented by me naming them. Developers, AIDS, and other factors contributed to the disappearance of many sites of pleasure. I originally titled the piece "Without Comment" because I did not want to sit in judgment of the scene created on the bus by the two black gay men, nor did I want to make judgments about what I have known and what I remember.

PROVINCETOWN, MASSACHUSETTS

THE PILGRIMS LANDED IN Provincetown in 1620, spent a month there, then took off for the solider mainland harborage of what was to be named Plymouth. Had the high-minded Calvinists of that first foundation known the Sodom Provincetown was to become, they probably would have left even sooner.

For Provincetown has continued to attract fugitives of varying kinds, not all of them pious. At the beginning of this century, it acquired the reputation of an artists' colony. Painters were drawn by the miraculous, clean light, and playwrights by an experimental theater company, the Provincetown Players. Fittingly, Eugene O'Neill, whose plays focus on the lives of outcasts, got his first play produced in Provincetown in 1916. Finally—completing the traditional unholy trinity of "theater people, gypsies, and queers"—came gay men and lesbians, seeking refuge from the hostility and disbelief of mainstream America. And though the Provincetown Players have long been dissolved, their theater turned into a craft mall, though painters and galleries are few and complacent, we queers have continued to come here—to such an extent that Provincetown is, if for anything, known for *us;* known for being one of the two or three places on the continent where gay people can be seen in something like their native habitat. It is one of our hometowns.

Unlike the first Pilgrims, gay people come to the tip of Cape Cod precisely to escape land, not to seek it. This seems to be some kind of pattern, in fact. Consider the places we have migrated to: among cities, New York, Boston, L.A., San Francisco; among resorts, Provincetown, Fire Island, Key West. We are drawn, it would seem, to the extremities of the Republic, poised as for urgent flight on the sandbars of our continent. We put down roots—if that's what they are—in dry shallow soil, and we travel light. We are detached from the world by reason of our sexual desires; at our best, we see through the fictions of "nature" by the very act of declaring ourselves gay, and thus "unnatural." We are placed in the position—some would say an enviable one—of creating the self we choose to live. We are like Walt Whitman's spider, patiently spinning filament after filament out of itself, then flinging it out into the universe and hoping it will anchor somewhere. What better physical place for us than spits of land not quite connected with the "world," where whatever comforts exist must be consciously made. What better air than the bracing, alien sea wind?

Or so it has seemed to me, over the fifteen years I've been coming here. I look forward as I drive down Route 3 to the sweet sense of alienation from the land that comes when you've crossed the Sagamore Bridge. (Cape Cod, because of its canal, is literally an island, a bent arm severed at the shoulder.) I welcome the scrub pines that gradually replace deciduous trees. I like to see the mysterious sign that warns of SAND DANGER IN HIGH WINDS and which is the visitor's first, ambiguous welcome to Provincetown.

Provincetown itself is situated on the inner side of the final curve of Cape Cod, a little knuckle that crooks in on itself at the very last moment. To many people's initial disappointment—to mine, the first time I came—the ocean and beach are actually a mile away from the town, on the bony side of the crooked finger. (This means there's no falling asleep to the sound of surf.) Between are acres of vast, lunar dunes, the so-called Province Lands, now part of a national park that extends halfway down the Cape. The town therefore is geographically confined to a rather small area. It is long, not wide, and stretches in parallel lines along the two main streets, Commercial and Bradford. Commercial Street is all shops, restaurants, and people. Bradford exists for cars, though barely, and only by charitable comparison with Commercial Street. Joining, or keeping them separate, are dozens of tiny residential streets, some no bigger than alleys. The whole town from the air would look like a long rope ladder hastily deposited on the shore.

As on all islands, you are very aware of the land because there is so little of it. Houses of every size and shape jostle each other on the small rises that pass for hills. Behind a peeling flower-entwined fence adjacent to a white house with green shutters is an infinitesimal cottage, also white with green shutters, its echo. A conversation between a bicyclist and a pedestrian stops traffic on Commercial Street at 5:00 P.M.

As if in compensation for the finiteness and aridity of the land, the town itself has blossomed in every kind of human commercial enterprise. A few years ago, for instance, I remember the pièce de résistance at a local store: a dressing table every centimeter of which—top, sides, handles—was encrusted with bright buttons that had then been drowned in a layer of almost edible varnish. (Who *buys* these things?) This year you could buy two-hundred-dollar Italian shirts in puce and mustard that paid solemnly ironic homage to the fifteen-dollar ones you wore in seventh grade. You can buy other beautiful irrelevant things: a Japanese obi, gorgeous and complicated kites, a wholistic massage by one of America's great poets, Olga Broumas.

But, for all its commercial exotica, Provincetown is surprisingly ordinary. It exists to gratify basic, not refined appetites— sex, food, music, sun, laughter, spending money, showing off. Fundamentally it is neither glamorous, rich, nor (in town, at least) picturesque. It is determinedly middle class. It is no longer an artists' colony and differs from other beach resorts only in being smaller and harder to reach. Even so, it's easy to understand what draws the thousands of tourists here. It is pleasant to be for once in a place where driving a car makes no sense at all, to see no golden arches, no Howard Johnson's or Hilton, to stay in a room where there may be no TV. There are surely worse ways of spending your time and dollars than watching a drag show or buying a painting. People do well to look wistfully at Provincetown's amiable bohemian seediness.

And of course at all the fags and dykes!

Sometimes I try to imagine what the straight visitors see when they walk down Commercial Street on a hot afternoon. Are they—as they sometimes seem—oblivious of the parade of same-sex couples all around them? Do they see us but pretend not to? Are they secretly fascinated by us? Disgusted? Do they (like the rest of us) just want to get laid? What exactly is in it for them?

I know what's in it for us—or for *me,* at least: freedom, outrageousness, and visibility. The last two, however, are strangely dependent on the presence of these mystifying, mystified strangers, these straight families from the suburbs of New York and Boston. I know that, by the strictest standards of gay liberation, one is not supposed to be beholden to straights for anything. But it is thanks to them, to their curiosity, however well- or ill-motivated, that I've had the experience of seeing myself through straight eyes—and of *surviving the glance.* This gives a sense of strength. At the same time, our sheer number permits us to see ourselves through our *own* eyes, to see what we look like and who we are. In both cases, the victory we win is visibility—to the straight world, but also to ourselves. Visibility, after all, is what we almost never have in the cities and towns we live in. Provincetown, with its puzzled tourists and impassive local fishermen, makes our invisible gay ink legible.

Oddly enough, the first time I came to Provincetown I might as well have *been* a straight tourist: I hated it. I was a timid graduate student, and as unsure of what to do as any nuclear family on its wary tour of Sodom. This seems paradoxical to me now, because gay liberation was the closest thing I had then to a religion. I theoretically believed in sexual freedom not only as an act of justice, but as a duty; and I practiced what I preached

("Just say Yes"). In all this I was (I still think) on the right track. What was missing, however, was any sense of exhilaration at gay life's possibilities, or any love for myself as a gay man, though I would have hotly denied it at the time. I was the exact opposite of the Pope: I loved the sin and hated (or rather, despised) the sinner. As a result I was completely unprepared for the real gay world that was being created, at that very time, in the very place I was visiting.

In my high-minded naïveté, I wasn't much different from the Pilgrims themselves. I imagined, and in fact required, Provincetown to be the "artists' colony" it no longer was. I wanted it to be a sort of Yaddo-on-the-Sea—plus homosexuals. I was, of course, disappointed. When my friends and I got to town, I remember finding it conventionally pretty, but hardly overwhelming. Commercial Street was, as it always is, crowded—and crowds did not fit with my idealized image of Provincetown. Worse, and to my horror, those crowds were *straight*. Betrayal! I had come, as many still do, looking primarily for a certifiably "safe" gay place, and instead felt conspicuous and "queer." I know now that part of my horror was unavoidable because I was horrified by *myself*. Then, I didn't feel the strength of our numbers nor the exaltation of "surviving the glance." I saw myself—not to mention all those other fags—through straight eyes, which I assumed to be as unmerciful as my own.

It's easy to laugh at earlier sketches of oneself. But my dilemma, however funny in the light of forty-one years, was frightening at twenty-six. Nor do I think it was that uncommon. Like many properly brought-up middle-class people, I expected, and sought, safety in life. To be gay was, no matter how I looked at it, *dangerous*. (Had I not, at age sixteen, been toppled from my unquestioned family eminence and sent to a shrink to be cured, when my kind, worried parents discovered I was gay?) And despite my liberationist beliefs—I would never have *lied* about my homosexuality—I was scared of myself.

Scared too, as a result, of the other gay people who acted as my mirror. Gay Provincetown was then at the height of its arrogance and glory. I dreaded (A student that I'd always been) not making the grade. What if I wasn't gay *enough?* What if there were *other ways* of being gay that I hadn't read about in books? High-mindedness had kept this alarming possibility at bay, but was of no use at all when confronted with actual gay men and women in large numbers.

What I eventually found in Provincetown was not safety, but salvation, a place not to hide, but to shine forth. But even Provincetown could not confer the benefits of experience overnight, and if asked I would have predicted that my first visit would be my last. I had hated (and feared) the crowds of straight people, but also the alien *gay* multitudes, who in their insouciant shopping, flirting, and gossiping were a living refutation of my belief that being gay meant being quietly superior or flagrantly outcast. (My ideology could embrace "outlaws" but not consumers.) Something I had clung to crumbled on that first trip. Provincetown was not an "artists' colony," nor were gay people all "artists." Indeed, the escape route I'd always kept secretly open—"eccentricity," that poor substitute for freedom—was now closed.

Thank God for sex, the one thing that can keep us honest if we let it! Without the disreputable pull of desire, I would probably never have been led back to Provincetown. But I *was* drawn back, and each time I went I became more at ease with my own sexuality and with the ordinariness of gay life there. What a relief it was (eventually) to realize that homosexuality didn't have to mean a lifetime sentence to respectability, that gay liberation could mean the freedom to *lower* your standards as well as raise them! Provincetown, friendly, tacky, and democratic, was exactly the right place to learn that lesson.

And one of the principal chapters in the P'town textbook was the institution of the guest house. Guest houses are the Provincetown lodging *par excellence,* and not staying at one the first time I came was probably why I had such a hard time making sense of the place. I don't know how many guest houses there are in Provincetown—dozens, anyway, most of them gay. They come in a variety of styles and range from the comparatively fancy to the dumpy; most are comfortable rather than luxurious, a little overdecorated, and cozy if not actually cramped. Typically their rooms are small, and often you share a bathroom with other guests on the hall. (This, like so much else about guest houses, leads to camaraderie.) Downstairs, there is usually a common room where the guests gather for morning coffee, late afternoon drinks, and twenty-four-hour gossip. The people staying at the house become your de facto friends, the people you go to the beach with at noon, and to Spiritus Pizza with at 1:00 A.M. You may or may not like them: that's immaterial. They are your jumping-off point in Provincetown.

Over the years I have stayed at half a dozen guest houses in Provincetown, but there was one I knew best and that now seems to exemplify everything I love about Provincetown. It was owned by a friend of mine named Vince. From the street, it looked like an ordinary shingled house, with, you'd imagine, two or three rooms on each of two floors. In fact it had three floors, was much deeper than it appeared to be, and was a rabbit warren of rooms, none of them identical. Two were rather grand, one with a cathedral ceiling, and one with its own deck. The one I usually stayed in was the reverse: a minute room with a single bed, small wooden dresser, and a view of the harbor. Its neatness, its shipshapeness delighted me. As in so many places in Provincetown, the sea was so much the motif of the house that you could imagine yourself being on shipboard.

Nothing about the place was glamorous or, seemingly, organized, and yet it somehow *worked*. Chores got done, breakfast made, guests perked up, all with a maximum of drama but a minimum of real fuss. (Everyone on staff, I suspect, felt that he was an actor in a potentially great role.) In addition to a truly astounding collection of objects of virtu, Vince's great achievement in the house was the creation of a hospitable place, one that welcomed people and asked no awkward questions. (As in the Old West—perhaps because so many of us are literal lawbreakers—people's pasts are held to be irrelevant in Provincetown.) There was room for every kind of person there, or so it seemed, from glamorous twinkies to world-weary leather men. There was even, I found, room for timid graduate students who were learning to be gay. I often went down for just a day or two, staying in my room much of the time with a book or a boy. But even unsociability did not disqualify me from inclusion in the activities of the house. It was one of the first places where my secret dream of a gay democracy began to come true.

One of the happiest single recollections of my life concerns this house. On New Year's Eve, 1984, my best friend Tom and I drove down from Boston to spend the night there. I remember that night vividly, and the exhilarating sense of being alone and free on the deserted highways. The cold black sky made our human company in Tom's car the more noticeable, and precious; the silence encouraged conversation. We talked all the way down, though I no longer remember anything but scraps of it: the gym and boys we fell in love with there, our families, a string quintet I couldn't get out of my mind. But of course the real topic, the palpable subtext, was friendship.

When we arrived at the house around 10:00 P.M., we discovered a party in progress. There were almost no real guests— that is, strangers—at the house, just members of Vince's astonishingly farflung "family." The house was warm, gaudy, friendly, and intoxicated. One member of the family, soaring above the rest of us on a combination of exhilarative drugs, had donned a frumpy brown woman's toque and was impersonating a Central European baroness of decayed fortunes. Incident was piled on pathetic incident till the climactic "revelation" that the poor baroness had been reduced to pilfering silverware. A photo of this event shows Vince indignantly ripping open the baroness's handbag, from which spills a glittering mound of forks and knives. To conceal her shame, the baroness has thrown her hands up before her face; the rest of us, like the observers of a Renaissance Nativity, gesture with hand or eye toward the stolen hoard.

A second photo from the same last hours of 1984 shows the group gathered around the bar, many of us by this time hatted and veiled ourselves. A bottle of poppers is making the rounds. Although most eyes are on the baroness, I am looking—glazed, but happy—at the camera. Tom is smiling at me. It is a moment that can never be repeated. Of the persons in that picture, at least three are dead, Tom and Vince among them. The smiles that came so easily to all our faces are hard to believe in now, and, since he died, no one has looked at me the way Tom did that night.

Now when I go to Provincetown I rent for a week or two, an economic step or two up from my days at guest houses. And while I miss the easy comradeship of the house, I must admit to enjoying the quiet and privacy of my own place. And even my rentals, so small and intense is Provincetown gay society, have seemed like "rooms" in a larger guest house. I stayed this summer, for example, next to a houseful of gay men from Boston and was given, as it were, visiting membership in their house. I was struck by their diversity. Two were schoolteachers, one a housecleaner, another an art student. One man spent his days at the farthest extremity of the gay beach, preferably nude, and had— or rather didn't have—the tan-line to prove it. Another was writing a novel and spent *his* days at the word processor. (For which of course there was nothing to show beyond a faint worried abstraction.) Almost none did the usual Provincetown things— shopping, Tea-Dance, post-bar cruising at Spiritus—except by accident. On the weekends, various lovers showed up from town, in addition to whom there were usually a few houseguests. Even with all these people, the house seemed full but seldom crowded.

I particularly admired the house's ability to do group things—cooking dinner, going dancing, or having a party— without imposing a group obligation. They ate together frequently, for example, but never to a plan. Dinner parties were casual enough to allow for more or fewer participants; and no one was miffed if a house member failed to show up. (Who knew what adventure might have detained him?) Conversation at dinner, or over morning coffee in the kitchen, was both witty and generous. The house managed, in other words, to have a group identity while still letting everybody do what he wanted.

This equilibrium of private and public existence seems to me the great strength of Provincetown, and indeed of gay life. Because many of us are either single, or live in somewhat open relationships, friendships of many degrees of intimacy are possible. By contrast, a straight woman I know, divorced with a grown daughter, lamented that as a single woman she had virtually no options in meeting people, male or female. She dislikes singles' bars, and feels herself to be persona non grata at her coupled friends' dinner tables. If she wants company, she has to work for it. Although this sort of isolation obviously occurs in gay society too—and occurs more and more to AIDS widowers—we gay men have a flexibility which that woman does not have. If you go to a party as a single person, you do not feel "set up" for a date; but if you meet someone at dinner whom you like, a date can easily come out of it.

The ingenuity that successfully brings such disparate people together, that turns the liability of living in a world of transient strangers into an advantage and an ornament, is what brings me back to Provincetown and makes me call it "home." Not a home, however, that has ever existed; we are not trying to re-create the homes of our parents or our straight friends. What distinguishes Provincetown from the homes we grew up in is precisely its democracy, its lack of hierarchies. There are "daddies," but no fathers, "boys" but no sons. People meet there, to an astonishing degree, as equals. It is even different from other gay resorts: if, as Ethan Mordden has aptly said, the Pines "may be the only gay colony in the history of the world," Provincetown can't really compete, precisely because of its large straight population. What it loses in sheer gay bravura it makes up for in cheerful, middle-class inclusiveness.

Having said which, I must admit that it has the deficiencies as well as the strengths of middle-class America. It has, for instance, a pronounced flavor of Yankee self-satisfaction. And the cowardly, but daunting "attitude" that has made Boston bars virtually uninhabitable gets reproduced down here too, and is a cause of many people's justifiable discomfort in the place. But the worst vice of Provincetown, as of middle-class America generally, is its total indifference, and probably hostility, to black Americans. You will not see many dark faces in Provincetown. For all its many virtues, then, it is nonetheless a faithful mirror of the grossest inequity of our nation.

Even so, the strengths of the place are virtually unique. They are, in my opinion, an unapologetic love of pleasure, a tolerance for wide differences of behavior and opinion, and a resourcefulness in seizing the moment. Our biological families don't possess exactly these virtues, nor do our love affairs. Family and love seem to be about exclusivity and possession, about defining who you are by who you are not; the flexible friendships I've seen in P'town, by contrast, are comparatively unboundaried: anybody can come in.

Provincetown is the place where I've come closest to realizing a long-sought dream: a house of friends. This house, whatever its material form—guest house, apartment, or even the town itself—is a kind of second chance at a family, a second chance at "home," a simulacrum (at times) of love. In Provincetown I've had the chance to get "family" right, and if not to go home *again*, to go there, happily, for the first time.

ANCHORAGE, ALASKA

IMAGINE NOVEMBER IN Anchorage, Alaska. The sun low on the horizon gives the brief day the quality of one long afternoon. From your deck in a part of the town called Hillside, about five hundred feet above the city, in the foothills of the Chugach Mountains, which rise like a cresting sea wave, the Anchorage bowl begins to sparkle in the early dusk. Lights spread all the way to Point Woronzoff overlooking the comma that is Fire Island in the shining waters of Cook Inlet. Just before that, the lights of the airport shimmer where the planes are long streaks as they arrive and depart for Europe, the Far East, and the Lower Forty-eight. To the west, the great Alaska Range sweeps north to rise in Mount Foraker and Mount McKinley, powerful against the deepening purple. Curving southward in a wide arc that flows on toward the distant Aleutians, the horizon is broken by Mount Susitna, the Sleeping Lady, then southwest by Mount Redoubt's smoking plume. Further down is Mount Iliamna. Beyond that is the dark. The bright sunset, pure as a bugle call, turns the mountains into blue silhouettes. If the night is fine, we can expect to see the velvet flicker, green, gold, and icy blue, of the aurora borealis spreading across the sky in rippling, cascading waves; then fading. There is a hard chill in the air and in the dank ruins of the flowers. Within one day a white frost has settled over the bare branches of the slim birches lining the roads. Nearly all of the gold and dull orange leaves have been blown away by the boisterous autumn windstorms, and in the woods stands of dark spruce anchor the landscape. In the light spreading over the hills there is a diminishing, a promise of winter.

The dark mornings are chill and windshields are white with frost. Snow has fallen briefly, leaving low mounds in the yard and a tracery in the dead grass around the crisp shrubs. Within the week it will come again, now thickly, for good. The season changes quickly, and the days' light drains away steadily, like water down a white bowl. Coming into winter excites me. In the twenty-two years I have lived and worked in Alaska, I feel this way each time a season changes: regret giving way to anticipation. To one having grown up in a region with only token winters, these seasons are dramatic. Now is the time when the light-deprived become sullen complainers. Not me. When I came to live at sixty-two degrees latitude (about the same as Leningrad and Helsinki) I *expected* it to be this way.

At the university where I teach, and in my office where I work with patients, there is an air of approaching holiday. Students are struggling by now, some doing their best to wing it until Thanksgiving. Patients anticipate indulgence without guilt. After this comes the Christmas exodus to Hawaii, Mexico, and other parts Outside. About a fourth of Anchorage's population, it seems, goes to Maui for the Christmas season. Because the Thanksgiving holiday has evolved for me and a group of close friends into a special time, a gathering and a celebration of our particular friendship, I write about it here and try to convey this atmosphere in a particular instance; an occasion that contains many others, too. It gives a glimpse into one of the many possibilities that make up Anchorage and Alaska for me, and what I have found as I live here.

Our crowd, always with additions and subtractions, has spent the last half dozen Thanksgivings at a tiny cabin about 125 miles up the road, in the bush. We get there by the state highway leading to the turnoff onto the back roads that finally peter out just beyond a sign nailed to a tree marking the descent to the place. The trip is not an easy one. The cabin sits on a shelf beneath a bluff beside medium-sized Wolverine Lake, which has a couple of small islands. Around the lake on three sides steep foothills covered with birch and spruce forest rise to Lazy Mountain in the southwest. In summer we push the small skiff across the shallow, weedy water to the islands or the other shore where we pick berries and explore. At Thanksgiving, for fun, for contrast, and perhaps as a small light in an immense darkness and cold, we gather as many exotic gourmet items as we can think of to take for a feast in the wilderness, in surroundings as primitive and beautiful as one could find. It started as the standard American Thanksgiving. We had such a good time together that after the first year we began to elaborate and improvise, enthusiastically thinking up variations that we could put together, surprising each other as the years passed. Guy Bassett and Jim Williams, whose place this is, organize it. Jim is the best cook I know.

"You're coming up to the cabin?" Jim always puts it as a question, to which the answer is always, "Sure. What do I bring?" Thanksgiving is near.

"Remember that great Danish movie we saw, *Babette's Feast?* We're doing the menu in it. Guy's got a printout for everybody."

Babette's Feast. It was a beautiful movie. I hadn't known what to expect when I saw it. When I left the little art theater, I was deeply moved. As a friend pointed out, the film was about a feast that was an act of thanksgiving, a celebration given in gratitude by an exile who had been taken in, welcomed. It was an act of thanks for a gift of community, of belonging; belonging, finally, to a place one has come to know and friends one has come to cherish.

I have many friends who were born in Alaska. I have more who were not, who came up from Outside to make a home here. "Outside," always capitalized in this context, means anywhere outside of Alaska. Unlike some of the older states, someone coming from Outside does not remain an outsider because of that. Alaska is generous and welcoming. But it isn't easy, with its climate and its isolation. Some never like it or adjust to it. There is an organization, only half joking, made up mostly of wives, called WHATWOLF: Women Held Against Their Will On the Last Frontier. That there is such a group says a lot about living here. That most of us choose to stay also speaks for itself. We are committed. When I considered all of this, using *Babette's Feast* as our theme was not just a game, but a fitting act for us, who gather here every year.

"We've already got most of the stuff," Jim continued, "and I'll get my Air France friend to look in Paris or New York for the turtle soup. He always brings caviar. Gets it in Tokyo. And I've ordered the birds."

"I'll bring a couple of the wines, then."

The day comes and all is ready, tasks assigned. In town the sunlight is wan. To the north in the Matanuska Valley, lush farmland in summer, there is a high band of flat gray clouds across the sky. Snow. I've put on my studded tires for winter. I load the truck, my two dogs jump in, and we start for the cabin 125 miles away up the Glenn Highway. Ten miles out of Anchorage we pass the town of Eagle River at the foot of a line of massive mountains, near that branch of Cook Inlet called Knick Arm. Past Chugiak, with the long glimpse on clear days of Mount McKinley, 250 miles north. Past the Native village of Eklutna, with its tiny onion-domed church and its graveyard with brightly painted wooden grave houses. I turn into the Old Palmer Highway just this side of the Matanuska Valley town of Palmer, then cross Knick Arm and the Matanuska River with its thickening skin of ice. Along the massive flank of Pioneer Peak (like McKinley, its native name—whatever it was—disregarded), crossing the narrow metal bridge with peeling silver paint; passing the steep ditches and streams, frozen now, where salmon come in late summer to spawn, turn polychrome with rot, still fighting, then die.

After a sharp turn into Wolverine Road, we take the final twelve miles up and down the ice-slicked washboard road to a broad upland meadow, now hard and white. Against the distant

Talkeetna Mountains the cliffs along the Matanuska River shine in the fading light. My big poodle, in her usual position behind me, breathes down my neck while my other dog curls up on the front seat, asleep.

In summer, going to the cabin, when we reach the meadow Jim and Guy let their Irish Setter range over the fields of grass, barking behind the car in the curling rolls of dust. He knows Wolverine Lake and the cabin are near, where he plunges joyously into the shallow, weedy water off the boat ramp as the tin skiff bobs in the commotion. Now it will have been hauled out for the winter and fitted against the cabin like a small ear.

A quarter of a mile ahead of us I can see the change in the air where the snow begins, a pale curtain across the landscape. We enter, and against my windshield the driving snow has a tiny frying sound. Reaching the woods again, I bounce along the road's trail in four-wheel drive. At last I see a van parked near a sign, a rose stenciled on a board banked with new snow. Here is the top of the switchback leading to the lake and the cabin. I park, stretch, and try to figure out how to carry everything in a single trip down those seventy-five steep feet. The dogs know the way and can shift for themselves. The big poodle plunges wetly into the drifts; my older dog hates the cold snow on her belly and goes fast and straight. Bottles of wine and brandy clink musically with every lurching step as I drag the bag behind me, my arms filled with other stuff, a pack with socks, skates, and long johns over my shoulder. No skating, though, unless the snow lets up. It is thick and silent in the trees, luminous enough for me to see my way. The sun has set. On the last turn I confront the privy, its wood door hanging at an angle from the leaning box propped against a large boulder. All of us know how gusty it is inside in any season, but our visits in winter are heroic, born of hard necessity.

There. A few yards in front of me I see the rosy square of the cabin window above a pile of snow-topped wood by the door. The door stays out of plumb; we must drag and slam it. I burst in, dropping all my stuff on the nearest of the five beds against the walls, bottles clanging dangerously. The dogs' collars jingle as they shake themselves dry behind me. The setter comes up to exchange smells; tails wave gently. One of my hosts stands with his back to the fire, our only heat. It crackles with a couple of half-burned logs. I greet him and we talk about our trip up, then I put my things away and take the wines to the counter. There is a burst of creaking hinges and slamming screen as my other host enters, slapping his gloves on his shoulders. His wool clothes smell like wet snow.

The cabin is one square room with a counter to serve on and a tiny propane oven, a metal sink, and some shelves in one corner. There is no running water. On the opposite side is our plank dining table with a chair at each end, a couple of benches, and the door to an unheated lean-to. In front of the fireplace, which is made of smooth round rocks in what looks like concrete chewing gum, are a low table and a couple of tattered, seat-sprung lounge chairs. The beds are piled with quilts and blankets. One summer, tracing a strange smell, we pulled a wild duck from beneath the largest one. The bird was mummified and as flat as run-over shoe. No one could figure out how or why it got in, but we guessed it had been there at least a year. Snaking up a narrow post near the fireplace are two copper tubes ending in delicate mantles glowing eerily with the white propane flame. These, with the fire, are our lights. Around the windows are torn paper curtains, and over the table hang decorations from past holidays—paper flags from the Fourth of July, yellow and black pumpkins, witches on broomsticks, turkeys, tinsel, and wreaths. Except for streaking snowflakes, the windows are black. The wind is rising. The temperature is falling. An old thermometer shows five degrees above zero. We can feel the world outside tightening with cold.

"When I got to the last turn I saw the window with the light behind it and I knew you two were here." Guy turned to the fire rubbing his hands, then laid them against his face. "It's funny how comforting that was. All of a sudden in the snow and the dark I was home."

A tearing wind has risen, driving away the snow clouds and sweeping bare the frozen lake's surface. It rattles the windows in booming gusts. The moon, a worn dime, is almost full. The light reflects off the snow in the woods and on the hills. Only the brightest stars are visible, and we know we won't see the aurora tonight. Supper is fried chicken and biscuits, and everyone is here except a couple of others who will drive up tomorrow. Firelight plays over our faces and over the dogs sprawled around the hearth. One friend's cairn terriers, nervous around the bigger animals, try to crowd onto his lap.

"Okay, guys, skates! I'm going skating. Who's coming?" Guy pulls his size twelve skates out of a lumpy bag and starts unbuckling his boots.

"That goddamned wind, Guy. . . ." Someone starts to complain. The dogs sit up, alert. The terriers yap sharply. "Well, shit! Go on, go on, then. I'm coming."

A friend grunts as he tries to jam a foot into his skate boot and lace it up. Pushing a dog off his down parka, he laughs. "We'll freeze."

We straggle outside, hobbling down to the boat ramp, flailing our arms for balance. Then we launch ourselves on the ice, now a full yard thick. Finding any gap in our scarves and mufflers, an exposed wrist, an ear tip, the savage wind makes us whirl and jump to pull everything tighter. It is so strong that we can spread our arms wide in our heavy clothes and sail wobbling off over the uneven surface, scoured bare. The temperature, with the wind chill, must be at least 20 degrees below zero. Down, down in the black crystalline thickness I can see great bubbles like flowers frozen as they ascended, glittering in the moonlight. The dogs run in a frenzy of joy, nails clicking as they scramble after us barking frantically. The moon rides high over Lazy Mountain's white shoulder. Firs lining the shore of the lake are black, and on the steep foothills bare birches cast rows of matchlike shadows on the gleaming snow. Soon my face feels frozen, rigid, and my breath is crystal ice against my silk balaclava. Someone falls sprawling. With the dogs, all us of skate over to help, glad for the respite. One skater in a circling stop, rows backward frantically then falls on top of the man on the ice. The dogs dance around the struggling heap, yelping. We all decide to go in for hot buttered rum and other warmers.

Later, the chill off, Guy shuffles the cards in three rapid

spatters then slaps the deck on the table. We've warmed and bitched and dished, but stave off sleep and bed, drowsily comfortable.

"Bridge," he states, "and Martin'll deal . . ."

I groan. I have always had card-game dyslexia and can barely get through a dilapidated game of hearts. Fighting drowsiness, I run through a mental check and find myself as befuddled as ever. The game begins. I feel as if I'm trying to run on snowshoes.

Well into the game, I ask, "What's trumps?" Guy laughs. My friends groan. One folds his suit and throws it on the table, disgusted. Another looks at me pityingly. The game ends.

"Well." I'm defensive. "Well, Martin Luther said that card playing is a harmless amusement for immature minds . . ."

"Martin Luther who?" Someone stretches widely.

Yawns. Covers pulled down. Dogs turn in small circles then thump to the floor. The terriers crawl under the covers to their master's feet, never yet having smothered. We turn in. In the darkening room the fire shifts in a cloud of tiny sparks, gleaming on the scattered cards and an almost empty bottle.

The cold draws closer as the night settles. A light snore rises from the mounded blankets on one bed. It ends in a snort as the sleeper turns. A dog's leg thumps the floor rapidly as it wakes to scratch. Someone drops an incoherent word into the colder darkness. Outside, the moon is bone white, the shadows pitch black. It is twenty-five degrees below zero. The wind has died; the air cuts the skin. Over the still hours the moon slowly draws to a shoulder of Lazy Mountain. The fire pops, settles, shrinks, now and then keening in a long whistle against a damp log. Paralyzing cold creeps nearer to the stone hearth. An animal whines briefly. No one stirs.

In the bare, pale light someone wakes, a dazed eye trying to make sense of the shadowed room. It is almost 10:00 A.M. Jim Williams rubs his hands with a feathery sound in the chill. He dresses and throws a log on the fire, sending a cloud of sparks up the chimney. Someone yawns, groans, rubs his face, throws the blankets back over his head. The room smells like sleeping men. The door bangs as someone stumbles out to the steps and begins peeing loudly on the frozen snow. Grabbing the roll of

toilet paper, another heads for the privy. Coins and suspenders
jingle as pants are pulled on. Water gurgles out of the ten-gallon
thermos as someone tips it to break the ice. Another riser hocks
up phlegm. Morning voices croak. Across the lake in a bare tree
two ravens dispute, echoing over the ice. The light grows and the
moon, just paler than the sky, is almost behind the mountain.
The last guests, loaded down, appear on the last turn. It is
Thanksgiving Day.

When I moved to Anchorage from New Orleans and started practicing in a local clinic I was glib about why I moved. Now, twenty-
two years later I'm at a loss to explain it. Sometimes a turn 180
degrees from the familiar, whatever the reason, can make one
wake up and greet himself. At this point I may not be able to say
precisely how I came to live in Alaska, but now I know why I've
stayed. Someone remarked that Americans know more about the
moon than they do about Alaska; that many people think it is in
that little box just off California and above the box containing
Hawaii. And that now it is slimed with crude oil. At a recent
family reunion in a southern state I solemnly told some relatives
that I live in a centrally heated igloo. For a while they believed
me. For most, the name conjures up a jumbled, mythical place.
In *Death of a Salesman,* Arthur Miller used it to symbolize Out
There, the exotic, where Ben made his fabulous fortune, seen
through Willy Loman's failing eyes. I think it has parts of all
these things. And it is true that it is a place of adventurers, those
who haven't fit in, from yuppies to roustabouts. Anchorage was
founded only in 1915. It is odd, when one comes from an older
region, to see ordinary kitchen tables and chairs of that era called
"antiques," and a railroad house built around that time now on
the National Register of Historic Buildings. But fitting. Since I
came, Anchorage has gone ripping through the oil boom, growing
from 75,000 people to 250,000, then shrinking to its present
population of 218,000. The appearance of the city ranges from
slum to elegance. It is expensive to live here, but anything one
wants, however exotic, can be found. Anchorage is also thor-
oughly middle class, middle America. In the majority of the people, what you see is what you get. It is a Third-World city, with

an underclass of badly treated Alaska Natives who make up most of the downtown drunks. Anchorage has a thriving criminal set; any drug available can be had. Rapes, murders; violence is common. Two permanent armed forces posts are here. It has some of the best restaurants I know of. It has smog and air pollution. It has two good universities. It supports two readable newspapers, one morning and one afternoon, with opposite political viewpoints. It has no criminal code regarding gay life-styles, and no entrapment. You can find any kind of auto here from Rolls to fifteen-year-old disintegrating hulks. Anchorage is run for the benefit mainly of white, middle-class, middle-aged, Christian heterosexual male businessmen. But the large Korean, Filipino, Japanese, Southeast Asian, African-American, and Hispanic populations, among others, are also a powerful factor. The Mob operates here, too. We have an opera and symphony season. We have a superb new main library. With a few exceptions, its U.S. senators and representatives remain in Washington after retiring.

It has a physical setting of awesome beauty. It, like Scandinavia, is mad about sports and stays outdoors as long as possible in the brief summer. It has a fine system of parks, greenbelts, and trails. When spring comes over a single weekend in late May, sweeping almost at once into summer, the green wind has a fragrance I have found nowhere else. The woods ring with returning songbirds—thrush, robins, song sparrows, warblers. Wild geese, ducks, shore birds nest in the city. Swans come to Potter marsh on their migrations. In winter moose munch on shrubs in city yards. First becoming noticeable in early March, the hours of daylight swell steadily through the months to a crescendo at the June solstice, when there is no night, just four and a half hours of cool twilight. The stars disappear in late April, not to return until mid-July. After June, the daylight drains, first slowly, then in a steady rush until in the December solstice, when there are only four hours of daylight, the cycle begins once more. On January days and nights when, at times, the temperature gets to thirty below zero, I look at the mountains that have no connection at all with this man-made flimsy. In the white shadow there is the breath of an abyss, an *other* that is palpable. On a summer day of endless, slowly turning light, flashing on the thick green of the trees, always cool, I don't want to be anywhere else. As the summer grows, then recedes, brief and intense, there is poignance in its passage.

> *A mountain range curves into dark.*
> *I watch the emptying light*
>   *answer this northern silence . . .*

In this part of Alaska trees do not grow as large as they do in the Lower Forty-eight except in sheltered places. This makes the sky appear vast and empty, where light, especially in the long days, does mysterious things. And it is still true that one can go twenty miles in almost any direction and find wilderness.

My close friends are the extended family that many of us create. Together we share Christmas, birthdays, celebrations, concerns. I am only one of a fluid circle we draw around ourselves, friends, lovers, acquaintances, strangers. Every season it expands and contracts as this one leaves, that one returns, someone Outside sends friends; new faces added to a constant core. In recent years death and illness have frayed us, but that, too, is a bond. Alaskans are friendly and surpassingly hospitable. We mark the season with each other, at our homes. Fur Rendezvous, in February, is one of my favorites. On Sunday, the last day of the sled dog races, we gather at brunch then straggle a half block to Cordova Street where the dogs and mushers pass. The animals are beautiful: small, lithe, muscular, poignant in their intense determination. They run down the snow-filled street in silence except for the hiss of the sleds' runners and the "Hup!" of the musher paddling with one foot. The cold is deep. If the day is fine, the world is dazzling blue and white. Things like this are in the glue that binds us together.

At the cabin, everyone is functioning now. We've finished a breakfast of hot cakes and sausage. We melt enough ice to wash our faces and the dishes. We've read the newspapers, magazines, and paperbacks lying around for the past ten years. Jim Williams stands by the table looking things over, fists on his hips. This means he is about to get down to some serious cooking, and it's time for us to leave him to his work. The day is clear when we cross the ice and explore the islands and the other shore of the lake. In late summer, hollows in the islands are filled with mushrooms. A Polish friend, a passionate mushroom hunter, taught me how to identify several kinds that are edible, and I found them on one of our island forays. When I returned with them for supper, proud of my find, the friend who was cooking looked at the mess of fungi without saying anything. No one else spoke either.

"If *you* want to eat them I'll cook them for you after I cook everything else," he said, finally.

"All right." I was stung. "I'll take them back and cook them myself. You'll see."

"I hope not." He was emphatic.

The matter was settled. They went in the lake. By then I was a doubter too. But I still think they were edible.

Today the air is still and frigid. The sun is low in the sky but bright. On one island, in a hollow where the clump of alders is thick, we come across a moose stand. In winter their droppings form a mounded nest of what looks exactly like small chocolate Easter eggs. In town these moose nuggets are shellacked and made into lapel pins and cuff links for tourists. Dogs like them, and we pull ours away. Alder tips and branches have been stripped, probably this morning. When they must, the huge beasts move in almost total silence, leaving deep cloven tracks in the snow. Winter drives them down from the hills. Black-polled chickadees in small groups dart among the trees, wings and tails flirting, *dee-dee-dee*. Two ravens fly past making a rhythmic feathery sound with their large wings. They are wary, turning one bright eye then the other, to watch us. These birds have an astonishing repertory, making sounds ranging from shrieks to a liquid mating call that sounds like water flowing over pebbles. When we're too clumsy with cold to climb over brush and trees, we head back to the cabin. The light is fading.

Inside, the cabin is fragrant and almost hot. The table is set, and the rest of us busy ourselves putting together the details of dinner while the cook concentrates on the tiny stove, a clutter of dishes beside him on the counter. The bottled propane hisses quietly. We get our menu cards printed with Babette's Feast. Thanksgiving is about to start, and we drag our chairs and benches to the table. Two candles in chipped glass holders shine on the paper tablecloth and the napkins with gaudy turkeys and Pilgrims. Our wineglasses are from 7-Eleven and our knives, forks, and spoons mix sterling with stainless steel and plastic. Two volunteers bring the first course: turtle soup from a gourmet store in Paris. It has small golden dumplings floating in it, and with it we sip Amontillado sherry. Next, Jim brings our blinis Demidoff with Sevruga caviar. With the caviar, the warm sour cream over the small pancakes has a rich, slightly salty taste as I burst the pellets against the roof of my mouth. With this course we drink Veuve Cliquot champagne, dry and tangy with bubbles. Since we have only one plastic glass, we finish and rinse or just mix as we go from wine to wine. The blending can be unusual. The cook gets a round of compliments. Now we're glad for a short rest; then the creaking spring on the oven door lets us get ready for what's coming. Jim lifts the platter high before he sets it on the table.

"Oh, yuck!" someone exclaims. The rest of us stare for a couple of deep breaths. Looking exhausted, small lids closed, a draggled crown of scorched pinfeathers on bald, yellow-beaked heads, their long necks curved, skinny claws curled, the quails *en sarcophage* are a sensation. Stuffed with foie gras and truffles in their nests of puff pastry, they are Jim's prize dish today. There are a variety of expressions on our faces, but no one chickens out. The rich Clos de Vougeot wine served with them, along with curiosity, helps us start. Soon we dismember them and savor their juicy, delicate taste. In the film an old general splits his bird's skull with his knife handle and slurps out the brain, I remember. I am thankful that no one suggests it today. A salad course cools us. Then the cheeses—Contal, Fourme d'Ambert, bleu d'Auvergne that our friend on Swissair fetched for us—are creamy, sharp, and delicious on the melba toast. We eat all of it. Everyone is talking: the week past, plans, the present gathering, what we'll do next year, who is here, who is gone. We're enjoying each other, as we always do. I'm content. I watch the fire play on faces, walls. I can see flakes of snow from time to time against the dark window. I am comfortable, reflective, a little melancholy. I think of past years, but I can't focus on a next year. I want to stay in this one.

The last course comes: It is a rich, spongy cake soaked in fragrant rum, topped with cream, a delicious baba au rhum from Alaska Silk Pie. While we pick at this, we can try the platter of candied fruits. Cognac finishes the meal. We sit for a while in silence. Some are in the old chairs by the fire; one person lies across the bed. Two of us start clearing the table, throwing the paper plates in the garbage with wet smacks. We'll have to drag it up the hill, bottles and all, when we leave.

A perfume of rum hangs in the air. A couple of us step outside in the sharp fresh air, snowflakes touching our faces. It is warmer than it was this morning, and the snow clouds are opaque. We go back inside.

"Okay, okay, everybody, coffee? More Cognac?" Jim Williams wipes his hands and stands as if he were going to start the whole dinner again. "We'll have the mince and pumpkin pies before we go to bed."

Protests and groans. "You're *kidding!*" someone says. But we know we'll eat the pies. We always do.

It is late. We've fed and walked the dogs. The fire is warm. Several start a game of poker. Others have gone to bed and are sleeping. I talk with a friend between comfortable silences.

"You know," he begins, but trails off, his expressive face serious. We sit without speaking. Yes, I say to myself. Yes, I *do* know. I pull myself out of the chair and get ready for bed. Others follow after a while. I watch the pale gaslight in the growing darkness as I think over the day. I fall asleep without realizing it. The room is cold again and full of sleep when I rise and dress the next morning, having to return to the city. In the light of the embers I see that it is seven o'clock.

I search out all my stuff with the help of a flashlight and pack it for the climb. The door scrapes open as Jim Williams, up and dressed, returns from the privy.

"Cold!" He whistles. "Leaving?"

"I've never had a better Thanksgiving." I am sincere as I hug him good-bye.

"You say that every year." He smiles.

I step out on the sagging porch, pulling the dogs with me. It has begun to snow again, the flakes falling straight down in the still air. Jim has revived the fire and I can see the rosy glow of the front window as I reach the first turn of the trail. After that only the luminous snow lights my way.

I think of my time in Alaska. Times of feeling isolated, even trapped, in this remote place. Sorrowful times, lonely times. I can't remember anytime in my life when I was not lonely; it is a kind of salvation. But then I think of the times when I am least lonely, and our gatherings here are among those times. Why do I stay in Alaska? I don't know. And then, sometimes, I do know. Years ago I lived in the tiny settlement of Indian about twenty miles from Anchorage. The drive to town in any season, in its splendor, is like no other I've ever taken. I thought of the fierce winter storms. I remembered early spring, the air chilly with a bright silvery mist. I always feel then as if I am about to go on an exciting journey, my destination unknown. I remember a hushed summer day down there at my cabin on the side of Indianhead Mountain. As I was repairing something in the yard the feeling grew that I was being watched. I stood very still and slowly studied the woods, finally seeing a lynx at the edge, his golden look fixed on me. After we had held each other's eyes for a long space, he silently withdrew. I thought of my work, the people I've known. I saw the great, distant mountains across the water, on the horizon, always changing in the clear subarctic light. Here we are forced to create whatever we have, transience in the midst of the totally impersonal, the potentially lethal. Perhaps this very precariousness forces one to become aware, to grow in awareness more than one might elsewhere. Because of this, other human beings seem precious.

I am near the top of the trail in the silent forest when I remember what we've said these past years when we get ready to leave. At first it was a joke; now it is a talisman. And today it slipped my mind.

"Next year in Jerusalem," I call, my breath a small cloud.

The snow-covered red truck waits like a patient little animal at the top of the trail. I open the door, heave my gear and garbage in, then whistle up the dogs who scatter snow all over the seats. The engine starts without a cough, and we're on our way back to Anchorage.

MAR VISTA, CALIFORNIA

As a boy, I dreamed of falling in love with a man with broad shoulders, strong, gentle hands, and a warm, sweet smile that crinkled the corners of his eyes; I imagined sharing my life with him, all of my life for as long as we lived. I pictured a house of our own on a clean, quiet street, with a patch of evenly mown lawn growing in the front and back. It was my gay child's variation on the old-fashioned Hollywood happy ending, crossed with my impression of the way my parents lived—only sans children and with fewer tchotchkes in the living room. I don't remember considering exactly where this little dream cottage might be located—Los Angeles native that I am, I likely assumed I would settle somewhere in Southern California. But geography was never my main concern: San Francisco, Saginaw, or Siberia, what mattered most was the guy, this broad-shouldered Jim, Joe, or Jack I hoped to meet someday. Wherever I lived with him, that would be home.

Sometimes, if you're lucky (and I suppose I am), dreams do

come true: nearly fifteen years ago, I met a man who fit the bill—broad shoulders and everything—and we fell in love. His name is Greg, and (knock wood) we're still together, and still in love. Not only that: I got the house, too. Well, actually, a large interstate bank still owns most of it; but as long as we keep up the mortgage payments, we can *say* it's our house.

We live in Mar Vista. Now, if you know the Los Angeles area well, you probably have some idea where Mar Vista is located. Otherwise, this will likely require some explanation, if not photocopied pages from the *Thomas Guide*. And I suppose it's only fair to mention that, like most Angelenos, I tend to measure the distance between one object and another not in miles, kilometers, or city blocks, but in minutes spent behind the wheel of a car. After all, L.A. is (as Dionne Warwicke once put it) a great big freeway; when estimating the distance between your home and your office, your favorite video store or that nice couple you met at Michael's party who have invited you over for Sunday brunch and Canasta, the number of miles as the crow flies is considerably less relevant than how long you're likely to be parked in the middle lane of the northbound San Diego Freeway, swearing under your breath and jabbing at the buttons on your car radio. And whether that time is likely to double on Friday afternoon as opposed to Thursday afternoon.

That having been said, Mar Vista is just north of Culver City, immediately southeast of Santa Monica, about two miles due east of Venice Beach—famous for the oil-slathered bodybuilders, Spandex-clad roller skaters, and encampments of homeless citizens that congregate there. The beach is a mere ten minutes from our house by bicycle; a little less by car, but you'll probably spend ten or fifteen minutes searching for a parking space once you get there. Hence the name—Mar Vista, which, in case your knowledge of the Spanish language is confined to words found on the menu at Del Taco, means "ocean view." What this means for Greg and me is that we can see the ocean if we sit on the roof—which we actually did one Fourth of July, drinking champagne and watching the fireworks from the Santa Monica pier. We're planning to add a second story to the house to take advantage of this potential view. Someday. When we have the money. Like when a long-lost uncle keels over and leaves me a fortune. In the meantime, we have the cooling ocean breezes to clean the air and take the edge off even the hottest summer day. Mar Vista is consistently five to ten degrees cooler and noticeably less smoggy than, say, West Hollywood, which is only about seven miles (or twenty minutes on surface streets in decent traffic) away. And there's always the roof.

A large part of what attracted Greg and me to Mar Vista when, early in the summer of 1984, we set out to buy what we somewhat naïvely referred to as our "first home" was that it was among the last areas of affordable single-family housing on L.A.'s "West Side"—"affordable" being a very relative term. So far as I know, there is no official, government-issue definition of the West Side, but I tend to think of it as the expanse of ever-more-expensive real estate from Culver City to the south, Brentwood to the north, Beverly Hills to the east, inclusive, and stopping at the Pacific Ocean to the west. It was important to Greg and me that we buy our house on the West Side, for a couple of reasons. For one, the West Side boasts considerably less litter, graffiti, and smog and consistently cooler temperatures than the San Fernando Valley, far less gang activity and crime (both violent and victimless) than Inglewood or Compton, and almost none of the overall sleaze quotient of Hollywood.

In addition, Greg and I had met and fallen in love while we were both students at UCLA—the University of California at Los Angeles—a West Side landmark. We'd first set up housekeeping together in an infinitesimal apartment within easy walking distance of the campus, and in the ensuing decade had resolutely refused to settle more than a few miles from our alma mater. By the time we began serious house hunting, the West Side was the indisputable center of our little universe, with both our jobs (Greg is a banker, while I toil by day as a legal secretary), our church, and a familiar and reliable collection of food markets, health spas, public libraries, movie theaters, record stores, and video outlets well within our preferred territory. Like good shoppers, we dutifully walked through open houses in the San Fernando Valley (thirty, maybe thirty-five minutes from the West Side in good traffic, up and over the hill on the San Diego Freeway North), where we knew we could get nearly twice the house for our hard-won dollar than on the West Side, but our hearts weren't in it. Sure, three bedrooms and a swimming pool would be nice, but it's so darned *hot* in the summertime, the air quality sucks, and jeez, it's the *Valley*. Location, it seems, had taken on a somewhat heightened importance for me over the years. We were, we discovered, West Side chauvinists.

We learned of Mar Vista through the real estate section of the *L.A. Times:* it was just a few miles from our apartment, and we'd been completely unaware of the area, so provincial had we become. Still, the descriptions and photographs looked promising, and the prices were reasonable—that is, having already scrimped and saved and made do with last year's fashions for four or five years in order to raise a down payment, if we could cope with being flat broke for six months or so (after which we were both due for pay increases), we could probably get into a house there. A fixer, more than likely, but something we could live in, in a neighborhood we could live *with*. We made an exploratory venture into Mar Vista one Sunday afternoon in May, just to check out the lay of the land. We bought the first house we walked into.

The street, Stewart Avenue, was everything we wanted: a quiet, tree-lined cul-de-sac with only single-family dwellings of pre–World War II vintage. No apartment buildings, no recently erected condo complexes. No wrought-iron bars over the windows, no graffiti sprayed across the fences. The house was a couple of blocks away from a fire station (safe) and a Mormon chapel (spiritual). It looked like the kind of neighborhood where we had both grown up—Greg in San Jose, fifty miles south of San Francisco (about an hour's drive on the freeway from the City)—and I in Inglewood, a couple of decades before drugs and gang violence would turn that L.A. area into a war zone. It was like finding a little pocket of suburbia a twenty-minute drive on surface streets from Beverly Hills, where we both worked.

As for the house itself, it was in fact a fixer: front yard overgrown in unsightly ivy, backyard thigh high in dead weeds, almost every room in immediate need of paint. And only one bathroom. It was of no immediately discernible style or era; just

one whitewashed-wood-and-stucco box parked on top of another—two-car garage below, house above—just sort of a *house*
house. But we fell in love with it immediately, simultaneously,
literally skidding to a halt in front of it. We liked the large garage
with a workbench and the fact that the house itself was built
above the street level, with fifteen concrete steps and a short
walkway leading to the front door. We liked the roomy rooms,
the twin lemon trees in the backyard, the flagpole in the front,
and the fact that the washer and dryer came with. And we both
agreed that it *felt* right. This was our house. We made an offer
on it the same day.

Nearly seven years later, we're still here. The ivy is gone
from the front yard—Greg removed it with a succession of hoes,
picks, shovels, and his bare hands—and replaced by one of the
neatest, greenest lawns on the block; the weed jungle in the backyard sliced down, yanked up, and chemically killed; and both
bedrooms and the bathroom painted. In fact, it's high time we
painted them again. Since we moved in, the teenage girls next
door have grown up and gone. Chuck and Doris, the sweet, in-
domitably cheerful grandparents directly across the street have
retired to the wine country, replaced by a classic yuppie lawyer-
and-housewife couple with a small child and one in the oven.
And property values in Mar Vista have gone berserk. We bought
our house in 1984 for $160,000, a sum that prompted my mother
to exclaim, "You're buying a *mansion?*" That same year she had
a four bedroom, two-and-a-half-bath house custom built from the
ground up on an acre of land for $170,000. Not in Los Angeles,
of course, let alone the *West Side,* but in Lancaster, some eighty-
five miles northeast of Los Angeles, or about an hour and a quarter on the freeway, if you break the law most of the way, driving
between sixty-five and seventy, as I do; a smallish (but rapidly
growing) area that my mother seems to love and my father often
refers to as "the sticks." Anyway, our house was last appraised
at over $450,000. No brag, just facts.

Aside from the joys of equity (among them a recent refi-
nancing that yielded us enough money to do a full renovation on
the kitchen), the things we like about Mar Vista are the things
that attracted us in the first place: the quiet, the notable lack of

high-rises in the immediate vicinity, and its proximity to the ocean, with its relatively clean, cool air, and to a particular strip of Venice Beach popular with gay men for sunning, splashing, and (shall we say) sightseeing.

I know what you're thinking. If we wanted to be with other gay men, why not live in West Hollywood? Well, first of all, West Hollywood lies just outside our preferred territory (see definition of the West Side, above). Besides, home prices there were way beyond our budget, even seven years ago. And while we do live relatively close to West Hollywood (an L -shaped drive, north on Centinela Avenue then due east on Santa Monica Boulevard or, as I've said, about twenty minutes if the traffic is with you), we've always thought of it as someplace to *visit,* like Disneyland or San Francisco. We've never seriously considered *living* there. Oh, we'll brunch a couple of Sundays a month at the Rose Tattoo (one of too-few gay-owned restaurants in the L.A. area—we saw Rock Hudson there a couple of years before he died), with its better-than-average eggs benedict and its somewhat overly familiar waiters standing hand-to-hip, pelvis forward, reading you the specials through an insinuating smile. We'll pay a visit to The Pleasure Chest (a veritable Bloomingdale's of sexual paraphernalia at Santa Monica near Fairfax, across the street from the Pussycat porno theater) to purchase our "personal lubricant" of choice, on an as-needed basis, checking the local bookstores for copies of my novels along the way. Once in a very great while (usually at the insistence—and in the company of—friends) we'll "do Boys' Town," barhopping up and down Santa Monica Boulevard; dancing up a good sweat on the tiny dance floor at Rage, alongside boys who were in the fifth grade when Greg and I first moved in together; slipping dollar bills into the G-strings of the exotic dancer/go-go boys at Studio One; shamelessly ogling the pretty young things strutting, standing, leaning in the classic one-foot-up-on-the-wall pose, all along the boulevard.

We have fun in West Hollywood. What's not to enjoy about great hordes of gay men? Even we old married couples like to *look.* And besides, we both find something very comforting, something . . . I don't know . . . *affirming* about large groups of gays. The sheer numbers and variety—big and small, blond and dark, younger, older—give us both a warm sense of (dare I say it) community that's like a spiritual booster shot. We never miss the Christopher Street West Gay Pride Festival, for the same reasons. On the other hand, those same great hordes of gay men, and the accompanying sense of sexual possibility around every corner, has always made West Hollywood seem less than ideally conducive to long-term gay relationships. And it's awfully far from the beach.

And how, you may well ask, have we fared in Mar Vista over the past almost seven years, an interracial male couple in a basically hetero middle-class reasonable facsimile of a suburban neighborhood?

Just fine, thanks. Our neighbors have ranged from pleasant and personable to standoffish and monosyllabic—mostly, they've just minded their own bloody business while we minded ours. Which, very frankly, is all we've ever wanted of the folks on our block. Perhaps naïvely, Greg and I never expected trouble from the neighbors, though my brother Lloyd (who helped us wrestle our furniture up those fifteen stairs and into the house) did warn us to be on guard for unpleasantness. Not for being gay, which, as Lloyd pointed out, is difficult to prove, but because I am black, and the neighborhood into which we were moving was largely Caucasian. A black family of Lloyd's acquaintance had recently moved into a mostly white neighborhood (I can't remember what area it was), only to find their neighbors hostile and cold, and racial epithets spray painted across the front of their house. Again, I suppose we've been lucky. We didn't expect trouble, and so far we haven't had any—no crosses aflame on the front lawn, no firebombings, not a word of off-color graffiti, ethnic or sexual.

As for our current relationships with the neighbors, they are generally confined to the exchange of smiles and waves hello, or a few words of heat-vs.-humidity small talk from our respective front lawns as we pick up our respective newspapers in the morning or wash our respective cars on a warm Sunday afternoon. Claire, the retired lady across the street (voice like a band saw, hair dyed the color of strawberry Kool-Aid) has popped over a couple of times in the past several years—once to check out our kitchen renovation, once to ask where we'd purchased the wind chimes that hang over the front porch. And if any of our neighbors have been shocked or disgusted by the sight of men (some-times groups of men) hugging and kissing one another on our front porch, in our doorway, or on the walk in front of our house, they have had the remarkable good taste never to say so.

We've never made any attempts to cultivate friendships among the neighbors. In fact, we've allowed attempts by a few of them to go by, mostly because Greg and I have created for our-selves an emotionally close-knit (if geographically scattered) neighborhood, which, of necessity, lies beyond Stewart Avenue, beyond Mar Vista.

Our closest friends are men Greg and I met when we were all boys in college (which takes us all back more years than any of us likes to admit aloud), those men's lovers, or people we've met through them. At one point, we all lived on the beloved West Side, within the shadow of UCLA's Royce Hall, within a mile or two of one another. Just "dropping by" was common. But as we came to purchase our respective "first houses," we began to dis-perse. Chris and Wef (that's right, *W-e-f)* moved to Long Beach (about half an hour on the freeway in good traffic, twelve or thirteen days in bad), buying for a song the huge, rambling three-bedroom, two-and-a-half-story beast left by Wef's grandmother. Stephen and Michael opted for Sepulveda, in the Valley (about the same relative distance as Long Beach, but in the opposite direction), where they purchased a better-than-decent house they could afford in an ever-tougher real estate market.

If Greg is my home, these men are my hometown. This despite the fact that seeing any one or more of them requires that one or more of us get into a fossil fuel–propelled vehicle and drive for half an hour at least. Just dropping by is out of the question.

But one adjusts. Schlepping all the way out to the Valley becomes the trade-off for a delicious dinner and a few games of rather casual bridge ("Two no trump, did you see k.d. lang on Carson last week?") with Stephen and Michael; packing an over-night bag and spending Friday night in Long Beach rather than trying to dredge up the wherewithal to drive back to Mar Vista after food and drink, after midnight, becomes part of the fun.

Still, there are times when we long for the geographical closeness of the years immediately post-college. When Wef, Chris's spouse of thirteen years, grew ill and died of AIDS last year, the miles between us and our friends suddenly seemed to expand. We longed to see Chris, newly widowed and our dearest friend, every day; to hug him, hold his hand, and share his grief daily. But the southbound San Diego Freeway can make for a frustratingly effective deterrent, and we had to make do with weekend visits and telephone calls. We still do.

Our Saturday nights tend to wrap up early. Our friends expect to be hugged, smooched, and sent on their way before twelve. People who don't know us well often look askance or think we're kidding when we take our leave from some Saturday night wingding, with the explanation that we need our beauty sleep and besides, there's church in the morning. The fact is, Greg and I are the very backbone of the tenor section of the Chancel Choir at Westwood Presbyterian Church.

We first met—as I've mentioned—at UCLA. What I didn't mention is that we were both singing tenor in the UCLA Men's Glee Club at the time. After graduation, eager for a musical outlet, I followed the choral director at UCLA to Westwood Presbyterian, where he is musical director. Not to go to church especially—I'm a somewhat bitter lapsed Baptist myself—but for the quality of the music. After a while, Greg (sort of a vague Protestant) followed me there. Westwood Pres is a smallish, unassuming concrete building wedged between a large condominium complex and the Avco Cinema movie theaters on Wilshire Boulevard in Westwood Village, easy walking distance from the UCLA campus. Directly behind the church is the cemetery where rest the remains of Marilyn Monroe. It's usually a quick drive from Mar Vista on a Sunday morning (nine minutes flat from garage to parking lot is our current record), but it can take as long as half an hour to get to 7:30 Thursday evening rehearsal if the San Diego Freeway is congested.

Though we do know three other gay men among the small, generally rather well-heeled congregation (two of which are also in the choir), Greg and I are the only openly gay couple, and Westwood Presbyterian is not a gay church, only a very open and loving one. Now, before I get myself into trouble, I must hasten to add that neither of us have anything against gay churches. We just happen to be very comfortable where we are, more so than we would have believed possible in a nongay church. We have attended services at gay churches from time to time, but we've always returned to Westwood.

Granted, it would take quite a lot to pry us away from Westwood. The music program continues to please and challenge us (the choir performs at least three major classical works per year, with orchestra), and we have formed sweet, years-long friendships among our fellow choir members. We feel respected as musicians, valued as people, and accepted as a couple. We pay our annual choir dues as a couple, and if one of us is absent from rehearsal or Sunday service, the other is invariably asked "Where's your other half?" The pastor of the church (a man of great love and human decency, who denounced Anita Bryant from the pulpit back in the seventies, and who condemns anti-AIDS homophobia from that same pulpit today) demonstrated his regard for us recently when he invited Greg and me to join the church, an invitation I sidestepped at the time and will likely decline. I consider the Christian church as an institution to be the greatest vehicle for homophobia the world has ever known. My own unpleasant experiences with the Baptist church (relax, I don't intend to recount them here) have left a taste in my mouth all the Listerine on the planet couldn't touch. So while I can enjoy attending a particular church where I have been made to feel welcome and accepted, I don't think I can go so far as to join.

The Mar Vista area is, of course, hardly devoid of gay life. Greg and I work out at the Sports Connection in Santa Monica. Only a couple of miles from us (I really should jog or bike there more often, but I usually drive—so sue me.), this Sports Connection is not to be confused with the West Hollywood branch, which is affectionately known as the "Sports Erection." In this bastion of hard-bodied, health-conscious heterosexuality (the movie "Perfect" was based on this Sports Connection and shot there), both Greg and I have not only been, shall we say, fondled in the hot tub by men not of our acquaintance (Have you ever noticed how difficult it is to say "no" convincingly while you're getting an erection?), but we have also become friendly—if not yet friends—with several other gays, having found one another with the combination of eye-contact and body language peculiar to gay men in nongay milieus.

On any given day, as I enter the Nautilus room, Jerry, a handsome silver-haired gentleman, pants a hello in my direction as he performs his umpteenth set of sit-ups, chipping away at the stubborn little pot belly he can't seem to get rid of despite daily workouts. Lee, a diminutive, doe-eyed young trust fund brat, winks and waves while monopolizing the Nautilus "ab" machine. Jim and Randy, a cute young couple (almost two years together) grin in tandem and ask me "Where's your wife today?" Perhaps in deference to the well-publicized overall heterosexual attitude of the place, or maybe just to be silly, these men often refer to Greg (in his absence) as my "wife."

Greg and I have discussed dinner with Jim and Randy, though no one's actually taken out his date book yet. It'll probably happen, sooner or later, our place or theirs. But even if it doesn't, if we never get beyond gym buddies with any of these guys, it's still nice to see them, smile and make small talk about the relative merits of dumbbells versus Nautilus with them. It's that *community* feeling again. Even in this hyperhetero atmosphere, it's nice to feel like we're not alone.

At the market where I do most of my food shopping (maybe two miles away, five minutes in the car), at least three of the checkers are gay. This fact is not nearly so interesting as the way they let me know they're gay. Since I go to the market three to five times a week (I buy most of our food fresh, and I'm not one for planning meals days in advance), I have engaged most of the checkers in some amount of small talk, and most of them know me by name. Shortly after an interview with me was published in *The Advocate* (which included a large photograph), one of the checkers—a tall, nice-looking blond named Bert—walked up to me and said, with a decidedly conspiratorial smile, "So, you're a writer, huh? I read an article about you." A couple of weeks later, Lee, a young black man with a Spike Lee geometric haircut, grinned a mouthful of braces at me and said, "I read an article about you." Mike, whose well-maintained short hair and moustache and gym-built biceps had already caused me to suspect he might be gay, never actually said anything to let me know he knew. He just suddenly got friendlier with me, making little jokes with me, always sotto voce—none of these guys is actually "out" on the job. Anyway, it's kind of nice for me. I mean, while none of these guys has become an actual friend or even yet bought any of my books, it's nice to know that any one of them would open up a check stand for me upon request.

And then there's Mrs. Gooch's Natural Food Store (just around the corner—I could walk there but I generally don't), where I do a good deal of what I call auxiliary food shopping (soy milk, protein powder, that sort of thing), and where every now and again some male shopper will attempt to engage me in a bit of patently transparent small talk, usually concerning my physique ("Boy, you're really in shape!") and how I achieved it ("Gee, how much do you bench press?"). This is also where Todd, a beautiful nineteen-year-old checker—imagine if you will the young Elvis Presley, if Gladys had been Mexican, with curly shoulder-length hair and a black velvet voice—scribbled his telephone number on the back of my receipt and tucked it into my grocery bag next to the whole-grain fruit-juice-sweetened oatmeal cookies.

All this, and an ocean view from the roof of my house. What can I say? It's home.

ARNIE KANTROWITZ

GREENWICH VILLAGE, NEW YORK

IT ISN'T SO BAD, I TOLD myself as I unpacked my few cartons of belongings in my first New York apartment. It wasn't quite the Greenwich Village "pad" of my dreams: that would have been several small rooms architected with charming nineteenth-century complexity in a quaint town house peopled by bohemian artists and actors on a narrow, winding street lined with curiosity shops. Instead it was one L -shaped room (inexplicably called "2½ rms" in the real estate section of *The Village Voice)* located at the back of a squat, plastic apartment house with cookie-cutter floor plans and barren white walls that laughed at individuality. The tenants were mostly business people and professionals, and the closest thing to a curiosity was the number of my apartment—4-X; but like it or not, it was going to be home.

I suppose I should be fairer. Bleecker Street isn't exactly winding, but it does have a curve or two, and it is set at an odd angle to Manhattan's gridded block plan. It was and still is lined with curiosity shops, but they specialized in antiques that were unaffordable to me then, and they were run by supercilious older gentlemen who were apt to be short-tempered with mere browsers like me. I thought how much help a few curiosities might be as I considered the sterility of my new quarters once all the books and dishes and pillowcases were unpacked. My furniture was a folding metal cot and a borrowed bridge table with a bent leg and the scars of some unknown accident on its top, a perfect environment to be depressed in. It was already after midnight, but there were still a few days before I had to begin teaching English to the reluctant freshmen at Staten Island Community College, so I decided to go for a walk. I might as well have been an innocent English girl named Alice deciding to follow a tardy White Rabbit into its burrow.

It was the night of Labor Day, 1966, and at first glance, the streets were simply a darkened version of what I'd seen when I'd been apartment hunting. I knew nothing about my new neighborhood except that it had a reputation for being tolerant and artistic, perhaps a bit eccentric, so I presumed it would be a little easier to continue my carefully closeted gay life there than it had been in Newark, New Jersey, where I had been living with my father. I was only a block from Christopher Street, but that had no particular meaning to me. Nonetheless, I was drawn in that direction, perhaps because there seemed to be a little more activity there.

As I turned the corner, my jaw dropped. It was as if I'd stepped into another dimension! Christopher Street was literally lined with obviously gay men, leaning against buildings, sitting on railings and stone stoops and car fenders, strutting and sashaying and celebrating the last moments of the holiday weekend with easy smiles and gladly leering glances. Most of them had left their shirts open almost to their navels to show off their summer tans and well-sculpted chests, which made me feel conspicuously pale and frumpy in my baggy academic tweed jacket. Compared to them, I looked middle-aged although I was still in my mid-twenties. I walked for blocks, my eyes wide with wonder. If they'd added a Mad Hatter and a Cheshire Cat, I couldn't have been more amazed, but by the following Labor Day I had accumulated a wardrobe for cruising and the manner to go with it, and at least after dark, I was one of the boys.

The Village was a far cry from where I'd grown up. Newark was less than an hour away but was a different world. My feelings about my hometown were summed up by Eve Arden in a film called *Goodbye My Fancy:* "I don't believe in nostalgia. I was born in Newark. When I pass through it on a train, I keep the shades drawn." Newark was no place to be different. The Weequahic section, where I was raised in the 1950s, was a landscape of tidy one- and two-family frame houses populated by suburbanites in training whose highest value was conformity. The merest hint of queerness brought smirks and ridicule in the form of a pinky tip, wetted on the tongue and painstakingly drawn across one eyebrow. I presume they were referring to the homosexual reputation for vanity, but I thought the gesture strange coming from young men who spent a full twenty minutes at the mirror in the high school gym locker room arranging the forecurls of their "Chicago box" haircuts (long on the sides and short on the top and stiffly held together with setting gel).

Fag bashing wasn't the style in my neighborhood, but it was okay downtown, which by day was populated by gray-faced office drones, who worshipped drabness. At night, however, it became the cruising ground of the desperate, the pathetic, the self-hating, and those who sought to victimize them. I spent my college days as an English major at the Rutgers campus in downtown Newark (including many hours wasted peering through a tiny hole in the wall of the men's room stall, which revealed only the heads of pissing penises and never once led to an active encounter).

Late at night I discovered that Washington Park, right in front of the school, was where I could find dicks to suck—and troubles to contend with—but I was willing to pay any price to pursue my desires. After graduation, I even moved into a furnished apartment a block from the park. A stream of cars, driven by nervous, middle-aged married men, or by cocky young men who still lived with their parents, would silently circle the park in search of furtive blow jobs. Lonely gays would walk around the park and peer into the darkened interiors of those cars, imagining they saw the silhouettes of their dream heroes beckoning them to eternal love, or at least to a moment of fleeting ecstasy that would hold them over until the real thing came along. We hated ourselves for what we were doing, but we felt that we were victims of an irresistible compulsion—and of each other.

The most pleasant encounters involved checking into fleabag hotels and kneeling on cracked linoleum to service embarrassed men or having my virgin ass popped by a hunky bread truck driver in a sleazy apartment without benefit of either a lubricant or the ability to cry out since the building superintendent was next door. The uglier moments included getting into a car with three—count 'em, three—swarthy young studs in white athletic undershirts with promising bulges in their jeans and soon finding myself on a dark side street in the neighboring town of Harrison with a gun pointed at me, pleading for my college ring and at least enough carfare to get back to my beloved Newark.

The most unforgettable experience was the time I allowed the handsomest man I had ever seen (that month) to drive me to the back of a closed parking lot. ("Make it quick," he said. "I have to meet my brother soon.") In a few minutes, I was lost in bliss, my face buried between his buttocks. ("You like that?" he said. "I think you're disgusting.") I was nodding my muffled assent when suddenly a bright light was shining on us, and two cops were loudly expressing their contempt for our kind and threatening us with arrest and exposure to our families and employers and possibly the clergy as well, unless, of course, we happened to have a little extra money. I gave them all I had, twenty-five dollars, and they left us with a warning of dire results if we were ever caught again. I sighed with relief. ("You got any money for gas?" my handsome hero responded. "I'm out of cash.") That was when I knew I didn't want to spend the rest of my life in that town.

When I finally escaped, I ended up someplace worse. I got my first teaching job at a college in the small town of Cortland, New York, which made Newark look glamorous. My students might as well have been the sex police because there was nowhere to go to avoid encountering them, but that didn't matter because there were no opportunities for sex, other than a faded false promise scrawled on the wall of the men's room in the town's only hotel. Aside from combing my hair to shreds in the mirror that faced the door to the men's locker room at school, I contented myself with fearful purchases of *Tomorrow's Man,* hoping that the storekeeper would think I was interested in my own muscle development despite my obvious evidence to the contrary. When I got back to my apartment, I would masturbate compulsively (up to six times a day) while imagining what pleasures lay waiting beneath the bathing suits and posing straps of the unattainably perfect models. Then I would cover the magazines with bricks at the bottom of a carton that I kept hidden at the back of the living room closet.

Eventually, my desperation led me to leave the house at two in the morning to patrol Main Street, a four-block stretch of silent banks and storefront displays featuring tasteless greeting cards, ominous prosthetic devices, and dusty mannequins clothed in dated fashions, all of which I inspected minutely. There, in a period of one and a half years, I had three encounters: one with a local man, in which any hint of pleasure was undermined by our anxieties, and two others with traveling salesmen, who were more interested in a free place to sleep than in true love or good sex or even mutual solace. Ultimately, I cut my wrists and landed back at my father's house in Newark, seriously depressed.

The only bright note was my weekly visit to New York to see a psychotherapist (who turned out to be as gay as I was but a lot better adjusted), and as soon as I was back on my feet, I found a job on Staten Island and moved to Greenwich Village, where I would never have to feel different again. I wandered the twisting streets of my new neighborhood, wondering like every newcomer how, if Manhattan was laid out in a grid pattern, West Fourth Street could possibly cross West Tenth Street. I explored the wonders of avant-garde film and Off-Broadway theater, ate in crowded exotic restaurants, and squeezed my way through tiny art galleries.

I spent my days teaching and my nights cruising, often until dawn. I saw more of Christopher Street than I did of my apartment. In the 1950s, a decade before I arrived, the cruising area had been the "meat rack" on the edge of Washington Square, where nannies had wheeled baby carriages by day and gays had

flaunted their wares late at night. In the early sixties, the scene
had moved a few blocks north and west to Greenwich Avenue,
where tourists had shopped in charming craft shops by day and
gays had continued to flaunt their wares late at night. When I
moved in, the flower children had begun to fill Washington
Square with the sound of guitars, and Greenwich Avenue had
grown seriously commercial. The gays were flaunting their wares
both day and night along Christopher Street, whose custom-
designed jewelry and homemade candle and chocolate shops and
bars grew increasingly gayer from Sheridan Square westward to
the Hudson River, on whose banks I could look across the water
at New Jersey and laugh because I was free.

During my early years in the Village, my friends were
straight, and my only contact with the homosexual world took
place in the streets since I was afraid to be seen going in and out
of gay bars. My quest often continued after the bars closed at
4:00 A.M., when scores of horny men were still trying to make a
last-minute connection, but while I was trying to think up an
opening line more clever than, "Nice night, isn't it?" or "Got a
match?" I was also preparing explanations of why I was out
window shopping at such bizarre hours, in case I ran into one of
my teaching colleagues who lived in the neighborhood. I was even
dating a woman regularly, for cover, in the hours before I began
my nightly search for the man of my dreams.

Some of the men I met were liberated hippies, who weren't
"into" relationships and some of them were paid hustlers. Many
of my tricks were tourists or furtive visitors from other parts of
the greater metropolitan area, who needed to get drunk far from
home in order to commit homosexual acts. We remained
strangers, often exchanging only first names, a suspiciously large
number of which were "John," and we never had breakfast together. If there was a gay community in the neighborhood, I
certainly wasn't part of it.

One June night in 1969, I was on my way home from my
weekly heterosexual date when I noticed a crowd gathered around
a small bar on Christopher Street. I knew nothing about the place,
and I had no idea what was happening there, so I passed on by,
unaware that my life and every gay life in America was being

changed. The police were raiding a gay bar called The Stonewall Inn. For the first time in history gays were fighting back and in the process were launching the modern gay liberation movement. I read about its progress in the local papers as I went about my usual closeted life, teaching and being psychoanalyzed, and finding furtive sex.

Eight months after Stonewall, however, gay liberation finally caught up with me. I was walking through Sheridan Square dressed in my academic tweeds to hide my vulnerable mood. A few days earlier, I had been threatened with blackmail by a junkie hustler whom I'd succeeded in wrestling out of my apartment doorway, but I didn't want to lead the life of a chronic victim. As I walked through the square, someone suddenly thrust a leaflet at me. The leaflet said that there was going to be a demonstration because another gay bar, The Snakepit, had been raided. One hundred eighty-seven people had been arrested, and a young visitor from Argentina, afraid of being deported, had fallen while trying to escape from the window of the police station, impaling himself on a spiked fence. My first thought was, "Why was the leaflet given to me? Do I look gay?"

The next day, I took a straight couple with me for camouflage and watched the demonstration. Members of the Gay Activists Alliance marched up Bleecker Street with angry shouts of, "Say it loud: Gay is proud!" and "Two-four-six-eight, gay is just as good as straight!" Their words rang in my ears because I knew they were true. We followed them to the police station and then to the hospital for a vigil. As I admired their courage, I began to see what was wrong with my life. I wanted to earn my self-respect as a gay man, and I knew that in order to do so I could no longer be a mere spectator because this was my battle, too. The next day I began to come out of the closet. My life on the gay side of the looking glass began, and Greenwich Village finally began to feel like home.

I saw an ad in *The Village Voice* later that week, and I went to my first meeting of the Gay Activists Alliance. I found myself in a roomful of strangely wonderful people: butch bodybuilders and angry drag queens, militant lesbians and sensitive artists. I had always struggled to avoid obviously gay people for fear they would attract attention to my secret life. Besides, I had always believed I was different from stereotypical gays, perhaps because my wrists weren't limp and I didn't lisp. Now, for the first time, I saw them for what they were: individuals. I knew that I was one of them, and I was happy to belong somewhere at last.

Within a few months I was elected first as GAA's secretary and then its vice-president. All my free time was spent sitting at meetings or going to demonstrations at magazine publishers' offices, insurance companies, and courthouses. After one protest in sympathy with the hustlers of Times Square, who were being harassed by the police, we marched all the way back to the Village, where we found a gay night club being harassed by the fire department. The result was the darker side of Wonderland: a night of rioting, with cars overturned and store windows broken, and policemen breaking potentially dangerous bottles with their nightsticks, filling the night with the sound of shattering glass. When we had worn ourselves out, my friends and I stopped for an innocent ice cream sundae only a few blocks from the nightmare our neighborhood had become. In the morning, life quietly returned to our special version of normality.

Emboldened by the new sense of strength such experiences gave me, I came out of my closet in newspaper articles, on television shows, and in classrooms. Since my colleagues and family and students and even some of the general public already knew I was gay, I integrated the different parts of my personality by teaching in the embroidered, rhinestoned dungarees I had made and wearing the colorful shirts I had purchased in hip Village boutiques. My neck and wrists and fingers were agleam with jewelry, which caused some curious stares and comments on conservative Staten Island, but I was determined to carry the concentrated gayness of Greenwich Village with me wherever I went.

I paid less and less attention to the strictures of the heterosexual world as I became part of a whole universe of liberated gay people. Openly gay shops and businesses were springing up everywhere. The gay liberation lambda symbol appeared on posters in store windows and was incorporated into clothing and greeting cards and jewelry. I spent holidays with my new gay friends rather than with my family. Soon I was writing regularly in the gay press, and—aside from textbooks—reading mostly gay material. I followed innumerable gay political meetings with gay parties and gay demonstrations and meals in gay restaurants and drinks in a great many gay Village bars, which were proliferating in a bewildering variety, segregated by tastes in clothing, age, gender, music, money, and orgasm, with friendly names like Ty's, Carr's, Julius's, Keller's, Uncle Peter's and Uncle Charlie's, or intriguing names like The Zodiac, The Barn, The Roadhouse, The Ninth Circle, The Monster, Boots and Saddle, Exiles, The Sewer, The Toilet, The Strap, The Anvil, The Cell Block, The Hellfire Club, The Locker Room, The Annex, Ramrod, Peter Rabbit's, Sneakers, The Stud, and a few blocks uptown, The Spike and The Eagle's Nest. The women went to bars like The Duchess, Moonshadow, and The Cubbyhole. Some bars lasted for decades, while over the years others disappeared with White Rabbit speed, but all of them afforded opportunities to be surrounded by gay people, so that it was easy to forget there was a larger world that began only a few blocks away. When my lease was up, I moved into a gay commune with five other men in an old house in SoHo, just south of the Village, but that meant nightly twenty-minute treks back to Christopher Street because no matter how gay my life had become at home and work, Greenwich Village was the place to put my principles into practice, i.e., to get laid. I cruised the Village streets proudly, as if they belonged to me at last, defiantly standing for hours beneath a grocery sign that read "Fancy Fruits" and looking everyone from nervously clutched straight couples to prospective sex partners right in the eye. When the commune disintegrated a couple of years later, of course I moved right back to the Village with a roommate, and that's when Wonderland finally grew a little too wonderful for me.

Our apartment was on the corner of Christopher and Bleecker Streets, which was like living next door to the Mad Hatter's tea party. Christopher Street had exploded into an all-night event, with gays coming from all over America and several other continents to be a part of its legendary freedom. The gay world was no longer a secret society. It had become a public circus. The sounds of its night life floated into my bedroom window until dawn: shrieks of "Get real, Mary!" accompanied by

antigay epithets shouted from passing cars full of drunken teenagers from New Jersey, occasional brawls, and cheers from the
revelers who gathered to watch the campy antics of Rollerina.
Rollerina was the Village's best example of spontaneous gay culture: a Wall Street businessman who at night and on weekends
turned himself into a fairy godmother on roller skates, dressed in
a granny gown topped with a demure little bonnet and glittering
harlequin glasses. As he skated in front of cars and waved his
magical wand, the traffic stopped, and the bemused drivers
honked their horns impatiently, raising gales of gay laughter and
irate complaints from annoyed straight neighbors.

Having visitors in the apartment meant trying to talk to
people who were looking over my shoulder to cruise the endless
parade of gay men outside. (I once counted them from my window. From 2:00 P.M. to 2:05 P.M. on a Saturday afternoon, there
were 104 passersby on the north side of Christopher Street. Forty-
seven of them appeared heterosexual, four of them were lesbians,
and fifty-three, judging by obvious signals of dress or manner,
were gay men.) Cruising from the window was not merely wishful
thinking, as I proved several times by successfully meeting sex
partners from my third-floor window (only to discover that everyone looks a lot better from three stories up). Going to the
corner market meant dressing for a possible sexual encounter and
enduring the uncomprehending stares of Midwesterners perched
two yards above street level in the tourist buses that rolled down
the block with tedious regularity.

Although it had its quiet side streets lined with brownstone
town houses and carefully nurtured trees, the heart of Greenwich
Village had long been like a theme park. First bohemians, then
beatniks, then hippies, then liberated gays drew crowds of spec-
tators and fellow travelers. The weekends were totally out of the
question. Locals stayed home to avoid the throngs of "bridge and
tunnel people" who come from other boroughs of the city and
from other states in search of colorful mementos, plain fun, cool
jazz, kinky sex, and trouble. Weekdays weren't much better. The
leftovers of the previous night's party were always to be found.
On the corner, in front of the Village Cigar Store on Sheridan
Square, smartly dressed businesspeople and old Italian grand-

mothers who'd lived in the neighborhood for decades would pass a semiconscious drag queen in a crushed red velvet dress sitting on the curb, her mascara running as she sobbed in the unforgiving sunlight. One morning I found an inexplicably naked man sitting on my doorstep and went upstairs to get him some clothes and shoes. Another time I opened my front door to be greeted raucously with, "I'll suck your ass if you give me a Tuinal!" (I politely declined.) Wonderland, I finally decided, was no place to live.

Christopher Street had grown progressively shabbier in the years since I'd arrived. The hard drug trade had established itself in Washington Square, where the gay cruising grounds had once flourished, but the drug peddlers had followed the gay market and hawked their wares openly. I walked the streets to their rhythmic intonations of, "Ups, downs, 'ludes, coke, acid, grass," and eventually, "crack." Along with the flower generation of the sixties, I had developed a taste for psychedelic mushroom delights of the sort offered to Alice by the caterpillar. I had danced until dawn at the Gay Activists Alliance Firehouse and later at The Saint (both of them now only memories) energized into phantasmagoric fantasies with the help of modern chemistry. I had been to wonderful parties. (My favorite had begun with a quaalude and a little grass smoked in a water pipe filled with amyl nitrite, then progressed to LSD, followed by a birthday cake laced with psilocybin, until the dancing of men in their homemade satin costumes covered with glitter looked nothing short of miraculous, while a tape of Janis Joplin sang, "Freedom is just another word for nothin' left to lose," and when a raging fire erupted in the next building, everyone gathered at the window to look at the pretty flames as if they were made of harmless ribbon.) But I eventually lost my taste for drugs, and I had never been interested in enslavement to heroin, which was what the street dealers were beginning to offer. I also had no interest in the violence and crime that seemed to gravitate to them.

Even if I had been willing to endure the night-and-day intensity of the Village for all its sexual pleasures, it still had not produced a steady lover for me. The very quantity of choices was working against my settling down. Hundreds of "clones," gay men dressed in dungarees and leather bomber jackets, looking as alike as Tweedle Dum and Tweedle Dee, produced a great statement of open homosexuality and solidarity and a new assertion of masculinity, but the concentrated gayness produced an altered sense of reality. For example, there were several blocks where gay men and lesbians could hold hands and kiss openly, and there were so many of us that even the taunts from carloads of visiting fag bashers couldn't terrorize us into abandoning that hard-won freedom. But sometimes it was a rude shock to walk around the wrong corner and realize that a mere block from dreamland, another reality continued to reign. Eventually, my cruising of the same several blocks of Christopher Street began to make me feel like an animal pacing in a cage, so I decided to expand my horizons and move uptown to explore other aspects of my identity. I wrote a painful farewell letter to Christopher Street and published it, which garnered a good deal of mail from gay men who felt the way I did, and I exiled myself to the Upper West Side.

My anger at Christopher Street lasted for a few years, but the sex downtown was more interesting and less complicated than the furtive, less celebratory uptown variety, so I often found myself taking the subway down to The Everard Baths in Chelsea or The Saint Marks Baths in the East Village (both of them later closed by the city). Eventually, even the baths seemed like too much effort, and I frequently found myself traveling down to the Village's most legendary leather sex supermarket, The Mineshaft, two floors of rooms equipped for heavy sex, where my fantasies could be fulfilled by merely reaching out my hand (sometimes up to the elbow), and I didn't get home until 7:00 A.M., reeking of pleasure and coolly breezing past the doorman's raised eyebrows into the staid marble lobby of my West End Avenue apartment house.

It was rarely long before I was on the train heading downtown again. Greenwich Village also remained the city's gay political center. Whenever we demonstrated—against the city council, which took fifteen years to pass a gay civil rights bill or against the use of our streets for the filming of homophobic movies or against the Supreme Court's infamously antigay Hardwick decision or against the random shooting of our friends at a local bar—or whenever we celebrated our gay pride, it began, as had the movement itself, in Sheridan Square. The small crowd of several hundred had gathered near there on Waverly Place for the first gay pride march in 1970, bravely heading out of our "ghetto" up to Central Park, where we had been moved to tears when we learned that 15,000 had joined us all along the route. Now the annual marches of 200,000 end on Christopher Street in a humongous street festival, with food and dancing and fireworks. Thanks to my political life and my sex life and my social life (since most of my friends lived downtown and complained of nosebleeds if they had to go north of Fourteenth Street), I found that I was spending most of my time on the Seventh Avenue IRT, traveling back to the gay heartland.

Ultimately, as I neared forty, my promiscuous life began to wear thin, and I gave it a rest and tried to concentrate on one man at a time. I did meet a lover uptown, but after two years we decided we weren't going to make it, so I returned to the baths, which is where I met Larry Mass, who has been my lover for the last eight years. Larry had a co-op apartment in Chelsea, which for gays is something like a suburb just north of the Village, so of course I ended up moving back downtown, which is where I live now, an address from which it's impossible to ignore the center of our gay universe. Whether we're visiting friends or politically demonstrating or going for a walk or shopping at one of the gay book stores or looking for a good restaurant for brunch, Larry and I usually find ourselves gravitating back to the vicinity of Sheridan Square.

Now, in the tenth year of the AIDS epidemic, the streets of the Village are full of ghostly reminders of the many friends who are ill and who have died. There is the restaurant where Vito Russo used to be a waiter, and from this corner you can look up and see Mark Mutchnik's apartment. On this street, David Summers left the People With AIDS contingent of the gay pride march to kiss me hello, the summer before he died, while his lover Sal Licata, now gone too, stood there, holding up the banner that read FIGHTING FOR OUR LIVES. Here is the bar founded by the late Ty Pinney, who told me he was a pussycat even though he looked like a tiger. That house is where Doric Wilson, a leather-man playwright, used to live before his best friend Billy Black-well, a drag performer, died and Doric split for the West Coast. Right upstairs was where Chuck Choset, the first openly gay candidate for citywide office, used to live, and around the corner is where I saw and hugged Artie Bressan for the last time. A few blocks south is where Marty Robinson used to mimeograph movement leaflets, and around the corner from that is where Tom Doerr, the designer of the gay liberation lambda, lived until his death. Here is where the candlelight vigil was held, and up and down Christopher is where John-John (whose last name I never knew) used to yell his political disagreements at us, and where Arthur Bell used to say, "Let's walk a few blocks and cast aspersions on people," and where "Bambi" wandered, always wise-cracking and looking for help. I never really knew Bambi. He was a street queen who looked more battered every year. Whenever he disappeared for a few months, there were rumors of his death, but he always turned up eventually. We used to joke that when Bambi finally did die, our era in the Village would be over. He hasn't been seen for years now.

The world of Greenwich Village has changed considerably from what it was when I arrived. Although some of the same bars are still popular, the younger generation is more apt to be found at newer places like Mars or The Roxy, or at East Village spots like The Bar or The Pyramid. The Gay Activists Alliance is long since gone, but thousands of people now fill the streets for demonstrations run by ACT UP (the AIDS Coalition to Unleash Power) or Queer Nation (which addresses the issue of antigay violence). Yet no matter how much change there is in the trends of fashion or the popularity of particular night spots or political organizations, one essential thing that remains unchanged is the Village's function as a place where young gay people come to learn the ropes.

At the Gay and Lesbian Community Services Center, housed in a former schoolhouse on Thirteenth Street, well over one hundred organizations meet, ranging from Gay Fathers Forum, Gay Overeaters Anonymous, and Bronx Lesbians United in Sisterhood to Senior Action in a Gay Environment, Gay Teachers Association, Gay Male S&M Activists, and the Committee for Outraged Lesbians. On the twentieth anniversary of Stonewall, a forum on the political movement of the early 1970s was announced, so I went, hoping to see some old faces. I was amazed that even though the main floor was so crowded I didn't recognize anyone, but I was gratified that hundreds of young people were interested in what was probably ancient history to them, so I slipped quietly into a chair in the back row. The leader of the panel asked, "How many of you are in this building for the first time?" and two-thirds of the audience raised their hands. Then she asked, "How many of you have never been to a gay event before?" and half the audience responded. Finally, she asked, "How many of you have never had any kind of gay experience before?" and when a quarter of the audience timidly raised their hands, I realized that I was at an orientation session for newcomers to the gay community. I nearly wept when I thought how valuable such an evening would have been for me when I was young. Then I went upstairs, where I found the Stonewall panel in a room equally crowded. There I recognized many familiar faces and had one happy reunion after another, and I knew that I was home.

Going back to the Village is like going back to visit a childhood school. The teachers look older and the desks look smaller, but there is still a great awe at how much one has learned there. The Village may be too much of a good thing to be quite real, and few people bring their daily selves there. What they bring is their psyches for education and exercise, and when they leave, they are never quite the same. Alice may have ended up back on an ordinary riverbank in England, but Wonderland will always be a major part of her, just as—wherever else I may be—Greenwich Village will always be a part of me.

LAURENCE TATE

SAN FRANCISCO, CALIFORNIA

"HOME," SAID T. S. ELIOT, "is where one starts from."

But my father was in the air force; we moved every year or two, all over the world. After I left for college, my parents moved twice more, to a town where I'd never lived.

So there's no going back. As for the gay angle:

In Whittier, California (junior high), I got hard-ons looking at the guys in the locker room. I knew it was wrong, but not why.

I realized I was gay on an air base in the Philippines, from an article in the *Stars and Stripes*. Age fourteen. At a school assembly, somebody wrote, "Weber is a queer" on a blackboard. (Weber was a teacher.) Talk, overheard, about "homos."

Deep cover in northern Michigan. Girlfriends. Nose clean. Very, very clean.

At Michigan State, a straight boy. First love, first kiss; first long grisly aftermath.

Nothing against these locales, as such; that's how it was. Most of my adult life I've been in the Bay Area, first Berkeley, now (ten years) San Francisco.

It didn't seem at the time that I came here for any major reason. It was the late sixties, I shared certain ideas of my generation about drugs, Vietnam, mystical stuff. There weren't that many places known to be hospitable to long hair and alternative notions, and Berkeley was certainly one of them.

At that point I'd been in the Midwest for six years, drove out across those vast, empty stretches (Nebraska, Wyoming, on and on) to a distant land's end.

This was before Stonewall, and though I knew I was gay and told (straight) friends, I hadn't done that much and wouldn't do much more for another five years. I didn't know other gay men could be people I might want to be around.

Multilayered city, by now. Era upon era.

Berkeley wasn't bad. Not much gay presence (eyes meeting, guys from the bar, etc.). I leafleted on Telegraph for gay raps; once a guy followed me, yelling, "Faggot on the street!" Normally I blended, like everybody else.

Coming into the city, I used to hate Castro Street. The air was thick with hormones, thump-thump beats from the bars, loitering, eye contact, bare skin. Always unsettling.

I was never into Mecca, gay culture, serious tricking. Lack of talent, mostly, also temperament.

Gay was always an edgy thing for me.

Over the years I've made a peace with San Francisco. You need a place to go. Your turf. Like being a Munchkin in Munchkin-land.

It's hard to look straight in San Francisco. I tell friends, you see groupings of men, women, children, you think: lesbians and their semen donors.

I work at an AIDS agency. Gay men, women of various preferences. You get out of the habit of straight men. There's one, a volunteer, young, with AIDS; hangs out with the ducks, walks and talks, but isn't. Protective coloration. (Even so, he told me he's "not homophobic"; leftover mind-sets, from a lost world.)

I visit my father in Oklahoma City. Shopping malls, every male over thirteen attached to a female, or female and kids. To me, the daddies look gay. Lóok like guys I see here. Look like guys. Guys are gay.

Mind-sets.

Once in a while, in a mall there, two men of a certain age. Fish out of water.

Coming back, getting off the plane, I have a little game: how long till I spot a no-doubt gay. I've never made it to baggage claim.

Not that it's that simple or peaceable.

Sure, straights run it even here. Go outside a few neighborhoods. (Still, you see gays: it ain't Oklahoma.)

"Most of us," Michael Nava says, "struggle against our homosexuality and never learn to trust our natures." Statistically, I think that's true.

I'm a difficult man in many ways, a loner set in a city existence. I don't think about places much, let alone communities. (Certainly not about scenery. Vistas, fog, gingerbread Victorians, etc.: calendar art in daily life.)

But you can make an alternative universe here. Squint a little, screen out things. You can not think of who hates you, how much, shit you eat. Doubts, fears, what, if anything, it means. Just don't think.

Welcome to Munchkinland. The best revenge.

I change as I get older.

In Berkeley, I was in a collective. People who weren't gay-first were called "straight identified." That was me, too many years. Like in the politically incorrect personal ads: "Straight acting." Straight thinking. Their eyes.

Now the straight world irritates me.

I don't want to hear about men wanting women. I'm sick of straight sex scenes. Sometimes I try to imagine what the world would be like if the dominant images of my culture were my stuff too. A whole world in your image. A whole reinforcing metaphysic. This is who you are, this is right, this is *it*. Literally inconceivable.

And now the epidemic. I don't relate so well to people who aren't affected. Who don't care. It's become what I do and who I am. And people who don't get that . . . fine. They don't. See ya.

There were gays in Berkeley, but it was still exotic, mostly secret. The whole question of "minorities," the unacknowledged. All of us know, in different ways, whoever runs it, it's not us.

In San Francisco, we're the world, as much as anybody is. And you can carry that with you, to shopping malls in Oklahoma, to . . . anywhere. There's a reference point, an actual place you can go and see. You get up in the morning and go out and live in it. Stores, papers, billboards, people on the street, everywhere you fucking *look*. Politicians, institutions, power struggles, Harvey Milk libraries and schools. All the ceremonial crap, just like real people. Bite down: It's there.

Frances Fitzgerald included the Castro among some "cities on a hill": communities in the air, actually lived in. San Francisco is a big scummy deteriorating city, with all the pressure and dread that that entails: beggars, crime, traffic, litter, faceless multitudes. Another hundred people.

And the gay atmosphere can get oppressive. A friend lives at Castro and Market: "I get so tired of the queens," he says. Brunch, pierced nipples, all that.

San Francisco isn't God's country, is no delivery from the exigencies of individual fortune, in this vale of tears.

But, hey: It's home.

CHRISTOPHER WITTKE

BOSTON, MASSACHUSETTS

THE STEAMY RED LINE CAR
with the broken air conditioner chugs to a stop. Its brakes hiss.
I'm trying to read a *Gay Community News* article to make the
subway ride go a little faster as a sweat droplet beads up on the
tip of my nose and drips onto the page. I'm squished between
two people with whom I haven't even made eye contact, although
I know their arms and legs intimately. The train is stalled on the
Longfellow Bridge and the driver announces that we should be
moving along "shawtly."

I roll my eyes and another drop of sweat drips around my
brow, across the bridge of my nose, and directly into my right
eye. I remember that a friend once told me that the first thing
you love about a man is the first thing you come to hate about
him, if the relationship lasts that long. Did you find his devil-
may-care, impulsive nature absolutely liberating and downright
charming when you first met him? Then your first fight will probably be about his irresponsibility.

It occurs to me that my love affair with Boston may be going through the same thing. I grew up outside of Hartford, Connecticut, in the working-class section of a town called Manchester. Early on I realized, to paraphrase Mac Davis (of all people) that happiness is Manchester, Connecticut, in the rearview mirror and eventually came to believe that happiness is Boston, Mass., getting nearer and nearer. Sometimes I wonder, what could I possibly have been thinking?

Once I graduated from high school it seemed obvious to me that Manchester just couldn't supply me with the stimulation—sexual, intellectual, you-name-it—that my inquisitive young mind and body needed to survive. Actually, I probably came to this realization earlier than that. After all, I wasn't the first queen to find suburbia boring, and I'm sure I won't be the last.

Hartford, a mere fifteen-minute ride away, seemed almost like a parody of a city. There was a quiet gay community to be found in a small handful of bars and cruising places in the early eighties, but given that the major industries center around insurance and airplane engine manufacture, it's no surprise that the overall attitude was one of conservativism, if not closetedness. The city in general didn't exactly bustle with joie de vivre.

One time, when Bette Midler gave a concert in Hartford (you can only imagine the pent-up energy in the crowd) she called Hartford "a sleepy little burg" and wondered aloud if the streets weren't rolled up at 5:15. Actually, they were rolled up at 5:00.

When it finally came time to move on, to strike out on my own, to get a life . . . I somehow landed in Boston. Given that Hartford lies about midway between Boston and New York City, I sometimes wonder why I didn't choose the Big Apple. Looking back, I realize that I had an opinion of Boston that is so common it's a cliché. "Boston seems so manageable," friends from bigger and apparently more fun cities like New York say to me to this day, as if they were the first to make this statement.

That's what I remember telling myself when I moved here in the spring of 1985, as a nontraditional (meaning not typically college-aged) transfer student at Emerson College. Manageable Boston, with its quaint cobblestone sidewalks and its out and proud—as opposed to Hartford's mostly quiet—gay and lesbian community. I came of this opinion by visiting Boston regularly before I moved here, especially on Pride Day. Thousands and thousands of gay men and lesbians parading through its manageable streets. There was even a big AIDS service organization, AIDS Action Committee—one of the first in the country—concerned with promoting safe sex and helping those living with AIDS. In Hartford I had found it difficult even to get tricks to talk about the epidemic.

There also seemed to be endless cruising possibilities (I'm a cruiser by nature) among the reed-shrouded paths of the notorious Fenway, the steamy porno theaters and crowded peep shows of the infamous Combat Zone, and the dozen bars. It was all so exciting in 1985, that in the midst of the very scary AIDS epidemic it still seemed possible to have a wild and safe sex life in the Big City. Well, Medium-Sized Manageable City. There seemed to be so much to do, so many places to go, it's almost as if there were more gay people around then.

This is my thought on the stalled subway: I know every gay man in Boston, at least by face, and there is absolutely nothing exciting to do in this city anymore. I wonder if the intense heat of this late-summer day is making me grouchy and I'm just imagining these things to be true, or if, in fact, I have a point.

Not only are you imagining it, you're getting very cynical for a person in his late twenties, a voice in my head says. Oh sure, I scoff to the voice in a frighteningly schizophrenic bit of dialogue I attribute to heatstroke, I'm cynical. Who wouldn't be cynical living in a city he can't afford, searching for community, a community he can't really define and certainly can't find? I realize I really am sounding crazy, even to myself, just as the train chugs back into motion.

About a hundred feet later the doors slam open at the Charles Street stop at the base of historic Beacon Hill. "Challs," the driver announces. I could have walked the rest of the way to work and back about a dozen times while the train was stuck and I remember that once a train makes frequent mid-route stops it happens again and again (Rule Number One of Boston subway travel), which reminds me of the old Beantown joke: "Should we walk or do we have time to take the subway?" I realize that I do have the time but decide to wander a bit on my way to work rather than make the transfer to the Orange or Green Lines for the trip into the South End. At any rate, it will give me the chance to cool off. I step onto the platform and even though it's at least eighty degrees outside, I feel like I've just stepped into an air-conditioned room.

I stuff my copy of *Gay Community News* into my backpack as I walk down Charles Street in the direction of the Boston Public Garden, home of the kitsch-but-cute Swan Boats. I find myself fixating on the notion of "community" and wondering exactly what it is that is making me so unhappy about the city I chose to adopt as my hometown.

When I first moved to Boston I lived on Beacon Hill with one of my best friends from back in Connecticut. Prudence and I shared a postage-stamp-sized hovel on Revere Street that was ridiculously expensive, but actually quite cheap compared to what rents are today. We made the best of our cockroach-infested apartment and seemed to find lots of fun things to do with almost no money. She had a new job and a new boyfriend—now her husband—and I was studying by day and cruising by night.

Prudence loved to hear of my adventures and always marveled at my ability to strike up conversation with other gay men while we shopped at the market. I realize this doesn't exactly square with my current impression that New Englanders—and Bostonians in particular—are cold and uninterested in others to the point of hostility. I wonder what was different then?

I decide to take a left and walk up the steep slope of Revere Street to see if I can remember what it was about that time that made it seem so fraught with potential. As I find myself somewhat short of breath from the climb I remember that walking up the hill on a daily basis quickly gave me calves of granite. As I cross at the intersection of West Cedar Street I remember going home once with a guy in a cop uniform who lived nearby and playing "You're Under Arrest" in his foyer. I realize I haven't seen him around town in years.

Getting closer to the site of the apartment I shared with Prudence, I remember a first I experienced when I lived there. A friend I had originally met at a nearby leather bar had been

involved with *Gay Community News* for over a decade and suggested that, seeing as how I was a student in the Emerson College
writing program, perhaps I would be interested in writing an
article for that paper. I hadn't seriously considered submitting
anything to any of the local gay papers in Boston, and *GCN* was
a paper with a national scope. It just never occurred to me that
I could write for them or anyone else. I was "just a student" and
"didn't all of those papers get hundreds of submissions a week,
and isn't it really hard to break into getting published in them?"
Actually my friend explained that *GCN* was a mostly volunteer-
written paper and that they were always looking for new writers.

I couldn't believe my luck when I was given my first assign-
ment, a feature article about gay male porno videos. Sex and
movies, my favorite things, and I was going to get to tell the
world just what I thought of the state of the industry at the time
(which, as I recall, wasn't much).

When the article was published several weeks later I was
surprised to find it in the center spread. Prudence and I celebrated my good fortune and I was so elated that I sent copies off
to my family and friends back home. I felt as if I was on my way.

Days later, sprawled on a beanbag chair in the Beacon Hill
apartment, I found myself nodding as my older brother yelled at
me over the phone from Connecticut. "Is this what you're going
to writing school for?" he asked, incredulously.

"Uh, yes," I said, a little defensively, "as a matter of fact I
am."

"I can't believe you sent this to your mother," he said.

"Is that what this is all about?"

"That language, what could you have been thinking?"

"It's kind of hard," I said, "to talk about porno videos
without being graphic."

"How did you think Mom would feel?"

"What? Reading words like *dick* or is it the fact that I mentioned something gave me a hard-on?"

"I wasn't even thinking of those words . . ." he said, and it
turned out that he was most upset at the fact that the word *cum*
was sprinkled liberally throughout the article. He also told me
that as he read my article he wanted to "poke my eyes out." My

brother was not prone to threats of violence, even distinctly Three Stooges–like violence, so I realized he was serious. I tried to explain.

"Frankly," I said, "I sent it to her so she could see my name in a byline. I had a feeling she wouldn't even be interested in reading the whole thing. I also don't think," given that she was in her early sixties at the time, "that *cum* is a word she's really familiar with. Though I could be wrong. Look, I could have just sent her the headline and the byline, and crossed out the text, but I thought that would be insulting."

He paused for a few seconds and asked, "Is this the kind of writing you're always going to do?"

"What? Porno reviews? No. . . ."

"I mean, are you a Gay Writer or a Writer who's Gay?" he asked.

Ugh. It was another one of those moments when I couldn't believe that a person had just made a statement that he thought was entirely original, as if no one had ever verbalized it in exactly the same way about a million times before. But it was also at that moment that I realized for sure what the answer was.

"A gay writer," I said, "in that that's the community I know—and it's always best to write what you know—and that that's the community I want to write for."

I remember my brother being shocked by this response, as if he had these visions of mainstream success for me. Perhaps he expected to see my mass market paperbacks on the racks in the Manchester CVS. Maybe he thought that since my whole family was (presumably) straight, and that they had been extremely supportive of my decision to go to writing school (right in the middle of the yuppie-student business school boom of the mid-eighties), I was going to produce things that they could completely relate to. I realize now that my brother was feeling left out, as if I was ignoring him in a deliberate attempt to alienate him and the things he held dear. Or maybe I'm overanalyzing and being too generous, maybe my brother was just being a fuckhead.

The conversation wound down with a quick discussion of the merit of pseudonyms and why I didn't use one (because I wanted to take credit for my work) and finally ended with one of those typical pronouncements that straight men like to make. It was something along the lines of "I don't believe this." As I hung up the phone I remember thinking that perhaps I should wear protective eye gear on my next visit home, but I also remember feeling somewhat triumphant. It was as if I had managed to get across to a family member that when I came out to him I wasn't kidding.

"I wasn't kidding." I find myself laughing about this as I stare across the street at the doorway of our old apartment on Revere Street. I wonder if I would send an article like that to my mother today. This makes me sad, almost as sad as the day they told us the rent on our Beacon Hill apartment was (deliberately?) being priced way out of our reach. We were reassured that this didn't even reflect the market standard, which was much higher. Prudence and I took cold comfort in this and sought separate refuge elsewhere.

I take a left down Grove Street, facing Mass. General Hospital, where John Wayne died, but not before making a last statement about how the United States needed to build the neutron bomb. This is also the site, years later, of one of the first ACT UP/Boston protests. At the bottom of the street, right where my lover was recently gay bashed, I take a right onto Cambridge Street, heading in the direction of Government Center.

Walking along, I feel somewhat amazed when I realize that the first real conflict I had after I moved to Boston—during that phone call with my brother—was over my community. There's that word again. It had never occurred to my brother that I might consider myself a member of a community different from his. And I wonder if back then I felt more a part of a community or if I had imagined this monolith standing behind me. A monolith that wasn't really there.

I pass by Sporters, a landmark gay bar that has been open for decades. This was a place where I made lots of friends when I lived in the neighborhood, not the least of which was my lover Sherman. I met him about six months after that big fight with my brother and—I know this is ridiculously cliché—that night as I watched him from across the room I knew that he was "the one." Even Prudence had mentioned that I never used the phrase

"This is it, this is the one" in describing a lust object before. And I was right, as I so often am, because we'll be celebrating our fifth anniversary soon. Even at my most anti-Boston I feel lucky about the roots I have put down with my lover, and the friends I have here. Sometimes I just feel that the soil here isn't particularly fertile.

Continuing up Cambridge Street, I encounter what can only be called a gaggle of college summer students walking in my direction while engaged in loud (very loud) conversation. In five years I have come to really resent students. Ironic, I suppose, when I consider that I moved here to complete my studies. Every fall the city is inundated with a whole new crop of students who have somehow come to believe that the world is their quadrangle. Since there are sixty-five colleges and universities in the area it's no surprise that the presence of students is always noticeable, often oppressive. On the flipside, the winter holiday season and summer breaks offer a noticeable respite for old grouches like me. When the estimated 250,000 students in the area leave the city to the folks who live here, it feels like you're sliding into a warm bath after a particularly stressful day. But these breaks end with the inevitability of the swallows' return to Capistrano, and Boston feels crowded and uncomfortable once again.

I pass through the gaggle and cut across Government Center, remembering the political meetings I've attended over the years at City Hall. I was part of the original group that formed Mass ACT OUT (a sort of ACT UP takeoff) right after the 1987 March on Washington for Lesbian and Gay Rights. Hundreds of us came back from the march energized and determined to bring that excitement to our hometowns. There were some exciting times for a while but eventually Mass ACT OUT withered and disbanded.

Recently, the controversial direct-action group Queer Nation has been meeting at City Hall, and sometimes it feels as exciting as the 1987 stuff, other times it feels as frustrating and silly. I still find myself pinning my political hopes on the group, hoping that internal squabbles aren't its undoing.

I walk through the Downtown Crossing section, past Filene's department store—with its famous bargain basement—and am struck, as always, by the fact that all the faces here aren't white. It's impossible to walk through Boston and not notice its racial divisions, that many sections are predominantly white. It's also depressing as hell to realize that many people would prefer to keep things that way. If I really want to examine the things that I hate about this city, I guess racism would be a good place to start. The problem did not begin with the protests over busing to end segregation in public schools in the mid-1970s. Nor did it end there.

The murder of pregnant Carol Stuart terrified the city in the fall of 1989. Her husband, Charles, wounded in the shooting, claimed that they were victimized by a black man. For weeks, police routinely stopped, and many say strip searched, black men in the Mission Hill district where the murder happened. On the day it was to be announced that Charles Stuart was himself a suspect in the case, he leaped to his death in a nearby river. This case played into the most profound prejudices of many Bostonians, and its aftereffects are still palpable on the street.

I continue down Washington Street and amble through what used to be the Combat Zone, an area in which dozens of adult businesses used to flourish. At this time there are exactly two adult movie theaters here, one showing straight films but very cruisy, the other showing gay films and heavily patrolled by staff. This strikes me as another example of Boston—and probably New England—behavior patterns. Men can have sex with each other in a straight porno theater with relative ease but they can barely sit next to each other in a gay theater without having flashlights shone in their faces.

There are three adult bookstores left here, all of which were stripped of their licenses to have peep shows in a late eighties clampdown on the Combat Zone. At that time the city decided that Combat Zone property was quite valuable and systematically worked to oust adult businesses from the area. The Licensing Board knew that there was nowhere else for these businesses to open as these blocks were in the only area zoned for such things.

The promise was, of course, that the old theaters would be refurbished and the area would soon become a hotbed of upscale performing arts centers and nightclubs. One theater has opened as an Emerson College theater space and one old restaurant has been replaced by a more yup-scale nightclub. As the Massachusetts economy has gradually done its nosedive, the sites of countless formerly thriving Combat Zone haunts have remained boarded up and unused. Gone are the dozens of spaces where men—gay, bi, and "straight"—could connect for quick sex. The memories of such times, many of them mine, are trapped behind the plywood lining the Combat Zone.

This is true of so many Boston hot spots, not just those along my walk to work. Even the venerable Fens on the other end of town, the only real outdoor cruising location in Boston proper, has recently fallen victim to the weed whackers determined to halt public sex practices. While there have been incidents of brutal violence against some of the men who cruise the Fens late at night, it's interesting to note that the Boston solution involves destroying an institution of the gay male community that is decades old, rather than trying to make it safer for men to do what men will do. Small wonder, then, that one of the more conservative gay weeklies in Boston has repeatedly called for reeds in the Fens to be cut down in order to stop men from responding to the "fire in their loins." It's a sign of the times.

As I cut through Bay Village, home of Boston's only full-time drag club, Jacques, and head toward the South End, I realize that both of these neighborhoods have reputations for being "gay." I'm not sure how gay Bay Village can be when I consider that Jacques is also being hassled by Boston Licensing Board, at the request of many neighbors, and faces a precarious future.

The South End is probably no more gay than most urban neighborhoods, it just gets the lion's share of the focus of Boston gay media. Except, of course, in the co-gender *Gay Community News,* with its office also located in the South End, which is where I have worked for the past three years.

I spent my first two and a half years typesetting the paper, a position I never realized was depressing until one longtime collective member mentioned that he wouldn't be able to stand processing so much bad news week after week after week. I realized that he was right. How many AIDS statistics can you type without it getting to you? How can you try to honor an institution's commitment to fight racism and sexism in Reagan/Bush's U.S.A.? How do you stop yourself from plunging into despair?

I guess I thought things would let up when I became Features Editor, the collective position I currently occupy. To some degree this is a less depressing position, but our paper is constantly reporting on legislative setbacks, the AIDS epidemic/genocide, censorship, queer bashing, and the general anti-gay and lesbian furor in this country. It's kind of hard not to get depressed, especially when the city you live in both reflects and contributes to these trends.

And of course, there's the naggingly elusive definition of community. Sometimes it's hard to convince people, both in the mainstream and queer media, that "gay community" doesn't necessarily mean white, doesn't have to mean male, doesn't always mean disposable income, doesn't mean the dozens of things that marketing geniuses have claimed it to mean. Perhaps the notion of "a" community, as a single entity, has been a spurious one all along. And perhaps Boston, which seems to have an even more refined and limited definition of gay as meaning either white, male, and in college or white, male, and semicloseted because of your job, needs a real shake-up to come out of its sleepy-lidded ways.

But recently I have noticed some interesting news coming from south of the Massachusetts border. A few summers ago, after a particularly brutal gay-bash murder outside of Hartford, the local gay and lesbian community began to become more vocal and militant. It is with great delight that we file stories about this development in *GCN;* I often find myself wondering who these people are and where they were when I lived there.

My lover and I have even attended a couple of Pride Days in Hartford—something I never seemed to manage to do when I was a citizen of Connecticut. These parades were rather exciting, perhaps because the participants numbered in the hundreds and we really did feel like a community. With chants in Spanish as well as English (something I can't imagine happening in Beantown) we defiantly strolled through the streets because we wanted to tell people that we were there. I found myself envious of the Hartford lesbian and gay community. When some of its members disrupted Connecticut's governor during a speech and caused him to be visibly upset, the thing that most appealed to me was the image of this group of queers seeming so . . . unmanageable.

SCOTT TUCKER

KEY WEST, FLORIDA

Not in Utopia,—subterranean fields,—
Or on some secret island, Heaven knows where!
But in this very world, which is the world
Of all of us,—the place where, in the end,
We find our happiness, or not at all!
                           —WILLIAM WORDSWORTH

1

"IT IS AN ODD AND NOVEL PLACE," WROTE ONE OB-
server in 1886 (under her married name of Mrs. L. D. Whitson,
in the travelogue *Away Down South*), "and the more interesting
on that account. There are peculiarities here that strike a stranger
very forcibly. Key West is intensely unlike any other place in the
Union." Key West lies at the end of a spinal archipelago of isles
curving from the mainland tip of Florida southwest into the Caribbean, the nation's southernmost point, with Cuba ninety miles

away. In comparison with many other more beautiful islands, Key West is only a small coral shelf where storms have eroded the few decent beaches. Yet for many years my lover and I kept returning there for a week in January. In 1986 I decided to live and work there through the winter.

The history is dim, but it seems the Calusa Indians originally inhabited the Florida Keys. In the 1760s, mainland tribes drove the Calusas down the island chain, and only a few survived a final battle in Key West, fleeing to Cuba. The Spaniards called the bone-strewn spot Cayo Hueso, the Island of Bones. It became a useful and contested piece of real estate among pirates, sea merchants, and salvagers, who were not above using the lighthouse to lure ships against the rocks so they could cash in on the cargo. On March 25, 1822, Lieutenant Matthew C. Perry—later known as Commodore Perry, who opened Japan to American trade—hoisted the American flag above Key West with a thirteen-gun salute from the USS *Shark*. In his report to the government, Perry wrote:

"Heretofore the Florida Keys have been the resort of smugglers, New Providence wreckers, and in fact of a Set of desperadoes who have paid but little regard to either Law or Honesty—the present establishment tho' on a small scale will, I conjecture, with the assistance of the Settlers be enabled to keep these lawless people from this Island. . . ."

Salvaging, or "wrecking," was the main industry, later augmented by sponging and cigar making, attracting Bahamian and Cuban immigrants. In 1861 Key West became a strategic outpost of the Union, from which Florida had just seceded; the Union Naval Station enforced a sea blockade throughout the Civil War. When the USS *Maine* exploded in Havana Harbor February 15, 1898, Key West became a naval boomtown. Epidemics such as yellow fever and AIDS, hurricanes, world wars, the Depression, the changing regimes in Cuba, the migrations of sailors, artists, and gays, the highs and lows of tourism have all defined the character of Key West.

In early 1934 the island economy was shot, the navy was almost gone, and eighty percent of the residents were on relief; there were serious proposals to abandon the island. But the island successfully sold itself as a tourist resort within the same year, and the population and economy rebounded with the military buildup during World War II. With thousands of sailors ashore at times, the sexual scene was lively. Artists and writers established seasonal and permanent homes on the island, including Robert Frost, John Dewey, Wallace Stevens, Hart Crane, S. J. Perelman, Archibald MacLeish, John Dos Passos, and Elizabeth Bishop.

And, of course, Ernest Hemingway and Tennessee Williams, each so representative in his own way of the butch/femme tango of American literature. This little island was big enough for these travelers from opposite poles of sex and psyche. Big enough for each to pursue his sport—deep-sea fishing and cruising sailors, to each his own—and to perfect his own persona. Beneath the machismo of the one and the dandyism of the other was a common struggle to be Americans, artists, and men, all three; the one more declarative and stoic, the other more lyrical and allusive; both dulling pain with their drugs of choice.

For me, the history of Key West is part of its mystery. The simple facts are goldenly suggestive, like finding a pirate hoard: scraps of maps, old coins, and bones. This was the place where Karl von Cosel, a bespectacled and bow-tied X-ray technician at the Marine Hospital, fell in love with a tubercular Cuban girl, Elena Hoyos Mesa. Seven years dead, preserved with wires and wax, and dressed in a wedding gown, she was discovered laid on a bed in von Cosel's home in 1940. He had removed her body from the cemetery hoping to resurrect her, and had first housed her in a homemade airplane. And this is the place where President Truman spent eleven working vacations at the Little White House on the naval base, surely a less appealing and far more sinister figure.

Key West is the place where Jose Martí, founder of the Cuban Revolutionary Party in 1892, stood on the balcony of a home at Duval and Catherine streets to orate for his cause: today the home is a guest house and restaurant known as La Terraza de Martí—or LaTeDa, in gay dialect, where we go for Tea Dance.

Key West is one of America's outer limits of sexuality and sensibility, if you care to venture further and longer than most

tourists; therefore, it is a place of shipwreck for so many. Is it
worth the risk? "Where danger is," wrote Hölderlin, "grow also
the rescuing powers."

2

Journal: Key West, January 13, 1986

Bravo!

I'm living and working in Key West now—I've turned my
world upside down for three months. I have $6 at the moment
and don't get paid till Friday. Passing moments of panic and
reserves of the old daring—which I'd almost come to doubt.

Worked a first short day, nine to noon—crew renovating
two connecting houses and grounds bought by a gay IBM lawyer,
very wealthy: this property in Key West, house in Southern
France, condo in NYC. Today I did prep work, cleaned and
sanded, will be painting later. A good crew—a good dozen, half
gay—carpenters, painters, gardeners.

Journal: Key West, January 14, 1986

"Life is a Breeze in the Florida Keys." Or as Matt likes to
say—who spends his life catering to the whims of the rich, working hard to afford his piece of paradise—"On Your Hands and
Knees in the Florida Keys."

Journal: Key West, January 15, 1986

Little Joe, my workmate who lives in the next apartment,
explained the hierarchy and tensions among crew. Exhausted by
long day at work. Hauling marble tiles upstairs for luxury bathrooms. Priming wooden doors and moldings. Little Joe saw checks
for carpenters—they are making nearly ten times an hour what
he is, and still expect him to clean and sweep after them. On
principle he refuses: "I clean my brushes after I paint, let them
sweep up their own sawdust." Half the crew is openly gay, though
I notice the two most "obvious" or "effeminate" gay guys (including Joe) end up with most of the servile shitwork. Of course
he's difficult—he is quite rightly an outraged queen! If Joe is
"insubordinate," what can or should I do? Unionize the crew

and hold consciousness-raising sessions at lunch break? Laughable in this situation. In some ways we're a real team with island ways and pride in craft, and in some ways we've just brought all the mainland crap and contradictions with us. Nor are we building a utopian commune, but the island chateau of a millionaire.

Understand: there is no Tahiti.

Journal: Key West, January 18, 1986

My hands badly blistered from digging a trench with pickax and shovel through an old cistern and coral rock. We considered quitting—with all the money going into this property, they break our backs to save what it would cost to rent a drill and backhoe. The next day we planted ficus trees in the trench—after hauling them off a flat-bed truck—and the hedge now looks long established. Received my first pay in cash, must buy a used bike to get around the island.

Journal: Key West, February 12, 1986

My apartment block is a classic slumlord property. I figured I would rough it for three months, but we have to complain even to get steady water. Little Joe was assaulted and injured one night by neighbors below. No heart to spin out details now. To work.

Journal: Key West, February 17, 1986

This morning I biked to the dock to see the cruise ship with 750 gay men come in—a marimba band to welcome them, hundreds of helium balloons released (an eco-error, that). Now, home from work, I listen to the conversation of neighbors, a teenage boy and his mother, in her late thirties and beautiful. The boy tells her how he "watched all those faggots come off the boat." He saw "two of them kiss"—disgust. She in turn tells of "two guys at sunset hugging each other—what can you do? Just ignore it." At no point did she discourage her darling from using a string of abuse against gays, and smiled even when her son suggested "they all deserve a beating." Injustice collecting, the shrinks would call what I write now. The boy: "Faggots with flowers in their hats and hair." Yes, lovely they looked, too, old and young men with flowers in their hats and hair.

Journal: Key West, March 2, 1986

Bike tires were slashed last night—I left my bike locked in court, and I suspect the bigots who live below. Nor is that all— a disturbed boy with an alcoholic mom has been opening the mail of tenants, leaving empty envelopes in the mailboxes and on the trail. We spoke with his mom, and she to him; he's now in a panic about cops—his mom's threat—whom none of us want involved, poor kid.

Journal: Key West, March 8, 1986

Audition Monday night for the Tennessee Williams Theatre production of *Best Little Whorehouse in Texas*. I biked from Key West to the Tennessee Williams Theatre on Stock Island (in the shadow of Mount Trashmore) and there was Al, registering people for chorus auditions. His first question was "Are you a navy boy?"—my hair cut short for the heat. He drove me back to Key West, my bike stowed in his van, and said, "We're getting too many faggots for the chorus." I strongly suspected that his gay baiting was his way of being buddies with trade, putting down cocksuckers as a prelude to sucking cock. I told him I was gay. He didn't apologize but invited me for a drink at his house. I drank orange juice, he downed one glass after another of the strong stuff. He told me he'd just lost his younger lover to another older man, seemed to blame this on moving to Key West. We listened and sang along to *West Side Story* until he began pawing me, drunker and drunker. So I thanked him for his company and left—by then he was stumbling and far gone. A dear man in a bad way.

Journal: Key West, March 9, 1986

J.B., an editor, invited me to his house for a drink—he was already soaked when I dropped by and wanted us to go to Tea Dance, where he'd certainly go over the edge. Drinking is an Olympic sport in Key West, the common culture between down-and-out conchs and shrimpers, and the comfy literati. This island also floats on coke, but that tends to be the drug of choice for yuppie entrepreneurs, disco bunnies, and hired help—the bartenders, waiters, salesclerks, guest-house servants, hustlers, and tour guides. Between paying rent and paying for nose candy, not all of these folks eat well, unless they smuggle food from the restaurants where they work. This is what happens when forbidden fruit becomes fast food. Sex and drugs require a real community and initiation, or folks get careless and greedy. Sex and drugs are strong natural magic, as the wiser bohemians and gay folks know. They would be sacramental if we had real community; otherwise they dull the pain of our disconnection.

J.B. has decided I'm a puritan and a hermit because I turn down too many drinks and leave parties early. He says literary life is hopping in Key West—I should meet them all, etc. "You're antisocial," he says. "Come out of your shell." I could have told him I'm the same guy who danced onstage in a bikini at the AIDS benefit at Lighthouse Court, and that friends here think I live a charmed life—dates, dinners, glamour. As they see it. I enjoy myself, but the island has an underside you have to live here to know, even among the "best" island society.

3

"A map of the world that does not include Utopia is not worth glancing at," wrote Oscar Wilde, "for it leaves out the one country at which Humanity is always landing. And when Humanity lands there, it looks out, and seeing a better country, sets sail. Progress is the realization of Utopias."

If you care to believe the boosterism of Key West emanating from certain gay citizens there, then you'll believe the island has achieved a utopian harmony of business interests and civic values, a utopian accommodation of gays and straights. I believe there's a better country and that it's time to set sail again; even if we circle the globe and return to the same place, we may learn to change it. In his book *In Search of Gay America*, Neil Miller wrote: "In Key West, they didn't seem to care very much about gay rights—or at least about having gay rights protection made into law. I could understand that in Bunceton, Missouri, with its six gay residents; in Key West, the city that a lot of people viewed as gay paradise, I found it odd and just a little smug."

Whenever the navy is reduced in Key West there is an economic slump, as happened in the early seventies. But in that decade there was also a major gay migration to the island, and today a high percentage of homes, guest houses, restaurants, and other businesses are owned and staffed by gays. In 1983 an openly gay art gallery owner named Richard Heyman was elected mayor. When Neil Miller asked him if he'd tried to get a gay rights bill enacted, he said there "was no need for gay issues in Key West"; such a bill would be "superfluous."

Miller asked the same question of Jim Stokes, co-owner of a large gay guest house and Heyman's appointee to the city's architectural review commission, and the answer was the same. But couldn't antigay employment or housing discrimination occur even in Key West? Stokes replied to Miller, "There is enough residential space in Key West that is owned or controlled by gay people to house all the gay people who want to come down here and are willing to work." Likewise, a gay strike would shut down the town (though Stokes spoke hypothetically, and hardly called for gay labor solidarity). "In short," as Miller paraphrased Stokes, "gay economic power meant there was no need for gay civil rights protection." When Miller spoke with Peter K. Ilchuk, Heyman's campaign manager, he received "the party line" once more: "In his view, gay tourists were just another part of the market."

If this sounds all too sweet, it is. Gay business owners in a resort economy are very privileged, and may well feel that what works for them does not need fixing. Gay tourists are privileged transients who want a break from everyday life and will hardly spend play time campaigning for a local gay rights bill they can't take back home. But if you are neither a businessperson nor a tourist but a gay worker, the free market hardly protects you like the hand of God. It is simply untrue that affordable housing is abundantly offered by gay owners to gay workers, or I and others on my work crew would have been glad to take it rather than live in a slumlord property.

Three gay crew members, including Little Joe and me, sat one evening on our collapsing balcony while the downstairs neighbors had a barbecue cookout directly below us, drunkenly hollering, "Let's smoke out the faggots!" It got worse: "Let's *gas* the faggots!'' A member of the party below kicked Little Joe's bike over, and he dashed down the steps to confront the man, who proceeded to batter his face and chest. Officer Joe Mote of the Key West Police Department filled out the offense form (a copy of which I have before me) and warned the offender to stay away from the building. End of story? No. After the cops left, our neighbors harangued us for a half hour, spewing every venomous prejudice and epithet they could dredge up.

Of course we reported these incidents and others to King Realty, one of the most powerful real estate companies on the island, and their response was simple: Somehow Little Joe "provoked the attack"—by being gay?—and "we're ready to evict all of you." So I told the story to a prominent gay politician, to a gay newspaper editor, and to a gay lawyer. The politician responded with stone-faced evasion, the editor promised a "general" piece on antigay violence sometime in the misty future, and the lawyer was not about to engage in a pro bono case against King Realty. Nor was I ready to organize a picket at their office just as I was due to return home. I had no heart to record this at any length in my journal.

This island paradise is largely built on migrant labor, from construction to cleaning toilets, with little union protection. Gay bashing in Key West became news when the victim happened to be Tennessee Williams; otherwise it is mostly unpublicized because then it is bad for business. There is no way all gay labor can be segregated in gay-owned housing and employment compounds, nor would this be a desirable solution. Neil Miller wrote of Key West, "Alliance with mainstream economic and political forces clearly was important for gay progress; some degree of 'amalgamation' made sense. But it seemed naïve to leave yourself defenseless, without institutions or laws to protect you. Even in paradise." In fact, for those with sufficient money and power, anyplace at all may be paradise enough. Others will have to raise hell.

In my journal I also had no heart to tell the story of a guy I'll name Carl, noting only that he was "dishonest, dangerous—and hot." Carl was a porn model who could be very charismatic. He was also a deeply angry and disturbed young man. He would shoot up drugs in front of his sexual partners, offer the same needle to them, and then try to fuck them without rubbers. Ideally, all of us without exception would refuse such offers. I and a friend named Brad did just that, but it's a fact we knew two other guys who had not. Carl later volunteered the information that he had been diagnosed with AIDS, and showed Brad and me a few small Kaposi's lesions.

Our reaction was similar: a mixture of helpless compassion and suppressed fury. At the very time he was endangering the lives of others, he was awaiting the final diagnosis for AIDS, but he already knew he was HIV positive. We insisted he needed serious counseling, and we felt obliged to spread the word to his partners that he could be dangerous. In this way we learned the risks others had taken. Carl assaulted Brad one night, blaming him for ruining his reputation on the island. Carl did call for help shortly thereafter, and a former lover from Los Angeles paid him a visit—an older man, a psychologist, who took Carl into his home again. Carl died about one year later.

Too many others I knew in Key West have died or are now ill; some are breaking drug habits. The editor I'd known, J.B., also died: rumors of cirrhosis, rumors of pneumonia. I remember a literary dinner party in the garden of a gay couple, with J.B. getting mildly soused while the manager of a guest house spun an elegy about a beautiful young man who had died of AIDS. I paraphrase, though I remember well the tone and certain refrains:

"Luke was the son of a well-established Key West family, a golden boy with charm to spare. Everybody was in love with him. Such a beauty! We were swimming together one day when a crab nipped him or he stepped on a sharp shell—he cried out like a little boy, and I put my arms round him. Such a beauty! A muscular boy with a heavy penis. And once I saw him lying nude in a hammock, with the breeze brushing his hair and moving his heavy penis from one thigh to the other—"

J.B. broke in to exclaim: "A breeze moved a cock that big? It must have been a fucking hurricane!" I spat my wine, I laughed so hard. Then J.B. got up from the table, stripped, and plunged into a hot tub. The teller of the story was unfazed, commenting, "J.B. is the most benign drunk I've ever known." Conversation drifted on, but I had a sudden attack of grief—maybe the delayed effect of the story, as it called to mind so many others dying young—and the night sky seemed to open like an abyss. I felt like I was falling into the dark. I quickly said good night, so quickly that the host followed me out the door. All I could do was apologize and go home.

Never in my life before or since have I lived so completely in my body as when I lived in Key West: physical work for pay, and then leisure at the gym and beach. I'd say this was the swan song of youth, and now I look into the mirror of that recent past and I have my Marschallin moods, knowing that I have less time now for sporting sex, less hair on my head, more weight round my middle. Women are sometimes mocked for their vanity; men just tend to be more dishonest. Queers are tagged with congenital narcissism in any case, so what can we lose if we tell what we know about aging and dying?

"By 'paradise'," wrote Paul Goodman, "I mean nothing but the world practical." *The world practical!* And that might be the best definition of any decent utopianism. Those who feel they already own their piece of paradise on Key West have also put up this sign above the island: DO NOT DISTURB. Trust *The New York Times* to purvey the chamber of commerce line unalloyed, quoting current mayor Tony Tarracino: "Gays are accepted here and respected here. The gays saved a lot of the oldest parts of town, and they brought in art and culture. They deserve a lot of credit for what Key West is today." So I read in the September 3, 1990 issue of the *Times* under this headline: "Hard-Hit Key West Battles AIDS with Communitywide Effort."

True enough, so far as it goes. But we may wonder just how wide that community is, and whether charity is sufficient without social change. Key West has a hospital and hospice, and citizens and businesses donated $700,000 to build a rest home for indigent people with AIDS. But as the *Times* reporter noted: "Local officials emphasize that such services are intended for residents and that even here, resources are stretched to the limit." So do not go to paradise for health care. Inevitably, gay meccas now attract not only the healthy, but those seeking medical and social support. San Francisco itself is now critically overburdened.

When Neil Miller asked Jim Stokes why Key West had no gay pride parade, this kind of whistling in the storm was still possible: "We have gay pride all the time. We don't need to demonstrate our numbers because there isn't anyone who doesn't know our numbers and appreciate the value of our numbers— or the value of our money!" But AIDS has aggravated prejudice against gays nationwide, including in Key West. Resorts are better at taking gay tourist dollars than in giving back fully adequate health and social care. Key West cannot be an island sufficient unto itself; it shares the health crisis of the mainland. Local charity won't meet the real need in a national epidemic and in a country where over thirty-five million people have no kind of health insurance at all.

Is it a curse or blessing to see the dark side of the moon? At times that's how I see Key West—as a lunar meteor that dropped into the ocean, and that we strange creatures have colonized. On the earth but not of it. Coral islands are fossils, and from this dead rock the islanders have carved out gardens, planting their palms and frangipani in graven plots, resting their corpses aboveground in marble trunks, so Key West still remains Cayo Hueso, the Isle of Bones. For a very small island, Key West has a very large cemetery.

In Mexico, the Day of the Dead is celebrated in cemeteries: graves and tombs become tables laden with flowers, food, and gifts; homes are decorated with skeletal figures of painted clay and tin, while the children eat sugar skulls and bones. Life can be deadly and death can be lively: that becomes common sense. Since AIDS has cut down so many in Key West, let the mad queens celebrate a Day of the Dead on the Isle of Bones. After all the funerals, let there be a carnival. Let it begin on winter solstice at the island cemetery, let the procession wander through the streets, let sorrows be cast to the wind and waves. Let there be remembrance, music, dancing, costumes, and fireworks. Let there be lunacy and lovemaking in the light of day and all night long.

A few more memories for good measure: the day the work crew fell silent during our lunch break in the garden, a radio newscaster describing the explosion of the *Challenger,* and I flashed on Shiva dancing amid flames, red hibiscus flowers around us, life in death and death in life; the gay guide pointing out the Octagon House to a group of tourists, informing them, "Calvin Klein used to own it, *but there wasn't enough closet space*"; and two of the sweetest gay men in Key West who lived in a renovated Baptist church with a psalm verse painted on a wide arch: "How Good and Pleasant a Thing it is for Brethren to Dwell Together in Unity."

FIRE ISLAND, NEW YORK

I WENT BACK ONE NIGHT this past July to the Sandpiper, the dance bar in Fire Island Pines that is called The Pavilion now. The place was not terribly crowded because it was only 12:30 on a Thursday night and because the island itself was not terribly crowded this year. But the music was good and the new panels installed beneath the ceiling went up and down on schedule. For the first two hours I recognized no one, and when a face from the old crowd—the crowd that was current when I first came to Fire Island ten years ago—did arrive, it belonged to a man I had never met personally. He had a decade ago a lover I thought the best catch in Manhattan. Since then they had broken up and the best catch moved away from New York. But here his other half survived, dancing now with a young man wearing the khaki walking shorts I eventually realized were this summer's contribution to fashion. But if he was a constant, nothing else was, and as I danced alone on the side of the floor, the building I was in was not the building in my heart—no, like a palimpsest, there was another structure whose outline, tables, crowd existed just beneath the one I was looking at (the old Sandpiper), and I realized that for me Fire Island consisted now in large part of memory.

In fact nearly every building I saw in the Pines and Cherry Grove as I walked around these towns during the next few days had beneath its outlines another building: a ghost structure, if you will, that existed as a blueprint in my mind. The Sea Shack had burned down, and the Ice Palace was refurbished, so I was glad to pass the Belvedere and see that something had not changed. The Belvedere still floats above the bulrushes, and the fountain still splashes into its basin—an odd mixture of tranquility and camp—in the middle of the hot, quiet afternoon. And for the most part the residential Grove remains unchanged. The Pines is another story. I was accustomed by now to the proliferation of swimming pools, new houses, and new façades, but strolling down Bay Walk I began to notice new wooden walls. The wooden walls seemed finally to confirm that psychological trait people in the Pines are often accused of: A certain reserve, a studied aloofness that prevents men spurred by hundreds of other men they find attractive from meeting a single one of them on a given weekend. As the town grew larger, the ferry fare was raised, and the homeowners asked that signs be put up on Long Island saying THERE ARE NO PUBLIC TOILETS IN THE PINES to discourage day-trippers. But the Pines is large enough without daily visitors to provide a sense of alienation—so large it leads the pedestrian faced with all this new building to wonder crazily what would happen if everyone in town flushed his toilet at the same time. Would the Pavilion explode?

In the Pines the predilection for making things attractive has extended to the harbor itself—one used to get off the boat at a nondescript dock, unhitch a wagon, and trundle off down a boardwalk that looked like any other. Now one disembarks at an entrance gate flanked by flower boxes and what wags have dubbed the Clarence La Fountain Shopping Mall, and they have built a house for the policeman, a new expanse of boardwalk on which to put the wagons that used to cluster beside the water's edge. It is all tasteful, as everything in the Pines is, and not significant, I suppose, except to the man who remembers the way it used to look. The way it used to look lies—in the minds of those who remember—beneath the way it looks now, like an old black-and-white photograph taken at night. The photograph looks like this: the white boats on black water dappled with silver light; the low white façade of the darkened Sandpiper; the single boardwalk stretching past an empty phone booth, a utility pole, an electric light, on into the darkness; and around it nothing but sand. That is what the harbor of a beach town should look like, I think as I walk by in July of 1983, and that is how the Pines looked before the harbor was gentrified.

In truth it was a forlorn harbor: white and skeletal, especially in late fall. It can never look forlorn again now, and it is only the love of times past that makes the man who sees it question the new wood, circular seats, stairs, awnings, and bulletin boards.

These ghostly blueprints he carries even to Tea Dance that afternoon, where he recognizes 2 men in the crowd of 300. This does not bother him. He is glad to see the 2 men he knows, and glad to see 298 he does not. One is comforting, the other exciting. He is able for the first time in years not only to attend a Tea Dance but enjoy it, and he is not in a critical mood, at any rate. Tea Dance is the reason he moved to New York: one afternoon in 1970, visiting Fire Island with three other men from Philadelphia, he wandered out of their room at the Botel to dry his hair with a towel, looked down, and shouted, "Tommy! Come here!" Four hundred men stood beneath him on the wooden deck with glasses and bottles in their hands. No one was drinking tea. Only a fraction were dancing. But this was Tea Dance. He had never seen so many stunning homosexual men gathered in one space in his life. He thought: I must move into this city.

Within five years of this initial discovery of homosexual New York, he could not go near Tea Dance—he considered it the most grotesque male preening rite north of the Amazon, a sterile parody of a bad cocktail party. In fact he could not think of a single advantage to Tea Dance except that, having suffered its profound superficiality, attending any other Tea Dance was a relief: the one in Cherry Grove or Provincetown, for instance, which was where he went rather than the Pines—because he was, well, angry with the Pines. He was angry with the Pines for not having given him what he thought it promised the first time he saw Tea Dance at the Botel: eternal happiness.

He thinks to himself as he stands there now watching Tea Dance how exaggerated and unfair both his love and disdain for this place were. He thinks to himself as he stands there watching these people he does not remotely know: We go to these beach resorts each year as very subjective people at different stages in our own lives. We go as poor youths who have no idea what career to pursue and ten years later as prosperous men entrenched in a vocation. We go, frantically—looking for lovers and emphatically not looking for anything of the sort. We go dejected and leave in defeat, to return several seasons later with that depression surmounted, those problems solved. We go back to recapture old times and to erase bad memories: to live free of a depression that ruined the place years ago—like the second visit I made to Provincetown because I spent the first one with a lover leaving me at the time, an experience so melancholy every corner of the town was soaked in tears. I went back to lay that ghost to rest, he thinks, and I did. But even so the Pines, the Island, is a place I have gone to far more frequently, and so the dunes here are filled with ghosts: people I kissed and watched the stars with and slept with in empty houses the night before they were to be surrendered to the owner late in the fall. A beach resort is both real and unreal—a collection of houses, streets, bars, dance places; a collection of memories, hopes, illusions, discoveries, distress we experience there at different summers of our lives.

In fact nearly every corner of the Pines has for him a memory of some sort—an invisible figure standing there in the sunlight of previous summers—as he goes back to the house he is staying in; all of them, accumulated, make him slightly crazy. They give to the island something it never had when he first came to it: a past. Talking about old times with friends by day he feels avuncular and wise, recalling people whose ups and downs he has been able to track over a long period of time—some of them to the final scene—but when he is alone, he feels very peculiar indeed, like a poltergeist who does not cruise so much as haunt.

He feels less peculiar, in fact, at night, when the reality of the place is obliterated by darkness, and he can wander like a proper ghost. The harbor of the Pines, after all, does not look so different after dark: the white boats, the dappled black water are still the prettiest sight he has ever seen on a summer night. And passing people on the boardwalk, he feels the same thrill he felt the first time this happened ten years ago: a form, a disembodied voice, brushes his shoulder, slows suddenly to get by, each trying to make the other one out like soldiers on a night patrol. Yet when one of these mysterious men stops and waits for him to approach, he feels once more like a ghost, a thousand years old, and wonders if, with a certain pressure at his lips (the right words, the right song), he might start talking endless trivia. He carries secrets within: secrets that form a rich and fabulous memory.

For this reason the Pavilion I danced in that Thursday evening was only an imposter—the real building was the old Sandpiper, with its low ceiling, crude sliding glass doors, and dining tables stacked against the wall. It would always be.

Ten years ago friends took me on an architectural walking tour along the beach, telling me the names of houses they had christened African Village, Broadway Arms, the House of Pain, the TV house, Camp Tommy, Tina's Mouth ("You'll see, when you meet Tina."). As I passed certain houses now I realized I could no longer remember what some of them looked like when I first saw them—particularly the ones renovated in the early seventies, before every landlord realized that by adding a pool and a modernistic shell he might ask ten thousand dollars for the beach shack he had been renting for only five. As I walked along I could only remember the nicknames. Camp Tommy was recognizable only by its location—the old suburban bungalow was now three glass cubes regarding a pool. The House of Pain I could not even remember in its original state, but now it had a low retaining wall and a man cultivating a garden between its swimming pool and the beach. One house that was unchanged had five strange youths lifting weights on the deck to the beat of Donna Summer, but I wanted to stop and say: "You don't live there. You're not the people I know who lived there. You're not real." They went on pressing their barbells as if they were; so that by the time I reached my favorite house in the Pines, I was not at all prepared for what I saw. Surely it was just a trick of perspective, I thought, an optical illusion: that large second story with the plate glass wall facing the sunset. Surely it belonged to the house behind it! No one would add to *that* house!

And I realized as I walked closer how proprietary I had become about the Pines' houses—as if they all belonged to me in some way, a mere pedestrian who became accustomed to admiring them for so many years. I came to a stop. It was not an optical illusion. The owners had added a second floor to this gem of a house, which had always had in my mind a sort of landmark status, had always stood for the best the Pines had to offer. I was so startled I went to the pay phones at the harbor and called my friend in Manhattan who one summer worked in the house as a cook. He knew about it already. "I was prepared to hate it," he said. "But I went to the party they threw in June to celebrate the new wing, and it's stunning. The most beautiful bathroom you've ever seen in your life!"

"Well," I sighed, "I guess that is what the Pines is all about on one level. The most beautiful bathroom you've ever seen in your life."

"To be able to watch deer grazing as you douche?" he said. "Where else in the world, I ask you?"

"Oh, Cuddles," I said, suddenly excited by the appearance of a handsome quartet passing the phone booth, "there are four youngsters beside me as I speak on their way to Tea Dance and on their faces is a mixture of terror and excitement, fear and happiness—an expression I haven't seen since . . ."

"When, Sugar?"

"It was on *your* face, *our* faces, when *we* went to Tea!"

"Isn't it wonderful," he said. "To think they still believe they're going to meet *him*. All tan and muscular and chatty, holding a margarita."

"Exactly!" I said, suddenly seeing my way out of my confusion. "Maybe the island exists in the heads of twenty-six-year-olds!"

"You bet it does, ducky," he said. "Not to mention their Speedos. Why don't you follow those tender young souls to Tea Dance yourself?"

"I went yesterday," I said. "Once every five years is enough."

"Then do go back to the House of All Cash, and drop in to see the new toilette. You recall what Oliver Wendell Holmes wrote about the chambered nautilus?"

"What?"

"Build three more stately bathrooms, oh my soul!" he said. *"That's* the Pines."

I hung up. It was sunset. I walked back to the beach—inexplicably deserted, as always, at this time—and strolled back down to the House of All Cash (given this nickname because that's how the current owner bought it). I did not own this house, I reminded myself. I did not own the harbor. I did not own the Sandpiper or the houses on Bay Walk. Those black-and-white photographs that existed in my mind, those spectral blueprints, these palimpsests, those other images—of people, dancers, boardwalks, houses—are the accumulated freight I carry with me in my mind and had nothing to do with the living reef that adds each winter, each summer, to the coral around me. The Pines is all about building a master bedroom that has a view of sunset over the dunes and a bathroom that is a state of the art. Dreamers drench a place in legend and memory. Carpenters hammer. Both contribute. Both towns are real—both bathrooms, for that matter: the one that does not exist (because it was not there when I had my fling on the island) and the one that indeed looks out on the sweep of dune grass shining on one side in the light of the setting sun. The same sun has turned the wash of foam on the beach a pale gold, and aureoled the velvet stubble of the antlers of the deer watching a lone man swim while the world is at Tea Dance. What matters most to dreamers or carpenters, what matters in the end, has been preserved: the beauty of the place is, thank God, in the hands of the federal government.

ROBIN METCALFE

HALIFAX, NOVA SCOTIA

IT WAS MILD EVENING IN
July. We had borrowed a cottage two hours' drive from the city:
a tipsy cabin perched on the edge of a cliff that was slowly crumbling into the Bay of Fundy. Jim was a dear friend I had known
since forever; Paul a handsome young acquaintance visiting from
Toronto. We were three gay companions sitting on a porch, chatting over drinks, and watching the fog drown the lights on the
far shore of the Minas Basin.

The talk turned to personal history—our private origin
myths—and the notion of a hometown. Paul and I had both had
wandering childhoods. Perhaps, I suggested, it was in reaction to
this that as an adult I had become so attached to the idea of
home.

Paul agreed. The youngest of the three, he did not feel he
had yet found his home, but knew he wanted one. He wondered
if Nova Scotia might be it.

Jim fixed me with a doubtful eye. My thesis didn't apply to

him, he said, delicately sipping his gin. He was as attached to place as I was but had spent his childhood in the grip of one Nova Scotian town. The security of a stable home had not made him footloose and fancy free.

Ah yes, I said, but his hometown had never been a home. It was a prison from which he had escaped at the earliest opportunity. Jim had grown up as homeless as I, even if he hadn't moved. Like me, he had finally made a home for himself as an adult; like me, he had done it in Halifax.

Halifax is surely nobody's idea of gay paradise. Relatively unknown to those who don't live here; relatively unappreciated by those who do. And yet, there are those, like me and Jim, who cling to it with a fierce loyalty. Somewhere in the North Atlantic fog we have glimpsed the outlines of a Halifax few people have dreamed of: a hidden city of myth and mystery—a city gay people can call their own.

At a quarter of a million people, Halifax is the closest thing to a metropolis in my part of the world: the region's political and cultural center of gravity. Atlantic Canada's two million inhabitants are sprinkled through four provinces, along a damp ragged fringe of headlands and islands where the map slides into the sea. In a continent that thrusts ever upward and to the west, we are the eastern shoals: the half-forgotten homestead of the first transatlantic settlers, a cut umbilical cord stretching back toward Europe.

Geographically and psychologically, we're about as far from gay and golden California as you can get without actually leaving North America. There's something undefinably different here. Outsiders notice it when they visit, and we notice its absence when economic or personal necessity drives us west or south into exile. Perhaps it is the strong sense of place. We know who we are, even if others have forgotten. In that respect, Atlantic Canada resembles the American South. Like Southerners, we bear ourselves with a sense of wounded dignity, but not from having been defeated in war. We suffered the more humiliating fate of being eclipsed.

We have a term for those foreigners, Canadian and American, who live on the rest of the continent: Come From Aways.

I was born in Atlantic Canada, but I was born an outsider. My parents married across heavily guarded ethnic barriers: my mother a Catholic and French-speaking Acadian, my father a Protestant of Newfoundland ancestry. We moved continually when I was young, wandering throughout the region, from town to country to city, and yet on to other cities. People here measure residence not in years but in generations. My ancestors may have walked these shores for four centuries, but none of the places I passed through as a child would claim me now as its own. I grew up under the curse of the Come From Away—without having any Away to go home to.

After I came out, in a distant western city, it might have seemed only logical to make a new life in a new place. I soon realized, however, that I am too much a child of my local culture, steeped in its own eccentric mythologies, to feel at home in the rootless bustle of urban North America.

I am a poet by vocation, and must draw on deep wells. The bones of my Acadian and Celtic ancestors sing to me out of the rocks, and from the farmland that they wrested from the sea. During a thousand years of European settlement, from the time of Leif the Lucky and possibly earlier, we have knit ourselves to this land. Only the Native cultures have a more ancient connection. Leaving this coast would be like severing an artery.

Halifax in 1975, however, was not a nurturing place for a young man with a radicalized gay consciousness. What to do when the place you inhabit is too small for comfort? You can leave, of course—or you can work to make it bigger.

If God did not exist, said Voltaire, it would be necessary to invent him. I realized early on that the city I needed to inhabit—my own hometown—did not exist; that it, like Voltaire's God, would have to be invented.

The road that leads to a gay identity is often a slow and difficult one, but it is not for any lack of gay desire, or even necessarily of gay experience. It is because, growing up in this culture, we are not exposed to stories and images that reflect that experience; we have no words with which to name it. We must learn—or invent—a vocabulary with which to call our gay selves into being. Wherever we grow up, gay people are always Come-From-Away. But where is this Away?

Literature plays a special part in many gay lives. It is often in the pages of a book that gay men and lesbians first make the momentous discovery that their feelings have a name. If Away does not exist as a physical country, it does exist as country of the mind, and every novel, play, and poem that speaks of gay experience enlarges the boundaries of that country.

When I read the words of another writer, I become a citizen of his republic. I walk with Isherwood under the lindens of Berlin. I cruise with Cavafy in the alleyways of Alexandria and feel the hands of his lovers, hot and urgent on my skin.

As a writer, I see it as part of my task to create the city I inhabit, not only for myself, but for the men of my community. By imagining it, I help to make a gay life possible in Halifax.

A city that exists only in steel and concrete is a mere phantom. Its inhabitants are like sleepwalkers; they pass through their environment with unseeing eyes while dreaming of distant places: of Paris, New York or Los Angeles, whose streets are real to them by grace of a thousand novels and movies. Before a city can become real to its inhabitants, it must be constructed in more durable materials: out of words, songs, images, and gestures.

To become real, a city or a country must lay claim to its own mythology. As a Canadian, I inhabit an imaginary country. To be Canadian today, in the age of free trade, depends on an act of will. It means sorting through thirty-six channels of American programming to find the CBC. Canada is a stubborn fiction, ever poised on the verge of becoming a fact.

A state like Canada may claim sovereignty over half a continent, but until its people have laid claim to their own imagination, they are not yet a nation. The same applies to gay people, and to particular gay communities such as the one in Halifax. Until we have imagined ourselves into our landscape, we do not really live here.

At the center of downtown Halifax is a great bald hill. Geologically, it is what's known as a drumlin: a heap of silt deposited by giant glaciers that retreated some twelve thousand years ago. Carved first by ice, Citadel Hill has been reshaped by British military engineers over the past two centuries. They dug huge moats and threw up stone walls for the defense of one of the North Atlantic's great naval harbors. At its crown they erected fortifications in the shape of a six-pointed star. From its walls, the Hill slopes away at geometrically calculated angles toward the harbor. Hemmed in by office towers, the Citadel holds its fire and dreams of the past.

Every evening at sunset a procession of cars circulates counterclockwise along the road that skirts the fortifications at the top of the Hill. The cars execute an intricate dance with the men who amble on foot, who pause to chat with the drivers, or sprawl seductively on the upper slopes. The Hill has been home to troops of lonesome and horny men since 1749. It is surely one of North America's oldest continuous cruising grounds.

One day when I was walking around the Hill, I ran into a friend, sitting on one of the granite blocks that line the edge of the moat. He was with a young man I'd never seen before, but who recognized my name. "You're the guy who writes those stories," he said.

I wrote "those stories" for various American gay skin magazines in the mid 1980s. Canada is the only major Western country that does not have its own national gay commercial press, so if a Canadian gay writer wants to speak directly to a certain Canadian gay readership, he has to send his manuscripts to New York or Los Angeles.

When I tell people that some of my writing is porn, their responses are interesting. Some politely smother an impulse to cringe. Others show a mixture of embarrassment and prurient fascination. Many wonder earnestly why I would choose to call my sexual fiction "porn," instead of using the more elevated term, "erotica." The question almost everyone asks is, Do I use my own name?

Of course I do. For me, the fact that these stories are intended to give the reader a hard-on does not make them any less literature than another story designed to make him laugh or cry. If I can tell a good story and please my reader, I am proud of my work and want the reader to know who did it.

When a magazine publishes one of these stories, therefore, I appear under my own name—and so does my community. I make a point of using local place names whenever possible. People who tell me they've read something I wrote may not remember the title, or even an intelligible gist of the plot. What they do tend to remember is the fact that a certain story took place on Gottingen Street.

You can see Gottingen Street from the Hill. In fact, you can see most of Halifax. It's true, some people do come here for the view.

Looking south from the Hill, beyond the distant harbor mouth, you can see the open Atlantic, where the Gulf Stream collides with the Labrador Current. Even on a clear summer day, a gray bank of fog looms on the horizon like an imaginary mountain range. As the sun sets, twin tendrils of fog creep up the harbor and along the Northwest Arm, ghostly hands reaching to embrace this city and claim it once again for the sea.

You can see the two suspension bridges that span the harbor. The newer one crosses the narrows at the mouth of the Bedford Basin, a protected bay that sheltered the combined Allied fleets during two world wars. Almost exactly where the bridge now stands, a munitions ship blew up on December 6, 1917, producing the largest manmade explosion before Hiroshima. The shock waves from the Halifax explosion flattened the northern half of the city and were responsible for two thousand deaths.

Halifax is a city made and unmade by war: the only city in North America to be devastated by military weapons in this century. In peacetime it is a sleepy provincial city in a minor corner of Canada. In times of global conflict, however, it is a bastion of empire, the fortress of the North Atlantic. Founded as an imperial garrison town in the mid-eighteenth century, Halifax quickly blossomed with the imported elegance of the Georgian court. In the nineteenth century, the city was in the forefront of literary and political culture in English Canada. If life in Halifax has often been hard, even brutal, it has never been rustic.

Like any busy port city, Halifax has always had some kind of gay life. As early as 1752, the local papers reported on soldiers and sailors being prosecuted for "sodomitical practices." Most local gay experience of the past two centuries, however, is undocumented, and could only be fleshed out now through the imagination of the fiction writer. Someday I hope my characters will lead me back to the Blue Bird Café, where you could pick up lonely servicemen in 1944.

Today's gay and lesbian Haligonians (yes, that's what we're called) are determined that future gay generations should not be left without a history. To have recorded and preserved some of that history is a contribution to my community of which I am particularly proud.

Gay liberation arrived in Halifax in 1972, brought home, like a strange flowering plant, by a visiting native son who had settled in Toronto. The planter disappeared again in the west; the transplant took root in the garden and was tended by local hands. The Gay Alliance for Equality appeared at a time when all-purpose gay organizations were springing up in cities across North America. After eighteen years, it is one of the few of its generation to have survived.

When GAE applied in 1973 for incorporation under the Societies Act of Nova Scotia, fifteen members registered themselves as the "first officers" of the organization. That document, a simple list of names, addresses, and occupations, is the kind to make social historians drool.

Those first officers were a cozy lot: they had only eight street addresses among them. Three men and a woman lived in one house. Another five women lived at two adjacent addresses. Of the fifteen names on the list, eight are women.

In stating their occupations, they were anxious to present themselves in the most credible light, and I know that some of them fudged a bit. The one "road supervisor" was a fairly ordinary railway porter. The "businessman—self-employed" lived in a tiny hole-in-the-wall next to the shoebox-sized unlicensed club that was the closest thing to a gay bar in Halifax when I started going to it in 1975. Their colleagues included three cooks, a baker, an office manager and an accounting clerk; a laundry worker, a day-care worker, two students, and a teacher. An assistant manager had set up housekeeping with a cook. The woman who lived with the lesbian baker listed herself as a "housewife."

In the heady days of the 1970s, when I was reporting from Halifax for the legendary Toronto gay paper, *The Body Politic,* I was used to hearing my fellow radicals tut-tutting about the male domination and middle-class bias of the gay movement. None of those smug New Left truisms, however, applied comfortably to Halifax. Gay Haligonians, whether men or women, hospital orderlies or law students, have had to learn to live together. Living cheek by jowl doesn't reduce the differences among us, but it certainly makes it harder to shut each other out and to live in ignorance of one another's lives.

Like other cities, Halifax has seen a burgeoning of specialized gay and lesbian organizations: an ecumenical Christian group, student organizations, a women's paper, the PWA Coalition, a human rights lobby group, a leather fraternity, women's and men's choirs. Unlike other cities, however, Halifax has retained its One Big Organization from the early 1970s. GAE is now called GALA—Gay And Lesbian Association of Nova Scotia—but it still functions as the town meeting hall of the gay and lesbian community. When the community feels threatened or is fractured by internal conflict or feels a need to celebrate, it is in GALA's space that people come together.

My connection with *The Body Politic* made Toronto my gay home away from home, and I would sometimes sit in on collective meetings when I was in town. I was amazed at the polite and slightly frosty Upper Canadian niceness with which they conducted business. Everyone spoke calmly and in turn: as anxious as the Japanese to avoid confrontation or a "scene." You knew they were having an argument if everyone spoke so quietly you couldn't hear them.

Gay politics in Halifax, by contrast, is a blood sport. It has not been unknown for people to launch vicious personal attacks, threaten lawsuits, burst into tears, or throw furniture at meetings. About once every six months, the organization has a huge blowout. The meeting hall is packed. Everybody and his/her dog arrives early to get a good seat. Returning to GALA from a national or international gay conference can be like going from Sunday tea to a bullfight.

Halifax may be hell on wheels, but it's wonderfully alive. There is a rough spark of democracy that never seems to die. People may sometimes be rude and crude, but they speak their minds honestly; they actually listen to one another. They know that after they speak their minds they will have to go on living together. I have reported on and participated in fifteen years of gladiatorial gay politics in Halifax, and I cannot remember any major controversy that did not end with community reconciliation.

There is still only one gay bar in Halifax, although it is a lot bigger and fancier than the shoebox of yore. Since 1976, GAE/GALA has operated a licensed social club. Its present incarnation, Rumours, occupies a renovated 1940s movie theater originally called the Vogue. (If we'd had our wits about us, we would have restored the original name in time to cash in on Madonna's monster dance hit.) The interior is a series of cascading levels. The lower house is for serious cruising; the Middle Deck, the former balcony, has pool tables and lookout spots; and a quiet lounge high up in the Projection Room commands a regal view all the way down to the dance floor and the stage. There is a changing room backstage for drag queens, performance artists, or lesbian a cappella acts, and the front lobby contains the offices of GALA.

There are not many cities whose main gay social space for the past fifteen years has been owned and operated by an organization that is community-based, nonprofit, gender-balanced, and politically active. Like many other aspects of Halifax, it is a distinction more evident to visitors than to the natives, who tend to take the whole thing for granted.

Standing in the Projection Room, looking down at the dancing crowds, I ponder the power of imagination: the audacity of the few young faggots and dykes who dared to dream this place into being.

The act of imagining is the most potent and subversive of political acts. We have to imagine the future before we can create it. But it is not only the future for which this is true: the present, also, needs to be imagined before it can be truly lived.

Jim and Paul, my companions in that foggy cabin last summer, represent two sources from which Halifax draws its gay male population: those fleeing roots, and those seeking them. The city where I live is something of a way station where those two journeys cross: a compromise, and, for some, a solution.

I did not live in Halifax until I was almost an adult, but it is this city that I have claimed as my hometown. For me, it is as rich in meaning as Florence was for Dante: a City of Sorrows who reveals her soul slowly to those who take the time to know her. In my writing, I want to show Halifax in all its mythic grandeur. I want to show it—and thus to create it—as a city where gay men live and love.

JOHN PRESTON

PORTLAND, MAINE

|GOT MY DRIVER'S LI-
cense in 1961, when I was sixteen. The great activity that year
was taking long trips in the family car. The periphery of my
courage and my parents' patience was Portland, Maine, a hundred miles and change from our home in Massachusetts.

It wasn't a very exciting place to go. Back then Portland was
a city that had been down so long no one could imagine it would
ever make it back up again. Portland had been a major seaport
when sailing ships ruled the sea, and its proximity to Maine's
great forests created a shipbuilding industry. It got a reprieve in
the days of the steamship because it was the closest warm-water
port to Montreal. When the St. Lawrence River froze, much of
Canada's commerce moved through Portland's waterfront. The
hectic activity during those three or four months of the year made
the longshoremen and chandlers rich and prosperous.

During the Depression, the Canadian government built a
new railroad from Montreal to the Maritime Provinces as a mat-

ter of national defense and national pride. Just as the shoe and textile industries around Maine were beginning to go broke, the economic lifeline was cut by the new rail route to Halifax. World War II brought a reprieve, but when it was over, Portland sank into a slump that lasted for decades.

I used to drive the station wagon down to the empty wharves and cruise around the abandoned warehouses. Congress Street, the main street of the city, was lined with styleless shops centered around an antiquated department store. Ugly plastic façades covered most of the commercial buildings in town that were still used, vain attempts to make the structures appear up-to-date. Portland seemed, really, just a place to pass through. It was where you got the ferries to the resort islands of Casco Bay, perhaps where you changed buses to go farther north to Bar Harbor and the other seaside resorts. Portland, itself, was a destination only for traveling salesmen and teenagers who had no place better to go.

So it was a shock when I was sitting in my apartment in Manhattan's East Village in 1979, trying to think of a place to move, that Portland came up on the top of the list. I had never considered living there, not once that I can remember.

I was looking for someplace to go to because I was tired of the cities. I had gone to college in Chicago, then, in quick succession, had lived in Minneapolis, Philadelphia, New York, Los Angeles, San Francisco, and now, again, New York. I had spent so much time in Denver, Houston, and Washington that I sometimes forgot I'd never actually lived in any one of them and put them on the list of places I had. Now I was in my mid-thirties and I had become a writer. It was time to change.

Having this vocation was as unexpected as thinking about moving to Portland. I had been a magazine editor and a public speaker, but I hadn't thought of myself as a writer until I had moved this second time to New York. I had begun by pushing out some erotic fiction, thinking it wasn't important—probably the reason I was able to do it in the first place—and I discovered that it was all being published. More than that, it was well received. I was quickly being asked for essays and reviews, even being encouraged to write a book. I could earn my living at this, I realized. This could become my life.

If I were going to be a writer, though, I needed to live somewhere else. The cities had become a distraction, they were no longer a stimulation. The pace and expense of New York was too much pressure. The struggle to survive economically and to block out the noise and turbulence of the streets was too much of a diversion from my work.

I also wanted to move back to New England. When I'd first left Massachusetts for college, I discovered myself returning as often as possible, at least once a year, to Provincetown. I had told myself that I was doing it because it was the capital of my new gay life, but I came to realize that I was going back to Provincetown in an attempt to return home. No matter how much of a gay center it might be, Provincetown was still a Yankee village. The sights, the sounds, the streets all made sense to me when I visited there. The resort was a lifeline that kept me precariously in touch with my roots.

Of course I considered Provincetown as a place I might go, but the idea of living there year round didn't appeal. I knew how deserted and isolated it is in the off-season. The crowds of people who swarm through the streets and decorate the beaches don't persist in the winter months on Cape Cod. They are home working to save the money for their return the next summer, or they'd gone to Florida or California on an annual migration.

I wasn't willing to spend the better part of the year alone. I didn't want to give up all the positive aspects of a city, just the oppressive ones. That meant that Boston also was out of the picture. It would have satisfied my desires to live in New England again, but there seemed little reason to trade the hassles of New York for those of Boston, a city almost as pressured and just as expensive as Manhattan.

I sat down in my apartment and wrote out the things that my new home should have. It should be something of a city. Though as small as possible, it should still have some kind of cultural life—theaters, decent movie houses, good restaurants. I wasn't at all ready to give up my gay life. I wanted a place with at least a few bars and perhaps an organization or two that could allow easy access to a social life and support system.

Those were very important considerations. The visible gay

communities back then were limited to the few resorts like Provincetown and Key West and Fire Island and certain neighborhoods like Greenwich Village and West Hollywood. We had just finished establishing those places as our own and we didn't really know if we could exist outside them.

There were noises of other locales where a gay man could find some safety and community. Certainly university cities like Madison and Boulder had something to offer, but I wasn't so sure that the new gay life in smaller cities like Portland was really viable. Above all, I didn't want to move to a hometown where I had to hide. I wasn't willing to go back into the closet just to enjoy life in New England. I had developed very strong opinions about myself and community and they didn't include that kind of payoff.

But as I went through the points on my list and considered other places, none of them made as much sense as Portland. Portsmouth, New Hampshire, was too much of a tourist community and too close to Boston, it would be like living in a suburb. Providence, Rhode Island, wasn't an attractive option. New London, Connecticut, and Burlington, Vermont, were too small.

There was another detail that had to be thought about. The idea of leaving New York wasn't without its risks. My contacts with the publishing world seemed frail. I wasn't sure I could maintain them if I didn't visit them often. I wanted someplace that gave me quick access to both Boston and Manhattan. No matter how little I wanted to reside in those places, I wanted to be able to get to them easily. Portland had regular airline service to New York, and not just prop commuter planes; it had jets that would get me to LaGuardia in less than an hour. It was also only a two-hour drive to Boston.

I made a visit to Portland that Thanksgiving. All those years of economic hardship had one positive outcome: It hadn't been worth anyone's effort to tear down all the old buildings and replace them with characterless modern structures. By the time Portland's economy began to resurrect itself—and it had just happened recently—attitudes about urban development had altered. A grand railroad station was gone and there was a glaring Holiday

Inn at the center of the city, but those were aberrations. Restoring and preserving the older buildings was the new goal. The plastic façades had been torn down and what was exposed was handsome architecture from the mid-nineteenth century. Most of Portland had burned to the ground as a result of an industrial accident in 1866. The core of the city had been reconstructed quickly and left the place with a unity of red brick and gray granite stone.

The waterfront was one of the centers of renovation. Where I had seen deserted warehouses twenty years earlier, there were now handsome office buildings and new restaurants. The pavements had been redone, asphalt was replaced with cobblestone streets and brick sidewalks. The area even had a name, The Old Port, to attract tourists and businessmen.

Gay life was much better than I'd remembered. There used to be a bar on Cumberland Avenue with a dance floor in the rear. Whenever a policeman or an unknown visitor came into the front, the bartender would press a silent button that would make the lights in the back room flicker, a warning for all the same-sex couples to stop touching one another and sit down, so they wouldn't be arrested. Now there were more bars, much less circumspect. I found a Maine gay newspaper stacked in the entrance to one of the pubs. It wasn't sophisticated, but it gave some hope that there was real political and cultural gay life in the city.

I moved to Portland that December. Most of my memories of the first few months are wonderful. I was happy to be in New England again, and Portland proved to be the archetypical Yankee city in many ways. Even the early winter snowfalls seemed romantic. I was at home.

Many of the first impressions of living in Maine were surprisingly erotic. I discovered that I loved, most of all, the voices of the men. When I'd gone to college, my accent had been the cause of cruel ridicule. I sounded as exotic as a Kennedy to my new schoolmates, but not nearly so sophisticated. My words had the weight of the country about them, and they knew it. I was humiliated by their jokes and retreated to my room, where I spent my freshman year learning how to talk in a way they wouldn't make fun of. I succeeded, and my social life and sense of comfort increased dramatically in my sophomore year.

I always knew that I had lost something important, though. I would always make a connection between changing my way of speaking with hiding my way of being. To have given up my accent for the sake of social peace was the same, in some profound way, as hiding my sexuality had been during those college years.

Now I was surrounded by the sounds of New England men, all of them speaking in just the way I had. The sounds of their voices were alluring. It was, somehow, a mingling of my open sexuality and my return to the region. I would find any way possible to keep the men talking, their heads on a pillow beside mine, or standing in a bar while we seduced one another, or dancing together on the open floors of the new bars.

New England men provided another erotic element, one that I thought was hilarious. Being gay in Portland doesn't have much to do with the media image of gay life. For one thing, most of the men I know here are working class. There's none of the ostentatious wealth that gay men are supposed to have. Most social occasions with other gay men in Portland consist of cheap restaurants or potluck suppers in someone's home. During all the years I had lived in the big cities, the emerging gay cultures had developed certain styles of dress whose purpose was frankly sexual. The carefully cultivated images of construction workers or motorcyclists or seamen were all affectations of office managers, lawyers, and editors. I was surprised that few of those likenesses were obvious in Portland bars. At first I took it as a sign of backwardness that none of the gay men here dressed in the fads of Greenwich Village or Castro Street. Then I got to know more of the men and I discovered the reason.

The men I would meet in the bars in Portland really *were* construction workers. They drove motorcycles because they were cheap transportation, not because they were stylish. They worked on the waterfront because the pay was good, not because it was sexy. When they went out at night, none of them wanted to draw attention to their working-class jobs. They dressed in sharply creased chinos and crew-neck sweaters because they didn't want to be reminded of what they did during the day.

I became known as the one who would ask others to come

over to his apartment right from work, so he could see them in their uniforms. A few began to understand what I was after and I remember, with great pleasure, the first time Mike gave me his hard hat, not one worn to a disco for appearance's sake, but the one he wore while he was a linesman for Central Maine Power Company. Then there was the day when Brian, who worked on the wharves, showed up wearing his hip boots, his yellow slicker hat, and layers of thermal underwear. He was embarrassed to be seen in that outfit. I could only tell him that he would make a fortune if he could package it and sell it in the Village. I had worried that my sexual fantasies wouldn't be possible in a small place like Portland; instead I discovered them being lived daily by all the men with whom I came in contact.

I didn't like a lot of other things about being gay in Portland those first few years. My concern about my connections with publishing led me to make sure that a post office box was my first purchase when I moved. The clerks began to eye me curiously as they handed over the packages from gay newspapers and magazines. Religious tracts were left conspicuously on their counters, sometimes I thought they were brought out especially for me, when they'd seen me coming into the station. I hated the hoops they made me jump through, and silently prepared to complain to the federal authorities if the local clerks dared step any further out of line.

Having been such a public figure in other, larger cities, I didn't think twice when asked to speak on gay views for newspapers and television. It was unheard of back then for local gay men to do that, even gay liberationists would speak on camera only if their faces would be shown in silhouette. Most of the guys I had been meeting were excited by my activism, which was very low-key so far as I was concerned. A few of them worked at L. L. Bean, one of the largest employers in the state, and they started to use their employee discounts to let me buy myself better clothes, so I would look more like a spokesman they'd admire.

Others were much less pleased. It came as a shock to be asked not to acknowledge a couple of acquaintances when we met on the street. They were frightened that my notoriety would wear off on them.

I was even more angered by the way the writing community dealt with me. My being gay overwhelmed whatever common interests we might have held. It was years before another writer in Maine would approach me or invite me to take part in community activities, even though the fact that I was working with large publishing houses was quickly well publicized. One of my goals when I moved to Portland was to write books. I accomplished that in the first year. When *Franny, the Queen of Provincetown* was published, *The Maine Sunday Telegram* sent a writer to interview me. He seemed uncomfortable and finally blurted out a question he'd obviously been holding inside for quite a while: How could I write a gay book that wasn't pornographic? What was the reason for a gay book if it weren't explicitly sexual? It didn't surprise me when the paper canceled the interview and when the review, written by this same man, was the most scathing gotten by that otherwise well-received sweet book.

Probably the most enraging incident occurred when the manager of the large state-of-the-art photocopying shop in town took me aside and told me that she no longer wanted my business. She was sure that my work, erotic or not, was something she wanted nothing to do with, and she let me know she *hoped* it was illegal as well. It didn't really help when I learned, years later, that the (numerous) gay employees had been illegally copying all my material and passing it around to their friends. They weren't about to defend me to their employer, but they were happy to have access to the stories and articles I was writing.

The tension from all these events built up. I had to move twice in the first year or so I was in town for utterly routine reasons. I had always admired the stolid line of Georgian buildings that lined one block in the center of the city. It was called "The Park Street Row" and held for me all the elegance and grandeur of Boston's Beacon Hill, whose architecture these structures mirrored. The last time I had to move, there were apartments for rent in a newly renovated building in the middle of the Row. I was one of the first people to show up on the first day they were being shown. Hugh, the landlord, led me to a flat on the second floor, the parlor floor in the days when this had been a Victorian mansion. The tall ceilings were lined with hand-painted cornices and the living room was crowned by a grand plaster of paris rosette. The apartment was perfect, with two large rooms for living and sleeping and a third small one, the perfect home office. I wanted to live here desperately, but I was bruised. I discovered myself bursting out to Hugh, "But you have to understand that I'm gay. I'm angry I even have to mention it. It's none of your business. But I don't want it to become an issue in the future." I would *never* had to have told a landlord in New York or San Francisco that I was gay. They could have assumed it, but here in a small city, I had been forced into being defensive.

Hugh looked at me and said quietly, "You're right. It's none of my business. And I couldn't care less."

I moved in the next week and I still live here. In fact, I've lived in this apartment for ten years, longer than I'd ever even lived in a city before in my entire adult life.

Life in Portland became almost all good. The annoyances seemed to disappear. Dale McCormick began her campaign to establish a gay and lesbian political organization and hundreds of people came out of the closet to join her statewide movement. Gay men and lesbians in Maine were no longer silhouettes on the screen, they had more and more faces of real neighbors, and the Maine Lesbian and Gay Coalition became one of the most successful organizations in the country.

I had my personal victories as well. The rest of the media didn't feel as constrained as the Sunday paper. Over the next few years, as I began to publish more, they took me on as a local figure, and I was profiled on the front page of the daily newspaper. When I won awards, the local television stations gave my trophies major play. When a friend visited from New York once, a bag boy at the supermarket made me eternally happy when he asked, in front of my guest, "Aren't you that famous writer?" To be known in one's supermarket is the final accolade a community can give.

I made some money by writing some mass market pulp adventure novels that had a certain pseudonymous success. There was a new crew at the post office, men my age with my own background, who loved them. I even ended up dedicating one of the series to "The Men of Station A." The world might have thought they were Cold War warriors, but my dedicatees were actually my postmen. While their predecessors had been guarded about any mention of where my mail came from, the new guys watched the return addresses and complimented me whenever one was Avon or Dell or St. Martin's.

They even got over my sexuality. Once a soft-core heterosexual porn magazine was mailed to me. I couldn't imagine how it had come to be addressed to me, but it was. There weren't any other customers in the place and when the clerk handed it over the counter, he yelled to the other postal workers, "Hey, look what Preston got! I knew it all the time. He's just faking that gay stuff. There must be money in it!" The rest of them laughed and made jokes about the way the world had changed. Everyone used to hide his homosexuality, they said, but now, here I was, cashing in on the new trend.

One of the few sumptuous social highlights of my year isn't even gay; it's an annual Christmas party that Hugh and his wife, Linda, give. Some years it's only been for the tenants, sometimes the list is made up of their business contacts or other homeowners on Park Street Row. Through sheer attrition, I'm the lodger who's been here the longest; whoever else is invited, I'm always on the list. Their apartment, on the fifth floor, is the most modern in the building. It's a stylish loft with windows that show a panoramic view of the harbor and Casco Bay. I dress up and climb the stairs right on time, anxious to see what Hugh, a gourmand, has cooked this holiday season.

I always stay the whole time, I'm not one of those who come in for a quick social nod and leave. By the end of the party, Hugh and I have usually had more than a fair share to drink. (Actually, while most people are satisfied with a glass of wine, Hugh usually has a bit of Scotch tucked away for the two of us.) A couple years ago, after we were both pleasantly blushed with holiday cheer, Hugh saw me to the door when the party was over. He asked me, "John, we hear all about this AIDS stuff. We're so concerned. You're okay, aren't you?" I looked at him blankly, I couldn't find any words, I couldn't lie to him.

"Oh, god, why did I ask?"

I had kept my diagnosis a secret. I had watched the spread

of the epidemic for years before I learned that I was infected myself. I had thought, quite frankly, that my move to Portland might have saved me. Sure, there had been trips back to New York, to Boston, to California, but I had learned the new rules of the sexual game early and there hadn't been many times in Maine when I thought I could have been infected.

But I had been. I had just learned a few months before Hugh asked the question. I had thought that the news would be easy for me to accept. I was trained as an educator and had been one of the people who had founded the first AIDS organizations in Maine. I was aware, conscious of what was happening, certainly I should have been able to deal with this. But I hadn't been able, not at all. I didn't know who to tell, I couldn't figure out what I would ask for. I was certain I'd find nothing but trouble when the news spread.

However I thought I should have handled the situation, I also knew very well how viciously so many people were treated when the news of their diagnosis had been spread. I had seen them abandoned by their lovers, kicked out of their apartments, scorned by their families. I might have information about the virus that I could use, but I didn't know what was going to happen to people when they found out.

Hugh was embarrassed by his question. He came to my apartment the next day and apologized for having intruded into my privacy, but I was glad he'd asked. I knew I couldn't sit alone in my apartment and take everything on myself forever. It was time to take some risks, time to test the waters. I had to find out what my supports were going to be.

The next year was tough. There were many choked conversations on the phone with friends and relatives and many awkward revelations over lunch or drinks. When I finally spoke to my brother, the person in my family with whom I had the strongest relationship, he asked what he should do with the information. I told him it was his. I didn't want to control it anymore. If it was appropriate and comfortable for him to tell others, he should. If not, he shouldn't feel an obligation. He did tell the other members of our family and they came to visit me, one by one, uncomfortably, but honestly.

When things got hardest, Hugh was one of the people I called. We went to lunch once when I phoned him in a panic. It was a day when I felt utterly out of control of my life. Over a decent meal and a glass of wine he sat there and listened and talked about his own aging. We were just a couple of guys sitting around talking about our mortality that afternoon. He and Linda began to ask questions about my therapies, what doctors was I seeing in Boston? Asking about my well-being wasn't something we saw as an intrusion anymore.

They were part of my healing, not my physical healing, but the restoration of my spirits. The way I finally had to complete that recovery was by writing. I wrote essays about my infection and collected my own and some others in an anthology, *Personal Dispatches*. The act of putting the words into type was the final reclaiming of my self. It was done. I had faced the disease and, even if I couldn't defeat it, I wasn't going to hide from it.

When the book was published, I accepted an invitation to be interviewed by Al Diamon on Maine Public Radio. He was one of the newspeople who'd spoken to me over the years, I think—I hope—he was one of those who'd respected me. The interview was hard for both of us, we spoke openly about my infection and my own thoughts on what was ahead for me.

I knew there'd be more publicity, especially now that I was out in the open about my diagnosis, but I didn't expect an interview on public radio to reach the masses. The next morning I walked unsuspectingly into my post office branch. As soon as they saw me, all the clerks gathered at one of the desks. They were staring at me, ignoring the other customers. "Come here," one of them said. I walked up to them, not sure what was happening. "Is it true? What we heard on the radio last night?" I nodded that it was. I had flashes of the religious tracts the other postal workers had kept on their desks. I began to worry about how these men were going to react. I had visions of all the ignorance about AIDS I'd seen flashed over the television. Instead, one of the men, who I now realize was designated as their spokesperson, said to me, calmly, and clearly, "Shit, we all gotta die, John, but it must be hell to be standing on the tracks, watching the locomotive coming with your name on it." I don't think anyone else, not the most eloquent author or the most inspired political leader, has ever put it better.

And that was it, for that morning and for the past three years. Like everyone else who knows me, they ask about potential cures they read about in the newspapers and they wonder about my health, asking how I'm doing. They're happy when I seem well and they become concerned when I look haggard.

They're like Hugh and Linda, like my fellow workers at The AIDS Project, like Al Diamon, they're people who live in the same place I do, bound together not just because of geography, but because we all share a hometown.

DEMING, NEW MEXICO

IN JANUARY OF 1987, MY lover came to me one night and said that he wanted to break up, that he was heterosexual and before he got too old he wanted a chance to get married and have children. At the time, we were living in Arlington, Texas. I had just lost my job; he had been promoted and was being transferred to El Paso, Texas. He said that this move was a good time for him to end our fourteen-year relationship. At first, I felt lost and angry, but by the end of the year, I began to realize that such a change in my life was good for me, too. I had to return to my hometown of Deming, New Mexico, however, to find this out.

After my lover and I managed an equitable separation of property and pets, I moved to Las Cruces, New Mexico—sixty miles east of my hometown—where I had gone to college years before and had got my start as a technical writer. I hoped that by returning there, I could get another start. Instead, for the ten months that I lived in Las Cruces, I was lonely and felt isolated.

I kept telling myself that my circumstances would change. In December of 1987, they did. My mother became ill and was hospitalized, so I moved from Las Cruces to Deming to help my father while my mother was in the hospital.

Right after her operation, when she was brought back to the hospital room, I watched her sleeping. My father was in the room with me. We spoke in whispers and agreed that, without her teeth, my mother looked like her mother had as an old woman, and I wanted to cry.

A week or so later, when we brought her home, my father and I tried to keep up with the housework. He cooked and I did dishes—mundane things that go unnoticed when someone else is doing them but that pile up and become reminders that the person in our lives who had always made a home was down the hall, in bed, recovering and probably worrying about us rather than herself. Then one day, my mother got up and cooked lunch, or swept the kitchen, and insisted that she could walk on her own. Her improvement seemed slow, at first, then accelerated, and I began to relax.

I might have gone away, then, resumed my life as a newly single adult, but as soon as my mother began to recover, my father had a heart attack. It seemed mild. Under his own strength, he walked into the hospital, but once he was admitted and placed in ICU, he grew worse immediately. He was there a week, his condition seeming to worsen every day. So the family was called in.

My oldest sister came from Colorado; my brother and other sisters came in from elsewhere in New Mexico. Relatives from up in the mountains in south-central New Mexico came in, too. We had not seen them since the death of one of them several years before. Soon my parents' home was filled with people, and I thought I was witnessing that time of life most adult children must face, when one's parents grow frail and ultimately pass on. I wondered if I would be up to this seeming imminent dissolution of the family home.

I watched it all, recalling times in my childhood, when my aunts and uncles were young as I am now. There were funerals for which the extended family gathered in one small town or another to bury their parents or their elderly relatives. There were many other times when these people gathered for the holidays, or gathered because their farms or ranches could run themselves during certain seasons of the year, when the nights were filled with fiddle playing and laughter. This time, there was no fiddle playing as in years past, none of Aunt Eva's cobbler. There were hushed whispers at the hospital and, at home, the saddened recalling of other days, and I thought that even the rememberers in this family would one day be gone.

Then my father took a turn for the better, and the relatives left, making us promise to call if anything went wrong or if there was anything that needed to be done. Eventually, the rest of my siblings had to leave, and it was just me and my mother at home. She and I traded vigil at the hospital. Daily, we got reports that my father's condition was improving, but the nurses told me he had to walk to get his strength back. When I helped him out of bed, he gripped my neck; as we walked the length of the corridor, both of us taking small, interdependent steps, both sweating from the effort, I felt awed at my father's strength of will, even in his frailty.

I began to see that there was something of great value at home. Besides helping my parents through their illnesses, I was beginning to feel serene, happy in a way that I had not been since I lost my lover. I wasn't yet ready to plunge headlong into some gay social mix without him, who was off plunging headlong into some heterosexual mix. Besides discovering that my parents needed me, I found that I needed to be here as well.

I was also waiting for word from a publisher about whether a novel I had written would be accepted for publication. The contract arrived in the mail in August of 1988 and I asked my parents if they minded if I stayed for a while. They said of course not.

So here I am, living with the help of my parents' generosity, able to spend the time I need writing. We've worked out an equitable agreement; I do the yard work, raise a large garden, summerize and winterize their home, do maintenance work on their vehicles, and, in exchange, they've let me move into a small one-room building on their place for minuscule rent. It has electricity, but no plumbing, a bare concrete floor, unfinished walls, and two naked windows looking south. Yet this room is a blessed place, where I can work when the desert is a blizzard of sand or snow. I've got a bed, a coffeepot, my computer, my books, and a musical keyboard upon which I make music of my own weird composition. In the evenings, when the sun is setting, I can watch the spectacular and long-lasting sunsets. The colors span the sky from west to east, and when the sun has sunk to the horizon, the Florida Mountains to the east become brilliantly lit, multicolored and dominant.

Once I knew that my novel was going to be published, I began to talk about it, forgetting that its theme might cause distress to those members of my family who didn't know that I was gay. To some of my nephews, cousins, siblings, the idea of someone in the family being a published writer was a kind of event, as was the notion that someone in the family would go to college. In fact, on the day that my book arrived, the dining room was full of relatives (coincidentally there). When my father opened the UPS box with his pocket knife and pulled out a copy of my book, it was passed from hand to hand. I was about fifth in line to touch it.

A nephew was the first to buy an autographed copy from me. He and his wife read it to each other each night. An elderly aunt with cataracts took a copy that I hesitantly loaned her. My parents know that I'm gay as do my brother and sisters, but I didn't think that many of my relatives did. My aunt read it within a week and returned it smiling, saying with a giggle and a wave of the hand, "It's a good book, for the kind of book it is." Her daughter also read it and told me she thought it was time that such books were published and wished me success with it.

Then one day as I came into my parents' house, my mother, who was in her usual spot at the dining-room table, turned and looked at me with a bright smile, her eyes lit with excitement.

"Oh, Ron, I'm glad you're back. The Deming *Headlight* called and they want to interview you about your book!"

"They do?"

I felt anxious about the local paper doing an interview. It

may be self-repressive, but I didn't want my family to suffer any ostracism from people in Deming at the expense of my "coming out of the closet" in my hometown—their town, really. I could pick up and leave anytime I wanted. I worried about the reaction of the family friends, distant relatives, and old classmates of mine still in Deming once the news was out.

So, when the article was published, I read it before anyone else had seen it. Right there in black and white, it said, "Donaghe is gay, and . . ." I sweated bullets that day as I knew many of Deming's fifteen thousand residents were reading the article as they settled down for the evening. What if the telephone suddenly began ringing off the hook? "Hey. You the Donaghes with the faggot son? Yeah? Well, you know what's good for you, you'll . . ."

The telephone rang once. I rushed to it, going a little dizzy with anticipation. My mouth was dry when I answered it. It was somebody from the Deming Center for the Arts wondering if I'd like to do a book signing. The voice on the other end was female. She said that the council had decided that the book signing would go well with an art exhibit that was currently running at the center. "But we've decided that your signing will be financed by contributions from the community, rather than with funding from the state—ah, considering the objections many people had to that recent Mapplethorpe thing."

I understood. But I was amazed. "You do know that my novel has a gay theme?"

"Yes. Will Sunday be all right?"

I agreed, was eager for it, but still couldn't relax. Where was the flack? The threatening telephone calls in the middle of the night? The invitation to be the guest of honor at a queer bashing?

I was used to being afraid of homophobia—much of that coming from places like San Francisco, where the ex-cop murdered Harvey Milk, or like Houston, where a gay man was castrated one night in a city park. My lover and I were visiting a friend there the weekend when it happened. He knew about the park as a cruising area, said that it was only a few blocks from where he worked. Such violence always hit home to me. Maybe its randomness gave it a sense of pervasiveness; the message from such terrorists: "If you're openly gay or flamboyant, you're likely to get attacked." This act of violence reminded me also of the perversions during the Anita Bryant campaigns in Dade County, Florida, where the message went out on bumper stickers: KILL A QUEER FOR CHRIST.

So, thinking about homophobia and the worsening rampage of the self-righteous, I couldn't relax about the book signing. I doubted that a crazed, gun-wielding, fundamentalist minister of some sort would walk into the arts center and, in front of a small crowd of arts lovers, blow me away, but I fully expected some member of some church to be among the audience and, during my reading of passages from *Common Sons*, to jump up and spew biblical quotes and self-righteous spittle. But that didn't happen either.

Instead, I sold a few more copies of my book. Among the well wishers at the book signing were a local high school teacher, members of the arts council, a dozen or so strangers, and three former classmates, one of whom was buying a copy for herself and a couple of copies for other people I had gone to school with thirty years before.

About a week later, I had lunch with one of the classmates to discuss my book. This woman, Donna, whom I'd known from the third grade through high school, and then hadn't seen for twenty-three years, was unchanged to me, except that we were now in our forties. After we ordered and were waiting for our food, I asked if she minded if I smoked. She smiled and said she'd been waiting to ask me the same thing. The conversation became relaxed as we lit up. We talked about diet and being older, changes in the town.

She seemed to have given a lot of thought to those of us who had moved away from Deming as soon as we left high school. She had become the keeper of the memories for those of us who went to the same country school—"our old gang," she called us—the entire eighth-grade graduating class of 1962. There were fourteen of us. She told me about those who stayed in Deming as she had, those who had prospered in the way their parents had, by hanging on to family property and changing methods of farming with the technology. Donna has been married for twenty years, has two adopted children, and lives fifteen miles northeast of Deming at the foot of Black Mountain. When I knew her in grade school, her family lived fifteen or so miles south of Deming at the foot of the Tres Hermanas Mountains.

"My husband and I liked your main character's religion," she said. Over the telephone, when we made our lunch date, she'd surprised me right away when she told me that her husband had read my novel. "Our religion is kind of like Joel Reece's in your story—except that we think God is in everything."

About my writing, she said two things that I recall vividly. One was that she thought I was going to be a "great" writer one of these days. The other was that at first, in reading my novel, she couldn't quite stomach the sexual scenes between the two male characters, until her husband, who'd finished the book first, told her to think of it as "love." That, she said, made the rest of the novel go down easily. I was flabbergasted—not that a heterosexual woman would have difficulty "stomaching" a sexual scene between two males, but that her husband could key into the essence of the affection between them, rather than just their sexual intimacy.

I liked Donna after all these years. We touched on my homosexuality. I told her about my lover and an ex-wife, my son going on eighteen. About my lover she said, "I imagine it was like a death, losing him."

On past visits to Deming, when I'd run into people I knew from school, our conversations were restrained, maybe because I had felt it necessary to keep my gay identity to myself. Now that people knew, as with Donna, we were both free to talk, although I still felt very conscious of being newly "out of the closet" with her.

There were other indications that people from my past who still lived in Deming knew about my book, my coming out. My mother kept me abreast of the reaction. Two women I'd dated in high school had read the newspaper article and when they met my mother at the grocery store, asked for copies of my novel. Later, one of them said she'd read it several times, and parts of it had made her cry. . . .

■   ■   ■

This is my hometown? Doesn't conventional wisdom have it that the smaller the community, the smaller the minds, and the higher the rate of homophobia? I get the impression that it's possible to be openly gay and "happy" here in the 1990s. Let me rephrase that; it's possible to be as open in my hometown as it is in most parts of most cities. It's definitely not possible to be as open in Deming as it is in the gay ghettos of New York, San Francisco, or Houston. But even though I came out in the local newspaper, I find that people are not hysterical about one of their native sons being gay. I haven't a clue why, unless it's something in the water supply.

Other than having a colorful history as a coal stop for the railroad in the 1800s with a collection of cathouses, saloons, and hotels for the railroad workers, Deming is not unique from its sister towns in the Southwest. The name is less poetic than those towns with Spanish heritages. It is less rich in history than Las Cruces, which was founded in the 1500s by the Spanish. In fact, there is no particular Southwestern heritage responsible for creating Deming; although, today, Deming is at least half Hispanic. The other half of the population is usually referred to as "Anglo," but it's a conglomeration of races and nationalities. The people share the same goals—just staying alive in this valley, making a living as they can while the world continues.

Most of the settlers came to Deming in the early 1900s. They populated the town and the county and established ranches and farms and businesses to deal with agriculture—selling farm equipment, ginning cotton, and shipping the county's products by rail to other places.

Today, agriculture is surging, and Deming is the seasonal home of what the locals call "snowbirds"—people from other states who make their winter home in this desert valley. It is also a retirement community, home of the Great American Duck Race, whose winner was once a guest on Johnny Carson; Deming is, well, a tourist trap, a quick stop off the interstate with one all-night truck stop, a McDonald's, an Arby's, a Pizza Hut, and a Kentucky Fried Chicken. There are local hamburger and taco joints, too, and a host of family-run restaurants. There are motels, gas stations, and bars along the main street, and off on side streets. There are all-night garages, where the traveler with car trouble can get repairs and get back on the road. That's about it, except for the businesses that stay afloat if the farmers and ranchers do.

There are at least fifteen hundred gay people in Deming, if one accepts statistical probability, yet I've only met a handful of those. After the newspaper article, I expected that several gay people would call me, if for no other reason than to make contact. One seventy-year-old man did call several months after the newspaper story. He said it took him that long to work up the courage.

So, I haven't changed history by making my gay identity public in this small town, haven't given others much courage to follow suit, either. I'm left with the conclusion that there's no particular reason that I should feel free to be gay here. Just like anywhere else, were I to go into a straight bar (there are no gay bars within a hundred miles of here), I would be a fool to attempt to make a date with another man. And I have found quiet discrimination that I could have predicted. I was substituting at the various schools—until the article came out in the local paper. I haven't been asked to substitute since. But then there have been no hot-headed book bannings; no teachers that I recall were ever expelled for poisoning a child's mind. And I have not experienced any *overt* hostility.

So far as I know, Deming is just an average Southwestern town, with average citizens. But like ceasing to care what "makes me gay," I've ceased to wonder what makes this town so casual about whether it has homosexuals in it. In the newspaper interview, I told the readers that there were many homosexuals among them. That didn't seem to rock the town with scandal, either.

Coming home, getting published, and especially coming out as a gay person has changed my perspectives—or at least made me question some basic assumptions I held about Deming and small-mindedness. I've discovered that my parents, my elderly relatives, and other people here have things to teach me about being judged and judging others, about neighborliness. I've also discovered that being in the middle of nowhere, having little contact with the outside world except through letters and telephone calls is about all I need at the moment. I'm not ready to go back to a city, even though there are things I miss.

Being home to help my parents through their illnesses has taught me a great deal about personal reward and gratitude. Other elderly relatives around Deming also call on me to drive them to the doctors in other towns, to pick up appliances that need to be repaired. I've become a reluctant mechanic but an enthusiastic carpenter. Six months after my father's heart attack, he and I built a free-standing roof over a mobile home down the road. My father outworked me, and I'm still learning about patience from him.

I'm also a general maintenance man. Calls for my new skills as a handyman have increased. These elderly people *need* younger people like me who are willing to help them with the heavy work they are no longer able to do. They take an active and generally good-natured interest in me and each other.

Curiosity was lively when I put in a garden. Several people stopped by when I was working there and asked the obvious. "What's that you're doing?" Later on, the regular drive-bys would stop to offer me horse or cow manure, seeds from their gardens, and of course, advice. Later, I passed the vegetables around as they came off. All mourned the worm infestation in the corn patch. All agreed that it was a bad year for tomatoes.

I've also become the letter writer in the family. Since I've written a book, my family and friends seem to think that I must know something about dealing with almost anything having to do with words—from writing résumés for my nephew and his wife to writing legislators and filling out Social Security forms. When the U.S. Congress was talking about a pay raise, I had half a dozen senior citizens telling me what they wanted written on the subject. I got tickled at one point at an elderly uncle's suggestion that the senators and representatives should serve one term, then we should "cut their heads off." His answer to everything is "Cut their heads off." Yet, he's really very astute, reads *Time, Newsweek*—a whole spectrum of national publications—and always votes Democratic. He knows I'm gay, too. But like others in my family, that doesn't prevent him from wanting to spend time with me, nor to get me to drive him to town, nor to take the opportunity to give me advice.

Although many of the people I run into in Deming know about my novel and its theme, they are more concerned with the price of cotton, farm subsidies, and Social Security than with someone being gay; in their private minds they may still equate my homosexuality with someone else's alcoholism. They excuse it because it doesn't concern them, maybe, or they've seen it all on television and it doesn't surprise them anymore. My father's casual acceptance of the *notion* of homosexuality made me smile. One day he and I were watching "Donahue." My mother called out from the dining room: "What are you watching, Cliff?" My father said, "Oh . . . Rock Hudson's lover."

Certainly homosexuality is no longer a taboo subject. And if it causes members of my family anxiety, they don't let me see it. Getting published and going public brought my immediate family out of the closet with me, and they may have learned as I have that fear itself is often worse than the thing being feared.

I feel free to take a lover, to live with him, to be seen together, and to make no bones about our relationship if asked about it. My family and family friends and some of the people I went to school with thirty years ago, those who've read my novel, have not only continued to treat me as one of them, but to treat me with a little more intimacy than they used to. One woman I met wanted to read me a poem. She said, "I thought you would understand. You people are so much more sensitive." I imagine that by "you people" she meant "gays and lesbians" and not writers.

Were it not for being single and sometimes lonely, I think I could make Deming a permanent home. In fact, the town of Deming could be wiped off the map and it would not diminish in value, because it's not the buildings, the streets, nor even the people of this small town that make Deming a special place to live. It's something much more valuable than that.

Sometimes I go out into the country miles away from the nearest human being. This is the real place, my hometown, that will be hard to leave when it comes time. Deming is built on the floor of the Mimbres Valley, surrounded by ribs of the Rocky Mountain chain that rise from the desert to 10,000 feet above sea level. The high plateau upon which even the valley rests is 4,300 feet. To the west and north runs the Continental Divide; east and south of Deming lie the Floridas, a jagged chain of mountains that dominate the area. It is to the Floridas that I find I'm frequently drawn.

If I drive to the foothills, then walk a little higher up the slope of ground, I can see beyond the mountains that surround the Mimbres Valley to another range and another beyond that, until the mountains themselves look like clouds on the distant horizon.

And the sky is equally endless. On a clear day, above the lines of the mountains, it's a piercing blue and turquoise, the purity of the color never to be captured on canvas or film, nor the depth of the color. Above me the air is thin, and through the clear atmosphere, the color of the blue seems to deepen, to hint at the blackness it soon becomes in outer space. Out here, the colors blend gently from the sandy color at my feet, to the browns of the close hills above me on the slope of the mountains, to the purple and shadow blue mysteries of the Floridas, themselves, their canyons and cliffs and secrets.

As a youth, I roamed this same region, but back then I was blind to the land, its mysteries, its subtleties. Now, even though I still carry a blind civilization of industry and commerce on my back, I've discovered a way to see this place like a newborn, to be cleansed by the desert fire, to burn away the debris of sadness that continues to hang over me from losing my lover, already three years ago. By coming to this private place as an adult, to think, to be alone for a while, I'm eventually getting over what was once the best thing in my life.

Here, I can remove my clothing and stand like naked truth, exposed to the desert.

The sun bathes my shoulders and back and genitals. The wind, with an icy breath, stirs the tiny hairs on my skin and chills it. I can open my arms and let the delicious warmth and chill wash over me, leap and run through the broad daylight celebrating the rush of raw energy that pumps through me.

When I go out into the desert and the mountains, I don't try to describe them in someone else's terms; I don't dredge up from my literature studies classical allusions to Nature.

Instead, as I climb out of the valley, I feel more vulnerable than the jackrabbits and coyotes I used to hunt when I was fully dressed and armed to the teeth, when I wore hiking boots spiked with metal and carried a rifle for blasting the brains out of a fellow animal. Naked as I am, I must listen with my senses, to smell rank danger on the wind, to run if need be, like prey.

I discover that every sense, every pore of my skin, every breath I draw, is open to the land, the scents and sounds on the wind, the way the wind changes constantly in swirls and eddies around me from the effect of the sun. The sun dominates the desert, casts all in stark detail. In the summer its fire licks the bones of dead animals dry of moisture and color. Evidence of that power is all around me, from the bleached-out bones at my feet to the patches of ash that were once tender shoots of grass.

Yet, in the shadows of the cliffs when I'm hiking I can find small streams, maybe a foot wide and an inch deep. If I'm thirsty, I can kneel and drink the water without fear of pollution. But out here, I'm constantly aware of what water is, how precious, how ephemeral. The sun will eventually claim it, cause it to evaporate and rise out of sight into the blue.

I forget that I'm saddened, tense, anxious. I become merely a dance of awareness, energy, trading heat and cold and moisture with my surroundings.

From up here, I can gaze into the blue haze of distance. A hundred miles away the earth, the land, looks like the ocean. In this immensity, my problems seem so minute that it makes me laugh aloud, and the echoes of my laughter come back eerily from the canyon walls, doubled and tripled even as the sound dies. I am merely one kind of sentient being in this desert, gazing out over a magnificence that defies human control. Binoculars are useless. Infinity can grow no closer.

When I hike into the shadowed canyons amid the rock cliffs, the silence is deafening, yet I think I must hear the same voice the Native Americans heard only a hundred or so years before me. The soul, the magic of the place, surrounds me; the stony silence diminishes all distracting sound of humanity, stirs the hair on the nape of my neck, sends thrills of awe down my spine. There is a primordial mystery here—a singing—a voice in the wind, that says the secret of the land is freedom.

When at last I feel cold, I become aware of my nakedness, again, and return to my pickup, where I gladly wrap myself in the warmth of my clothing, feeling refreshed.

Such a life, especially with the serenity of the country surrounding me, makes me *feel* more integrated than I ever felt in the city. Working in the yard on a clear crisp fall day, working in my garden, hiking in the desert, all these things nurture me. I didn't know that I missed this simple life so much until I came home.

I know that I risk being alone. Sometimes I ache for the touch of a man, the comfort of sharing a home, intimate companionship. Sometimes I wonder if I'm putting too much importance on my serenity, rather than on interpersonal relationships with other gay people. I've met a few gay people here in Deming. But other than an occasional dinner, an occasional connection, I'm basically alone.

It seems like only yesterday that I thought of myself as an outsider when I came home to visit. During fourteen of those years, when my lover came with me, our bedroom was always waiting for us when we pulled in late at night after a long drive. My mother or father would meet us at the door and say something as casual as, "We've got your bed ready." My youngest brother and sister were only eight and six when my lover met the family for the first time. The youngest is now twenty-five. Both my parents are doing well, these days, so there is a tension in me about staying on or submerging myself in the life of some city. But this time, I wouldn't leave my hometown thinking that it holds nothing for me. A few miles from here, high above the valley, it offers the world.

THE EPISCOPAL CHURCH: SAN JOSE, CALIFORNIA

I SIT, NOW, AS I DO MOST days, licking the last of my healing wounds. Below, in the valley, lies the city of San Jose, the third largest, the latest census says, of the hometowns in California. But up here in the dry, brown hills, home is smaller: sheep, pygmy goats, a Shetland sheepdog, a Swiss-Mexican-Sioux lover, and our five-year-old Honduran-born son.

They are gone most of the day—my lover at work, our son at day care—and I tend to the daily chores of land, animal, and house. By midmorning my work is complete; I have time to consider my home, not the home of my childhood, although that was where I first, as a boy, let them have the knife. . . .

I grew up on a reservation in the Bitterroot Mountains of northern Idaho, in a valley shared by loggers and Indians, the son of a Germanic mother and (how can I say it cautiously, tenderly?) a dark, blue-eyed father. Her parents were descendants of successful immigrants: substantial, well-off—they belonged—in their hometown; while his parents descended from the wreckage of the American West: products of furtive and undocumented matings, moving continually, always camping near land not their own, belonging to none.

Because of her marriage, my mother's family rejected her, and their rejection extended to her children. As first-born, I was raised at the time her wounds were freshest, most open, and her parents became for me the symbol of a powerful, nonmongrel world: one to which I, because I was my father's child, could never belong. But deeper, more terrifying than their rejection— always lurking, ready to whirl and kill—lay their final conclusion: I should not be.

So, that was why: belonging to no one, trapped between two peoples, I surrendered, tossed them my knife.

Not, I think, that anyone knew. Disarmed, I bluffed and feinted, acted as though I could be dangerous. And I used my noncombative skills to the hilt: my intelligence, personality, and above all my desire to please. I would do—be—believe anything, if they would prove to me that I was all right, if they would prove it by taking me in, by letting me belong.

And it worked; I lived.

My childhood was filled with baseball, football, swimming, camping, bicycles, and even the delights of sex as I crossed the barriers into both camps, belonging with the closeness of my body, pleasing and being pleased.

People had prepared me and the other boys for the time of becoming a man, for the time when we would become interested in girls. Suddenly, the time erupted and our balls, cocks, and hair grew; our bodies shot up, out; imaginations followed the swelling of cocks as they demanded freedom from tightened pants—freedom to explore this girl and this girl and this girl. My cock swelled, too—maybe more so—demanded freedom like the rest, but those who had prepared us for the time of becoming a man had not guessed the truth. I didn't belong.

Although on reservations and in logging towns, the dint of Puritan morality is slight (alcohol and sex—an easy, almost careless sex—abound), but it is a world of heterosexuality. There are exceptions. Among the whites there are sissies who, as soon as they can, disappear to Seattle, Portland, or California. Among the Indians there are men who dress in feminine-looking trousers, blouses, wrap themselves in sweaters or blankets, and put rouge on their cheeks.

The knife swung at my Levi's, next to my balls.

I feigned great interest in girls, turned out for football and track, won my letter, did everything I could to convince anyone, everyone, that I was all right, that I should belong. They agreed. Popular in both camps, I was elected class president, student body vice-president, student body president. And I graduated from high school, uncastrated.

Underneath, in the hollow of my success, I was frightened, afraid they would uncover the truth, afraid they would give me the choice: running as a white sissy or staying as a blue-eyed berdache. I dreamed of a place where I could belong, a hometown where my birth would be unimportant, where I could still be a man, where instead of liking girls, I could like boys.

Even deep in the Bitterroots, people knew of Paris. Veterans snickered, newspapers insinuated, magazines exposed: in Paris, there lived, with the scandalous French, a group of American expatriots who wrote banned books, who painted pictures of naked people, and who openly engaged in behavior too outrageous to print. I got a job driving a truck, tried to save enough money so I could leave, so I could join the exiles, the others who belonged to no one. Money piled up slower than I planned, and I was naïve, unsure that I could support myself in Paris. Reluctantly, I gave in to the advice of others: use your intelligence; first, get a college education. I enrolled in the University of Idaho, returned to the reservation each summer to pile lumber in the sawmill, and with what I could earn between studies, paid my way through college.

One Sunday morning, a sissy professor, anxious to keep me for the day, bribing me with more spending money and the promise of lunch and another dinner, invited me to the Episcopal church. I expected cold drabness, but instead found colored light pouring from the windows; flags, banners, flowers, candles crowding the interior; and then, unbelievably, a procession of people, all white—boys and men, girls and women—dressed in costumes of red and white, some singing, some carrying large, shining crosses, some more candles. At the last came their priest, dressed in an ornate costume of white and gold. Those in the procession crowded to the front, and began an intricate dance of bowing, kneeling, sitting, standing, processing. And surrounding me, everyone joined the dance.

In the midst of the service, the priest began to chant, a soaring, weird, wild, forlorn chant, and the people answered, chanted back. The beauty of these people's ceremony matched the beauty of the Indians'. I was swept away, and in my excitement, I failed to notice: unlike the barren costumes of the Indians, the long, flowing costumes of these people contained many dark places to hide the knife.

Back in his apartment, the professor was amused, then annoyed, for, rather than wanting to spend the entire afternoon probing his body, I wanted, also, to probe him about his church. That evening he took me to dinner with two other professors, and though only one was an Episcopalian, they all told stories about the Episcopal church. It sounded like Paris.

That week I made an appointment, told their priest that I wanted to become a priest, too. He had been warned, amused also, by the naïveté of my decision: I had attended only one service and had never been baptized. But I was familiar with barriers, knew how to surmount them, and one by one, sacrament and ceremony, pleasing, feinting, studying, bluffing, I passed them all and went, unarmed, to seminary.

Paris pales next to the Episcopal church, for Paris is but a city, confined to the banks of the Seine, while the Episcopal church, like some scattered, rich tribe, dwells throughout the world, its people and clergy easily flowing from one place to the next. In the sixties, the Episcopal church was still deeply rooted in the Renaissance; in love with freedom, in love with learning, in love with excess; composed of quarreling factions who had their own history, signs, code words as intricate as those of any Renaissance Italian city (and making the same kind of sense—none—to an outsider).

And the professors had been right: parties and sex abounded.

Not to say that all people engaged in sex or that all single men engaged in homosexual sex or that all married men engaged in heterosexual sex, but the lines blurred, broke, changed, enough to confuse and dizzy the most advanced of Paris's expatriots.

In the midst of seminary, I married. At the time, it seemed to be a wise decision, because although not as exciting, I enjoyed heterosexual sex, and in the places and at the times it mattered, marriage would hide my desire for males. I, also, loved the woman; I could have children and my parents, grandchildren.

Seven years later, after two successful and exciting cures (pastorates) in Arizona, and after the birth of three children, I was called as rector to the Salinas Valley, to King City, California, John's Steinbeck's East of Eden. There, new to the valley and having no friends, the marriage closed in, became oppressive, a prison of my own making, a hell which, I believed, was worse than anything I would have endured had I stayed on the reservation.

And Stonewall had happened. The sissies and berdaches who had fled to the cities were now heroes. Unlike me, they had exposed their balls, had refused to run anymore, had refused to hide from the hail of knives.

I got divorced, expected the knife, no one threw it. But alone in a small town, I was miserable.

A new work was opening in San Francisco. Indian Episcopalians, still on the reservations, were concerned that their families and friends who had left their hometowns and moved to the Bay Area were being ignored by their own church because of their race, culture, and poverty. The reservation people wanted a priest to walk the streets, visit the centers, be a liaison with the reservation churches, and to discover what, if anything, Indians of the city wanted with or from the church.

Offered the job, I accepted, moved to San Francisco, and followed the tradition of my father's people: I lived on the edge of someone else's land. I walked the streets of the Mission District, South of Market, the Tenderloin; contacting the centers in Oakland and San Jose. Those on the reservations had been right: the Indians had been forgotten.

It was an exciting time. People wanted a church similar to

home, to have their own kind of services, to feel comfortable in their casual clothing, where their children were welcome during the ceremonies, where they could gather for meals, talk, where the people could sew, where they could take care of one another, where there was someone for them in the time of crisis.

The group moved from the street to a storefront; took back a large community center, abandoned years before by the Episcopal church; took back the church next door. In eight years the center offered a preschool, community recreation, meetings and dinners, emergency clothing and food, after-school tutoring, crisis counseling, employment services, sewing, arts and crafts. From its Indian base, it reached out and new organizations formed—Latinos, Haitians, and elderly whites—and all joined together to run the center.

In the meantime, my personal, financial, and social life blossomed, too. My lover moved in, completed law school, was hired by a major firm. We bought two flats, four flats, became part of gaynewal, and thanks to the democracy of the clerical collar, our gay friends stretched from the law partners of Pacific Heights to the berdaches of the Tenderloin.

Flush with success, I decided to return to the mainstream of the church and thought it would be good for the center, its staff and people, to find a director who bore a badge other than founder. My lover's hometown is San Jose, and his home parish was looking for a rector. I submitted my name.

The selection narrowed to three names, but before a vote could be taken, their new bishop (the new diocese had recently been carved from the one centered in San Francisco) exercised his right, removed my name, refused to give the vestry a reason. Wounded, convinced there was a mistake, I called him. He refused to restore my name, saying that he wanted a priest from his new diocese. But of the two names left, there was the name of another priest from San Francisco, married. They chose the other San Francisco priest.

Hurting, I confronted the bishop again, asked him if his veto precluded my ever coming to his diocese. It did not, he said, for they might open an Indian work, and if so he would want me, for Indian work, he understood, was my "thing." A stab next to my heart.

Bleeding profusely, in September I told my bishop and his priest-administrator that I would resign from the center, effective December 31. As the door was closing, the knife hit my back. Although each year we had faithfully submitted the books for the required audit, and I and the all-Indian (with the exception of one elderly white man) staff that handled the finances checked each other continually, making sure all money was handled honestly, the diocesan priest-administrator relieved me of all responsibilities except for duties liturgical and pastoral and sent in a retired bank vice-president to pore over the financial records. Gossip flew, and as the meticulous audit later discovered, everyone, including me, had been scrupulously honest. Nothing was missing: there was no reason to subject me or anyone to the rumors. We could have been trusted.

My lover and I moved to San Jose. I decided to get another master's degree and enrolled in counseling psychology with the Jesuits at Santa Clara University. Licensed to function as a priest in the new diocese, I was invited to attend their Clergy Conference. Foolishly, I went.

After the evening session, I returned to the common room to socialize, and attempted to join the group. Feeling cold-shouldered, unwelcome, I moved across the room, picked up a magazine. The rector of one of the most powerful parishes of the diocese held forth, complaining about the bishop, saying loudly, with a nod toward me, that the bishop had better check with the clergy before he opened the diocesan doors to my ilk.

Walking upright, without uttering a moan, I made it back to my room, the knife deep in my gut. The bishop's veto, his acceptance of me only for an Indian "thing"; the suspicion and my removal by the administrator in San Francisco; and now, even at a conference of my fellow priests, I am unwanted.

Alone, I pulled at the knife, twisted, stirred, pushed deeper, pulled with both hands, but was unable to remove it, the blade had entered too far, had hit too many dark, hidden guts. They wrenched and bled: my mother's parents; my father's darkness; the reservation, my childhood, the years of becoming a man; my birth which should never have been. And now, after eighteen years in the priesthood—the Church, my Paris, my hometown— I was unwanted. I didn't belong.

But they weren't quite through with me, for I strayed another time, came too near. Excited about my new master's degree and confident of my work experience for the church, I decided to explore private companies for work in personnel. Someone mentioned an Episcopal deacon (now a priest) who was a personnel director at a Silicon Valley company. I made an appointment to see him, I liked him and the interview went well, and I was confident that, even though I might not be employed in his office, he would recommend other interviews, so I could begin to network.

Too trusting, I was unconcerned that he served at the same church as the powerful rector at the clergy conference. The personnel director had promised to call me but didn't, and after trying to call him several times, one of his underlings bruskly told me they were not interested. I asked him if he had any advice or names for me to use in networking. The underling suggested I should try to get a job at Goodwill, teaching people how to assemble cardboard boxes. Even a mongrel can get the point.

So now I sit on the dry, brown hillside, safely torn from the bonds of the church. I have taken back the knife, guard it securely. I hear again the wisdom of the old people. And I have returned to the paganism of my childhood.

As for the knife—I realize now that it is holy, that I should have never tossed it to them. For it was given to me at the time of my creation in order to cut myself open, to examine my heart; it was wrong to let the others cut me, open me, to listen to them as they told of what they saw, to listen to them as they told of my belonging, my worth, my existence.

As for my return to paganism—no more do I have the desire to please, to do-be-believe anything to belong. I have walked the circle and have found healing in the old ways: in relying on who I truly am; in knowing again of the Great Spirit and truth, earth and sky, heart and spirit, strength and bravery; in standing cleansed, alone before the rising sun; in rediscovering the wisdom of visions and dreams.

The Plains Indians, in some places, hold a ceremony that people call the Sundance where (unlike the Judeo-Christians who only symbolically reenact their sacrifices) the dancers physically join the spiritual reality. As the dancers play out the sweeping reenactments of life—Capture, Torture, Captivity, and Release— they are captured, thrown down, cut beneath the muscles of their chests or backs, pierced with sticks. Leather thongs are tied to the sticks and are attached to the Sun Pole and captivity is reenacted as they dance, attached to the pole, gazing into the power of the sun. During the fourth dance of the captivity, they can begin their struggle for freedom, to tear their flesh or, using only their weight, snap the thongs.

Each dancer is rewarded with a vision, and afterward walks, proven, with those who stand tall on the earth, who stand tall among everything under the sun.

Some say that beyond the grief of Kübler-Ross, beyond acceptance, there lies another dimension: celebration. Certainly, these dancers reach it, and I suspect successful warriors reach it. Charging into battle as boy, wounded, returning with the badge of wound and scar, the warrior shrugs away what he endured, lets others see, touch, the intimacy of his pain, his experience, his manhood.

It is blasphemy to compare my wounds with those of the Sundance or those of battle, but I hope, someday, to walk through the grief of my rejection and reach celebration. Sometimes I draw close, for I realize, without the pain of their wounds, I would never have taken back the knife, and I would still gaze at them and not the sun. And without their wounds, I would never have thrashed and yanked, tore myself free from their bonds, discovered the delight of being who I am, of walking with pride as a man, of finding, deep within myself, my real hometown.

And I have had a vision. Through the strength of the vision—through the strength of my scars—through the strength of being who I truly am—I can rise up from the hillside and discover a fourth strength. I can reach out to others, not demanding proof of my worth or acceptance but delighting in everyone as brothers and sisters, delighting in their differences, standing with them, fighting for them, protecting their right to be who they are.

Because ultimately, says part of the vision, we all belong to each other—all things, plants, animals, people—all races, sexes, nations, mongrels, gays, and straights—and, in the Heart of our Creator, we all belong to one hometown.

CONTRIBUTORS

CHRISTOPHER BRAM grew up outside Norfolk, Virginia, where he was an Eagle Scout and morning paperboy. He studied English at the College of William and Mary and moved to New York City in 1978, working initially for the Social Security Administration, then for Scribner's Bookstore. He published his first novel, *Surprising Myself,* in 1987, followed by *Hold Tight* and *In Memory of Angel Clare.* He has reviewed books for *Christopher Street, Newsday,* and *The New York Times Book Review,* movies for *The New York Native* and *Premiere,* and has written a couple of screenplays. He is currently finishing a new novel, *Almost History.*

MICHAEL BRONSKI is the author of *Culture Clash: The Making of Gay Sensibility.* He is a columnist for *Z Magazine, First Hand,* and *The Guide.* His articles on books, film, culture, politics, and sexuality have appeared in *Gay Community News, The Boston Globe, Fag Rag, Radical America, American Book Review,* and *The Advocate,* as well as numerous anthologies including *Personal Dispatches:*

Writers Confront AIDS, Leatherfolk, and *Gay Spirit,* He has been involved in gay liberation for more than twenty years.

JOHN CHAMPAGNE attended three other undergraduate schools before completing his B.A. at Hunter College in New York. He also planned seminars for dentists, taught day care, worked in wholesale, and played piano for ballet classes and cabaret acts. He completed an M.A. in Cinema Studies at New York University in 1988. He is currently a Ph.D. candidate at the University of Pittsburgh, where he also teaches. Champagne's first novel, *The Blue Lady's Hands,* was called "pornographic and sacrilegious" by the *West Coast Review of Books* and "too middle class" by *Inches.* His second novel, *When the Parrot Boy Sings,* was published in 1990. Champagne's work on film has appeared in *CineAction!*

RONALD DONAGHE, after working as a technical writer for many years, is now working as an openly gay writer in his hometown. He has published one novel, *Common Sons,* and is working on a sequel. He enjoys gardening, hiking, carpentry, and music between sessions at his word processor. Becoming reacquainted with his home state is now a research project that he plans to turn into nonfiction articles in addition to providing background for his novels. He wants to demystify gay people in his work, to show their ordinariness and their relationship with the rest of humanity.

LARRY DUPLECHAN is the author of three critically acclaimed novels: *Eight Days a Week, Blackbird,* and *Tangled Up in Blue.* Duplechan's work has appeared in *L.A. Style, The New York Native,* and *Black American Literature Forum* and in the anthologies *Black Men/White Men* and *Revelations: A Collection of Gay Male Coming Out Stories.* He holds a B.A. in English Literature from the University of California, Los Angeles, where he teaches writing as part of the Continuing Education Program. A native of Los Angeles, Duplechan lives there with his spouse of fifteen years. He has recently begun work on his fourth novel, which has the working title *Jazzin' for Blue Jean.*

PHILIP GAMBONE has published short stores in over a dozen magazines including *Gettysburg Review*, *Tribe*, and *NER/BLQ* as well as in *Men on Men 3*. A former fellow of the MacDowell Colony, he has also been listed in *Best American Short Stories, 1989*. A collection of his short stories has been published as *The Language We Use Up Here*. He has taught writing at the University of Massachusetts and Boston College; currently he works at the Park School in Brookline, Massachusetts, and teaches at Harvard. He makes his home in Boston and Provincetown.

HARLAN GREENE is the author of the novels *Why We Never Danced the Charleston* and *What the Dead Remember;* and of the nonfiction *Charleston: City of Memory* (with photographs by N. Jane Iseley). He lives in Chapel Hill, North Carolina.

ESSEX HEMPHILL is the author of *Earth Life* and *Conditions*. He is the editor of *Brother to Brother: New Writings by Black Gay Men*. He is the recipient of fellowships in literature from the District of Columbia Commission for the Arts and the National Endowment for the Arts. His poetry has been widely published in journals and his essays have recently appeared in *High Performance*, *Gay Community News*, *The Advocate*, *Pyramid Periodical*, and *Essence*. His poetry is featured in the black gay films *Looking for Langston* and *Tongues Untied*.

ANDREW HOLLERAN is the author of the novels *Dancer from the Dance* and *Nights in Aruba*, and a book of essays, *Ground Zero*.

ARNIE KANTROWITZ is an associate professor of English at the College of Staten Island, City University of New York. His essays have appeared in *The Advocate*, *The Village Voice*, London's *Gay News*, *The New York Times*, and other publications. His poetry has appeared in *Trace*, *Descant*, *The Mouth of the Dragon*, and other literary magazines. He is the author of an autobiography, *Under the Rainbow: Growing Up Gay*, and he has recently completed a novel about a modern disciple of Walt Whitman.

MICHAEL LASSELL is the author of two volumes of poetry: *Poems for Lost and Un-Lost Boys* and *Decade Dance*. His poetry and fiction have been included in *Gay and Lesbian Poetry in Our Time, Poets for Life: 76 Poets Respond to AIDS, High Risk, Men on Men 3,* and *Indivisible.* He has published poetry in many periodicals including *City Lights Review, The James White Review, Fag Rag, Outweek, Bay Windows, The Literary Review, Kansas Quarterly, Mid-American Review, Central Park, Hanging Loose, Colorado-North Review, ON THE BUS, Poetry/LA* and *ZYZZYVA.* As a journalist and critic he has written regularly for the *Los Angeles Herald Examiner, L.A. Weekly,* and *L.A. Style.* A native and resident of New York City, he holds degrees from Colgate University, California Institute of the Arts, and Yale. He has never been a Boy Scout.

R. NIKOLAUS MERRELL is a Westerner, born in Spokane, Washington, and raised in Montana and Idaho on Indian reservations and in logging towns. He attended graduate school in Mexico City and holds an M.Div. from the Church Divinity School of the Pacific in Berkeley, California, and an M.A. in counseling psychology from Santa Clara University. An Episcopal priest, he now lives with his lover and their adopted five-year-old Honduran-born son near San Jose, California. He is currently finishing his first novel, *Bitterroot,* a German-American heroic adventure set in the Pacific Northwest.

ROBIN METCALFE abandoned a career as a sleeping car porter for Canadian National Railways in 1985. Since then he has earned his livelihood writing art criticism and gay porn. He has edited several periodicals, including a gay and lesbian regional journal, a literary annual, and a crafts magazine. Over the years he has been Halifax, Nova Scotia's Official Homosexual, a two-time cover boy for *The Body Politic,* and a founding member of the Bad Boys Club. He likes to take his shirt off when he dances.

JESSE MONTEAGUDO is an editorial journalist and literary critic for *The Weekly News* (Miami). His reviews and essays have been featured in a variety of lesbian/gay publications, including *The Front Page* (Raleigh), *Lambda Book Report,* and *Chicago Gay Life.* Recognized as an authority on gay literature, his essay "Books and the Gay Identity" appeared in the anthology *Gay Life.* A long-time activist who has served on the boards of several community organizations, he lives with his lifemate in Ft. Lauderdale.

MICHAEL NAVA was born in 1954 and raised in Sacramento, California. At seventeen, he left home for Colorado College where he wrote poetry and eventually obtained a degree in history. He spent the following year in Buenos Aires where he studied and translated the poetry of Ruben Dario. In 1978, he entered law school at Stanford, graduating in 1981. While working as a prosecutor for the City of Los Angeles, he wrote his first book, *The Little Death,* a mystery featuring gay Chicano attorney Henry Rios. There have been two other Rios books, *Goldenboy* and *How Town.* He lives in West Hollywood with his lover, Andy Ferrero, still practices law, and is currently at work on a new novel.

MARTIN PALMER was born and educated in Florida. He is a graduate of Johns Hopkins Medical School and trained afterward at Tulane University Medical School in New Orleans, where he lived until he moved to Alaska in 1968. He teaches English and Speech at the University of Alaska–Anchorage, where he received his M.F.A. He lives in Anchorage where he practices internal medicine. He is a poet and finds the land, the people, the progression of the seasons, and above all the quality of light in the Far North an inexhaustible source of renewal. His fiction has appeared in *Men on Men 3.*

JOHN PRESTON is the author of many books including *Franny, the Queen of Provincetown* and the Alex Kane adventure series. He co-authored *Safe Sex: The Ultimate Erotic Guide* with Glenn Swann and edited *Personal Dispatches: Writers Confront AIDS.* The former editor of *The Advocate,* he now lives in Portland, Maine, where he is president of the board of directors of The AIDS Project.

LEV RAPHAEL has published nearly thirty stories in *Redbook, Commentary, Christopher Street, The James White Review, Midstream, Hadassah, Amelia,* and elsewhere. He contributed stories to *Men on Men 2, Certain Voices,* and the *Faber Anthology of Gay Short Fiction.*

He is the author of the 1990 Lambda Literary Award-winning short story collection, *Dancing on Tisha B'Av,* and a nonfiction work, *Edith Wharton's Prisoners of Shame* and has also co-authored *The Dynamics of Power* and *Stick Up for Yourself!* with Gershen Kaufman. He is a winner of the Harvey Swados and Reed Smith Fiction prizes. He holds a Ph.D. in American Studies from Michigan State University, where he taught Creative Writing, Women's Studies, and Jewish-American Fiction.

STEVEN SAYLOR's first short story was published when he was twelve and won first place in a nationwide contest sponsored by the Methodist magazine *Accent on Youth.* Fifteen years later he was editing the gay leather-and-SM magazine *Drummer.* Under the pen name Aaron Travis he wrote the erotic novel *Slaves of the Empire,* and his short stories have appeared in numerous magazines. His more mainstream fiction includes stories in *The San Francisco Bay Guardian, The Magazine of Fantasy and Science Fiction,* and the gaming journal *Dragon,* as well as the historical mystery novel *Roman Blood* about Cicero's first murder case. He lives in San Francisco with his lover of many years.

JAN-MITCHELL SHERRILL is the author of *Blind Leading the Blind,* published by the New Poets Series. Most recently his work has appeared in *Carolina Quarterly, South Coast Poetry Journal,* and *James White Review.*

GEORGE SNYDER is the author of *Maps of the Heavens,* on the history and development of celestial cartography. He received his B.A. from Baldwin-Wallace College, Ohio, and an M.A. from the University of Chicago. After teaching private school in Pittsburgh and New York, he joined the staff of a New York auction house where he catalogued Hebrew printed books and manuscripts. He returned to Chicago in 1986, where he has lived since, writing two unpublished novels and intermittently pursuing research for a Ph.D. He is currently registrar of a midwestern corporate art collection. He lives on the far north side of the city in a converted resort hotel built in 1923, on Lake Michigan.

BOB SUMMER lives in Nashville, where he has chaired the Tennessee Arts Commission's literary panel and helps plan the annual Southern Festival of Books. A founder of the Publishers Association of the South, he held marketing positions at several university presses before moving from publishing into writing for his livelihood. Since then he has co-authored *Getting Strong, Looking Strong: A Guide to Successful Bodybuilding* and contributed book reviews, columns, and articles on bodybuilding, travel, art, authors, and the book industry to a variety of magazines and newspapers.

LAURENCE TATE lives in San Francisco and works at Project Inform. He has written articles for *Arrival, Body Politic,* and other publications and had an essay included in *Personal Dispatches: Writers Confront AIDS.*

MARK THOMPSON helped found the Gay Students Coalition at San Francisco State University in 1973, and has worked for gay and feminist causes since that time. Thompson is the Senior Editor of *The Advocate* and has contributed numerous feature articles, essays, and interviews with prominent artists and writers and others in the past fifteen years. In 1987, Thompson published *Gay Spirit: Myth and Meaning.* He is also the editor of the anthology *Leatherfolk: Radical Sex, People, Politics, and Practices,* and has most recently completed a retelling of the Gilgamesh myth for gay men. He lives in Los Angeles where he continues to expand his understanding of gay identity through the exploration of gay men's dreams, myths, and stories.

SCOTT TUCKER is a writer and activist whose work has appeared in *Christopher Street, The New York Native, Gay Community News, The Advocate, Body Politic,* and other publications. He is currently working on a book combining politics and autobiography.

CHRISTOPHER WITTKE is the Features Editor of *Gay Community News,* the Boston-based national lesbian and gay weekly. He has been a *GCN* collective member since 1987 and has written for the paper since 1985. His articles have also appeared in *In Touch,*

The Weekly News (Miami), *Art Issues* (Los Angeles), and other periodicals. He lives with his lover, Sherman Hanke, and their many tropical fish.

REED WOODHOUSE divides his time among literature, opera, and homosexuality. A Lecturer in literature at Massachusetts Institute of Technology since 1985, he is also Music Director of Opera at Boston Conservatory of Music. He is in current demand both as a free-lance writer and as an opera coach and conductor. He co-teaches (with writer Michael Schwartz) a popular course on gay male fiction at the Cambridge Center for Adult Education, and taught MIT's first gay and lesbian literature course in the spring of 1991. For the past eleven years, he has made his home in Boston's gay ghetto, the South End, where he still lives.

LES WRIGHT recently completed his Ph.D. in Comparative Literature at the University of California, Berkeley. His dissertation, *The Chiasmic War: AIDS Writing and Gay Countermemory* is the first of three projected volumes that examine the social mythologies and ideals that express collective gay identity. The completed volume examines the United States, the projected volumes will address German and Dutch subculture. He is a founding member of the Gay and Lesbian Historical Society of Northern California and currently serves as editor-in-chief of *OurStories*. He has been involved with the San Francisco Gay History Project since 1984, and returns to writing and publishing after a twelve-year hiatus. He first became a gay activist in Germany in the 1970s and currently writes a regular column for *Bear* magazine.